STEEL

A DARK AND DIRTY SINNERS' MC: FOUR

SERENA AKEROYD

Copyright © 2020 by Serena Akeroyd

All rights reserved.

No part of this book may be reproduced in any form or by any electronic or mechanical means, including information storage and retrieval systems, without written permission from the author, except for the use of brief quotations in a book review.

❦ Created with Vellum

STEEL

DEDICATION

TO THE PEOPLE who put up with me.
And to Trev. My Mrs. Biggins.

UNIVERSE READING ORDER

FILTHY
NYX
LINK
FILTHY RICH
SIN
STEEL
FILTHY DARK
CRUZ
MAVERICK
FILTHY SEX
HAWK
FILTHY HOT
STORM
THE DON
THE LADY
FILTHY SECRET (COMING NOVEMBER 2021)

PLAYLIST

IF YOU'D LIKE to hear a curated soundtrack, with songs that are featured in the book, as well as songs that inspired it, then here's the link:

https://open.spotify.com/playlist/36ajArZjZ9ZHFEp1nawkjk

STEEL

WHERE IT ALL WENT WRONG...

"YOU GOTTA FUCKING DO THIS."

I stared at myself in the mirror, pumping myself up for the evening ahead. I was almost ashamed of the fact that I was a Sinner, and I was giving myself a pep talk like I was a senior back in goddamn high school, but fuck, that was what Stone did to me.

She fucked with my head.

She screwed with it in the best possible way, until all I saw was her, until all I wanted was her.

She was fifteen.

I was nineteen.

The age gap wasn't right, and I had enough shit on my shoes without getting into something with someone who was technically a minor. I'd already been sent up last year for a minor drug charge, and I had no intention of being sent back for statutory rape, so I'd have to take this slow.

Until next month when she was sixteen.

Fuck, I felt like I'd been waiting for a lifetime...

Maybe I had.

Maybe I'd been waiting all my fucked-up life for the chance to make her mine. To own her, to have her own me.

I sucked in a breath as I stared at my face in the mirror.

I was, technically, handsome. Not as hot as my bros Nyx and Link, and the pussies were all melting for Rex, but I got mine. I had long brown hair that tangled when I slept and was a cunt to brush, a goatee that I was contemplating shaving, brown eyes, and kinda brown lips.

One big brown blur, you could call me, except everything in between was pretty. *Pretty.*

Exactly what a mean biker fucker wanted to be called.

The goatee and messy hair were a mask, a means of looking tougher than I was, but whatever, if Stone preferred me without a goddamn beard or with short hair, I'd get the clippers out.

Call me pussy whipped, I'd take it. I didn't give a shit. I just wanted her on my arm, riding bitch at my back, in my bed, around my cock.

Everything she had to give, I wanted.

Shuddering at the thought, I slapped some aftershave onto my face, sprayed a little too much deodorant under my pits, and headed out into my room.

I'd ironed my goddamn jeans, my Henley too, and my cut was spick-and-span, as were my boots.

I looked like a biker who was going on a first date, and honestly, that was true, except for the fact that Stone didn't know this was our first date.

After dressing, I managed to get out of the clubhouse without many of my brothers seeing me. If they had, I knew they'd give me shit about how clean I looked. Not that we were dirty, but I looked like an Abercrombie & Fitch version of a biker...not good for the rep.

All the way to West Orange, not far, even though we were on a large plot of land that was ours and accessed only by one road, I second-guessed myself. Worrying about what I'd do, what I'd say. How I'd get her to agree to be mine, and by the time I fucking made it outside her shack of a house, I'd admit that the excessive deodorant had been imperative.

When the rumble of my hog died and I'd parked, I peered at the door, unsurprised that it was wide open and she was standing there. She had the biggest fucking grin on her mouth, the prettiest smile in her eyes. Everything about her was wholesome and real, everything I'd never had in my miserable existence, and I wanted her so goddamn badly, I just couldn't see straight.

I had to stay on my bike, had no fucking choice, because my boner was pounding away like I'd grown a second heart and I was shaken.

Absolutely floored by the sight of her in denim short-shorts, a small cami that had a lacy insert at the deep V-neck, and bright pink Converse that she'd used a Sharpie to scrawl some of her favorite bands on. The kitten I'd bought her was playing with the shoelaces, and Mrs. Biggins—only fuck knew why she'd called the cat that—was too busy with them to hiss at me like she usually did.

When she arched a brow at me, evidently wondering why I was taking ages getting off my bike, I decided to man up and get the fucking afternoon underway.

She needed math help, and math was my shit.

So I sucked in a breath, climbed off my hog, then strolled toward her once the kickstand was in place.

With every step I took, I felt like there was a magnetic rope between us, one that pinged into place, and I knew I wasn't the only one who felt it.

I was pretty sure she felt the same way about me, but she'd never said shit, so that was why I was nervous. She'd never indicated that she might want me as anything other than a friend and a tutor—uh-huh, me, a goddamn tutor—and I was bricking it because if she fucked with my heart, she was going to fuck with my head.

When I was a step away, I heard her breath hitch, and I just knew.

It was like...

Fuck, it was like everything aligned. Suddenly, it all made sense.

Sure, she wanted me.

But she was fifteen, almost a woman, and I was a man. Why would she come on to me? I was a Sinner. She was a sophomore. She'd never have the guts to go for what she wanted, but at that moment, I saw *I* was what she wanted, and I took affirmative action.

Before she could say a word, I was in her face, and my mouth hovered an inch above hers.

"Tell me to fuck off," I rasped, my breath brushing against her lips.

She stuttered, "W-What? Why?"

"Because I'm too old for you. Because I'm wrong for you. Because I'm a Sinner and you want to have a future—"

She bridged the gap. My hands slid over her hair and gripped the short locks, but that was nothing compared to how her fingers tangled in mine. Nothing at all. She held me closer than I held her, her body molding to mine like it was born to. She melted into me, her lips taking everything I had to give, her tongue seeking mine, hungry for more, needing everything, and fuck, I was willing to give it to her.

We stood there for over ten minutes, eating each other's mouths on the doorstep of her shithole house, and the rightness of the moment was impossible to deny. Impossible to get away from.

Everything felt right about this.

Everything.

I let my hands smooth over her waist, down to her hips, and I clung to her ass. I couldn't have her—not yet—but fuck, I could feel, and she loved it. Little hitching breaths escaped her, small moans as she rippled against me, her body quivering like she was on the brink of coming.

I'd never know what she could have done, because Lana Jane, her mom, hollered, "Stone? What the fuck are you doing? Did you forget I asked for milk?"

We both froze.

Our lips still clung to the other, even as I slowly pulled back with a promise in my eyes that there was more, always more for both of us.

She gulped at the sight, licked her pink, sore lips, then called out, "Two minutes, Momma."

She darted off, and I watched her go, that tight ass of hers an obsession of mine as she wandered away, and I closed the door behind me before heading down the hall.

Lana Jane was a cunt, and if anyone deserved to be dying of cancer at thirty-nine, it was her.

Sure, I knew that was an evil thing to say, but she was a shitty mom to a really good kid. Maybe there was no physical abuse, but there were other ways to hurt a kid. To always put them down, to always make them feel lesser.

I wandered toward her room, unsurprised by all the IVs she was hooked up to. She was on the last stage of cancer, close to death, and she looked it. Her skin was like porcelain, frail and milky white, so white in fact, you could see the blue of her veins beneath the surface of her skin. She was all bone, no fat, and her eyes were a strange yellow.

One of the reasons Stone wanted to be a doctor was because of her ma, who'd been fighting cancer for a long time, but if I was going to be Stone's Old Man, which was going to happen the day she turned fucking eighteen, then shit needed to be said.

When I strolled in there, her gaze drifted from *Jeopardy* on the crap TV to me. Her eyes flared wide at the sight, but once a club-whore, always a clubwhore. She started fussing with her hair, trying to sit upright, settling herself in a way that'd show her good side.

I'd seen it a thousand times already, and I was barely nineteen. The last person I needed it from was a cancer patient who was on the brink of a death I was grateful for.

She'd always treated Stone like she was a piece of shit. I figured that was because of who her daddy *wasn't*, but that wasn't anyone else's fault but Lana Jane's.

"Steel! What are you doing here?"

Her voice was a little less shrill than it had been before, but I could hear a dazedness to it, and that, combined with what Stone had told me about her treatment, confirmed that she was as high as a kite.

Her pinpricks for pupils also gave that shit away.

Before I could say a word, her gaze drifted over me again, and when her eyes lit on my mouth, she smirked. It was a smirk of a person who knew something, who was going to hold it against me.

A snicker wheezed from her mean lips. "Like father, like son." She winked at me. "If I'd known you swung your father's way, Steel, I'd have let you have Stone when she was a kid."

Her words had me freezing.

For a second, I wasn't even sure what to process first. The fact that she had essentially told me she would have sold my fucking soulmate's body when she was a child if she'd known I was into kids. Or the fact that she referenced my father.

A father I didn't know.

But the father shit was neither here nor there. A part of me wondered if Lana Jane had pimped Stone out before, but then I thought about her kiss, and even if she was confident with me, there was a hesitance to everything she did that told me she was new to this shit. New as in untouched.

My throat closed at the bitch's inference, and how I didn't

stride over to her, take her by her miserable throat, and squeeze the life out of her, I'd never know.

"You don't know who my father is," I growled, trying to focus on that rather than the other point she'd made, because if I did, she really would be dying ahead of her time, and after that?

I wanted her to suffer.

I wanted the cancer to eat her away from the inside out.

If that made me a cunt, then so be it. I'd deal with that.

Hell, I'd make *her* deal with it without even giving her fucking morphine.

Rage swirled around inside me, and it only tripled in strength when she muttered, "Course she knew. A woman knows." She winked at me. "Always knows."

"Come on then, if you fucking know who it is, tell me, bitch."

She pouted. "Why are you being so mean to me? I was being generous!"

Generous? Selling her daughter...

My heartbeat doubled.

"You know shit," I snapped and, striding forward, I carried on, "Now, while I'm here, you need to—"

"You're Kevin's boy, of course. Should have known that shit was in the blood." She sniffed at me. "Pervert. Look at you, mouth all red. What were you doing? Sucking on my little girl's tits? Fucking her?" She roared out a laugh. "Pervert just like your papa."

Kevin.

My throat felt too thick at her words.

She was bullshitting me, right?

She had to be.

My father wasn't the fucker who'd raped Nyx's sister, Carly, since she was a little kid. Who'd prompted her to kill herself. Who'd died at Nyx's hand.

No.

It couldn't be.

She smiled at me, dazed but somehow lucid, and I'd never loathed anyone in my life more than I did her.

Just from her smugness, I knew she was enjoying this, savoring the ruination of my world, wrecking me from the bottom to the top.

Deep inside, everything started to shatter on its very foundations, but the only thing I could think of was to end her.

So I strode over to the IV line that I'd seen Stone change for her momma when the nurse who was supposed to come never did. I knew which was which, knew which was the morphine too.

And I felt no compunction in switching off that line.

Her eyes flared wide, distress flashing in them as I leaned down and pressed my hand over her mouth. "Don't worry, I won't kill you. But when you wake up, and you've been without the morphine, you'll wish you were dead."

I raised her bony ass arm, tipped her head to the side and, ignoring her struggles, didn't relent until she passed out.

My hatred for her made me want to grab a pillow and shove it over her face, but Stone would never forgive me for that, and even though my entire world had just been ruined, I wasn't about to have her hate me.

Throat thick, I rushed out of the room, and when I saw her approaching me, her mouth as pink as before, her eyes lazy with slumberous arousal, everything inside me locked up tight.

I couldn't taint her.

I just couldn't.

I—

My mouth was dry as I rasped, "She fell asleep while I was talking to her."

Her brows rose. "Huh. That's unusual. I doctored her milk so it's probably a good thing she slept on her own." Her smile widened as she held out her other hand. "Want to come sit in the living room?"

I heard the promise in her voice, knew what she was really asking, and I wanted it so much that my body ached with it. But deep down, I needed confirmation that Lana Jane wasn't being a bitch.

I believed her, but I'd be a fool to wreck my life over something some sour bitch said while she was high on morphine.

So I sucked in a breath, and mumbled, "I can't, baby doll." Her cheeks pinkened at the endearment, something that flew off my tongue as it always did. "Been called in."

Her nose crinkled, but she was also used to my having to go away at odd times, hell, she was friends with the guys I deemed brothers, and she was used to us being sent off at random all over the country.

"That's a shame," she whispered, her eyes filled with a promise I wanted to take as my own but couldn't.

Not yet.

Maybe not ever, if Lana Jane wasn't lying.

Fuck.

She had to be lying, didn't she?

I moved toward her, swept my hand to the center of her back, and held her close.

It felt so good. Too good.

Too perfect.

I breathed her in, absorbed the scent of honeysuckle and vanilla, absorbed it because it might be the very last time I got to hold her that way, and then I squeezed her before striding off.

She shouted after me, but I didn't wait. I ran to my hog, climbed on it, and headed for the clubhouse.

Bear would know. He knew everything. He'd be able to tell me if I'd been spawned by a pedophile fuck.

If she was lying, I'd make her pay, but God, I hoped she was. I hoped she was wrong.

For the first time in my life, I prayed, but unfortunately for me, that prayer was too little.

Too late.

ONE

QUIN
TODAY

SAYING I was nervous was like saying the Ferrari 458 Spider was easy to jack.

Which it wasn't.

The 2015 model was pretty fucking impossible to steal, but I'd give my left nut to try...of course, this was the equivalent of said carjacking.

I'd never killed someone before. I knew that becoming a Sinner often meant getting your hands 'dirty,' but in all honesty, I'd just never thought I'd have to do *that*. But here I was, in prison after my sentencing was skewed, with an unenvious job.

Nervous, I bit my lip as I thought about my plan.

I had no idea why Fieri was on my Prez's shit list, but my place was not to question why. My place was just to...you guessed it—*do or fucking die.*

Still, it wasn't hard to figure out. Fieri was a fucker, high up in the Italian mob, and when I said high up, I meant he was like the heir to the *Famiglia's* throne or something. As a result, he was the kingpin of the prison, so getting to him made figuring out who was going to sit on the Iron Throne look simple.

The easiest place was also the hardest—the showers. Accessing him was going to be nearly impossible, what with his guards around him, but I'd been planning this for a little while.

I worked in the kitchen, and some eye drops in their food today was, I prayed, going to give me some time while giving them the shits.

That was why I was nervous.

I'd heard that crap about the eye drops before, but I wasn't sure if it would work, and I didn't exactly have access to Wikipedia in here. Yeah, I had a phone I stashed in my briefs, just under my dick—I knew the radiation would probably boil my balls—but it wasn't a smartphone. It was just a simple boring burner that I'd only managed to get recently when my sis had visited.

It wasn't like I could ask for an upgrade, was it?

I didn't think Verizon was going to be willing to give me some perks for a job well done. *Congrats, Quin, you made it to a federal prison!*

"Focus, Quin. Fucking focus," I muttered under my breath, gulping as I glanced over my shoulder, just waiting on Fieri to walk by.

While he was cautious, he was also arrogant. The guards weren't his idea, but his father's, and I knew he chafed at their presence because he didn't like to look weak.

In the time since I'd received the call from my Prez, I'd been watching him, waiting. Planning.

That didn't take my nerves away any.

I sucked in a breath when I heard rustling, and when he moved past me, I darted out of my cubicle and slipped into the one opposite, making it look like I was walking out of the shower room when I wasn't. I knew his cubicle came with a camera blackout for his privacy, he even had a shower curtain the guards put up temporarily, and I intended on taking advantage of both privileges.

The showers were at half capacity when Fieri took his bathroom break, so I knew I'd be one of the suspects in his murder, but I was also hoping that the governor's dislike for the prick would be on my side.

I didn't have a shank, was armed only with my bare hands, and I hoped that my somewhat slender appearance was going to work to my advantage.

In comparison to my brother, Nyx, I was puny. I'd been working on that inside, and while I was getting there, I wasn't as big as him—life goals.

Still, with my scrawny fucking arms, I knew they'd mistake me for a weakling. I'd already had four guys try to make me their fucking bitch, and they were all talking at a higher octave as a result, but that was when the idea had struck me.

How to get away with murder.

It wasn't foolproof, could totally go wrong, but I just had to have faith.

This was the first time Rex had ever asked anything of me, and I wasn't going to let him down or show Nyx up. My brother's opinion of me was already low for getting caught and sent up, so I needed to make this better somehow. Needed to make shit right.

When I heard Fieri start to hum under his breath, I slipped past the stall wall, and darted into his cubicle.

He didn't even notice I was there, and I saw why—he had music in his ears.

Fucking music.

I almost drooled at the prospect of stealing his waterproof headphones, but I didn't, *couldn't* steal them, even though stealing was what I did best. All they'd have to do was search my cell to find them and realize I was the one behind Fieri's death, but sweet God, the temptation was hard.

If I'd learned anything in my relatively short life, it was that me and temptation didn't work well together.

Only thinking of Indy's glum face the last time I'd seen her and Nyx's disapproval had me staying on course.

Instead of stealing the headphones, I took advantage of his idiocy, grabbed him by the hair, held him tight, then kicked his feet out from under him.

In the slippery stall, he crumpled, unable to gain purchase on the floor, even as his arms flailed, and I took the opportunity to jerk his neck to the side.

The distinct crack had my heart pounding as I stared into his lifeless eyes.

I'd done it.

My mouth quivered.

How had that been so easy?

Who the fuck knew killing someone would be so—

Jesus.

I wanted to puke.

I—

Barely holding my gut in line, I grimaced as I slipped out of the stall, leaving the corpse behind. I rushed down the corridor, using the blackout spots to my advantage, peering up at the cameras all the while to make sure they hadn't moved since Fieri had strolled in, and then I darted out toward the exit where a couple of guards were waiting. I hoped I'd been fast enough to make it look like the departure from my shower to the guards' stand wasn't too long

I could have called attention to a 'scuffle' I'd heard, try to cast the net wider, but instead, I decided not to muddy the waters, kept my wits about me, and just strolled out like nothing had happened.

The second I made it back to my cell, I got into bed, ignored my cellmate, and rolled onto my side.

My tears shamed me, but fuck. That was my first kill.

I had to pray it would be the last.

TWO

STEEL

"MY ASS IS GROWING A RAINFOREST."

Rex sighed down the line. "Have you turned into Link? Do you think I give a fuck about your ass?"

"You should. I swear to fuck there's sweat on top of sweat on top of goddamn sweat, and then there's this place." I stared out onto Phnom Penh's harbor, where modern humanity clashed with an ancient culture that seemed to be winning the war.

Mostly, I missed AC and food that didn't make more than my ass crack burn.

I hated fucking spicy foods, and for some reason, whatever I picked up was hotter than fucking hell.

It was safe to say that I wasn't as happy as fucking Larry, but my mission was about to end, and I'd never been happier.

I'd lay down my life for the Satan's Sinners MC, but coming to Cambodia again?

I'd prefer to die.

Then I winced, because I knew I was being harsh on a pretty great country. The people were so fucking friendly, it made me realize how miserable we were in the States. The place was great too. But the weather? I'd been to Texas in midsummer where I was less miserable.

The rainforest shit was no joke. I had a whole subculture of flora and fauna growing between my butt cheeks now, no matter how often I showered.

And I was on my eighth shower today already.

Raising an arm, I leaned it against the window as I gazed out onto the dying sun. Naturally, my forehead stuck to my forearm, but that was just my luck right now.

"Not turning into Link," I muttered, annoyed. "It's not all about the ass. Just telling you my predicament."

"And I'll get you some fucking Butt Paste for your boo-boos when you're back home," he grumbled with a snort. "Now, for the reason why I actually fucking called, is everything down for tonight?"

"I already told you that," I retorted. "We didn't need this powwow."

"Sure I did. You're a sneaky fucker. Like to make sure things are all copacetic *verbally*," he scoffed, making my eye roll even more imperative, though he couldn't see it. "FYI, all travel arrangements are set."

I grunted. "Good. I don't feel like being arrested on my way back to the States."

He snorted. "We've got friends in high places, and they want Donavan down as much as we do."

"Okay, good. What's the deal?"

"I'll send you the address where you can pick the bastard up, and when you arrive, you'll be given horse tranquilizers. Don't fuck this up, Steel. Don't kill the bastard. You know Link wants blood."

"Like I'm going to kill the fucker."

"Since when are you a doctor?"

My brow furrowed at that. "Is this your way of getting me to ask Stone?"

"Maybe."

"Why?"

"Just think she'd like to talk to you is all."

That had my brow doing the Macarena, never mind fucking furrowing. "Stone? Are we talking about the same bitch here?"

"Yeah, we're talking about the girl who followed you around like a puppy until you found a way to fuck it up."

Rex's long-suffering sigh grated on my last nerve, and I gritted my teeth.

He knew I hated talking about Stone, knew I loathed it. It was one of my only 'do not touch' subjects, and that he was touching it when I was all the way across the fucking world and unable to beat the shit out of him only pissed me off even more.

I grunted. "She likes to hear from me when she thinks I'm dying."

"Yeah, well, shit's changed."

"What's changed?" I retorted. "I've only been gone three weeks."

It had taken that fucking long for our contacts to bring the bastard in.

He hummed. "Not my place to discuss this shit."

"Not your place? Since goddamn when?" If I sounded confused, that was because I was. Jesus Christ. That was all Rex fucking did—stick his nose where it wasn't wanted.

Dude should have a pussy.

If he wasn't one of the meanest fuckers I knew, he'd have a rep for giving too much of a shit about people.

"I'm not calling her."

"You need to make sure you don't kill him," he countered. "He needs to be out cold for the entirety of the trip."

"How's he being shipped back?"

"Cargo crate."

"What if they mess with the temps? I've heard about animals being killed down there."

"Then if that happens, it's tough shit. Nothing we can do. But I don't want him overdosing."

"You seriously want me to call Stone over ketamine and appropriate dosing?"

He heaved a sigh. "It would be a kindness."

I pulled my cell away to gape at it. "A kindness? Since when am I fucking kind?"

"Since you broke her fucking heart and left her a wreck? I think she deserves some shitty piece of niceness from you right now."

Getting mad was an understatement to how I was feeling, but I gritted my teeth. "I'll call her." He'd left me no choice. Just because I kept distance between us at all times didn't mean it didn't kill me to hear that she needed a 'shitty piece of niceness' from me.

"Good. When you find out the dosages, you're to give him the drug, then you're to pack him in the crate. There'll be an official there who'll load him on board. You'll be taking the same flight with him for that first leg."

"Okay," I said softly, still annoyed and still at a loss. No matter how down Stone was, she wouldn't want to hear from me. Rex knew that. Had someone died?

No, he'd tell me if that was the case. And anyway, the only people who mattered to Stone, who were her family, were mine too, right? So, no, it wasn't a death.

"Your name isn't linked to his shipping crate, so there shouldn't be any issues when you land in Belfast. From there, you'll be grabbing a transatlantic flight to JFK while he gets shipped over in a cargo plane."

I hummed. "Even better. I don't feel like serving twenty to life for trafficking that piece of shit."

Rex laughed. "As if I wouldn't look after you."

I laughed back, even though I was uneasy. Not about business, just about Stone. "Is everything okay over there?"

"Yeah, just a little…"

"What?" I prompted when he hesitated.

"Link's beating himself up over this shit."

"Can't say I blame him. He was a dumb fuck for not tying Lily to him in the first place."

"Yeah. I'm not sure where his head is at with that. Sin's already claimed Tiff. Lock, stock, and barrel. Ring's on her finger, and I know the second she's good to travel, he's taking her away to get married for real now that they did the deed in court." I could hear his cut rustle as he shrugged. "It's clear he's a fucking fool for Lily so—"

"I guess we never know what goes on behind closed doors, but there must be a reason why he's put shit off the way he did."

"Knowing Link, it'll be sentimental."

My lips curved at that. Even though they didn't particularly want to. Link was a stone-cold killer. He had a larger rap sheet than some death row inmates, but yeah, he could be sentimental.

I could see that.

"He still hasn't put a ring on her finger?"

"No. Not even a diamond." Another sigh. "I wish he would. He'd stop moping around the place. Both Tiff and Lily look like shit, Steel. Fuck, I wish their bruises would heal. It's a constant reminder of my fuck up."

I winced. "It's all our fuck up. We shouldn't have set Prospects on them. Should have put a full-time brother on each woman."

"We don't have the men for that," Rex countered.

"No, but there are ways of making sure they're safe. I'll talk to Sin about it."

"It's the new businesses. We've stretched ourselves thin, bro."

"Yeah, we have," I conceded, and as Secretary, I knew that

more than anyone as I had to deal with most of the rotas and schedules for the brothers.

While we outsourced a lot of the jobs to people in town, our new businesses—a strip joint, garage, diner, and bar—were mostly secured by our people. Some jobs were held by brothers too, like with security in the strip joint.

"Fucking money laundering—why's it gotta suck so hard getting rich?"

My lips twitched. "Would you prefer to pay taxes?"

He sniffed. "Okay. I'll stop whining."

I rubbed my chin. "How's it going without Storm there?"

"Didn't realize how much the dumb fuck did, to be honest."

"Ain't it always the way. I'm sure he's glad you miss him."

Rex snorted. "You're all heart."

I grinned. "I know. We might need to bring in staff to man the strip joint," I said slowly, thinking out loud. It wasn't my place to think about security—that was Sin's role as our new Enforcer. And though Nyx was the new VP, having taken over Storm's position, Nyx's heart wasn't in admin like it was in mine and Storm's.

Yeah, how cool was I?

My heart was in fucking paper pushing.

But only for my brothers.

If you'd stuck me in an office and had me working a nine to five from twenty, I'd have lost my fucking mind. For my family? My MC? Sure, I could do this shit, and I was pretty goddamn good at it too.

"Nyx and Sin have already suggested that, but they don't trust anyone."

"What about the security company who manned the Donavan place? We looked into them. They're shady as fuck."

"Do we really want a shady as fuck corporate security team in our little strip joint?"

"Maybe not, but how about we poach a couple of men? I'd prefer them on the joint and our guys on our women."

Rex heaved a sigh. "True. Honestly, I'm thinking about setting someone on Rachel."

Ah, his lady love.

Almost snickering, I told him dryly, "I'm sure she'd love that."

His lack of a reply told me how little he was looking forward to that conversation.

Rachel was as independent as Stone, and if I made the suggestion to her, she'd give me the dead eye.

I wondered if Stone would need the extra security, but I figured she'd be safe because she was in New York City, not back at the compound anymore.

I tried not to think about that and how much the distance between us fucking hurt.

Everything was for a reason, and even if the reason sucked balls, it didn't take away what mattered most.

At least, it didn't to me.

I dug my thumb and forefinger into my eyes and rubbed away some of the sleep gathered there. Jet lag had been a bitch to get over, and while it wasn't the first time I'd endured it, throw in the heat and some killer allergies, I was glad this stay in Cambodia was over.

I was ready for home in a big way.

Heaving a sigh, Rex grunted. "I'll pass on the suggestion to Nyx. Maybe it'll work itself out."

I just hummed. I knew we needed outside help, or we needed to start pushing our brothers into doing more for the club.

The notion had me muttering, "Guys like Cruz are wasted just dicking around the clubhouse, Rex." Well, Cruz had other nastier jobs around the place, but mostly he was on hand at the compound.

"Yeah, I know."

"Same with Hawk. He's a good security guy. Might be time to step up the game so he can be patched in."

"What about North?"

"He's useless. More interested in pussy, but Hawk? He's a serious motherfucker, and he's invested. Giulia got hurt, and even though they're stupid taking Dog's" —their father— "side, he loves her. It's clear to see."

"We need to have a reshuffle. Jaxson is probably ready to be patched in too. Things have been busy. We need to get shit back on track." He sighed. "Trouble is, I keep saying that and some other clusterfuck goes down, and I can't get shit back in order."

His OCD was probably messing with his mind more than anything else.

Dude was *beyond* anal-retentive, and that wasn't me being like Link and being butt-minded. It was just how it was.

No way could we run as much as we did, with as few men as we had, without someone like Rex in charge.

"Once this dumb fuck is no more, things will calm down some," I soothed.

Rex snorted. "If you think that's true, then you're the one who's fucking high on ketamine."

My lips curved. "If only," I replied mournfully. "Maybe it would take away from the petri dish in my butt crack."

"Again with the ass?" Rex chuckled. "Anyway, you'll get the details in a text. Maverick will be sending it on the secure burner."

"Understood."

"Talk to Stone, Steel."

The order got my back up, but I blew out a breath and muttered, "Okay."

"Be good to have you back home, brother."

"Same, Rex. Same. See you soon."

"You will."

The confidence in his voice set my nerves on the right track.

Truth was, I'd known when I'd been sent over here that there was a risk I'd land in jail. Not twenty to life in a pretty Fed joint either, but some shithole prison in Asia. But to hook as big of a cunt as Donavan Lancaster? That was something I'd risk shit for.

I liked Lily. Didn't necessarily like that she'd tied my bro down, but fuck, if it could happen to Nyx, it could happen to anyone, so why not Link?

In fact, all my brothers were starting to drop like flies.

Three Old Ladies in less than six months?

Jesus.

Something was in the fucking water.

Speaking of Old Ladies... I twisted my phone around and stared at the cover photo I'd had as my background for way too fucking long to count.

It was Stone.

Of course.

She was twenty-three in this pic. It was one of my favorites.

She didn't know how many pictures I had of her, and I knew if she did, she'd call me a stalker psycho, which I probably was, but this one made me fucking happy.

It was her first day at med school—a year younger than her classmates because she was a true overachiever—her first day on the path to a new life, and it was both a reminder and a reset.

A reminder because it gave me the wherewithal to stay the fuck away from her.

A reset because I loved looking at her and it set me back on track.

Still, the idea of calling her, especially over this, made my balls crawl up into my body.

She and Giulia, Nyx's bitch, were cut from the same cloth—ball busters. But Stone hadn't always been that way. I'd turned her into that.

A part of me wondered if she'd still be soft and gooey in the fucking middle, like a s'more that I never stopped wanting to lap up, but I knew I wasn't allowed that anymore.

She was my favorite treat that was denied to me because of choices I'd made along the way, ones I'd had no say in, but primarily because of what I wanted for her.

That made her all the more tantalizing, of course.

Grunting at my stupidity, I tried to stop gawking at her picture, but it was hard.

In all these years, she hadn't changed that much. Her light brown hair still curled more than she liked, so she wore it in a pixie cut. Back then, it had made her look like a little fairy, but having hit her thirties, the short cut made her cheekbones pop.

She looked like an ice queen now, and I had to admit it looked good on her.

Those light brown locks were shorn at the sides with a little length on top. Just enough to soften shit up without making her look butch, but not enough to get in her face.

I loved long hair on a bitch. Loved tangling my hand in it and tugging her head back, but on Stone? She was perfect as she was.

With those glinting gray eyes, lips that were cushioned and pillowy, made to suck me off, and a facial structure that belonged on a catwalk, she was my kryptonite.

Everything about her, from her abundant curves to her height, was forged to make me burn.

I gritted my teeth, physically pained by the notion of calling her, but I did as my Prez asked, because Rex wouldn't have made me do this unless I needed to.

So obey I would.

Even if it fucking killed me.

THREE
STONE

I RUBBED a hand over my face, trying not to get overwhelmed with what I was dealing with.

So much was up in the air right now, and I was at a complete and utter loss as to how to process it. All I wanted was to be sitting in my tiny apartment with Mrs. Biggins, my cat, curled up on my lap, hissing and spitting at every loud noise the TV made. But I wasn't there.

I wasn't at home, I was at work, and I'd just learned that we'd lost Angela, a stage four pancreatic cancer patient who'd been such a fucking fighter that greeting her at the start of every shift had become a way to set up my day.

Sneaking in there to talk smack with her had been the highlight of my working hours, and learning she'd died while I was sleeping?

It screwed with my head.

Big time.

I'd never get used to patients dying. I couldn't harden my heart to it, couldn't make myself turn to ice. I worked with doctors and surgeons who could do that, and I was pretty sure it made them shittier at their jobs for it, but who was I to judge?

My method wasn't working, but I couldn't face the prospect of changing.

This was me.

This was what made patients respond to my care.

I blew out a breath, rubbing a hand through my greasy hair as I stared out at the parking lot.

It was crammed because it was a holiday weekend, and for the first time, I was glad I wasn't in the ER today. I didn't need that shit on top of everything else.

Just learning that Angela died had devastated me. Throw in a bunch of drunk nutcases who really needed headbutting when I had to be nice to them and patch them up for their dumb fuck antics?

A mood killer *par excellence.*

I heaved in a breath, trying not to cry, but it was hard.

So damn hard.

Indy: *You doing okay, babe? You've been quiet today.*

I gulped at the screen, gulped at my best friend's concern, and wanted to answer, I really did, but I just couldn't.

I just fucking couldn't.

I wasn't okay.

Angela had died at thirty-two, and she'd left behind a husband who actually gave a fuck about her and a three-year-old.

A toddler.

Oliver was going to grow up without his mom now, and while I knew it wasn't my fault, it felt that way.

I wasn't behind her treatment plan, but still, it just felt—

I rubbed a hand over my face.

Sucked in some air.

Ignored the burning in my eyes.

Indy: *Here to talk when you need to.*

Appreciation filtered through me, and I felt bad for ignoring her text, but I just couldn't speak to anyone right now. I just couldn't.

Something wasn't right in this hospital. My gut told me that. It told me it in so many fucking ways, and I'd been denying it for so long, but no one listened to me.

I was lucky to be working at High Lidren Hospital. It was where the elite came to have their noses worked on and their asses tightened up. More than that, it had a rep for being a great teaching hospital, and when I'd gotten my place here, I'd been so pumped because I knew it meant good things for the future.

But being excited about a reputation and actually living with it were two separate things.

The doctors here believed their shit smelled like roses, the administration was more of a money-grubbing whore than my mama, and something...someone wasn't right in the wards.

I refused to think it.

Refused to think what I was *thinking*, but the goddamn words still popped up anyway.

Angel.

Of.

Death

I gulped.

Reaching up to rub the back of my neck, I smiled when Indy sent me another text.

Indy: *I'll beat your ass if you're reading this and not opening it.*

Indy was a friend from another life, another time. We shouldn't still be friends, but we were. When I'd moved away from West Orange, New Jersey, when I'd taken my life from the Satan's Sinners MC and merged it into this world, I thought she'd drop me, even though her life wasn't tangled up with the MC either, and as a result, we were on completely different paths. Total opposites.

But she hadn't.

And I was so grateful for that.

In a world of change, she was one of my only constants, someone I trusted with all of me.

I wondered if she knew how much I appreciated her. How grateful I was for her friendship—

My cell buzzed.

I blinked, taken aback by the name that crossed my screen.

"My Bloody Valentine" by Good Charlotte played, because I'd set that to his ringtone a long time ago.

Steel was my bloody valentine, and he didn't even fucking know it.

I cleared my throat, and my thumb hovered over the disconnect call button. If I couldn't deal with talking to Indy, I sure as shit couldn't deal with Steel and all his crap. His attitude stank, had for years, so I didn't need that now, but when he hung up and started again?

My heart skipped a beat.

There'd already been one health scare this year when I'd been shipped into the Sinners' compound to tend to three human trafficking victims. I'd been brought there because Nyx had called me from Steel's phone, making me think the fucker was injured.

I felt sick at the sight of the name on the screen.

Since before that initial call a few months back, he hadn't called me in years.

And now he was calling again?

I couldn't, even if I wanted to, reject the call, but neither was I feeling up to talking.

My eyes burned as the past and present seemed to collide, but I hit the green button and murmured, "Steel? Are you okay?"

A sigh sounded down the line. "I swear, you're only interested in me if I'm bleeding."

My jaw clenched. "I think you'll find it's the opposite."

It would be so easy to snap at him, to argue and give him shit, but I just didn't have the energy for it.

Clearing my throat, I questioned, "What do you want?"

He paused, hesitating more than I was used to from him. He was decisive by nature. Always had been. That's what made his actions hard to swallow.

Whatever he did came with a purpose, and there was no fighting that. No hiding it.

If he wanted me to hurt, it was because he wanted me to hurt.

So screwed up.

What was more screwed up? Him doing that or me still loving him, even though he hurt me every day in ways he didn't even know? Or, maybe he did know, and didn't give a shit—either way, it sucked.

I bit my bottom lip as he murmured, "I need a favor."

Of course he did.

Why else would he call?

"I'm not in the mood," I said tiredly.

"It's—"

"Let me guess? Club business?" When he said nothing, I shook my head. "Not even a 'how are you?' before you get straight down to it." I huffed out a bitter laugh. "Sounds about right. Look, call someone else."

Steel sighed. "I didn't want to call."

And even though it shouldn't have, that made things hurt even fucking more.

"Of course you didn't," I replied flatly. "So why did you?"

"You know Ghost, Tatána, and Amara?"

My brow puckered. "How could I forget? Are they okay?" They were the women I'd helped bring back from death's door at the Sinners' compound a short while back.

"Yeah, they're fine. Getting better every day." Another sigh. "You know the person behind their situation?"

My eyes widened. "Yeah."

"I need help with him."

Warily, I stared at a Chevy's license plate. It read '2Hot 4Luv' as I contemplated what was going on here.

"I need to know how to knock someone out with ketamine."

A hiss escaped me, as did the air in my lungs. I felt like a balloon that had just been deflated. What with Angela and everything else that was happening here?

This was just the cherry on the sundae.

So, I probably stunned the shit out of him as I gave him an answer. When I heard him scratch it down, I didn't say another word, just cut the call.

He phoned back once, to his credit, but I ignored it and him, and instead, got to my feet and walked back into the hospital.

Sometimes, somedays, you could only take so much pain, and I'd just hit my limit.

The rest of my shift went by in a blur, and for the first time, I was grateful that I wouldn't be staying here for much longer.

I'd thought I'd start my career here—I knew I was good enough to be taken on the staff permanently, but something wasn't right. Something was most definitely wrong, and the day I managed to leave this place, even if it meant I had to return to West Orange like Rex had declared he wanted the last time we'd spoken face to face, suddenly, I was glad about that.

Even if it put me in Steel's path.

I'd deal with it, because the weird thing was that in *this* world, people weren't supposed to be killed. Sure, I knew that sounded strange. I wanted to specialize in trauma, for fuck's sake. I was working in NYC, where murder was no stranger to the cops, but here, death was different.

In the MC, it was part of the life, as well as being jailed for twenty-five years.

But here I was, walking the same corridors as someone who was supposedly giving patients who didn't need it *peace*.

Maybe I was wrong. I hoped I was. But I just knew I wasn't.

I'd been around murderers all my life. I knew what it felt like.

Angela shouldn't have died today.

She'd been responding well to treatment. Enough for her to live a little longer, for her to have more time with Oliver.

For cancer patients, even those who were knocking on death's door, every day mattered, and Oliver and Angela had been denied that time.

I bit my lip to stop more tears from welling up, then I shoved my feelings aside and got back to work.

I'd already been raked over the coals this week, and I didn't need to be given shit from my supervisor tonight either.

It was time to pull up my big girl panties and get on with shit.

FOUR

STEEL

THE OFFICIAL REX had told me about was tiny. Donavan, on the other hand, wasn't. But that was the joy of mechanical engineering.

There was a crate on one of those metal lifts that the small guy in an olive uniform wheeled in, one that managed to make him look even smaller than he already was, and I knew my prize was inside. Something I was grateful for, because it meant there'd be less of my DNA on Donavan's body now that I didn't have to manhandle him into the shipping container.

"He knocked out."

The first words from the guy had me smiling at him as I packed away the deck of cards I'd been shuffling into my pocket. "Good to know." I reached into my bag and handed him an envelope that was stuffed with dollars. He accepted it with a slickness that told me this wasn't and wouldn't be his first bribe for the night, and then crammed it in the briefcase he had plunked on top of the crate.

From there, he also pulled out another bag. "Your Mr. Rex told me this another request."

I nodded when he passed me the paper bag, wondering if this was the equivalent of a soldier genie, and I peered in, saw the vial and needle, and was grateful Stone had given me the info I needed, even if she'd been weird about it as she'd done so.

To be honest, I'd thought she'd give me more shit than she had, and I was grateful she hadn't, while a part of me was also concerned.

Stone was my personal ball buster, after all. Scared of nothing and no one. Capable of going toe-to-toe with any brother in the MC, but I was used to a different side of her.

A side where she'd melt. Where all the walls would come tumbling down and I was allowed inside.

I hadn't expected to miss that on that call, but I had.

Her voice hadn't softened at all like it used to once upon a time, and even though I knew I deserved that, it still made something inside me feel like I was being gnawed on by big fucking rats.

And trust me, I'd seen big fucking rats in this place.

"You fine, Mr. Steel?"

This 'mister' shit would have given me a laugh a few days back, but with Stone's words and lackluster voice still ringing in my head, I just cleared my throat and asked, "You'll be putting him on the flight for me according to Mr. Rex's instructions?"

The man dipped his chin. "This correct. He currently sleeping thanks to blow to head. But it not enough. He need that so sleep more."

I nodded. "I'll deal with that."

The official grunted. "He a bad man."

"Very bad man," I rasped, surprised by the statement, and even more surprised by the hand he'd put on my forearm as I strolled by him to reach the crate.

We were in a weird ante-office that reminded me of a loading bay back home.

There were squeaky concrete floors and lots of these crates all around me, and none of them were stacked in a way that was good for health and safety.

On the back wall, there was a window that overlooked a small runway, but I knew just around the corner was the larger airport. One I'd be transferring to for my flight home the second this business was over with.

"My sister," the official rasped. "She gone."

I blinked. "I'm sorry for your loss."

He shook his head. "No. Not dead. Alive. Gone." His gaze cut to the box. "He a Triad?"

"He has ties with them." We'd learned that much. I rubbed my thumb against my middle and forefinger, the universal sign for money. "He's the money man."

He gritted his teeth. "I thought so. Looked into him. Saw much. Can't find sister. Mother sad. Help?"

The broken, disjointed English somehow made his request all the more poignant. I hadn't expected this, had just thought it was business, not personal, but I guessed it fit.

This guy wore an army uniform. He was an official in more ways than one, and while I knew corruption was rife in every country at all levels, this was just a tad too unusual to be true.

"I'll set some people on it."

The soldier's eyes narrowed on me. "Thank you."

I shrugged. "I make no promises."

"Understand that. She might be gone for good." His nostrils flared, the pain of that hard truth hitting home, so I reached over, grabbed his shoulder, and squeezed.

"I'll do my best." I cleared my throat. "You got a pen?"

He nodded, pulled one out of a front flap on his chest, and gave it to me. On the paper bag, I wrote out my burner number, tore off the slip from the bag, and handed it to him.

"I'll be home in thirty-six hours. Call me or send me info then."

"I will. Thank you."

I nodded, then moved past him to get to Donavan. When I opened up the box, which hadn't been nailed shut yet, I grimaced at the smell of piss and shit. The fucker had evidently messed himself in there, which made this a real fucking blast.

The place had no AC, not outside of my hotel room, and the fetid odor was even worse than what I'd dealt with when I'd gone into that pit of hell where we'd found Amara, Ghost, and Tatána.

I'd been with Link, Nyx, and Giulia that night as we rode into the dark, potentially on a wild goose chase that had led to this moment in time.

The bastard was definitely thinner than the pictures I'd seen flashing on the screen of late. He had warrants out for his arrest, now that Ghost, my brother Maverick's woman, had gone to the cops to end him, and the stubbled gaunt cheeks, the thinning hair, the lines on his face, and the sunburn that randomly stained his skin, all spoke of a man who'd gone from an easy life to poverty.

That pleased me.

After what I'd seen in that fun box of his, I figured a man like him deserved such a fate.

"Smells bad," the official grunted.

"Yes."

A bag crinkled, and I peered up and saw that he'd opened up his briefcase. The thing was like a fucking carpet bag, Mary Poppin's style, because he pulled out ten bags of what I recognized as moth balls.

My nose twitched, unsure which scent I fucking preferred. Determining that Link owed me a shot of tequila every day until I died as the guy started opening bags and tossing moth balls to neutralize the stench into the crate, I roughly calculated Donavan's weight—he looked to be about one-seventy with how emaciated he was—and then I did the math Stone had given me.

With the dosage calculated, I went a little heavy by five ml and dosed up the syringe.

Leaning into the crate made it even harder to do as Stone had directed.

If I took this too fast, he'd go into respiratory arrest. I needed to stick him in the thigh, which meant getting way too close to all the nasty, so I sucked it up, held my breath so I didn't breathe in too much of his shit, and I did my thing, letting the drug fuck with his system and not his heart.

I wasn't sure how long he'd be out of it for, but with the concussion he already had—he had a goose egg the size of my face, and it was cracked and bleeding, which added to his currently rakish appearance—I figured both would work together to keep him asleep.

Fingers crossed.

Or we were fucked.

I wasn't a religious man, not at all. You couldn't live in my world, do the shit I did, and think God existed.

But at that moment, I really hoped he did. Not to save my ass, but so that Lily could get her own back. She deserved that, and God, after putting her through all the stuff she'd gone through, owed her that much at least.

And that wasn't anything compared to what Ghost, Tatána, and Amara owed him either.

I plucked my lip between my teeth as I helped the soldier, whose name I genuinely couldn't read on the stitching on his uniform, and we carried on pouring mothballs in there until he looked like he was in some kind of *Gulliver's Travels* kiddie ball pit.

The sight of him, this billionaire magnate, so disheveled, amused me, and I wanted nothing more than to take a photo, but fuck, that led to prison and I wasn't an idiot.

The official pulled out a hammer and some nails, apparently

uncaring that Lancaster might choke on whatever the fuck was in moth balls—not that I blamed him—and we put the lid back on and started to nail him in place.

It felt very much like I was nailing him in a coffin, and I actually thought that might be a fitting end.

Link wanted Lily to be the one to end him. I wasn't sure if she was strong enough for that. Sure, she was strong enough to deal with what her cunt father had done to her, but outright murder?

Naw.

That was hard.

Burying him alive though?

What a way to end this fucker.

Humming at the thought, I said, "Thank you for your help."

The official shrugged. "You paid me for it."

My lips twitched. "Above and beyond the call of duty."

The other man's smile was small. "True." He bowed to me, and though I was awkward, I bowed back, and he moved over to the handle of the pulley and started walking toward the door.

Well, that was business accounted for.

I strode out the other way, the way I'd come in which was like the customer entrance, and as I peered back at the warehouse once I was outside, the scent of filth still in my nostrils, I smirked as I climbed into the cab that would take me to the airport.

This wasn't my idea of a good vacation, but it sure had ended sweetly.

FIVE

REX

I WAS NERVOUS.

I'd admit it.

So much could have gone wrong, and Steel was my brother. Not just the MC variety either. He, Nyx, Link, Maverick, and Storm were like my fucking kin. Sin was too, but he actually was blood. We were tied in other ways, but the strength of my links with the other guys was tight enough to be blood too.

The idea of sending Steel off to another country, risking him being caught up in a human trafficking ring when that was the exact opposite of our intention, had me gnawing on antacids every night of the three weeks he'd been away.

Until he was here, until the crate was on the back of our truck, my stomach lining would be attacked by my gut.

I grunted when Nyx muttered at my side, "Wonder how long this is going to fucking take."

I shrugged. "No idea. As long as it needs to, I guess."

We were outside JFK, waiting on Steel with his bike on the back of the cage that Hawk, Giulia's brother, was driving.

We'd switch that out for the crate when we maneuvered to the cargo area of the airport the second Steel was back with us.

Truth was, we weren't going to be hitting a home run until we were on Sinners' territory. Only then could I breathe a deep sigh of relief.

It was shitty of me to put Hawk in the position of driving around with a man in a crate on his truck bed, but it was three AM and I was hoping we'd be left alone.

The Five Pointers had helped bribe their people until we hit the state line, and then our own markers with the state and county police would see us through when we rolled across Jersey.

Still, sometimes someone got greedy, and now wasn't the time for that.

What we were doing was stupid.

So fucking stupid.

I shouldn't be here. Neither should the rest of the council, but we were because this was personal.

This fucker had hurt our women, and we needed to make him pay.

The only person who wasn't here, which filled me with some comfort because he could take over as Prez in a heartbeat, was Maverick.

He'd refused to come, but I knew he'd be waiting, knew he wanted to get his licks in too.

That he was starting to feel again was a relief. I just wished that things were simpler for him and Ghost, because I was beyond ready to get my brother back.

Eyes scanning the front of the airport, I almost missed Steel until I caught sight of him strolling through the doors like he owned the fucking place.

The fucker wasn't dumb enough to wear his cut through the airport, so he just wore a wifebeater, jeans, and boots with a satchel on his back. I wasn't used to him looking so normal, so I'd almost missed him.

Around me, my brothers stiffened, straightening up on their rides as we watched him look for us.

I hadn't told him we'd be waiting—I didn't need to.

Some shit went unspoken.

When he saw us, he directed his path toward us. As he approached, he clapped hands with Sin, Link, and Nyx before he headed over to me. We butted shoulders in greeting, and I asked, "Everything go okay?"

"I'm not in cuffs, so I figure that's a yes," he replied wryly, but he peered up at the sky then popped his neck. "Fuck, it's good to be home."

"You just flew in first class," Link grumbled. "Only you'd be happy for it to be over."

He grinned. "Yeah, and it was fucking fine too. But still, even if one of the flight attendants sucked me off, I'm sick of fucking sweating."

My lips twitched at that. "Trust you to join the mile-high club."

He winked. "You bet your sweet ass I did."

"Thanks. My ass is still sweet. I was so nervous you'd stopped loving it."

He grinned at me, slapped me on the arm, then dumped his bag on the floor before rummaging around and grabbing his cut.

When he dragged it on, he sighed. "Now that feels better." He peered at the truck bed, strode over to it, and muttered, "Let's get Baby on the road."

I rolled my eyes at the nickname for his ugly ass hog that had bright orange flames on top of a burnt orange background. It wasn't even sexy, just tacky.

He never had much taste for his rides. Though it was tuned to perfection, it definitely wasn't classy like my sweet black hog.

I hummed as Hawk and Nyx got the bike down with Steel's help, and when he was on the back of it, he grinned.

I got it.

If he was glad to be back, then we were glad to have him back too.

It was always disconcerting when one of my council was away too long. It reminded me of prison.

It wasn't like we had that many vacations in this life, and if we did, they were for a few days and involved a cluster of the MC tagging along for security reasons.

Steel had been out of the country for three weeks, and he'd been on a job that might have seen him never coming home.

So, fuck yeah, it was good to have him back.

"We ready to collect that piece of shit?" I hollered over the rumble of our engines when we all started up our bikes.

"Fuck yeah."

It happened so smoothly, the transfer, that I wasn't sure I could have planned it better—trust me, I'd planned this shit down to the nth degree.

The crate was moved onto the truck bed, and then we drove through the city, out toward the state line, and into our home state without a single issue.

Not a single boy in blue drove past us, and when we made it to the clubhouse, I knew we were all amazed by how easily that had gone.

If I was a religious man, I'd have said God was on our side, and I saw Link fiddling with his rosary a little more than he usually did, evidently deep in gratitude for how fucking 'swimmingly' that had gone down.

We'd been a time bomb ticking away, just waiting for it to explode in our faces.

He could have woken up, could have slammed his fists into the side of the crate and made himself known. Just because no cops had passed us didn't mean another car couldn't have noticed how weird shit was and reported us, so for us to be riding as if we weren't transporting a fugitive on the back of a truck?

More than good luck was on our side.

As we pulled up at the front of the clubhouse, I climbed off my hog the second I was standing and strode over to Hawk, who rolled down his window. "I'll send someone over to help you get the crate down. Don't open it. Leave it for the council."

He nodded, his chin dipping, and though he was curious, he wasn't going to ask.

I respected that about him.

Sure, he had a rep for being a miserable cunt, but I could deal with that. Better than stupid and cheerful like his twin. Hawk was serious, but he knew when to toe the line, and I knew he'd go far in the club if he kept it up and didn't let his brother drag him down.

I knew the pair of them were fucking clubwhores, which was a direct rule break, but fuck, there was plenty of pussy to go around, and I knew Prospects always fucked on the sly, still, I was curious what would happen when Hawk got patched in sooner than North.

Would things change?

Their dynamic had to. They were twins, after all. Used to doing shit together.

I hummed at the thought, feeling like I was playing God with their familial ties, but truth was, it wasn't Hawk's fault that North was just shit at most tasks the MC gave him. When the truck started up and Hawk drove to the Fridge, I watched him go and felt someone move up behind me.

I wasn't surprised when it was Nyx, because the fucker was quiet but not quiet enough for me not to hear him.

In our world, your senses either turned supernatural fast or you ended up in a body bag.

"What's the next step?"

I blew out a breath. "Honestly? I don't fucking know. It took so much to get to this point, I never thought it would happen."

"But it did. You played it smart, Rex. Thank you. Not just from me, but from us all, bro."

I shrugged. "Thanks aren't necessary. You'd do the same for me if it was—"

I couldn't finish the sentence, because I didn't want to.

I didn't want to say her name, not at that moment. I figured everyone fucking knew what I felt for Rachel Laker, the MC's attorney, but saying it then?

It would have been a lot more revealing than I could handle.

So I said shit. Nyx clapped me on the shoulder, and muttered, "Maybe we should call church once he's situated in the Fridge?"

I cut him a look. "Sure. We're all awake anyway. Want to call it?"

His nose crinkled, and I laughed. He'd called two churches since Storm had left, and it always made me laugh because he wasn't a natural leader, even if he was fucking good at it.

"Just do it, dumb fuck."

His lips twisted in a snarl, but he grabbed his cell. The group message we all had pinged to life, making my own phone buzz, and I nodded at him before I strode off.

I needed to clear my head before church, needed to figure out what the fuck our next step was.

We'd invested a lot in bringing Donavan back, and while it was for revenge, I wanted to make it worth our while too.

Our allies were at war with the *Famiglia*, and that was a war we'd just joined, thanks to one of the don's sons coming after Lily and attempting to kidnap her.

In the hostage attempt, Tiffany, Sin's woman, had been hurt and had lost their kid, and Lily was badly beat up from her car going off road and colliding with a tree.

The don's kid was dead now, drained of both lifeblood and

information, and I saw no reason why we couldn't do the same with Donavan.

It would be even better, because unlike the dumb fuck son behind the hostage attempt, who was an idiot the father spent most of his time shoving into rehab, Donavan Lancaster?

He was one of his close friends. They'd gone to college together.

With the right persuasion, there was nothing Donavan couldn't tell us about the *Famiglia's* operations.

Turning to watch Hawk drive the bastard away, I started to stroll slowly, letting myself process things, toward the bunkhouse where the three women were living.

Girls, Tiffany insisted we call them, and for lack of a better word, I had no alternative to use.

"Where you going, Prez?" Steel tossed out.

I didn't answer because I didn't need to. I just raised a hand over my head and pointed at the bunkhouse where the women, 'girls,' were staying.

As I approached, I saw a small face through the window, and my lips twisted, because somehow, the compound had become a kind of halfway house for chicks of all ages.

I wasn't sure how that had happened.

How we'd managed to tuck a technically kidnapped child into the mix alongside three trafficking victims and a lunatic hacker who usually got us into more shit than she got us out of. Then there was Giulia, a bloodthirsty bitch who was the only one capable of soothing the torment in my brother's soul. Lily, whose fucking eyes made me feel like I was having a come-to-Jesus moment every time I stared deep into them, and who, I figured, did the same for Link—made him feel things that he hadn't felt in nearly forty years of living. Then there was Tiff. Lost, adrift, tied to us while somehow being even more of a part of this clusterfuck than anyone else.

She was the don's secret daughter.

A secret daughter, for fuck's sake.

It was like something from one of those Harlequin novels my mom had loved reading, except this shit had life and death consequences.

Katina, Ghost's kid sister, ducked out of the window, and I figured she was rushing into the living room where most of the women were undoubtedly sitting.

Having known our intent tonight, I had no doubt that Mav would be in the sitting room too, so when I made it around there, opened up the door, and saw seven women, one child, and a brother staring back at me expectantly, even though it wasn't even five AM yet, I just shrugged and said, "The boogeyman is no more."

SIX

STONE

"I FEEL like I'm losing my mind."

I smiled at Harriet, who was in the hospital for aggressive radiation therapy, and tried to soothe her by rubbing her shoulder. "Harriet, you're not losing your mind."

"Just a part of my brain," she replied with a sniff.

My lips twisted because she was one of the strongest people I knew. In fact, the more I stayed around the oncology unit, the more I realized exactly how strong the human race could be.

Every single one of the patients here were fighters. They had their down days, they had their moments where they needed to cry, just to slump in their chairs as the poison that we pumped into their veins swept everything, good and bad, from their system. But for the most part, they were strong.

Warriors of old in a modern facility.

"You're not losing your mind," I repeated.

She shook her head. "I feel like I am."

My brow puckered. "What makes you say that?"

She sucked in a breath. "I saw someone in Angela's room the other night, Stone."

My mouth worked at that. "You mean Alex?"

"No, it was too late for visitors. Alex left with Oliver with everyone else, the same time my Frank went home." She blew out a breath. "I wanted to tell you sooner, but it was your day off, and then..." Her shoulders shook. "I thought you'd think I was crazy, so I put it off."

Compassion filled me but, keeping my voice calm, I asked, "Who was it, Harriet?"

"I don't know, but I heard Angela cry out." She quivered. "I called for the nurse, but no matter how many times I pushed the buzzer, no one came." She bit her lip. "I was going to—I thought about pushing the emergency button, but I couldn't reach."

"You had a nasty dose that day, Harriet. There's no need to sound so mad at yourself."

"What if someone was hurting her?"

"Why would anyone hurt Angela?" I asked, even though my heart was beating like a fucking drum.

This was the first time a patient had confirmed my suspicions, but the truth was, I didn't have a clue what to do with it.

Did I go to the cops?

If I did, what would I say?

Grievously ill patients in the hospital were dying?

Angela wasn't going to have an autopsy. This would get swept under the rug again, just like it had with Louis and Thomas two months ago.

Once, well, I could have made a mistake.

Louis had been old. Nearly a hundred, he was blind in both eyes and deaf in both ears, and he was bedridden.

His death had been a blessing, thanks to an aggressive pancreatic carcinoma.

Technically.

A *technical* blessing.

When he'd died, he'd been brighter than usual. Not on the brink of death's door—not more so than usual.

There were always ways of telling if someone was close to passing over, and it boiled down to something that medical science would never agree with.

One: gut instinct.

Sometimes, the scent of death lingered in the air, as if the Grim Reaper himself was wearing aftershave.

Two: food.

A dying man or woman didn't care what they ate. They just ate. Sometimes they didn't, sometimes they did. But a favorite food? It lost the taste, that very essence that made it a favorite.

I knew it sounded stupid.

Truly, I did. And I knew my colleagues would mock me for it, but I'd seen it so many times that it was true to me.

My grandmother—she who loved KFC more than she loved me—that final month of her life had told us, "Ain't got none of the flavor no more."

My mother, who adored dill pickles, and even more the juice in which they came, had turned her nose up even at the pickles in a MickyD Big Mac—and everyone knew they were the best dill pickles around—when breast cancer had robbed us of her.

As for Louis, his favorite had been orange Jell-O. I'd sneaked him cups when I shouldn't. The old man went through as many as I could procure for him, until I started to feel like an orange Jell-O bandit, but he'd had no sight, no hearing. What joy was there in the world for him if he couldn't have that too?

And that last day?

He'd eaten eight of the damn cups I'd brought him.

And Thomas? He was in for palliative care as he went through rounds of chemo for lung tumors. The morning before his death, his wife had brought him a picnic basket filled with his favorite foods.

He'd even offered me a blini with caviar on top, for God's sake. They'd been sitting in the room like they were having a romantic picnic!

And sure, it could be said that people just died. They did, and I knew that. But this felt wrong.

Just...wrong.

It wasn't like I could say anything to Harriet. Fuck, I couldn't say *anything* to *anyone*.

Speaking out about Angels of Death was notoriously difficult, because getting the word out wasn't something the hospital itself would actually want.

I'd noticed three patients had passed, and this was since I'd joined the department.

How many other people had died in odd ways?

How many other deaths required investigations?

It meant compensation and expensive research into who the perpetrator had treated.

I sucked in my cheeks, pinching them with my teeth, even as I told Harriet, "I'm sure it was a bad dream, sweetie. Lottie said she was fine in the morning."

Harriet bit her bottom lip. "She did?"

I nodded. Even though it was a lie.

Harriet sank back against her pillow and whispered, "Thank the Lord for that."

Well, I wouldn't go that far...

I finished checking the site of her IV line, which had grown infected, and made notes on her chart about the subsequent direction of her treatment.

When I was done, I smiled at her and said, "I'll see you before I leave for the day."

Her eyes sparkled. "Thanks, Stone."

I winked. "My pleasure."

My smile lasted for as long as it took me to make it out through the door, and the guilt hit me next, as did one of the pharmacy assistants who was heading into Harriet's room.

My brow rose at the sight of her, but I smiled and informed her, "One of the nurses will confirm her new meds."

"Thanks, doctor."

Nodding, I peered back at Harriet, who waved at me, prompting me to wave back. I wasn't supposed to get close to my patients, and everywhere else, I'd been fine. I'd been able to stay away, keep my distance, but here? It was impossible.

That was why I told the ones I liked and who liked me to call me Stone.

They needed the personal touch, and it wasn't something they got often in a place where protocol was king.

I knew I'd get into shit if anyone found out, and patients were under strict requests to only call me Stone if we were alone. Thus far, there'd been no issues.

But that alone told me something about this ward.

Secret conversations.

Secret interactions.

I'd been looking up Angels of Death, and had seen how they got to know each person they decided to 'treat.' They were doing their duty, they thought. Trying to ease the pain of those who were beyond saving...

It was bullshit. Total and utter bullshit, but in this ward, it was doable.

I had a deal with the patients to call me Stone. Why couldn't someone else have something similar going down?

With me, there was no nefarious intent. But with someone else? Who the fuck knew?

As I passed a few nurses, a couple of med students, some junior residents and some senior, I avoided them, grateful I was on my break.

When I got to the nurses' station, I handed over Harriet's chart and told Raina, who was in charge today, about the change in Harriet's dosage as the infection site wasn't improving.

She nodded, cast me a concerned look, which told me I wasn't holding up under the strain that well, and asked, "You doing okay, Stone?"

I shook my head. "I'm just tired."

Her nose curled up. "Aren't we all, darling?"

I laughed. "True." I looked at the clock, which sat behind her desk, and told her, "I'll be back in an hour."

She waved me off, but instead of going down to the cafeteria to fill my grumbling stomach, I headed for the fire exit that had a faulty door at the back of the department.

It was supposed to have been repaired, but staff who smoked came out here for a quick fix since it was faster than going around to the main entrance.

I slipped out, took a seat on the step, and pulled out my phone.

I'd given up smoking two years ago, but just sitting here in the corner with cigarette butts around me and the scent of tobacco staining the air?

Damn, it made me wish for one.

I could almost feel the nicotine-tinged smoke penetrating my being as I sucked in a deep, calming breath.

It didn't work.

I knew the psychology behind it. Knew that smokers sucked in deep breaths that controlled the autonomous respiratory system like they were in a meditation or something.

I'd tried meditating without tobacco.

It hadn't worked.

Grunting, I unlocked my phone and dialed Indy's number.

"Bitch. Where the fuck have you been?"

Her greeting had me crinkling my nose. "You always know how to say the sweetest things."

"Fuck that. Where. The. Fuck. Have. You. Been?"

I sighed. "I want a cigarette."

"A cigarette?" Like I'd known it would, that shut her up. "You? Why?"

"Because I'm an addict, and once an addict, always an addict."

She snorted. "Bullshit. You're the strongest woman I know. You dropped coke, doll face. You sure as fuck don't need that stuff."

"I genuinely think I was more hooked to the cigs than the coke. I mean, the coke was a, what? Three-time thing?" I grumbled glumly, eying one of the butts on the ground, soggy and leaking brown water, with interest.

I mean, I wasn't going to pick one up, but still, they were bizarrely tempting.

"What's going on?"

"You busy?"

"You caught me at the right moment. I'm between clients."

Indy ran the best tattoo shop this side of the Hudson. She was based in the small town of Verona, and if the mayor didn't give her the key to the city for all the traffic she brought into the place soon, then there was no justice in the world.

Of course, that was more than true.

Sadly.

Huffing out a breath, I inquired, "How's Quin?"

"Still inside."

My brow puckered. "I know that. I meant you were going to see him the other day, weren't you?"

"Yeah. He was talking all kinds of cryptic shit."

I fell silent at that. "Oh."

Her silence said it all too.

"Oh. Yeah."

MC business.

Fuck.

It was everywhere. Like a venomous snake that kept on growing with each bite, with each kill.

It never died, but it could infect everything in its vicinity.

"He's only in there on a short sentence, why would they get him involved in something—"

"We can't talk about this," I warned her, and my voice was hard because even though I knew she wanted to, and I got it, there was nothing to say.

When you patched in and became a member, you signed yourself over to the club.

I hadn't even done that, but I was just as tied.

Money.

Rex had knotted me in with my tuition. I was one of the only people not struggling to get by, thanks to student loan debt, but my debts would last a helluva lot longer than most people's would.

I blew out a breath. "Aside from the cryptic stuff, he doing okay?"

"He's buff."

"They always are."

"They work out more in there. I swear, if he wasn't my baby brother, I'd think he was fine."

"You're an artist. You can think he's fine."

She sniffed. "It's wrong, but dayum, he's pretty."

I laughed. "You get a picture?"

"Just sent it."

I pulled the phone away, went to the messaging app, and whistled the second I set eyes on him.

Fuck, Caleb *was* pretty. Even in a blue jumpsuit.

I whistled again, unable to stop myself. "When did that happen?" I muttered.

"What? When did he get beautiful? Or when did we get old?"

"Fuck off, if you're old then what the hell am I?"

She snickered. "Ancient."

There was a four-year age gap between us, and while that had never presented itself as an issue aside from when we were at school and we were in different years and classes, now that we were older, it meant bupkis.

"Fuck. He's like 'robbing the cradle' beautiful."

She sniffed. "Now you see my predicament."

"I do. Oy vey." My heart clutched at the thought of him in prison though. "Be better when he's home, love."

"Yeah. I miss the little shit. I can't believe he got put away like two weeks after getting patched in."

"Sucks."

It did, but that was the life. Fuck, that was the major problem with every part of the life.

Jail.

It was always at the other end of things.

That, and death. But hell, death came to us all. Didn't matter if you were in an MC or not.

I couldn't even say that you could guarantee a nicer death by being a good person. Good people died in shitty ways too.

Case in point, what was going down at the hospital.

"How's he doing?"

"He's okay."

Her voice alone told me that she didn't get it, and neither did I, but we weren't in the life. Both of us had made specific choices and decisions that took us away from it, yet somehow, we were all tangled up with them regardless.

Indiana, because both her brothers were patched in with the MC.

Me, because when it had come down to it, and I'd had the rug pulled out from under me when my scholarship had fallen through, I'd had no alternative but to rely on the MC to achieve my goals.

The only constant in my life was a desire, a *need*, a burning fucking urge that was like a decade-long UTI, to be a doctor.

It was my dream. My passion. My goal.

Rex had helped me achieve that, and sure, I'd sold my soul to the devil to get it, but at least I'd be able to do what I was born to do.

I pursed my lips at the thought, then murmured, "What did they ask?"

"To take some pictures in." She sighed. "Don't like getting involved with that shit, you know that."

"I do." And I didn't blame her. It was a shitty thing for her to have to do. Take something inside that might eventually lead to extra time tacked onto Caleb's sentence.

But I got it. *That was the life.*

The fucking life.

"What pictures?"

"That's what made no sense. Of this fucking bike Link had just tuned up. It was this massive fucking issue too, because I was late in going."

"Why?" She was never late.

She huffed. "You'll get mad."

I hummed. "Sure I will. Doesn't mean I won't give you a wedgie the next time I see you if you don't tell me now."

"I took some of that Remeron you told me not to take."

My brows lifted. "The shit I specifically said your quack of a doctor shouldn't have prescribed? That shit?"

"Yeah. It worked the first night, but the second? Jesus, I felt like death warmed over. I went to the ER with it."

"And you didn't tell me?"

"What? And get served a dose of 'I told you so'?"

I snorted. "Since when has that stopped us from ever telling each other shit?"

Her gulp was audible. "This was different."

"Why?"

"'Cause I'm fucking exhausted, Stone. I'm not sleeping. At all. And fuck, the dreams are back. I'm pretty sure I'm losing my mind."

The words resonated with me in a way I couldn't even begin to describe. "It's funny you should say that." What with Harriet, now Indy, and me? Maybe insanity was airborne right now.

"Funny?" She huffed. "Thanks, babe."

"No, not funny har-har, but funny as in strange. I'm pretty sure I'm losing my sanity too."

I didn't have to see her face to know that she was probably glowering at my words.

We both knew what her problems were.

Nyx.

Quin, aka Caleb.

Her bros.

Both men were in a one-percenter club. Both men were leading violent lives.

More than that, she'd been having nightmares since she was a kid, and I knew why too.

She'd seen her bro fuck around with her uncle's shotgun before said uncle had been killed in an 'accident.'

The uncle who'd been screwing her older sister, Carly, and who'd messed with her some as a kid too.

I was the only person in the fucking world who knew all those things, and that was why she suffered.

If Nyx knew that the cunt had touched her as well?

We both knew he'd go insane, and Nyx was already pretty fucking mental. He didn't need any help becoming a weirder motherfucker.

I didn't have to be an integral part of the MC anymore to know there were ways he'd found to release his anger at the world.

I hadn't failed to miss the recent uptick in vigilante-style deaths of pedophiles in states that were linked to the Sinners' chapters.

Just because I stayed out of the life didn't mean I couldn't figure out what the fuck they were doing.

It was just a wonder they weren't on the FBI's radar. That'd make more fucking sense than a doctor picking up on shit.

I hummed under my breath. "I'm pretty sure there's an angel of death."

"A what?"

I sighed. "Some sick fuck who wants to end people's suffering, even if they're not ready to die yet."

She exhaled sharply. "You mean a murderer? A murderer is walking around the fucking hospital where you work?"

"I don't know. I think so. I think I'm also paranoid just because of where we come from. There isn't murder and mayhem wherever we go. I just need to take a chill pill and stop seeing monsters in the closet—"

"Stone, darlin', you're not paranoid. You're sensible. You and I both know how this shitty, fucked-up world works. It sucks. It does. And you're not losing your mind. If you truly think that, then maybe you should alert someone—"

"I don't know *who* to alert. Crap like this gets swept under the rug."

"Surely there's protocol?"

"There is, but it's ignored. Especially in places like this one. They're all swanky and shit here. No one would dare kill rich people," I mocked.

She snorted out a laugh. "Yeah, death is only for the poor."

My lips twitched. "Exactly." I rubbed my brow, then I twisted around when I heard the door behind me squeak.

Not wanting to be overheard, I muttered, "Indy, I'd better go—"

That was when I felt them behind me.

A second later, I felt the stab of the pinprick in my throat, and I tried to cry out, "Indy!"

But it was too late.

A cloth with the cloyingly sickly-sweet stench of chloroform on it was pressed to my mouth and nose, and it had me struggling with my attacker until I didn't even have the impetus to do that.

Whatever they hit me with, combined with the chloroform, I could already feel my faculties starting to be affected.

Fuck!

What was that?

I tried to keep myself alert by going through my symptoms, but no matter what I did, registering that I had to have been dosed with diazepam for the chloroform to be working so fast, maybe a dose of adrenaline too—

My thoughts blurred until I could feel all cognitive function starting to slip away.

I felt sure Indy's tinny voice from my cellphone speaker was a dream, but maybe it wasn't.

One second, it was there, and the next, it wasn't.

Just like my consciousness.

SEVEN

INDY

MY HEART WAS POUNDING in my chest so hard that it made the nightmares that tormented me nightly look like a walk in the park.

So far, in my life, only the people who'd deserved to die had died. I'd never dealt with death on a regular basis like Stone had, like my bro Nyx did.

But here, now? I knew what I was facing.

Someone had just hurt Stone.

Someone had hurt her after what she just told me.

An angel of death.

I sucked in a sharp breath, trying to reason that nothing was wrong. Maybe her service had just cut out. Shit like that happened all the time, didn't it?

And the only answer that resonated with me was the fact that, yeah, this shit happened all the time to *normal* people. Coverage cut out, batteries died—on normal folk.

Nothing about Stone or me was normal. We tried to be, fuck how we tried, but we weren't.

By blood and bone, we were tied to the Satan's Sinners MC, and that meant karma liked fucking with us.

I stared at a mandala I'd photographed three weeks ago, one that sat on Sin's woman's finger and hand.

Her brand.

The mandala gave me a kind of peace that couldn't be feigned. There was an eternal beauty to mandalas, a repetitive symmetry that gave me a deep sense of comfort.

I found no comfort in that today.

Stone was...

Fuck, I didn't know what Stone was.

Needing more calm than I was currently feeling, I ceased listening to the blank space on the other end of the line and quickly called the hospital where she worked.

I had them as a contact because I was her ICE, but when I connected through, without waiting on the receptionist to greet me, I asked, "Can you please page Dr. Walker?"

"Dr. Walker? Of course. Which unit?"

My eyes widened at the simple question, and for too long, I just gaped even harder at the wall opposite me—*I couldn't remember.*

She'd transferred a few months ago, and oddly enough, even though people died a lot there, she loved it.

Trouble was, people died in every unit.

Which fucking unit was this one in particular?

"Ma'am? Do you know? Because I have other people waiting on the other lines."

My lips were dried out from how long I gaped, then I croaked, "Oncology."

I prayed that was the correct one, prayed with all my heart and fucking soul that was right and that I hadn't gotten it wrong, and when she replied, "I'll page her right now. Is there a message you'd like to give her?" I breathed a sigh of relief.

"Tell her to contact Indiana?"

"The state?" the woman questioned, confused.

"No. Family. Please, just do so quickly. I have bad news she needs to hear."

"Oh, I'm so sorry! I'll contact her now."

"Thank you," I rasped, then when she disconnected the call, I reached up and pinched the bridge of my nose.

There was a difference between a nightmare being real and a nightmare happening and unfolding while I was in bed.

This was, most definitely, the former.

I could feel my heart starting to pound once more, and the rushing of blood in my ears was so deafening that I didn't hear the door to my section open, and when it did, I jerked when a scent I recognized filled my nostrils.

Nyx.

He always smelled like that—like musk, bikes, and aftershave. Like he'd doused himself in Axe so much as a kid that his skin forever held the imprint of it now. Somehow, it worked on him though.

When I recognized it was him, I stared at his face, terrified beyond belief.

I knew why he was here. He was trying to get me to ink his next tattoo, and while I'd agreed to do Giulia's the last time they were here, I'd refused to do his because I was mad at him.

He was pissed at Caleb for getting caught, and I was pissed at him for not even calling our baby bro, who was doing his first stint inside.

None of that mattered now. I jerked up, slipped my arms around his waist, and whimpered, "Nyx, it's Stone."

He tensed in my hold, and I knew why, but I wasn't saddened by it. We weren't tactile by nature, any of us, so for me to hug him, that meant shit was real.

"Stone? As in Steel's Stone?"

The state I was in could be considered panicked, but even I had to roll my eyes at that. "She isn't Steel's Stone."

He scoffed, "I beg to differ."

"Shame *he* isn't begging," I groused, then I shook my head. "Anyway, now isn't the time for this conversation! Someone took Stone."

"Someone took her?" He pulled back so he could look down at me. "Is this a joke?"

"Do I look like I'm having fun?" I snapped, pissed that he'd think that.

"Why do you think someone took her?"

"It's crazy, I know, but she was just telling me that she thought there was an angel of death at the hospital, and then the line went dead, it was like she dropped her phone, but I could hear her breathing still. Like she was rasping or something."

"Rasping? You sure you're not misreading things?"

"No, I'm pretty fucking sure I'm not misreading things, Nyx! How do you misread those things?" I snarled at him, shoving him away now that he was starting to piss me off. "I called the hospital and asked them to have her paged, but they haven't gotten back in touch with me yet."

"Yet being the operative word." He patted me on the back. "I'm sure everything is fine."

"You think there's no correlation that after she told me someone was murdering patients in her unit she goes quiet?"

My words were cool, calm.

But there was iron behind them, and he heard it, so he eyed me warily.

"Angels of death are, what? The fucked-up weirdos who kill sick patients as a kind of euthanasia, right? There's a difference between actively doing that and then murdering someone."

"No, there fucking isn't, dipshit. Do you even hear yourself right now?" I scowled at him. "Anyway, less of the fucking judgment. We both know murder is murder." I tipped my chin up at him, watching his eyes narrow into slits.

"What do you want me to do, Indy?"

"Get her fucking back."

"And what if she hasn't gone anywhere? What if her battery just died?"

"It didn't. I'm telling you. She cut off mid-sentence, then she was breathing, and then nothing. Someone else cut the call!"

When I saw my urgency was finally starting to get through, I almost wanted to cry, because if he believed me, then he'd act.

His new patch that was tacked onto the front of his cut declared him VP of the Satan's Sinners MC, now that Storm had traipsed down to Ohio to become the Prez of the chapter down there. Leaving his kid and wife behind.

Dumb fuck.

If anyone could help Stone, it was Nyx.

I tugged the wrist of his Henley. "Please, bro, do something. I swear, I'm not making this shit up."

He bit the inside of his cheek for a second, then he reached into his pocket and grabbed his cell.

I watched him, too wary to hope, and when he muttered, "Rex, there's an issue with Stone—" I felt the relief hit me.

The Sinners were better than the cops at getting shit done. I knew in my gut something was wrong, a gut that hadn't led me astray in all these years.

Stone would have figured out a way to have messaged me back by now if something had happened to her phone. We knew each other's numbers like they were our own. She could have sent me a text or called me from a landline. She knew I liked things done a certain way.

I liked to end each call by telling her that she was a pain in my ass, and she liked to tell me that I was a stitch in her side.

Not exactly loving words, but they were ours.

That was how we did shit.

Jesus.

How had our conversation derailed so badly?

And what the fuck would I do if she was hurt? For real hurt?

She was my lifeline some nights. When I couldn't sleep and I knew she was on night shift, she was the only person who could get me back into bed without feeling like it was a hot tin roof and I was a cat.

She had to be okay.

Not just for me, but for all the hundreds and thousands of people she was supposed to save in her life.

She couldn't die.

She just... She couldn't.

Could she?

The thought made me want to sob, but that was the life. People died. I'd just never thought Stone would be one of them when she was a hundred miles away from the Sinners' compound.

EIGHT

STEEL
BEFORE

"BEAR?"

The Prez raised his head, his brows lowering as he stared at me. "Steel? You okay, son?"

We weren't related, but Bear always treated Rex's friends as if they were his kids. I didn't know why, had no clue why he always called us 'son,' but at that moment, that he did was particularly fucking painful.

The time I'd been recovering from a steel plate to the head pretty much covered exactly how painful this was.

I felt it like a knife to the gut, a knee to the balls.

I had never given a fuck about who my father was before, but now that I had an answer to the question in my mind, it resonated with me in ways I just couldn't let go of.

If anyone would know who sired me, it'd be Bear. Bear knew everything. I wasn't sure how, but he and Rex were cut from the same cloth, and when, one day, Rex took over the position of Prez, when Bear was comfortable in letting shit slide toward his son or if, God forbid, he died, I knew Rex would rule in the same way.

Knowing everything, controlling it all, and making it look fucking easy as he kept his hands on all the puppet strings.

I pretty much staggered into the office, an office that hadn't changed in years, and when Bear studied me, his bushy brows doing the fucking tango as he took me in, I begged, "Who's my father?"

The begging tone didn't suit me. Sinners didn't plead for anything. Not for mercy or for cunt.

But in this, I pleaded. And I'd carry on doing so because the prospect of sharing DNA with that sick fuck?

Hell. On. Earth.

He tensed at my question, his back straightening up, and the distance he shoved between us by leaning back and away from me was the first nail in the coffin.

He knew.

And when he lied, saying, "Steel, what are you bringing that up for?" I knew it was because he didn't know what else to say.

He didn't want to admit to the truth, not when it had repercussions past me finding out who my sperm donor had been.

I felt itchy all over, like my skin was too tight for my frame, and I dipped my chin at him, grinding out, "Don't bullshit me, Bear."

"Don't use that tone with me," he barked. "I'm your fucking Prez. Don't forget about that."

My jaw tensed, and I stabbed the air in front of me with my finger. "You know who he is."

"Your ma was club snatch, son. How the fuck am I supposed to know who she spread her legs for?"

Another time, I might have thought he was trying to divert me by casting accusations at my mom's nature, but who the fuck was I kidding?

She was a slut.

Had been born from one, had died one. I'd probably be in her image if I had a pussy. Instead, I had a dick, thank fuck for that.

I gritted my teeth, and whispered, "Lana Jane told me Kevin was my father."

"You know not to mention that fucker's name inside these walls," Bear rasped, his leonine head turning bright red as he stared at me, earnest anger growing at my daring to voice the sick fuck's name in his presence.

When Nyx had killed Kevin, he'd done so in a way that could look accidental. The fuck went hunting, Nyx messed with his shotgun, and boom, the kickback had separated Kevin's skull from his neck.

Bear had gotten involved though, because the police had come sniffing around, wanting to know if Kevin had ties to the MC.

He didn't. He was the brother of an MC brother, but that didn't make him a part of the club.

Bear had to grease some palms, avert the investigation away from the Sinners, and all the while, he'd known, just like everyone else had, Nyx's Pop included, that Nyx had done what no one else had.

Taken out the goddamn trash.

My skin started itching again, and the buzz in my head made me feel like I was high. I'd smoked some weed before I patched in as a Prospect, and this was pretty much how I'd felt back then.

Like I was losing my mind.

I was a control freak by nature, liked to keep all my ducks in a row, and I didn't even like to get that drunk, but the fuzzies from beer and vodka were nothing compared to this.

I knew, point blank, that tonight, I'd be getting shit-faced because I had to. I had to do something to beat back these thoughts that were crowding me like a circle of demons intent on eating my soul.

"He's my father, isn't he?" I rasped, softer this time, calm when I felt anything but.

He narrowed his eyes at me. "Why do you wanna rake up this shit, boy?"

"Because Lana Jane fucking told me. Said if she'd known I was cut from the same fucking cloth as my daddy, she'd have fucking sold me Stone years ago."

Bear tensed at that, and if I'd thought he was angry before, that was nothing compared to now. A vein started pulsing at his temple, and his entire being seemed to swell with his rage.

We all knew the story.

Bear was pretty playful with the kids, a joker among his men, kind to the Old Ladies, unless they started getting too big for their boots...until he wasn't playful, kind, or a joker. Until the bear came out and he'd kill to defend and protect the people in his care.

"She said those specific words?"

His grating question filled me with relief. "She did."

His eyes flickered from left to right, darting around as he processed shit that only he knew—the things that entered the Prez's vault that lived between his ears.

He didn't say anything, but I knew he'd be saying shit to Lana Jane, and probably Stone too—asking if anyone had touched her.

Stone was like a daughter to him. She'd always hung around us. Tagging behind when she was younger, and along when she was older.

We were used to her being around, and what had started as her helping us with our homework at school—because the kid was fucking smart and we were the opposite of book smart, except for Mav and Rex—had turned into her always being there.

Bear wasn't the only one who'd castrate any motherfucker who'd dared touch her.

"Explain to me what happened," he rumbled.

My brow furrowed, but I admitted, "I went to ask her out on a date."

His eyes narrowed. "Thought you were tutoring her for

math?"

"I was." It was the one subject that she couldn't get a hold on, and I was good at it—I'd sat up half the fucking night learning the shit so I could teach it to her in a way that she'd be able to learn. Math, for me, was instinctive. I just got it. But that didn't help her, did it?

"And you went to ask her for a date?"

My nod had him tipping his chin up. "You better not be fucking around with her, Steel."

I scowled at him. "The second she's sixteen, I was going to fucking claim her. At eighteen, I was gonna make her my Old Lady."

His squinty-eyed look morphed into a swift grin. "About time you saw the lay of the land—"

I shook my head. "This changes shit, Bear. This changes everything. I ain't gonna claim her if Kevin is my father."

Bear scowled back at me. "Fuck, Steel, any sperm donor does exactly that—donates fucking cum. It takes more than that to become—"

"To become what? I've always fucking wanted her. Since she grew a set of tits and an ass." My mouth worked. "What if I'm like him?"

His brows lowered. "You didn't act on it."

"Of course I didn't," I snarled. "She's still a kid now. I wasn't going to push shit anyway, just wanted a fucking kiss."

He scraped a hand over his chin. "I was fifteen when I met Rene, and she was thirteen. It felt weird then, even though it was only two years, because in our world, two years means a fuck ton of a difference. I was a man at fifteen, but she wasn't a woman. It felt wrong, and I avoided her and my feelings for her. That's what men of honor do, Steel. That's exactly what you did, but you're wrong.

"Stone ain't like Rene. She's a woman. Her bitch of a mother saw to that, exposing her to the shit she did, and I wish that weren't true, but there's only so much I can fucking do. I ain't running a daycare here—" He blew out a breath. "But you ain't nothing like your father."

Our eyes clashed and held, and suddenly, there was a chasm between us. A whole fucking world, because he'd just confirmed it.

My father was—

I couldn't say it.

Wouldn't say it again.

But I knew.

He knew.

And the apology in his eyes killed me.

I scraped a hand over my face, trying to hide the tears in my eyes. "I understand if you want my cut," I said stiffly. "And if you want to watch me around the kids, I get it."

"Fuck, son, you ain't like him." He burst upright, looming over the desk as he growled, "I wouldn't have given you a cut if I thought you were—"

"Steel, don't be stupid."

The voice stunned me, and I whipped around, horrified to see that Rex was sitting there in the corner of the office, still as a rock.

I gaped at him, unbelieving that he was here to hear this shit. That he witnessed my downfall.

I'd never been more mortified or humiliated in my entire life.

He grimaced with apology, but I didn't stick around to hear shit.

I just took off. Shame beyond belief roared through me, to the point where I heard nothing, saw nothing, just darted into the bar, grabbed three bottles of vodka from behind the counter, rushed out of the clubhouse, and jumped onto my hog.

I had no idea where I was going, what I was going to do either, but I just knew that I needed out of here, stat.

NINE

STEEL
TODAY

I YAWNED past the jet lag, because to be honest, I was well rested. I'd been fed like a fucking prince on that plane, and my seat? The best couple of grand I could imagine spending, because I'd slept like a baby all while getting to drink the good shit.

I'd even had fucking champagne and caviar served by a pretty doll who'd sucked me off like a champion.

Close to purring at the memory, I washed my hair and started rinsing off. One thing that hadn't changed by shifting up a couple of classes from the cattle mart of economy—the stink.

What the fuck was it about planes that made you stink like shit?

The air was controlled and filtered, the temperature regulated...so what the hell was that about?

As I cleaned off, I heard someone pounding on my door, but I ignored it. A man's shower was sacrosanct, for fuck's sake. If ever there was time for a moment's peace, it was now.

Contemplating jacking off, or alternatively calling in JoJo or Jingles and having one of them suck me off because my balls were aching again, I soaped up my abs, and then I heard it.

"Steel! You open the motherfucking door right now!"

That was Rex.

My brows rose at the fact that he was hollering at me through the closed door, because Rex rarely raised his voice.

For a second, I was unsure what to fucking do, then I unfroze when I realized I had to act.

Shutting off the water, I heard him better now, and I grabbed a towel, dragged it around my waist, then grabbed another and draped it over my shoulders as I strode into the bedroom and yanked the door open after I unlocked it.

"What the fuck?"

Rex was pale, his features pinched, and his face was lined with both fury and...*terror*.

"What the fuck is it, Rex?" I snapped, freaked out by the state of him.

"Stone...she's been kidnapped."

My mouth worked. "The *Famiglia*? Those fucking cunts. I'll skin the bastards alive—"

Even as I spoke, I was turning my back to him as I headed toward the dresser to get some jeans and a shirt to cover up with.

But before I dropped the towel, Rex ground out, "No. Someone at the hospital took her."

I whipped around at that. "What? Who the fuck took her from the hospital?"

"I don't know. Nyx is trying to figure that out. Trying to see if he can get in touch with someone who will give us access to the CCTV footage, but—"

"But what?"

Rex blew out a breath. "She was on the phone with Indy."

I stilled at that. "What was she doing calling Indy? Was there a problem?"

Rex waved a hand. "Indy insists that they were talking, then mid-sentence, Stone just stopped."

My brow puckered. "Stone wouldn't do that. We all know how Indy is."

"Yeah. We do." His mouth tightened. "But she did. She just cut her off, and that was that. Indy contacted the hospital, asked them to page her, but when Nyx called again, the receptionist said that they couldn't get in touch with her."

"That doesn't mean someone's taken her—"

"No, it doesn't, but I know something's been weird with her for a few days now."

As confusion started to welter up inside me, I stared at my Prez.

Fear and panic were shoved aside as doubt laced my words. "You stay in touch with her?"

"You know I fucking do." His nostrils flared. "Now isn't the time to be getting into this shit."

"Isn't it? Sure as fuck feels like this is pertinent to the facts. You fucker, you know I kept her out of the MC on purpose!"

"I just fucking told you this has nothing to do with the *Famiglia*!"

"Bullshit. Of course it is. We go to war, and then one of our own gets taken? So soon after Lily and Tiff were kidnapped?"

"You know why they were. Stone has no ties to anyone."

"She has ties to us, you dumb piece of shit. That's enough for these people. And she's even easier. She's in New York. Christ, all they have to do is go down the fucking street to snatch her." I rubbed my brow, trying to figure this out, trying to figure out a way of getting her back. I'd never figured they'd be interested in her. If I had, she'd have had a guard. "I can pull some contacts, get someone to break rank to confirm they have her—"

Rex shook his head. "I think Indy is right. Stone called me the other day, your last night in Cambodia. I knew something was wrong with her, and she was pretty closemouthed—"

"As per fucking usual."

Rex shook his head and sealed a nail in his coffin. "Not with me."

"You fuck, are you seeing her? You know she's mine."

The words spewed out of me, even though I hadn't meant to let them. The truth was, Stone had been mine for as long as she'd been alive, and I was the one who was sacrificing my fucking world for her sake.

Yet, here this cunt was, trying to take my woman away from me, all while dragging her into the life I was trying to save her from.

It was bad enough the first thing she'd done was go to Rex to get him to fund her med degree and all the other shit she needed to become a doctor.

She was tied to us in ways I'd never be able to totally sever, but that was one thing.

This was another.

Just thinking of Stone and Rex fucking had me seeing red, and when I slammed my fist into his face, I didn't even fucking remember leaping across the room.

When I went to hit him again, I heard a, "Holy shit!" and then there was a palm catching my fist and shoving me back and away.

Within seconds, four or five brothers were in my bedroom, keeping me apart from Rex, who didn't even bother to catch the blood that was dripping down his face from my punch.

He glared at me, anger and irritation working their way into his expression, but he snarled, "Get your shit together, Steel. No, I'm not fucking Stone. She's like my goddamn sister. You should know that. And you should also know that if you're too chicken shit to claim her, then one of these days when she stops being so involved in her work, when she stops thinking about work and only work and that fucking cat of hers, that someone is going to come along and snatch her right out from under you."

"That's what I've wanted all along, just not someone from the life," I snarled at him, furious that he was bringing this shit up at all.

For once in my life, I didn't care that Hawk, Cruz, Sin, Link, and Jaxson were the ones to overhear this shit. Didn't give a fuck about anyone knowing my business.

I was just pissed that Rex was shoving this shit in my face, the bastard.

My fists ached with how hard I clenched them, my knuckles pinging to life as they absorbed how hard I'd smacked the fuck out of Rex.

But it wasn't enough.

"If I find out you've been fucking her—"

He sneered, "You'll what? Do fucking nothing, that's what you always do where she's concerned. If a real man decided to take her off the fucking singles market, then good for them. I won't be that guy, because she's my goddamn sister, and I swear to fuck, if you try to hit me again, I will break your hand." He growled under his breath at me, then snapped, "Okay, you listening with something other than your cock? I'm telling you that someone has her. It isn't *Famiglia* related. It has to do with this shit at the hospital.

"She happened to mention something to me the last time we talked, and I looked into it. There are a lot of fucking deaths going on in that ward of hers. Like, more than usual. And they tend to cluster around certain times, and when certain people are on the ward."

I shook my head at that, because there were more investigations going on than he was letting on if he could just reel off that information that way. Scowling at him, I barked, "You thought she was in danger?"

He gritted his teeth. "I thought it might be a possibility."

"That's why you said I needed to call her the other goddamn day. Because you knew—"

"I knew someone she liked, a patient that was close to her, had died. That's what I knew. So I looked into it, because she sounded really confused and upset, because that's what family should do for each other—"

"Fuck you, Rex. You know why I stay away from her."

"Yeah, and I thought it was a dumb fucking reason then, and I think it's a dumb fucking reason now."

Link tensed at that. "What? Why? You know what happened between them, Rex? And you never fucking shared anything?"

Rex snapped, "This isn't the time, Link. Christ. Stop being a gossiping cunt and get with the program. A murderer has Stone. We need to get on the road."

Link winced at Rex's insult, but he didn't argue, just muttered, "Come on, Steel, get changed. Rex is right. We need to be heading into the city."

I didn't respond, just shoved myself away from Hawk and Jaxson, who were clinging onto me like koala bears did to a eucalyptus tree.

"All right, I'm fine," I snapped. "I'm going to get dressed."

"Good, you have ten minutes, then we ride."

I tightened my mouth at his irritation—I was the one who deserved to be fucking irritated, but I didn't go for him. Not again. Even though I wanted to, because I knew he *would* break my hand, and I needed that to ride my bike, especially now.

They were right.

I'd gotten caught up, snagged in all the stupid shit, and I didn't have time for that.

Stone didn't have time for that.

If someone had taken her, be it the *Famiglia* like I thought or this—what did they call them? Those weirdos who trawled the wards for victims?—angel of death fucker in the hospital, either way, they weren't going to treat her to a Valentine's dinner and a bunch of goddamn roses, were they?

I tugged a wifebeater over my head, dragged on my jeans, and then slipped on my boots and laced them on tight.

When I went out, I grabbed my cut from the dresser where I'd placed it before, and once I was dressed, I gave Link a look.

He was pouting.

Of course.

Fuck.

I glared at him. "I don't want to talk about this. We don't have time."

"I can't believe you told Rex and not me."

"I didn't tell him. He found out by accident."

Link scowled. "That doesn't make it better."

I rolled my eyes at him as I started out of the bedroom that had been mine since I was patched in at nineteen. "This isn't *The Baby-Sitters' Club*, Link. I don't share all my secrets."

He sniffed. "No fucking shit." He grunted then. "Since when do you know what *The Baby-Sitters' Club* is?"

I flipped him the bird. He knew the answer to that.

The series had been Stone's favorite books as a kid.

He heaved a sigh. "What do you think's going on, Steel?"

"I don't know, bro. I have no fucking clue either."

"Think it's the *Famiglia*?" Link asked under his breath, and I knew that was just in case the walls had ears and those ears belonged to Rex.

The bastard somehow knew whenever we weren't in agreement with him.

"I don't know. I think it's more likely than this random theory that Rex has going on, but what the fuck can I say? His instincts rarely lie."

Link huffed. "I'm not sure what's worse."

"Either way, they don't want to hug her. We need to get her back."

"Stat," Link agreed, just in time for the two of us to make it to the door.

When we headed for our bikes, we split up because he was parked across the way near the bunkhouse where Lily and Tiffany usually sat with the women who'd been Donavan and Luke Lancaster's victims. I climbed astride mine, tipped my chin at Rex when he glared at me, and as a unit, we set off, our engines revving and the bass making the earth throb.

I had no idea what the fuck was happening, no idea what shit was going down, no idea if this was some kind of stunt, all I knew was that if anyone had laid a hand on Stone?

It would be the last time they took a breath.

She was mine.

She knew it.

I knew it.

I just never let that fact get in the way of what I was doing—leading my life while letting her lead hers.

She had a potential that few could ever understand. Rachel Laker, Rex's woman, was just the same.

Sometimes, it was a selfish man who got in the way of his woman's hopes and dreams, her goals and a future that she'd been idolizing since she was small.

I might have wanted to beat the shit out of Rex, but if anyone understood, I'd thought it was him.

Until today.

Of course, he was staying away from Rachel for his own reasons, and mine were a lot more complex.

He wasn't the son of a pedophile fuck.

He wasn't the one with tainted blood.

No.

I was.

That was me.

And there was no way I was tainting Stone with that, no way in fuck.

If she was in danger, I'd save her. But I wouldn't stain her.

I couldn't.

I'd made that promise to myself years ago, and it was the only promise, the only vow I'd ever kept with the intention of holding true to it until the day I died.

TEN

STONE

MY HEAD ACHED LIKE A MOTHERFUCKER.

In fact, a motherfucker was an understatement, because this was a level of excruciating agony that I'd never experienced before.

For someone who wanted to heal sick people, I'd been relatively healthy all my life. I'd never taken a sick day from work, for God's sake. The last time I had? It had been an excuse to grab a few more days at the Sinners' compound to help Amara, Ghost, and Tatána.

But that was how hardy I was. Pennsylvania stock...that's what my grandfather had called us. Had said we were made of sterner stuff and that we were held to a different standard as a result.

The irony was, I'd lived by that creed all my life.

Even when I'd overdosed, I'd thought I was okay. I'd forced myself to carry on, to keep on moving, not stopping until the drugs had made me.

I bit my lip hard, then when I realized what was happening—that this wasn't just an epic hangover that made every other hangover I'd experienced in my life look paltry—I was careful to peer out through my lashes and force myself to stillness.

Someone had taken me.

I didn't know who, but I had to figure I knew why.

The angel of death.

Shit.

Who was it?

I was still feeling it, so whoever had taken me knew their meds.

My mouth was like cotton, my body ached, and I knew I'd been tied to a chair for a good long while, because my limbs were so sore they were numb.

Which brought with it its own agony, because when they eventually started to work again, there would be even more excruciating agony to have to deal with.

I peered through my lashes and saw only a simple living room.

It was such a shock to see the furniture that I jerked back, my head flopping on my neck as though it wasn't attached.

When it rolled some more, the ache made me want to pass out. Little dots danced in my vision, and I had to work hard not to puke, because if I did, I might fucking choke on it, and while that was more amenable than whatever the hell my kidnapper had in store for me, I was a fighter.

I refused to quit.

Always had, always would.

I'd only ever quit on one thing in my life, and that was because he was more trouble than he was worth… Okay, maybe now wasn't the time to bullshit myself.

He was worth all the trouble in the world, but he didn't want me. I wasn't worth it to him.

So, I'd made it a point to strive hard for every other thing in my life that didn't come shaped like a biker.

When I managed to control the need to puke by holding my breath which, in turn, calmed down the frantic pace of my heart, the next point of contention was to make my head roll forward.

It took a disgusting amount of time to figure out how to do that, but from the angle I was in, I could see I was alone in the living room.

All alone.

In fact...my ears prickled with just how silent it was in here. I couldn't hear traffic either, which was impossible in New York.

There was traffic *everywhere*, for fuck's sake. Even on the tiniest and smallest of streets. Traffic was like bird shit.

A fact of life in NYC.

The room was decorated in a way that reminded me of my childhood. A kind of teal matte green that looked a little like puke mixed with lime, then there was a kind of rail around the center of the room that I knew had a name, but I could never remember it. A pale peach sofa matched two armchairs that looked rather comfortable. A coffee table had been shoved aside, and there was a TV stand as well as a dresser with a glass vase on it. There were boards on the floor, shiny with varnish, and a highly ornate carpet was beneath my feet where—when I shifted them—I felt the stickiness and wanted to die.

Fuck, had I pissed myself?

Oh God!

"Now isn't the time to be feeling mortified, Stone," I whispered under my breath, pretty certain that I was alone in the apartment now.

Unless the person who'd kidnapped me was asleep, of course, but I doubted it. Whoever was behind it had to have been working the day shift. I wouldn't be surprised if they'd snatched me, shuffled me into their car, and then driven me to their apartment all before getting back to work so that no suspicions were raised.

I'd been on the phone to Indy, hadn't I?

I could hear her voice in my head, but I couldn't recall the conversation. Not aside from me telling her about my theories.

Had I told her she was like a stitch in my side?

I couldn't remember.

Fuck!

I hated that I couldn't, because that was my clue as to whether or not I was screwed.

I was more than that if I had said it and she'd cut the call, gone merrily on her way just thinking that I was okay when I was the exact opposite.

If I hadn't said it, that made all the difference. We always said goodbye. We had no choice. She freaked out otherwise.

Indy played a good game. She looked normal on the outside, but the truth was she only looked it.

She was anything but normal.

Not necessarily in a bad way, but just in a 'life' way.

It had fucked with her, and she did her damnedest to fuck with it right back, but sometimes, she fell short of the mark.

I got it, I did. And it was one of the reasons why we were so close. The part of her that was broken was a part I felt compelled to heal.

It had always been that way, but over the years, that compulsion had died, morphing into a friendship that was rock solid and, ironically enough, we kept under wraps.

Very few people even knew that we were close, and we kept it that way because the fewer who knew that truth, the better.

We weren't being duplicitous, but sometimes, in our world, our ties put us in danger.

Both of us worked hard to stay on the sidelines of the MC. If we were both friends and people knew about it, then it could be used against us.

It was also ironic that, truthfully, I wished this was an MC thing. If it was, then I knew they'd be on their way. I wasn't sure if they'd come if Indy told them her suspicions. I mean, I figured she had her own way of dealing with them too, but it wasn't like *our* thing. It wasn't as if they knew how close we were, and that we ended shit a certain way every single time we spoke...

Unless she told them.

Would she do that?

It had become a point of pride for us to keep things from the brothers. Not out of malice, but because they had their whole secret boys' club shit going down. Why wouldn't we do the same?

But I was in danger. She had to know that, right?

She had to know that I'd find a way to say bye to her.

I blew out a breath because there was no point in worrying about this. No point in fretting over whether or not she'd managed to call in the devil's handymen, because if she had, they were on their way, but they didn't have a clue who had taken me.

So, regardless, I was fucked.

Unless I helped myself.

It always came down to that.

I'd forgotten that, but then I figured I'd be forgiven, because things had definitely taken a turn for the worse since I'd woken up.

I'd gone from having a headache from a bad hangover to realizing that I'd been kidnapped.

That I'd pissed myself.

And that the person who had taken me wasn't doing so because he or she wanted to be friends.

Nope.

This wasn't going to end well for someone, and I refused to let that be me.

So I sucked it up, sucked it in, and forced my head upright.

My neck twinged, but that's what necks did, and I stared around, trying to get a picture on where I was. Who it was that had taken me.

There were no photos on the wall, nothing that gave me a clue if it was Tonya, one of the auxiliary nurses, or Jason, a doctor with a god complex who fit the fucking profile of an angel of death to a

T, if it wasn't for the fact that he was too vain to think about ruining his life and his career over a little something like murder to grant a sick person peace.

I bit the inside of my cheek when my vision wavered, and then I began struggling against the tape on my wrists when I started to worry that I'd fall asleep or pass out again.

I needed to make a move.

Now.

I stared down at the clear tape, something that was definitely not duct tape, and that gave me an in, right?

After all, that stuff was fragile, even if the person had tied it around my wrists in a large swathe.

Duct tape, I was screwed. This tape? Maybe not.

Okay, so I took one thing from this situation.

Whoever had taken me wasn't as good at kidnapping as a Sinner's brat who'd been reared on a compound full of killers.

Jesus.

Serial Killing 101 was to have duct tape or cable ties as a means of securing people.

Christ.

I grimaced when the tape stuck fast, then I peered around, looking for something that I could maybe use to my benefit, and that was when I felt my feet coming online.

The ache and the sting and the pins and needles all morphed together in a way that was beyond agonizing.

I almost cried out, but just to be on the safe side, I didn't. If there was someone in the apartment, then they'd hear I was awake, and I needed all the time in the world to try to figure out how to get myself out of this situation.

When I began to move my feet, I realized the person hadn't tied them down. Just my arms.

Relief swirled inside me at the murderer's incompetence, and I started flexing my feet and my toes, trying to get the blood flowing back into them.

With a sigh when the pain cut off and they returned back to normal, I used that to shuffle forward toward the window.

There were two, oddly enough, not just one, even though the room was small, and as I rocked my chair, trying to gain some momentum to reach the window where there was a kind of sticky-outy clasp that I could use to nick the tape, *maybe*, I over-rocked.

Any desire to stay quiet, to stay under the radar, fled when the chair toppled over with me in it, and the boom was enough to make my ears roar with the sound.

The desire to be sick hit me again, and only knowing that, this time, I wouldn't choke on it, but I might drown in it, helped me contain it. This nausea came from fear, pure and simple.

But no one came running.

No one at all.

I let out a breath that was loaded with relief, and when I started trying to edge my way across the floor, I cursed the carpets which didn't aid me.

With a groan, I started rocking again, but this time, when I did, I realized the tape on my hands was looser. Everything about this was a mess, and it was clear that something had gone wrong with the meds I'd been given.

The kidnapper evidently calculated that I'd still be asleep in time for him or her to get back and deal with me then.

Thank God I was a grower not a shower.

I looked slimmer in my scrubs than I was in real life, and I'd never been happier for those extra twenty pounds I couldn't seem to drop.

Those twenty pounds had saved me, and I'd celebrate them when I got out of this fucking mess by eating two Big Macs and a double portion of extra-large fries. That meme about being harder to kidnap the more you weighed felt particularly on point right about now.

Sucking in a breath, I tried to cheer myself on as I worked at the tape, trying harder and harder to loosen it.

My skin felt raw, and the scent of blood powered through the air, making me realize just how badly adjusted my body was—some parts working, other parts numb and tingling.

I couldn't feel the pain yet, but I would soon, that was for sure, and I needed to be a million miles away from this place when everything started to work at the same time.

Groaning as I finally got my arm free, I rolled my head and began pulling and tugging at the other hand.

Thanking God it was my right hand I'd freed, my dominant one, I started to work faster and faster, only, as I did so, as the tape grew looser, I heard a door click.

It wasn't to this room, but it was definitely in this apartment.

The click echoed around me like it was a gunshot, and to me, it might as well have been.

Fuck, this was worse than 'ask not for whom the bell tolls,' because it was definitely tolling for me.

Feeling sick to my stomach once more, I hissed out a breath and worked double time on the tape. I had only God knew how long to get myself in a better position than the one I was currently in, and there was that vase on the dresser across the room with my name on it.

I heard footsteps, and my heart seemed to beat in time to them as I finally managed to liberate myself, and when I did, I crawled onto my knees with great difficulty.

It felt like half of me was numb and the other half was overactive. I struggled to crawl, but I knew I didn't have much choice.

It was either maim the fucker before they maimed me, or...

Well, yeah. Those were my options.

No bueno.

Managing to get my knees under me, I surged up just in time to get my hands on the edge of the dresser. When I hauled myself onto my feet, I toddled there like an overgrown fourteen-month-old, trying to find my balance, before I grabbed the vase and started to cling to that godawful railing that ran around the wall in what was supposed to be a decorative manner.

When I made it to the other side of the room, having edged my way around it now, I groaned when the door finally opened.

I lifted the vase high and timed it just so.

When the person peered into the room, I gripped the doorknob for support and put all my weight behind it.

As I brought the vase down, I wanted to weep with relief as it collided with the very feminine head.

When she shrieked then twisted around, I saw her surprised glare, but I also saw the blood spouting from the wound.

I looked down, and I realized the vase was made of thin glass, which had shattered around the rim while the body remained intact in my hold.

I stared at it for a second, not even registering the pharmacy assistant who I knew darted in and out of wards like a frightened mouse, whose name I didn't even know. When the jagged edge of the vase penetrated my sensibilities, I knew what I had to do.

Just as the bitch screamed and started coming for me, I stuck the vase out and sliced through the air.

When it snagged on her throat, I carried on with the momentum and watched as the arterial spray arced around the room like a symphony of color, coating me in her blood.

Her surprise was clear, her shock and pain evident, but I felt bupkis, because just as she quivered on her feet, hovering there until she slumped on the ground, I did the same.

Except knowing I was safe now, I flopped back and onto my side, uncaring that I was lying in her blood, uncaring that my eyes were on hers as she died, taken from this miserable world and hopefully into one that was even more fucking miserable.

As I passed out, I promised myself *four* Big Macs and *four* portions of fries as a reward for a job well done, because if ever I'd deserved to break my diet, it was today.

ELEVEN

STEEL

NO ONE KNEW where she was. No one recalled seeing her leave. They just knew she wasn't answering her pages, her cell phone wasn't working, and that she was nowhere on site.

I only knew that much because Rex had called in some favors with our allies, the Five Points, and some of their doctors—including one of the foundation's heads—actually worked on their payroll. With their help, we had access to the hospital in a way we'd never have been granted legally.

I knew Lodestar and Maverick were working on things from their end, hacking into the CCTV around the vicinity of the hospital, but it was like she'd disappeared into thin fucking air.

Where the fuck was she?

This slick move just made me feel like the *Famiglia* was behind all this, and it would totally explain why we couldn't seem to find her, why we didn't know which direction they'd taken her—

My cell buzzed, and I stopped tugging at my hair as I peered around the parking lot and grabbed it from my pocket.

Unknown number.

I frowned but answered it. "Hello?" I asked warily.

"Steel?"

Her voice sent relief surging through me. "Where the hell have you been?" I snarled, and the second I did, I wondered what the fuck was wrong with me.

Why was it so goddamn hard to be nice to her?

I blew out a breath, almost missing the quiver that told me she'd just started crying, and as I bit my lip, feeling like an evil cunt, I rasped, "I'm sorry, Stone. You've just had me worried, baby. Where the fuck are you?"

"I-I don't know where I am," she croaked, but her voice was stronger now, and I knew why.

I'd pissed her off and hurt her feelings. Talk about a double whammy.

Blowing out another breath, I rumbled, "Who took you?"

"A woman from work." She cleared her throat. "She's dead."

"You took care of her?"

"Yeah. It was either that or be taken care of myself."

I gnawed on the inside of my cheek, hating that she knew what it was like to take someone's life.

Death in a hospital and death on the gnarly streets were two separate things entirely.

I'd never wanted that for her, and that was one of the reasons why I'd tried to keep her out of it. Tried to keep her away from this shit.

I plucked at my bottom lip as I turned on my heel and headed into the hospital.

Security eyed me warily, as did the rest of the staff, and I knew all my brothers had been getting weird looks too but, so far, the in with the hospital was working and we were allowed full sway, even if our presence set everyone on edge.

When I saw Sin hovering by the corridor that led to the oncology unit, I waved him down. "She's okay. She's on the phone," I mouthed, as Stone was saying, "There's so much blood, Steel."

"You probably know the exact amount being all book smart and all."

She sniffed. "Book smart and seeing it on the carpet beneath you are two separate things." Her second sniff morphed into a gulp. "It was so easy, Steel. So easy to take her life."

I cringed inside. "I'm sorry, baby."

She started sobbing, and I swore to fuck it tore my heart out.

"When did—"

"I passed out afterward. She drugged me to get me here, and whatever it was, it knocked me out twice." She released a shaky breath. "I-I have no idea where I am."

"You need to go outside."

"Steel, I'm doused in blood. I look like I'm the one who should be locked up, not her."

I scowled at that. "You've done nothing wrong."

"Isn't that my word against hers?" She gulped. "What if they—"

"What if they, what? You haven't done anything wrong," I repeated. "We've had people looking for you, and the hospital knows you were missing—"

"They won't want to get involved. She was one of the pharmacy techs, Steel. She was killing patients. They won't want the scandal."

I shook my head. "This is nuts."

"What about our world isn't?" A panicked sob escaped her. "Oh my God, I'm going to lose everything, aren't I?"

"No!" I growled under my breath, hearing her breathing start to tick over to double time. "Stone, you calm the fuck down, do you hear me? Nothing is going to go wrong. Nothing at all. You did nothing wrong, she did it. She was the one who took you. You're the one who had to defend yourself. You did the right thing."

"Why does it feel like I did the wrong thing then?"

"I don't know, because you're crazy, maybe?"

She snorted out a laugh. "That's it, Steel. Kick a girl when she's down."

I chuckled. "That's how I roll. Look, stay on the line, but I'll talk to Rex about this."

Like my words had been whispered from my lips to God's ears, Rex, Sin, and the others stormed around the corner to meet me.

When we were face to face, Rex demanded, "Give me the phone."

When he held out his hand, I was loath to give it to him, especially after our last argument, the signs of which he was wearing on his face. But I got it. I did. Even if I was glad he was sporting a black eye too.

Reality was, Stone was like a sister to all of the guys. Shit, she should be one to me as well, but my feelings for her had never been and never would be brotherly.

I wished they had been.

I wished she was just miserable over unrequited love.

Only she wasn't.

I did love her. Always had and always would. But love made a person selfish, and where she was concerned, I'd always think of her first and foremost.

When he snagged the phone from me, biting off, "Stone? Tell me you're okay."

I heard her weeping, saw Rex and the others flinch, and I leaned back against the wall. There was a plastic rail that dug into my back, but I didn't care. I just pressed my skull against the wall, needing to ground myself to the moment.

I'd tried to take Stone away from the world I lived in, a world where death didn't come from sickness but from another's hand. Here she was with blood on her soul and all without her even being tied to the MC. I'd never wanted her to know what that felt like. Never. But she knew now.

She'd experienced it, and the worst thing of all?

She'd been in danger.

A danger that had been unknown to me because I'd put that much fucking distance between us—

"We're coming."

"How? I don't know where I am, so why should you?" she whispered, sounding distressed and distraught, the exact opposite of how she usually sounded.

I was used to her being strong and harsh, but at the moment, she was weak, and fuck if I didn't want to be the one who got her through this.

Who made shit right for her.

My throat felt thick. Not from tears, but from a cluster of emotions that I didn't need to be dealing with right now.

"I'm going to get Maverick on it," Rex rasped, and I realized that she was still on the line, still listening into all this.

I reached for my cell and told her, "One second, baby. Just stay calm and stay on the line until I say otherwise."

"O-Okay. You're coming for me, aren't you, Robin?" she whispered, and I didn't even cringe at my fucking name.

I got it.

I did.

"You bet your damn ass I am."

She released a shaky sigh that billowed in my ears as I put the call on mute. I saw Rex was already barking out orders to Mav, and I knew that soon enough, we'd have all our ducks in a row.

When he was off the line, when Mav was working on pinpointing my girl, I demanded, "I don't give a fuck how much it costs, don't care what you have to do, you make sure that she's transferred to the hospital near us."

He gritted his teeth. "Snapping orders at me is only one way to have the shit kicked out of you."

I stuck my finger in his chest, even though I knew I was baiting a bear. "You think she should stay here? That she should be around for the fallout? She's terrified of going to prison, for fuck's sake."

"Prison? Why would she be in danger of that?" Link questioned.

"I don't know, but she's got it all mapped out in her head." I rubbed the bridge of my nose. "Is she right? She said the kidnapper was the bitch who was killing patients. Is it likely that the hospital would help cover shit up?"

Rex eyed me warily. "Depends how deep the investigation would need to go."

My mouth tightened. "We already know the Five Points have their fingers in this pot. Who's to say the rest of the admin on board here isn't shady as fuck?"

He rubbed his chin, and I watched him flicker through the options.

"If there's a body, we could dispose of it, but she hasn't done anything wrong. There's no need to cover this up."

"We can't get involved," Nyx muttered. "If we do, that taints shit. As it stands, they won't think anything of it. She's a woman who was kidnapped—"

"She said she was drugged, so the drugs are in her system from when she was kidnapped. They'd still be in there, wouldn't they?" Rex questioned.

"Yeah," Nyx muttered, then he heaved a sigh. "I know what you said, but we can't go to her. We have to get the cops involved from the start. It's already shady that we were asking questions, and the staff will report our presence."

Rex scratched his jaw. "We're making this too complicated."

I shook my head and repeated Stone's words. "What isn't complicated in our life?"

He hissed at that, then he ground out, "Okay. I hear you. We'll let the cops deal with this, but the second I can, I'll have her transferred."

"It's time she came home anyway," Nyx groused, eying me with a disdain that got my back up.

If he fucking knew the reason why I was keeping my distance from her, he'd get it, but I wouldn't tell him because Nyx was my brother, and I didn't want him to look at me with loathing.

That would kill me.

I hit the mute button, then muttered, "Stone, baby?"

"Y-Yes, Robin."

"I need you to call the cops."

"The cops?" she shrieked. "Oh my God, why?"

"Because this can't be handled in-house," I whispered. "You need to do this right, and the second we can, we'll get you out of here and back to West Orange—"

"West Orange? Why? I don't want to go there."

"You might not want to, but it's time you came home. At least there, you'll be fucking safe."

"I was fucking safe here until this bitch started to go Grim Reaper on the wards."

"Yeah, well, there's shit you don't know about, shit that's making things change in the city. This isn't only coming from me," I rasped, then I shoved the phone at Rex, hating that she'd listen to him more than she would me.

Fuck, I'd sacrificed so much for her, changed my world for her, and she was listening to my Prez over me.

Goddamn typical.

Rex took the phone, and for the first time he looked apologetic. "He's right, Stone. It's time you came back to Jersey. This place is too hot for you now."

I didn't need to be the one with my ear to the earpiece to hear her scream, "Hot? It's NYC. When isn't it hot?"

"It's worse than ever before. You have to know that the Italians and Russians are at fucking war, and that half the city is against the *Famiglia*? At least in West Orange, you'll be safe.

"Now, do as you're told. Call the police, tell them what happened, and get them to come to you. When you need to call for next of kin, contact Indy and she'll be there. She'll bring you home, and I'll work on getting you transferred out of this hospital."

"But I don't want to—"

"You haven't got a choice. Shit's changing, Stone. I've already been thinking about getting a guard on you, but you're too far out, and this isn't our territory. It would cause shit, so the simplest solution is to bring you under our roof again."

"Fuck that! I'm not even tied to the club—"

"Bullshit. You and him might not get it, but the rest of the fucking universe is well aware that you're Steel's, and that puts you in danger. Now, get off the line, call the cops, and get everything set.

"The second we can get involved without muddying things for you, we'll be there."

Everything inside me cringed at what he was asking of me.

Not to go to her.

Just like I'd said I would. Breaking a promise I'd barely finished giving her before it was snatched away.

I sucked in a breath, hating that she whispered, "But I'll be alone."

Rex's face softened, and I grabbed the cell from him before he could say a word because I needed her to hear my voice.

"You won't be alone. You're never alone. I'm always with you." I twisted around to utter those words in a semblance of privacy, but they weren't enough to stop her from sobbing.

I could hear her heartache and hurt and horror, and all three just fucked with my head, making me want to tear my own heart out at the sound of her pain.

I'd caused her enough pain in this life, and I'd done that to protect her. No one, and I meant no one, was allowed to do the same thing to her.

I rasped, "Stone, you hear me. You do what Rex says, and things will roll easier. The second we get involved, you know unnecessary questions will be asked. You have to know that I'm there with you all the way, and I'll be there to get you the second Indy gives the word."

Her mouth trembled—I knew it because her words were shaky. "I-I'll call the cops now."

"You do that, baby doll. You do that."

She whispered, "It's been years since you called me that."

"Been years since I needed to," I admitted, no shame in my voice. "Let's get you home, hmm?"

Stone whispered, "Okay," and then she cut the call. She might as well have cut my fucking wrists for me because that's how it felt.

The finality of the blankness at the end of the line was enough to make me want to hurl my phone against the wall. The only thing that stopped me was the fact that she might call me later, even though she wasn't supposed to. I needed my number to be active so she could be in touch when she needed to.

My cheek ached from where I gnawed on it, and I jerked in surprise when one of my brothers clapped me on my shoulder and squeezed down hard. "You got this, bro."

I should have known it would be Link.

I cut him a look. "Why does that feel like the exact opposite of me having got this?"

He shrugged. "That's when you know you've fallen. Hook, line, and fucking sinker."

My mouth tightened. "I knew that a long time ago. I didn't need the memo."

TWELVE

STONE

THE BLOOD WAS EVERYWHERE.

On me, my skin, my clothes, and the carpet and the walls. It looked like a massacre.

Was I going to get blamed for this?

I just kept thinking I would.

I didn't have a rap sheet, but I had a sealed record from the stupid stunts I'd pulled when I was sixteen and dealing with the first wave of chaos in the aftermath of Steel's initial rejection, Mama's death, and my life starting to go down the crapper.

Gnawing on my bottom lip at the memory, I tapped in 911 and waited for the operator to answer.

"I-I've been kidnapped."

Instantly, the man's voice tightened with urgency. "You've been kidnapped? Is there anyone—"

Before he could continue, I rasped, "I-I managed to stop her."

"Her? You know who the assailant it?"

My throat grew thick. "I'm looking at her. She's dead."

My brain started to whir at that as I tried to figure out how this was possible. How any of *this* was even happening.

I reached up and rubbed my eyes, but when I did, I could feel the crispiness on my skin where the blood had dried after I passed out.

When he asked for my name, I gave it to him, then I explained it all, everything that I thought I knew from beginning to end, and I knew it would only be the first time that evening that I told my story, that I recounted it.

When the operator asked me to peer out of the window to see if there were any landmarks, I blinked in a daze, because why hadn't I thought to do that before?

Hissing with irritation at myself, I clambered onto my knees and winced when a wash of dizziness whispered over me—oh, yeah. *That* was why.

Just crawling around the body, tugging her from her front to her back so I could get into her jacket pocket and grab her phone had been hard, but going over to the window felt like I was being asked to cross the Sahara.

Sucking in a sharp breath, I rasped, "M-My head hurts. I don't know what she drugged me with, but it's still in my system."

"Take it slowly, Stone. It's okay. We've got all the time in the world."

But we didn't, we didn't have all the time in the world. I knew he was just trying to calm me, but it didn't work, because that was the last thing he should have said.

If I had to stay in this fucking apartment one more minute, I felt certain I would scream.

I peered out of the window, and as my gaze drifted around the area, seeking out a landmark, something that would give me a clue as to where we were staying, I happened to see it.

A street sign.

It was on the side of a building that was a little awkwardly placed, and it required me to squint, but I managed to read it and whispered it to the operator.

"I have two units and an ambulance on their way, Stone. Just stay on the line with me until they get there. You've been through a lot of trauma tonight."

I snorted out a laugh. "You think?"

His amusement was cautious, like he was trying to remain unaffected but my response had surprised him. "I suppose you're right."

"I'm a doctor," I told him. "I'm used to this. I'm just not used to being on the other side of it."

"I don't think you ever get used to it."

There was a nightmare in his voice, one that told me this was just one call in a career of calls he'd fielded where terrified men, women, and children contacted him, scared for their lives.

Being on the front line, in a word, *sucked*. He didn't know that I knew that, but I felt for him nonetheless.

Exhaustion hit me again, and I rubbed my eyes, covering my face with my hand as I tried to stop the room from spinning.

Whatever she gave me had been a doozy. I'd never felt anything so fast-acting but also so quick to drain off, to leave me able to function while still affecting everything I did.

I heard the sirens before I saw the flashing lights, and a whispered sob escaped me as I realized they were here.

At last.

I was strong, I was positive. I was used to being on my own, and I was independent.

But I'd admit, and I felt no shame in it, that at that moment, I wanted to give it all up and lean on the one man who was strong enough to hold me upright.

Steel.

And he wasn't here.

I'd have given up Big Macs for life if it meant he was the one coming to me, not the cops.

I bit my lip again, wincing as I realized that I'd actually bitten through it at some point without even knowing it. "They're here," I rasped.

"You need to get their attention, considering we have no specifics as to your actual location."

I stared at the window clasp, wishing that it didn't look like a maze, and somehow, managed to unfasten it.

When I thrust myself out of the window, hanging out of it so I could call out, "Help!" my brain started to whirl again as not only the dash of fresh air hit me square in the face, but the way the burst of action made my equilibrium waver.

For a second, I wasn't sure if I was going to fall out of the window, and then I heard a, "Ma'am? Just stay put!"

What could have been minutes or seconds later, I heard a pounding at the door, and when I just slumped over the windowsill, knowing I was safe, I heard the door being kicked in, and I let go.

I slouched against the low wall and passed out because that used every single ounce of my energy reserves and then some.

When I woke up, only God knew how long later, it was to find I was strapped into a stretcher. A red blanket covered me, and I had a drip attached to my arm while two EMTs worked around me.

I wasn't in an ambulance, I was outside, and nearby, I saw another stretcher.

This one with a body on it.

I gulped at the sight of the black plastic bag, knowing that I'd been the one to put that woman in there, and I stared at the EMTs, watching them work, registering their actions as I went through the checklist of what they were doing.

"Ma'am, how are you feeling?" one of them asked. The woman. She'd just seen that I was awake.

"I feel like death."

Her lips twisted. "I promise you, you're not."

"My head says otherwise." My mouth quivered as I asked for something I knew they couldn't give me. "I need meds for the pain."

"We need to figure out what you were given."

I nodded, accepting the answer, even as I rolled my gaze from hers and let my head droop onto my shoulder.

When I faded out of consciousness again, I didn't try to fight it.

It was either that, or deal with a long and bumpy hospital ride, where each jolt would make me feel like my skull was caving in.

In this instance, being unconscious was the kinder fate, so I embraced it and let myself go.

THIRTEEN

STEEL
BEFORE

"SHIT. FUCK!"

The words were whispered in my ear, but I knew they were actually a scream.

Rex didn't whisper.

He hollered.

I squinted up at nothing, my eyelashes flickering and fluttering as I tried to stop the blur from overtaking my eyes, but it wouldn't work.

My head fell back and rolled against the—

Floor?

I half sat up, then my stomach protested the move almost as fiercely as my brain, which told me that movement wasn't the best option at this moment.

So what? I was lying on the ground.

So what? I was being hustled onto my side by my brother.

So. Fucking. What.

"Leave me alone," I rumbled, the words slurred, making me realize my tongue was suddenly as heavy as my entire head.

Huh.

"Can't. We need to get you to the hospital, you dumb fuck."

"Hospital?" I sniffed. "I'm fiiiiiine. Don't need no hospital."

"You need your stomach pumped. I refuse to let you go to Lana Jane's funeral like this—"

If anything could have sobered me up, it was that bitch's name.

"Hate her."

"I know, man. I know." Rex heaved a sigh. "Can't say that I blame you."

I squinted at him. "Why did you have to hear that?"

The utterance of her name made it a shit ton easier to read his expression.

Guilt.

Fucking guilt.

"I'm sorry, bro." He hung his head. "We were working on club business, and you just stormed in. I didn't think—not until it was too late."

I reached up and slapped a hand over my face. "Rex?"

"Yeah?"

"I may have done something stupid."

"What like?" he asked warily. "You ain't why Lana Jane's dead, are you?"

I sniffed at that. "And have Stone hate me forever? She loved her ma, for some stupid reason."

"Not sure that makes me feel better. If you didn't, and I doubt she did, then that means my pop might have had something to do with it."

I squinted up at him, but my smirk was gleeful. "Hope so. You should have heard her, Rex. She meant it. Every vicious, venomous, clusterfuck of a word."

"I can't believe she'd have sold her, man—" He shook his head. "But they're all mercenary. You know what club snatch is like."

"I do." And I did. Too well. I was reared from one. Only the

Old Ladies seemed to have any honor, and that was why they were revered.

Maybe not by their Old Men, ironically enough, but by the MC on the whole, definitely.

We'd kill for any woman who wore a brother's brand. Shit, we'd go to war for one.

I rubbed my cheek against the grass, deciding it was a good time to ask, "Where am I?"

"You're in the swamp."

My nose crinkled at that. We didn't have any wetlands in West Orange, but behind the clubhouse, close to where the Fridge was, there was a little section where the ground was kind of, well, odd. You stood on it long enough, and it would shift beneath your feet.

The young kids, myself, and my friends included, all tended to ride out here to have parties. It was club land, so our parents usually let us get away with shit, and we never had to worry about the cops breaking us up.

"You're lucky I found you, dumb fuck. Now come on, what's the stupid shit you've done?"

I heaved a sigh. "Took some pills."

He tensed. "Fuck, Steel. Fuck! What kind of pills?"

I shrugged. "Don't know. Went riding into Verona. Bought as much as three hundred bucks would buy. Came back with my vodka, and I had myself a party."

"Why you telling me this if you wanted to die?"

"'Cause I don't want to die anymore."

He snorted. "Fuck. I'm lucky you're awake, but then the puddles of vomit around you are probably why you're even talking to me right now."

I sniffed the air and discovered he was right.

It did stink of puke.

And vodka.

Shit, it reeked of it.

"Thank you for coming for me, Rex," I slurred.

He heaved a sigh. "Thank me later when you've been deep throated by a bitchy nurse who's about to clean out your guts."

I sniffed. "Kinky."

His laugh hurt my ears and made my head ache, but I was glad he'd found me.

What had seemed like the best thing to do, suddenly didn't feel like that.

If anything, I realized how stupid I'd been. How fucking dumb.

As Rex helped me onto my feet, my knees gave out beneath me the second I was standing. When he caught me with a grunt, my limbs turned to spaghetti, and he heaved out a sigh. "Remind me why you're worth it?"

I thanked him by puking down his cut.

FOURTEEN

STEEL

WAITING on Indy to get the call was nerve-racking. She was sitting opposite me, having driven over from Jersey and to the city, arriving an hour ago.

We were camped out in a diner, just getting ready for things to get underway, but this was the first step.

She lit up like a dashboard when she got the call, and the second she heard Stone's voice, I saw the tears in her eyes and felt her relief as if it was my own, which was weird, considering I loved her and she barely knew Stone.

Still, Indy was weird. She felt shit more than most, but hell, she couldn't feel more relieved than I felt.

I hated that I wasn't with her.

Hated that I couldn't go to her, but Nyx was right. The fucker. By getting involved with my rep, with the Sinners' rep behind me, it would only muddy the waters.

She didn't need that.

Especially not in NYC, which wasn't our town.

Back home, we could deal with the authorities, but here, it was a different situation.

Fuck, I'd be glad when she was back in West Orange.

Rubbing the back of my neck, I watched Indy nod, then she scrambled out of the booth where we were seated, put down the phone, and rasped, "She's at Franklin Mercy Hospital. They're keeping her overnight for observation."

I nodded, relieved to know where she was, even if I couldn't go visit her.

Rex muttered, "Go and be with her, but the second you can get her out of there, bring her back to your place. She needs to come home."

Indy scowled at him, then at me. "This is her home."

"No, it isn't. It's her temporary home."

"Stop splitting hairs," Indy snapped. "Her life is here. This is where her job is."

"I'm going to work on getting her transferred to West Orange General."

Indy's mouth worked like a goldfish. "You're shitting me, right? You can't make that kind of decision for her!"

"Yeah, I fucking can," I growled, annoyed that she was even thinking about this shit when Stone needed her at her side, not fighting in her corner over an argument that was already fucking lost.

Her face scrunched up as she stared at me and Rex, then her eyes flashed over to Nyx, who grumbled, "Indy, this isn't the war you want to be fighting right now."

Her nostrils flared. "It's the exact war I need to be fighting. You making decisions for her is just going to piss her the fuck off. I can't say that I'd goddamn blame her either."

"You have no idea what we have going on right now," I snapped at her. "If you did, you'd be shitting yourself.

"If you were in NYC, I'm pretty sure that Nyx would be bringing you home too, so be grateful you're in Verona and not here, because that would change everything."

Her mouth tightened. "You can't make these decisions for us."

"Yeah, we can," Rex rumbled, weighing in with a heavy tone that was like Solomon making a life or death decision. "Like he said, you have no idea what's going on in this world of ours. Whether or not you like it, you're a part of the family, and we don't want you dead. The goal isn't to piss you off or to irritate you as we force you to accept our decisions, it's to keep you alive, and in the run up to that, we'll do whatever it takes to keep you safe." He stared at her, glowered at her when she glowered at him, then tacked on, "Even if you hate us for it."

An exasperated gust exploded from her lungs, just as she veered away from the table and started to storm off, striding down the small corridor of the diner like she couldn't bear to look at us.

Truly, I'd be pissed off as well if I was her, but it was just tough shit.

We weren't doing this to be pricks.

For once.

"Indy," Nyx called out.

She froze, hands balling into fists at her sides, before she growled, "What?"

"Heads up."

She twisted around, just in time to catch Stone's phone. "Stone's?" she asked warily, eying the cracked screen.

Nyx nodded. "Found it when we did a sweep of the hospital. Figure she'd like it back."

She gulped, and I knew the words 'thank you' burned on her tongue. She fought the urge and carried on storming off, slamming the diner door behind her for good measure.

If my world wasn't crashing down around me, I'd have laughed at their antics. As it was, I was barely keeping shit together.

Like he knew... a hand clapped on my shoulder and squeezed. Like always, it was Link. "It'll be okay, bro."

But it was going to be the opposite of okay.

Indy's reaction was nothing compared to what Stone's would be when she got over what had happened today.

She'd been dazed when we'd dropped the bombshell on her. Confused and scared. When she was in her right mind, she would go apeshit. Her initial angry reaction was child's play in contrast to the fallout that would drop down when she was awake and aware.

I blew out a breath and told them, "I don't care if she goes mental over this. She'll be safe."

"She isn't in danger now," Sin replied, his tone cautious.

"Maybe not, but we don't know, do we? I wouldn't want anyone I gave a shit about walking around unprotected. The closer we are to the clubhouse, the better," Rex rasped.

"What about Rachel?" Link questioned gruffly.

None of us were pussies. We'd each gone to war for the MC in our own way, and had killed or almost died to uphold it…but at his inquiry, I wasn't going to lie, most of us fucking froze.

Link might as well have tossed a live hand grenade into the diner…that was the incendiary power of his question.

Before I wondered if Rex was going to explode, he blew out a breath and muttered, "I have as much of a chance of getting Rachel to stick closer to home than I have of getting a porcupine to keep its quills in. I'll fight some battles but not that one.

"Rachel lives on her own land, in her own compound that we helped secure, and it's close to our place at least. She isn't in the city, and her office staff comes to her place to work. It's not ideal, but I can handle those odds."

I cut him a look. "Is it going to be hard transferring Stone?"

"It's already happening as we speak."

My brow puckered. "Really?"

His mouth twisted. "Ever since that fucker snatched Tiff and Lily, I've been determining just how easy it would be to bring Stone home. I wasn't lying when I told you she was like a sister to me. I'm not about to lose her over some dumb shit where the *Famiglia* thinks they've spotted a weakness. I'm having to quicken the pace on things, but the ball is rolling."

Because I could hear the caring in his voice, I didn't give him shit for it, just dipped my chin. "Thanks, brother."

"You don't have to thank me."

Our gazes clashed and held, and truthfully, I saw his warning in them.

I knew what he was saying.

Man the fuck up.

Take her.

Claim her.

Make her yours at long fucking last, but Rex didn't know what it was like to be me.

He didn't know what it was like to have the weight on your soul like I did.

I averted my eyes and just stared at some stuffing that was popping out of the red vinyl seating beside me.

Thankfully, Sin, being the good brother he was, picked up on the fact that I wasn't necessarily agreeing with Rex, and started a conversation that I didn't bother to focus on.

We were minutes away from the hospital we'd figured the ambulance would take Stone to, and ironically enough, we'd got it wrong.

In about twenty minutes, though, Indy would be there.

My woman wouldn't be alone anymore, and only that would ease the panic that was growing inside me. It was unfurling wide open, making me realize that shit was changing, whether I wanted it to or not.

I was like ice where Stone was concerned. I had to be.

If I wasn't, I'd relent, and I couldn't do that, and that was what was happening here.

I'd already started calling her fucking 'baby doll,' and the next thing I knew, I'd be kissing her the second that I caught a glimpse of her.

My nostrils flared as I burst upright into a standing position. The brothers looked at me like I'd lost my fucking mind, and I had. Maybe I fucking had.

"I'm going back to the compound."

Rex's mouth worked noiselessly for a second, then rage filtered into his expression. "You're fucking not," he grated out, slamming his fists onto the table, making all the dishes rattle, and a hush overcome the diner. The waitress even braked on her heels, squeaking to a halt before shuffling away from our table.

"Don't be a dick," Nyx argued, but I shook my head.

"I need to get out of here."

"Fuck this bullshit," Rex snarled. "She needs you. That's exactly what she needs. We couldn't let her have you until she was discharged from the hospital, but the second she's out, you could help her get back on her feet. She has to be shaky."

"I can't."

Two words, and I hated them.

My grandmother used to say that those two words didn't exist, but it was bullshit.

They did.

I couldn't go to her, I couldn't be there for her, I couldn't wait on her to come out of the hospital.

I needed to go home.

I needed to build up my walls, and I needed to make sure she couldn't get inside them, because if she did, she was lost.

Before they could stop me, I surged out of the booth and strolled down the linoleum-lined corridor that Indy had just hurried down.

When I made it outside, I ignored my brothers who'd followed me and were hollering at me from the diner's doorway, headed for my bike, and climbed on.

The second the beast was rumbling beneath me, I could feel the air fill my lungs a lot easier.

Freedom.

This beast gave me freedom like nothing else could.

I sighed as I rolled back out of the parking spaces we'd taken up with our cluster of bikes, and then I began to merge onto the street the second the ignition was rumbling.

As I maneuvered through busy morning rush hour traffic, I felt the distance I was putting between us pinging away inside me like I had my own personal Google Maps syncing with each mile I traveled, warning me just how far I was pushing it. Just how much space there was between us.

But I had to ignore it.

I had to.

I leaned over the handlebars, pushing shit so much that I knew I could get a traffic violation for how fast I was going, but I didn't give a fuck.

I didn't.

Right until I was stopped.

Not by a cop, not even by a traffic jam.

By a fucking bullet.

Right to the goddamn shoulder.

It shot through me, tearing the fucker up as it went, and I had to withhold a groan as the agony ripped through my body.

Sucking in a sharp breath, I focused on not crashing my bike, on not losing control of the hog, because that would fuck me over royally. I could skid under any of the massive trucks I was riding between.

As close to the Lincoln Tunnel as it was, I had to figure this was a chance shot by one of the *Famiglia* who'd maybe spotted my cut.

My teeth clenched as I thought about my next move.

I could already feel the damage it'd done, so did I stop now and roll back to another hospital, or did I—

Another bullet

Fuck.

This time, I had no choice about maintaining control of my bike.

Control was ripped out from under me as I slammed to the ground as if the momentum of it had shoved me off the seat and onto the asphalt. There was nothing I could do to ease the collision of my body into the pavement apart from watch the chaos of the traffic braking to a halt around me.

As my bones settled on the ground, I just waited to be run over when I saw Baby's fate as a car piled into it, and all I could think was…if this was death, did that mean my vow to Stone was over?

Maybe.

FIFTEEN

STONE
BEFORE

I WATCHED as Mom was lowered into the earth, the casket covering her far grander than anything she'd had in this life.

In death, she was having more spent on her than she'd had while living. Mostly because what she'd earned on her back had granted her a basic income. She'd begun whoring herself out when she couldn't get my father to take her on as an Old Lady, and when she became too old for that, she'd never had all that much to spare.

I'd been working two jobs since I was old enough to get a position at the diner in the next town over, Verona, and the local store, and I was used to giving her half of my money.

With her dying, and I knew this was a horrible thing to say, but I'd be better off financially. My half went to drink and cigs...not exactly staples, but she paid the rent and I lived there, eating food she bought. I figured that was the least I could do.

Still, as much as I'd loved my mom, I hadn't liked her. She'd been cruel, dismissive, and had I been prettier, I wasn't too sure whether or not she'd have pimped me out.

That thought flashed through my mind, washed away by the shame of thinking so badly of her when she was dead, but still sort of stuck in place with Gorilla Glue since I knew she was exactly that type of person.

Always on the lookout for what she could get. Always seeking the best way to hurt people. Never thinking about anyone other than herself. Money-grubbing...

Wow.

The bitterness was definitely new, and funny how it only spewed out of me now.

When she was dead.

And when I couldn't say anything to her.

I pursed my lips at that, then jerked when someone's hand slipped into mine. I hoped it was Steel, but I knew from the scent alone that it wasn't.

I cut Mav a look, surprised to see him, surprised because he wasn't supposed to be on leave for at least another two months. I turned into him, pressing my face into the cut he only wore when he was back home, and whispered, "You didn't have to come."

"Course I did."

I squeezed him tightly, hugging him like I'd never let myself before because the men were all men's men, and I didn't like to remind them I was a girl. If I did, then they'd probably stop hanging around me, and they were my lifeline.

In the limited time I had to myself, I wanted to be with them.

They were my friends, sure, but they were my family, and I'd missed Mav ever since he'd enlisted.

He was buffer than before, and when I peered up at him, staring into the eyes that had always seen far too much, I noticed they were harder.

A little fiercer.

I wasn't sure I wanted to know what had done that to him, not when he'd been reared in the life and had already seen too much shit for someone his age, but I didn't think about that. Just carried on hugging him.

"Where's Steel?"

That the question came from him and not from me had me stunned.

"You don't know? Isn't he at the clubhouse?"

He shrugged. "I don't know. I just rolled in. But I thought he'd be here."

"You did? Why?"

His smile was slow, but when he hit me with it, damn, I had to admit to myself, if no one else, he was pretty.

Not just pretty, but fine.

Except he'd never been mine. That was Steel. Who was just as pretty, but in a different way.

Steel looked like he could roll down a catwalk. His features were interesting. All high cheekbones and wide, clear eyes. His face was made up of angles, from the goatee he had now, to the sharp uptick of his brows.

His lips, the Cupid's bow, was sharply delineated too, and throw in the almond-shaped eyes and he was just one big Pi lover's wet dream.

Mav, on the other hand, reminded me of Brad Pitt. Except he was cuter. And with his shaved head, he looked like a bruiser, but in my world, being a bruiser wasn't a bad thing.

If a man could protect you, that was something to celebrate, not hate.

I rubbed my cheek against his cut, wishing like hell he was Steel, even while I was so glad that Mav was back.

"I think he's mad at me," I muttered softly, unsure what else to say, but somehow blurting the words out made me feel better.

The MC was at the funeral, as well as a few of Mom's other friends from around town, but it was a pretty informal event. That was how we rolled in these parts, so my talking to Maverick while being in his arms didn't raise any eyebrows.

It would have if Steel had claimed me, of course, and that was what Mav was implying.

My heart raced as I stared up at him, hoping beyond hope that was Steel's intention.

"How long have you known?"

He hummed, pushed his cheek to my hair, then asked, "That you've loved him, little bit?" When I nodded, he laughed. "Since forever."

Embarrassment made my stomach feel like a million butterflies had started dancing in there. I clenched my eyes closed as I whispered, "You guys all knew, didn't you?"

"That you loved him?" He snorted. "Yeah. But I wouldn't worry. We also knew that he loved you."

My whole body clenched at that. "Don't say shit like that when it isn't true."

"Isn't true?" He pshawed. "We ribbed him about it for years. Figured he was waiting on your sixteenth birthday to make shit permanent."

I bit my lip. "So why isn't he here?"

"Don't have an answer for that."

"I do." Nyx's voice sounded grim, so I looked up at him, surprised to see his usually expressionless face was loaded with irritation.

"What's wrong?"

"He's at the hospital. Rex just called. He tried to get him here in time, but he fuc—"

Mav bit off, "Watch your mouth, Nyx."

He rolled his eyes. "Stone's used to hearing me curse."

My lips quirked because that was an understatement. Yeah, I was definitely used to hearing him swear.

"Not next to her momma's dead body she ain't."

Nyx grunted. "Now who reminded her that her momma's dead?"

Even though the situation wasn't supposed to be amusing, it actually was. I snickered a little, muttering, "Look, don't worry about it. Why's Steel at the hospital?"

Just the thought made the bubble of amusement I'd felt seem treacherous. I needed to get to him and fast if he was sick.

"Dumb fuck drank too much or something. Had to have his stomach pumped."

My brow furrowed. "Huh? Steel? He never drinks."

"Well, he decided to do it with a bang."

I scrubbed a hand over my face as I pulled away from Mav.

I hadn't seen him for ten days, not since that kiss. Mom had died the next day, and things had been crazy in the aftermath.

I'd been hurt at his absence, confused, and when I'd tried to call him, the line had always gone to his voicemail.

"How long has he been in the hospital?"

Nyx and Mav were bickering now, like only true brothers could. "Huh?" Nyx asked.

I sighed. "How long has he been in the hospital for?"

"Overnight, right? That's how long it takes to get your stomach pumped?"

I elbowed Mav in the stomach. "Don't put words in his mouth."

I knew how these guys worked. They were surprisingly open with me, but at the same time, they had the bro code thing going down.

Something about how Mav had spoken up just before Nyx could say a word told me he was giving Nyx an out.

"How long?"

"Rex didn't say," Nyx hedged.

Steel had gone from kissing me like we were in a romance movie, where at the end, the hero finally got his girl, to walking away from me without a backward glance while looking like he'd been sucker punched.

I'd figured Mom had said something to him, but what that was specifically, I didn't know.

She was very good with her words, capable of using them like they were a weapon, and she'd honed that skill like I figured the army was honing Maverick—making him one of the fiercest fighters around.

She'd done something to break the moment I'd been dreaming about since I'd learned what it meant when boys and girls kissed.

I just knew she'd wrecked it for me.

She'd known how I felt about Steel, had mocked me for my crush for years, and even though she couldn't have seen us kiss, not when she was stuck in bed and we'd been in the hall, maybe she'd heard something?

Had I moaned?

I couldn't remember, but just thinking about that kiss had been enough to make me slip my hand between my legs to get myself off that night. So I had to figure that during it, I'd been pretty turned on too. Maybe I *had* moaned, or made a noise. Something that had clued her in. Sex had been her business for most of her adult life, if anyone would recognize the signs, it was her.

What had she said to him?

It had been enough to make him turn from me, for him to… what? Make himself sick by drinking?

Steel didn't drink.

Whatever she'd told him, it had fucked with his head to the point where he'd made himself sick with it.

"I need to see him," I stated decisively.

"Honey, the funeral's still going on."

I didn't care about any of that.

I'd paid my respects to the mom I wished I'd had, and now that my duty was done, I had other duties to attend to.

The people around us wouldn't care if I stood here until the rest of the crowd had tossed dirt on her coffin, but I cared about being away from Steel.

Nyx shook his head though. "Rex wouldn't let you in. He's in a bad way, Stone."

"And I'm not?" I murmured, my throat suddenly feeling thick with an onset of tears.

My world just collapsed around me, and the one man who could make it better had suddenly gone AWOL...

I blew out a breath. "I should be used to people letting me down," I rasped, including him and Mav in that look as I shoved myself away from them and retreated to the car where my mom's friend, Maria, was going to take me home.

I heard Mav call after me, but I didn't glance back. I should have known they'd stand with Rex and Steel over me.

They always did, and always would. That's what brothers did. And being a brother was something I'd never, could *never* be. So being reminded that I was an outsider, at this particular moment, was just the stab to the heart I didn't need.

As much of a family as they were to me, they'd always take Steel's side over mine. And that realization hurt.

Badly.

SIXTEEN

LILY

MY STOMACH WAS TWISTING and my nerves wouldn't let up as I watched Tiff.

The pair of us were a little battered and a lot broken, with casts here and there and bandages still covering the worst of our injuries, and I knew she was taking meds for the concussion headaches she had while I was trying *not* to.

I was still in pain now whenever I turned my head to the side, and I was just dealing with it because I had a nasty feeling that if I took some of the meds the doctors had prescribed, I'd get hooked.

Maybe that was a stupid thing to think, a little irrational, but I needed control right now.

I needed it more than ever.

So, I sat there, in pain, quiet as I processed it, and watched her pretty much do the same thing.

We'd both been quieter since the accident, quieter and more thoughtful, like we were taking the time to register just how fucking lucky we were.

But I didn't feel lucky.

I felt like I had a burden on my shoulders that wasn't going anywhere.

"What do you think's going on?" Tiff asked, her fingers swirling around the pattern on the armrest of the chair she was sitting on. "Why do you think they cut out of here so fast, so soon after they brought...you know who home?"

I shrugged. "I don't know. Link wouldn't tell me."

"Sin wouldn't tell me either. They just rolled on out and haven't messaged since."

I hummed. "Link hasn't either, and you know we text all the time."

She bit her lip. "Christ."

"What is it?" I pressed, concerned for her.

She shrugged. "I don't know."

My lips twitched. "Bullshit. You and I both know that you know exactly what you're thinking."

Her nose crinkled. "What are you? A mind reader?"

"Pretty much where you're concerned. You might as well spill it. After all, you'll tell me eventually."

She blew a raspberry at me. "I was just thinking that I'd love some of those OxyContin right now."

I snickered at her. "Me too. Jesus, I swear I was thinking the exact same thing."

Her lips twisted, and she muttered, "I really don't want that shit either, but fuck, some days it just really goddamn hurts."

I nodded. "Today is one of those days, and I don't think it's helping that we know something is going on and no one is telling us shit."

"Probably isn't helping that you know your father is somewhere on the compound."

My throat felt thick at her statement. "You think that's what Rex meant?"

She snorted. "Of course it is."

"I thought… Well, I was hoping it meant that he was dead."

She shook her head. "No way. Steel only just got back, and I know for a fact he wasn't going to be killing that fuck over there."

Last I'd heard about my father, he'd been in Hong Kong before his arrest warrants had gone wide, and he'd started hopping around countries that had a non-extradition order with the U.S. like he was a party boy on coke with a passport to burn and a bank account so padded, he could see the world in style. Unluckily for him, his padded bank account was now mine.

I tugged on my bottom lip. "I don't know how I feel about that."

"Katina said she saw a big box on a pickup truck when the bikes rolled in."

The soft voice had me jolting in surprise. I twisted around, instantly regretting it when my neck and shoulders twinged, then seeing Ghost, I relaxed.

I was in the bunkhouse I'd been given when I'd had to stay on the compound, and while it wasn't the most comfortable of places, it would do. It was better than the clubhouse, where people would and could fuck anywhere their hearts desired.

I wondered why the men were okay with that.

It was like…

This place was like a funhouse for kids but adult style. It was irritating, wondering if somewhere had been Lysoled, and it was even more irritating when you'd be sitting down and drinking something or eating something, and a few feet away, someone would either be boning or on the brink of boning.

I'd never seen as many pussies in my life, truth be told, and I'd watched a lot of porn before Link. A lot. But seriously, I'd never seen as much of a woman's body as I had until recently.

So, this bunkhouse?

The safest place to be for a non-coitus spoiled area.

My lips twitched at the thought, even as I asked Ghost, "What did she see?"

She spoke perfect English, but sometimes a word would come out thickened by an accent.

"A cr-ah-te."

My eyes flared wide at that and what it might mean... "You think my father's alive in there?"

Ghost shrugged. "I hope he is."

My jaw tensed as so many emotions washed through me, I wasn't sure which to process first.

Hell, I didn't know what I wanted to be going down on the compound right about now.

Whatever had sent the brothers shooting off, well, I knew it wasn't related to my father, because they'd only just gotten back from wherever they'd collected Steel and this crate from.

I assumed an airport, because it hadn't been that long, and I thought it took a couple of months for shipping containers to make land when it was from Asia.

"He's alive," I murmured, somehow feeling it in my bones. "Link would have told me if he wasn't."

"Why would he? Isn't that making you a coconspirator?"

I sniffed at Tiff's reasoning. "Aren't I that already?" I shrugged when she clucked her tongue, and muttered, "He wants me to help kill him."

Tiff's eyes widened, and I knew that was because whatever she'd expected me to say, it wasn't that.

Ghost whispered in, as was her way, moving over from the doorway, which she'd managed to open without a sliver of a sound, and as she took a seat opposite me, I stared at her warily.

"You're braver than me for even thinking of it."

Her words didn't get my back up, neither did they soothe me.

Had I thought she'd be jealous?

I cocked a brow at her. "Don't you want to twist the knife in?"

She shook her head. "No. I-I don't think I could bear to look at him," she muttered earnestly. "I just couldn't look upon him without wanting to puke."

"You could always puke on him," Tiff suggested helpfully. "Right in his smug face. I'm sure he'd love that."

Ghost gave her a small smile. "I'm sure he would. While he deserves it and more, I-I don't want those feelings in my life."

"What feelings?" I queried hesitantly. I wanted to know more, while being terrified she'd open up too much.

It was one thing to know someone evil had spawned you, but it was something else to realize that you, maybe, were just as bad as the person whose seed gave you life.

I cleared my throat at the unsettling thought, then tuned in as Ghost answered, "The anger, the rage…it's toxic. As is the fear and the hurt. I know Tatána and Amara feel the same way. Maybe even worse. I feel like I'm dealing with it better than them. I told Katina not to tell them what she told me, and I don't think they would deal well with the situation if they found out he was still alive."

"You told them he was dead?" Tiff asked.

She nodded. "I did. They asked me what they thought Rex had meant, and when they found out, they were relieved and they cried." Ghost shrugged. "That is enough for them to cope with. Knowing he can't hurt them anymore, knowing Luke is dead, and that they are safe? It is enough. It has to be." She cut me a look then, her delicate face softening from its pinched tension as she studied me. "But you are different than us, Lily. You're not a victim—"

"I am!" I whispered, finding it strange how strident my tone was at that, how eager I was to accept that label.

When she shook her head, I felt like crying. "This isn't a bad thing, *kohana*," she whispered softly. "You are very strong, stronger than any of us."

"You survived hell," I bit off fiercely.

"She's right, Ghost, you did," Tiff inserted calmly, her watchful eyes taking in the conversation in a way that I knew meant her brain had ticked into therapist mode.

The idea pissed me off, but also, I was glad.

I needed all the help I could get, and Tiffany knew the lay of the land in so many ways that no other shrink could ever learn.

Sure, she wasn't fully trained. Sure, she wasn't an actual shrink, but I'd take it.

I'd take it all the way to the bank.

I gulped, swallowing down my rage and hurt. "I'm strong because I had to be strong," I whispered, reaching up and rubbing my face. When I rubbed my eyes, though, I dug a little too hard and I knew I'd be feeling that ache for a while, but it was better that than anything else.

And that was when the need for drugs whispered through me.

Just like it had since the car crash.

A drug that would mellow me out. Take away the pain, a pain that was both mental and emotional, physical and psychological.

I closed my eyes, wishing I was different, wishing I wasn't *me*.

Here I was, all torn up inside, not because my father was somewhere in the compound, maybe being tortured as we spoke. But because I didn't know how much input I wanted in his death.

Once upon a time, I'd wanted to be the one to kill him. I'd wanted to reap unto him what he'd reaped unto my mother, but in the here and now, I wasn't so sure.

I was, I'd admit, a little lost, and without Link here, I felt that even more so.

Blowing out a breath, I listened in as Ghost murmured, "I'm strong, I know this, and so are the others, but we are strong in different ways, no? There are many ways to be strong, and the truth is, I'm content with my lot. I'm free, and that's all I ever wanted. I had the man who hurt me running around, chasing his tail, and more than that, his son is dead, and his empire is crumbling down around him. That gives me satisfaction. It makes me happy. But Lily is different. Her background is not mine. She was raised expecting more, expecting to have it all—"

"I never got it," I snapped, angered by her words to the point where I clenched my fists, which had my broken bones jarring like fuck.

Before I could even wince, Tiffany snapped, "This isn't a contest, Lily. Stop hurting yourself. It won't make things better."

"What are you talking about?" I whispered, wounded by her tone.

"You know what I'm talking about. There's no oblivion worth seeking that would make all this go away. You're an adult, let's act like one, and let's make sure that you're ready for whatever you're faced with."

I blinked at her, then slowly shook my head. "You think I should do it, don't you?"

There was a flatness to her expression that I'd never seen before. A cool reasoning, a logic that made me more twisted up inside than ever before.

I thought she'd try to talk me out of it, not lead me into hell like Link was doing.

Of course, he was only trying to give me what I'd told him I wanted. I'd said I wanted to take my father out, and Link, being the good man he was—even if good was relative to some people like Tiff's mother—was trying to give me what my heart supposedly desired.

"I don't know if I have what it takes," I admitted rawly. And that was the crux of the matter.

When it boiled down to it, I wasn't sure if I was talking all game.

A breath gusted from my lips as I made the admission, and her lips twisted as she murmured, "Sweetheart, you can do whatever you set your mind to. If you think it would give you closure, then if anyone deserves to die a horrible death, it's Donavan."

I gnawed on the inside of my cheek, but it provided no comfort. "I know he deserves to die, I just don't know if I want to be the one who's sliding the knife into his heart."

Ghost snorted. "I think if you wanted it, you could do it, but do you want that? Do you want to end his life?"

For a second, I thought about that, then I huffed. "The funny thing is, since I was a child when I saw him push Mom down the stairs, that's all I thought about. That was like my one aim—to make him pay, to get him back. Now the opportunity is here, and in a way that will never have any repercussions because I'd hazard a guess and say that the authorities still think he's in Asia, and I'm being chicken shit."

Tiffany pshawed. "Hardly chicken shit. Taking a life is a big deal. But his life doesn't mean anything, does it? In the grand scheme of things, I think you'd be getting good karma for the shit he put you through, for what he did to your mom, and then with his business practices. That's nothing compared to what he did to women like Ghost, Tatána, and Amara because, let's face it, they're not their first and only victims, are they?"

"What are you talking about?"

I jumped at Giulia's voice, and scowled at her through the window she was leaning in, her head peeking through the empty space.

"Is there no privacy on this compound?"

"Umm, nope. You can't live with so many people and expect privacy. You might as well ask for a genie to give you three wishes." She chuckled at her own shitty joke. "It always drove me crazy when I was growing up. How everyone was in each other's business. Now?" She shrugged. "I find it therapeutic."

Of course, that was Tiffany's trigger—her shoulders rolled

back as I watched her morph into a shrink before she inquired, "Why do you think that is?"

Giulia huffed. "I ain't getting into shit with you."

"No? Why not?" Tiff's smile was wicked, and it was a challenge to anyone with Giulia's temperament. "Scared?"

"I ain't scared of shit." She tipped her chin up, and muttered, "Anyway, I heard what you were saying. The walls have ears, babe," she told me, surprising me with the endearment. "It's all good for me to hear. I ain't gonna say shit, am I? But those clubwhores? Nasty fucking skanks."

Ghost's nose crinkled at that. "Why do they have them?"

Giulia heaved out a sigh. "Because they're men, and those women will spread their legs at any time of the day or night for them. Plus, before me, they cleaned, even if their version of cleaning was beyond unhygienic, and they cooked." She shrugged. "Sounds like any man's idea of a palace. Pussy on hand, doesn't have to feed himself or clean up after himself?"

I shuddered at the thought of what went down in the clubhouse. "I don't like it," I admitted.

"You know how I feel about them," Tiff grumbled, sniffing as she pulled down her tailored shorts so that they covered her knees.

Her mandala mark on her hand flashed at me, and I smiled at the sight because it did my heart good to see that on her.

Knowing she was safe, knowing that she was one of us, that we could talk like this, that we could be open in a way I hadn't been able to be before she'd become an Old Lady, it made me realize that our friendship wasn't going to crash and burn.

And I needed that.

I needed the constancy of our relationship.

"It's not like we can say anything, is it?" I groused. "We knew getting into this that was how things were."

Giulia sniffed. "Speak for yourself. I didn't get into this knowing I was going to be accepting those skanks sniffing around my man. The second a bitch does, I'm gonna rip her throat out."

And from the mean smirk in her eyes, I actually thought she meant it.

She wouldn't wimp out over it, like I was with my father. No, she'd go straight for the jugular.

"Anyway, I'm going to be making some changes around the place."

"Oh?" Tiff questioned, her ears pricking up with interest.

I laughed faintly at the sight of her eagerness, and I tuned into Giulia's conversation as she muttered, "Rex has told me that the clubhouse is in a state and that I need to get the place cleaned up. Apparently, now that we have more Old Ladies, it's time we started acting like it."

My brow puckered at that. "What's that supposed to mean?"

"It means that he's been putting this off for a while, and he's decided that now's the time for change."

"Why?"

Tiff's question had Giulia shrugging. She placed her hands on the windowsill, then let her weight fall back, her head rolling on her shoulders so she could stare up at the sky. "I'd hazard a guess and say it's because of Storm."

"Storm? What about him?"

"Well, his Old Lady left him over this shit, and his kid and woman are refusing to go to Ohio to be with him. They want to stay here." She sighed. "That's wrong. I mean, she wants to stay here and the kid wants to go be with her father. It's a mess."

My heart ached for them all, because it was so much more than a mess.

"Who is she?" Ghost asked softly.

"Name's Keira. Actually, I've never met her, I just know of her, and I know Storm is a dick."

"I didn't even know he had an Old Lady until recently," Tiff admitted. "The parties I came to before, when I first met Sin, they were all the same, but Storm's a real manwhore."

"Yeah, he's his own worst enemy. And things got worse, too, because he found out she was dating."

Ghost snorted at that. "God forbid she be allowed to move on while he's sowing his oats here, there, and everywhere."

The three of us laughed at her antiquated, if spot on, phrasing.

Giulia winked at her. "Exactly. She was smart getting out of that shit, if you ask me. But no one is asking me. So I'm just gonna take advantage of the gift Rex gave me and crack some skulls together if they don't toe the line."

I could hear the zealousness in her tone and knew she was stoked to be heading up this little task force that Rex had set up.

Truth was, I didn't know how Rex had the time to micromanage every aspect of club life, but somehow, he did.

I plucked at my bottom lip again, and questioned, "Are you going to make them stop having sex in the bar?"

Giulia grinned. "What do you think?"

Snickering, I thought about how that was going to go down—like a lead balloon. "They're going to love you."

She winked. "Oh, they will when I start telling them that if they fuck out in the open, I won't be making them any food." She tapped her nose with her pointer finger. "Way to any man's brain is through his stomach. Good thing for us, I'm a brilliant cook. They won't want to miss out on any of my food."

"You got it all worked out."

She smiled at my statement, which I'd admit was wistful.

"Babe, I've got shit worked out, but I'm gonna do what feels right, and that's what I think you should do. I got my revenge." She cleared her throat, and a shadow whispered over her eyes. "I know what it feels like to watch the bastard who was hurting me bleed out. If you want to do the same, then the ball is in your court, but don't think you're weak if you just don't have the stomach for it.

"Trust me, taking a life isn't something you should be easy with doing. It doesn't make you chicken shit. It makes you strong, and it makes you a good person." Her smile was gentle, accepting, then she clapped her hands together, rubbed them, and chirpily asked, "Who'd like to help me wake up the club snatch and get them scrubbing the staircase?"

Tiff laughed at that. "Is the key to get them to do all the miserable chores so they'll leave?"

Giulia winked at her. "Method to my madness, babe, method to my madness."

SEVENTEEN

STONE

WHEN INDY STRODE into the hospital room, it was like she brought in a thousand kilowatts of energy with her.

In fact, she might have been coming in off the back of a mushroom bomb. I felt the aftershocks in the floor as they traveled up to the bed I was lying on.

Seeing her, though, made my heart settle down. I was on edge, shaky, and whatever the woman had drugged me with—something the doctors had taken blood tests to discern—was making me feel sluggish at the same time.

But at the sight of her?

I had no choice but to just cry.

And cry.

And cry.

Her face crumpled, and she was there, in my space, sobbing too, as I clung to her and she clung to me.

"Fuck, I was so frightened, Stone," she whimpered into my hair, making it wet, but those tears were good tears.

I loved them, because they were real, honest. They meant she loved me, and I was so happy that she did, because I felt that right back at her.

I sobbed into the neck of her tee. "I was fucking petrified. I'm so lucky she was a dipshit, Indy, because if she wasn't, I'd have been a goner."

She sobbed harder at that, then I did too. As she squeezed me and I squeezed her, something settled inside me, a resolve that I needed this woman in my life.

I was tired of hiding our friendship, tired of keeping shit a secret.

Steel and Rex had told me that my life would be changing. That they'd be transferring me from NYC to West Orange, and while I didn't need to know how the fuck they were going to make that happen, while I'd been angry at first, in the silence after their call, I actually wasn't anymore.

I was accepting of it, because I knew where my place was.

And it wasn't in Manhattan.

If anything, a sense of peace washed over me as I accepted so many things I'd been struggling with.

I'd fought Steel's rejection for so many years, but here, now? I was so tired of fighting it. He could do whatever he wanted, and I wasn't going to be hurting anymore.

I didn't need to be in Manhattan to put space between us. I could focus on the sick, deal with my career, aim for more, all while being closer to home.

Yeah, *home*.

West Orange had always been that, and I'd just forced myself to think that it wasn't.

I was, by nature, a home body. And I missed my family.

The last time I'd gone back to the compound, Nyx had been sulking with me because he'd said I'd left them behind, and I had.

There was more to my family than just Steel, and even though we'd had our ups and downs, after I'd moved in with Rex's family after Mom's death, my relationships had tightened with almost all of the brothers.

Didn't Rex call me every couple of weeks? Wasn't I still in touch with Link via text? Was there a day that went by when he wasn't sending me some stupid GIF that made me laugh?

And Sin and Storm—weren't they just a phone call away? Always on the other end of the line if I needed them to come raging into battle for me.

And Maverick? What about our weekly emails? An email that I felt sure no one knew about, one that was my lifeline to the family and that was his way of expressing himself to me and to me alone.

He called on the Hippocratic Oath that I'd sworn to abide by when I'd first started practicing medicine, but we both knew that was bullshit.

I'd keep his secrets because he kept mine. We were each other's vault of truth.

But the trouble was, I had so many fucking secrets. So many of them. They were eating me up inside.

Maybe now was the time to let some of them slip.

Not the ones from Maverick or anything like that, just the ones with Indy. No one knew about how close we were. They just thought we were friends because we were linked by the MC. But I was tired of that.

I was sick of hiding my connections. Sick of being a little lost amid the ties that bound me to the clubhouse.

If I was going home, then I was going home with style.

"Did you tell them how close we are?"

She tensed at that. "Huh?"

When she pulled back to look at me with red-rimmed eyes, I smiled at her, reached up, and rubbed my thumb down her cheek.

I'd known she'd be nervous about that. Lifelines weren't always something you wanted broadcasted, and Indy was tougher than most. She felt she had to be that way, even though no one asked it of her.

Not even Nyx.

And their relationship was just one big mess.

"I think it's time, don't you?"

She winced a little. "I guess. But I didn't actually say anything. It was weird. Nyx strode into my room like he owned the fucking place, and there I was, just starting to lose my shit. He realized something was going on, and he helped."

"He realized something was going on, huh? Just helped out of the kindness of his heart?" I questioned with a snort.

Her lips twisted. "With a bit of persuasion."

"I'll bet." I grinned at her, even though I was exhausted and tired and the drugs were still in my system.

I felt like I could rest now that she was here though. I felt like I could let my guard down, and that no one would hurt me.

I was in a different hospital than the one I worked in, but Jesus, that didn't matter, did it? Was I safe anywhere?

Grunting at the thought, I muttered, "Love, I'm so tired right now. Do you mind if I sleep?"

"No! Of course I don't," she whispered, her voice as soggy as her eyes. "I'll take a seat over there and just sit here if you don't mind?"

"Don't mind? Jesus, Indy, I'd be grateful. I don't have the energy to keep my eyes open much longer, and the truth is, I couldn't rest knowing I was alone." I sucked in a breath. "I wanted Steel to come for me, but he said he couldn't."

"They told me their logic." Her mouth tightened. "I didn't approve."

I shrugged. "I don't mind."

Her mouth dropped open. "You don't mind?"

"No."

She peered at me. "Did you get hit on the head?"

"Maybe? I don't know what happened after I passed out."

She scowled at that, then her fingers were running over my head, slipping through my hair, like she was trying to find some lumps and bumps.

I laughed at her antics, then muttered, "Indy, it's okay. I'm okay with this."

"Your life is here. They can't just make decisions for you." Her remark keyed me into the fact that they'd cut her into the loop.

"Yeah, they can. They care about me. I realized that today. It surprised me. I just..." I shrugged.

She got it, of course. She was one of us, even if she tried not to be as well. "Of course they care, they just have a fucked up way of showing it."

I nodded at that, then dropped my head back against the pillows. "I know I was close to home anyway, but I'll be happy to be back there."

"You will? Why?"

The scoff in her voice was audible, and I got it. She'd moved a town over to be outside of West Orange, but she hadn't gone much farther than that for Nyx's and Caleb's sake. I hadn't been sure what her game plan would be once Caleb had hit eighteen and he'd started prospecting for the club, but she'd stuck around as he was patched in, and now with him in Riker's? She wasn't going to be moving while he was so close.

"Home is where my roots are, and I've been running from them long enough."

"You mean Steel too?"

I must have sounded more on the ball than I was actually feeling, because that she picked up on that didn't blow my mind.

"Yeah," I replied on a sleepy sigh, rolling my head to the side as I followed her path from my bedside over to the chair where she could sit next to me. Before she plunked her butt down, she reached into her purse and wiggled a phone with a cracked screen at me. "Yours. They found it."

God.

How was our phone conversation so recent yet still somehow like a lifetime ago?

"I have a charger," she told me as she plugged it in, then when she was seated, she scooted the chair forward so it was closer to the bed, and then she leaned her arm on the sheets.

Her skin was darker than mine, thanks to her Algonquin heritage, but as our hands knotted together, heritage, gender, history, all of it was lost as I found comfort in my best friend. The woman who was like a sister to me.

I sucked in a breath, finally feeling like I could relax, then I closed my eyes and whispered, "It's time to let him go."

"Dumb fuck that he is," she whispered.

I smiled, humming as I allowed my body and my brain to relax. "Yeah, he is, but it's his loss."

"That's what I've been telling you for years," she muttered grumpily, and I heard the tapping of her phone and knew she was on it.

That was the last thing I heard before I passed out.

EIGHTEEN

SIN

"YOU'RE THE NEW LINK, HUH?"

I narrowed my eyes at nothing in particular, but kept my voice polite as I rasped, "Link with what?"

"The Five Points, of course." A hum sounded down the line. "I'm Brennan O'Donnelly."

I scowled at Rex, who shrugged his shoulders, evidently not getting why I was pissed at him. "Who gave you this number?" My question had my brothers' conversations breaking off as they turned to look at me.

There was a snort down the line. "We have our ways and means of doing business, as I'm sure you do. But in this instance, Nyx gave it to me. As far as I'm aware, you're the new Enforcer, aren't you? He's the VP, isn't that right?"

I dipped my chin. "That's right. Pleasure to make your acquaintance, Brennan," I said, keying my brothers in on who was on the phone.

Nyx smirked at me, *fucker*, so I flipped him the bird but everyone else's attention reverted to what they'd been talking about before—plans for drawing Stone back into the fold.

Brennan snickered. "Acquaintance? Padraig? I think that's taking things a little too far, especially when a little birdie told me exactly who you are."

My mouth grew taut at that, and it didn't take much to figure out who'd opened their mouth. "She's an untrustworthy slut. I wouldn't put much mind to whatever shit she's spouting."

"Mary Catherine is a slut?"

For the first time, I felt like I'd stunned the shit out of him, and I couldn't blame him.

"Oh. Fuck! No. Not MaryCat. I meant—"

He chuckled, evidently back on an even keel while I was left squirming like a butterfly under a pin. "You mean your slut of a mother." He hummed. "Yes, she's an issue, but her husband is fairly capable of keeping her and her habits in line."

"Until he gets sick of her and trades her in for a newer model," I countered meanly.

"No one leaves the life. You know that," he rumbled, and I did. I truly did, and I was happy about that.

That meant if she was traded in and thought to run her mouth, she'd be dead.

I could think of no kinder fate for a cunt like my ma than that.

"Anyway, what's this about? This isn't family time."

I heard him shrug. "Thought you'd like to know that one of your men was shot down on 8th Avenue."

My heart fucking stopped at that—I swore it did. "What?" I rasped.

"One of our men saw it happen. We're not sure if he was a target, or if it was just an expedient hit because the dumb fuck was wearing his colors in the middle of disputed territory. There was another shooting a few minutes later, and a Bratva *boyevik* was taken down, so we think he was the original target and your boy was just collateral damage."

"Hardly collateral if it was the fucking *Famiglia* behind the hit. They're at war with us now."

"I heard. Nice to have you on board. The Irish, Russians, and the Americans...a new set of Allied Forces."

I muttered, "Fingers crossed you're painting them as the Nazis and not us."

Brennan laughed. "It's the victor who gets to write the history books."

"True." My brothers had tensed at my words, and I knew I needed to get shit back on track. "Was Steel taken to a hospital?" I questioned.

"Yeah. The second my man saw it go down, he was there, helping a fellow ally out."

"Many thanks to you for that," I told him cordially, but my words dripped with polite gratitude. Respect as well.

If their people had saved Steel from being run over, then fuck, we owed them more than just a thank you.

We owed them a blood debt.

Brennan hummed. "It's all good, *deartháir*, it's all good."

I flinched at that. "My Gaelic isn't that good, but I know you're not my brother."

"Maybe you are, maybe you aren't. Not by blood, but that's how it works in the MC, isn't it? You're all brothers in arms, so I don't see why you can't be for us too. I think it's fitting we have a liaison who's born from both our lines doing the running between our families."

I narrowed my eyes at that. "MaryCat is the one with ties. Not me. My father was a brother in the MC."

"I'm sure he was, but your mother has always been tied to the Five Points."

Surprise hit me. "What?"

Brennan hummed. "You don't think her husband picked up some skank off the street, do you?" He snorted. "She's the daughter of a lieutenant who went off the rails. When she was corralled in, she was married off. You know how it works."

I'd admit to being stunned as hell, and my gaping mouth confirmed it. "You're shitting me?"

Brennan snorted. "No. I'm not. We don't let our women float away, you know that."

"You let MaryCat—"

"MaryCat sneaked away. That's true. And she was smart. She got married, otherwise, we'd have hauled her back. She knew the deal. Clever girl, that one. Always did like her." Another hum. "Your ma wasn't as smart. Never wanted to be tied down, but if she had, that was the second she'd have been free from us."

I hoped that logic held true for Tiff. Fuck.

Rubbing my eyes after I pinched the bridge of my nose, I rasped, "Okay, less of the family time, I need to focus on my brother. Where's Steel?"

Brennan reeled off the information, then he murmured, "The last I heard, which was minutes before I called you, he's stable.

"We've had news, by the way. While things were derailed with the *Famiglia* war, we'll have a shipment landing soon. I've been in touch with the Rabid Wolves. They know to be on red alert, I'm warning you to do the same."

He didn't wait to say goodbye, and I didn't wait to give him a parting greeting either. We both clicked off, and I was surrounded by a bunch of brothers who were concerned to hell.

"Steel's down?" Nyx ground out.

"Either a stray shot, unlucky moment where he was in the wrong place at the wrong time, or it was a targeted hit. Brennan says he's stable." The irony had me shaking my head though. "You'll never guess where the fuck he is."

Rex heaved a sigh. "Of course he's in Stone's hospital."

"Yeah."

"If he dies, I'll fucking kill him." Rex rubbed his chin. But if he lives, I'll still kill him if he doesn't wake the fuck up and finally take what's his."

Link's focus shifted from me to Rex at that, and he asked, "Rex? What the fuck is going on between them?"

"Isn't my shit to spill. You know how it works, Link," Rex replied tiredly.

"You need to share this with us. Whatever the fuck is eating him up, it ain't going to stop," Link ground out.

From our reactions, I knew the lot of us were concerned about Steel, and the fact that I wasn't racing off probably showed we had time to make it to the hospital, which was close by but we wanted answers. And our Prez knew it.

Anyway, we knew how hospitals worked.

We weren't blood relatives, any of us. That meant they'd tell us sweet FA, even if we threatened them.

All that was waiting on us was a waiting room and no fucking answers as to how he was doing.

Rubbing my chin in irritation at the thought of yet another frustrating night being spent apart from Tiffany, I cursed Steel for being a prick and heading off into the unknown by himself.

I knew for a fact no lone sniper would have hit us all en masse, not without wanting to bring war down on himself and his side. But that Rex was keeping this tucked close to his chest was enough of a clue as to how fucked up Steel's secret was.

Rex cut each of us a look, but as he glanced over us, he connected with Nyx longer than anyone.

"Some shit doesn't need to be shared, and that's where Steel is at."

Nyx scowled. "What kind of fucking logic is that? You trying to mess with my head or something? If you've got something to say, fucking say it."

Rex narrowed his eyes back at him. "Why the fuck are all of you jumping down my throat on this? I've got secrets that I keep for everyone. If you want me to start spilling shit, then you're the ones who need to be buying me more JD so I'll open my mouth, because as it stands, I ain't saying nothing to no one. You hear me?"

He grunted when Link glared at him. "You can't be serious, Rex."

The Prez scowled at him. "Why can't I be? Your secrets are my secrets. I'm like a fucking priest. Don't you know that?"

"It's eating him up on the inside. He ain't gonna do shit when it's still rotting his guts away."

Interestingly enough, Rex flinched at that. Then, he scrubbed a hand over his face. "This ain't my business to tell."

"Maybe we can help."

Rex shook his head. "Link, sometimes you just can't fix everything for brothers you give a damn about."

"Why can't I? I have to try. Maybe there's something we can do—"

"There's nothing you can do about this. It's about his blood. He thinks it's tainted, and fuck, if I were him, maybe I'd feel the exact same way. Bear is many things, and I know he's committed enough sins to see him sitting on the electric chair, but I'm not tainted... Steel?" Air gusted from his lips. "I can understand why he might think it, even if I think he's a dumbass for denying what he and Stone have together."

My brow puckered at that, and I muttered, "Rex, you have to know you can't leave it like that. We understand that you're uncomfortable telling secrets that aren't yours to tell, but anyone can see Steel is goddamn miserable."

"And Stone is too. You know being in the city has to be killing her," Nyx rasped, and I knew why. Stone had always been a part of their friendship.

While I'd always been a bit of an outsider, thanks to arriving at the clubhouse later than the others, most of the council had grown up together, had been raised as a family almost.

They knew each other's shit, and while I was a part of the fam now, it wasn't the same as having been reared together.

I wasn't jealous, but I knew how they felt about Stone. She'd been one of them until Steel had changed, and suddenly, she wasn't anymore.

Stone had remained like a sister to most of the guys, with Steel pushing her further and further away, until shit had almost turned to tragedy.

I could still remember the shock in the clubhouse the day Stone had almost died.

She'd taken some drugs from a local Colombian gang that had been lacing their shit with weedkiller. She'd nearly died that day, and still, Steel had stayed the fuck away from her. Two more 'chemical' attempts at seeking his attention had gone wrong too, and all she'd gained in the end? Losing her college scholarship and derailing her future.

She'd almost lost everything, would have done if Rex and the MC hadn't stepped up to the plate when Steel had failed her.

Truth was, I had no idea why she was still pining for him. All the random shit he'd done to her, all the hurt he'd caused, none of it would have made me stick around the guy, that was for fucking sure. But hell, wasn't that love?

Just because I didn't get it, didn't mean I didn't get what love meant. I knew Tiffany could run me ragged and the love wouldn't die. We'd be having fucking words, but my feelings wouldn't be torn from me.

Sometimes, a love like this just endured, and I actually pitied the pair of them, Stone and Steel, because whatever the hell it was that was keeping them apart, it sucked.

Hard.

Rex looked tortured though, and I repeated, "Maybe we can't fix shit, but maybe we can ease his concern about what it is he's going through."

He grimaced. "Me telling you guys is only going to make shit worse."

"What's it about?" Nyx questioned softly, evidently sensing, as the rest of us were, that Rex was softening up some.

"His father."

My mouth dropped open at that. Whatever I'd thought he'd say, I'd never expected that. "His dad? I thought no one knew. Wasn't his mom one of the clubwhores back in the day?"

Rex nodded. "She was. And that's the issue." He rubbed a hand over his chin.

"The issue is that she was snatch or that his dad was someone —" I blinked. "Someone, what? I mean, Grizzly wasn't exactly a great daddy."

Rex gnawed on the inside of his cheek. "We need to get going."

"No." Nyx shoved a hand on his shoulder and kept him down. Anger flared in the Prez's eyes, but Nyx didn't care.

Fuck, we all knew what Nyx and Rex were capable of. Every brother here was aware things between them would end up with them both in a coma if we didn't stop them, but we also knew that Nyx's temper far outweighed Rex's.

"Steel would only be this messed up over one thing," Nyx rasped. "You don't have to say a fucking word, Rex, but just nod if what I say is right." Rex's nostrils flared, but Nyx, who'd turned a curious shade of white, muttered, "He's Kevin's kid, isn't he?"

Rex's mouth turned white, but he nodded.

And hell, that had us all blowing out a breath. All of us stared down at the scratches on the table, because suddenly, we got it.

Kevin was the cunt who'd been raping Nyx's sister since she was almost a toddler.

He was the fucker who'd threatened Nyx with the same fate if he ever said shit to anyone.

And he was the same bastard who was Nyx's first kill. I wasn't sure if he haunted my brother's dreams, but I knew Kevin had ruined his life. Nyx was on an eternal mission to stamp out any pedophilic bastard who roamed around freely.

He made them pay for Kevin's sins. Made them burn for the torment they caused their victims. Until one man blurred into Kevin, and Nyx was killing the same man over and over again for the crimes he'd committed.

"Just because he's his son, doesn't mean he's tainted."

Unsurprisingly, Link was the first one to speak up, and though Nyx stunned me by nodding, Rex muttered, "Doesn't help that Stone's ma told him that the apple doesn't fall far from the tree."

Link hissed, "Always hated that bitch."

And that was saying something.

Link was the most easygoing bastard I'd ever met.

"If anyone deserved to get cancer," Nyx agreed, "it was that old cunt."

"Fucking clubwhores," Rex rasped. "Make shitty mothers."

I nodded, but I couldn't argue or agree. My mother, apparently, was a daughter of a high-ranking Five Pointer. Fuck, talk about night and day. High-ranking or not, she'd still sucked as badly as the clubwhores as a mom.

Still, most of us around this table knew what it was like to have shitty parents. Only Rex, really, had had a good relationship with his folks.

He'd adored his mom, Rene, and I had too. Most of us had. She'd kept us going when things were bad. Link had a close relationship with his grandma, but as for the rest of us, we came from rotten backgrounds.

I had to figure it was why we were all nearly forty, and it had taken us a long ass time to even think about settling down. When we had, every one of us had gone for a woman who was the antithesis of the walking wombs who'd carried us.

Giulia was honest to a fault, willing to take on Nyx's burdens and ease his woes. Tiffany was a good, kind woman, generous with herself, even if it unduly affected her. Lily was gentle while also strong, capable of hitting back after a lifetime of being taught to be one thing, and able to open her arms to a man like Link, who was the exact opposite of what she should probably be looking for in a life mate.

Rene was a woman to look up to, but Rex had done her proud by falling for Rachel, the MC's lawyer. She wouldn't take any bullshit, and when he eventually got around to claiming her, I knew she'd make a brilliant Old Lady, who'd lead the bitches and would do a fucking great job at it.

I rubbed my chin as I thought about how we could help our brother, but I had to admit—I came up blank.

"What did she say to him?"

"I only know any of this, Link, because Steel barged into Bear's office while I was there. He didn't see me, so I overheard something I wish I hadn't. But...everything happens for a reason. He almost killed himself over this—I was the one who found him because I knew to go looking for him."

"You're shitting me?" Nyx rasped, his eyes wide with horror.

"Not kidding. Nothing funny about this messed up situation." Rex rubbed his eyes. "Look, now you know, and you can't let on that you do either. If he finds out I told you, he'll freak out, and that's the last thing any of us need—him acting out because he thinks he has something to prove.

"Steel is one of the most stubborn bastards I know. He's denied himself Stone all these years, when he's loved her longer than she's loved him, all because he didn't want to mar her with his taint.

"That tells you how powerful his will is. If we start treating him differently, then you know exactly what he'll do."

We all fell silent at that, because we knew just how steel-headed Steel was. He hadn't just gotten his nickname for the plate in his head, but for the fact that he was a stubborn fuck.

Running my hand over my face, I muttered, "I think it's time to head to the hospital now."

Because none of us had a clue what else to say, the others just nodded, then shuffled onto their feet.

I, for one, didn't feel a lick better for knowing the truth, and though I was glad I did, because if I could help him, I would, I was still as in the dark as ever.

The worst thing was, I knew my brothers felt the exact same way. And suddenly, all the shit we'd given him over Stone, the distance he'd shoved between them... I got it. It made sense. Steel was a man of honor, but we'd painted him as the villain. Yet the only villain in this story was Kevin.

I just wished Steel was aware of that too, and because I knew him well, I knew he never would.

NINETEEN

STONE
BEFORE

"YOU SURE YOU want me staying here, Bear?" I asked, lowering my rucksack to the ground as I peered at the small bunkhouse.

Normally, visiting chapters, friendly clubs, they'd stay in these places, especially the top ranks, but that Bear was letting me live here was a testament to how close I was to him and his family.

"Of course, darlin'. Didn't want you living out there by yourself. Could have covered the rent, easy, but why have you so far away from family when here's where you need to be?"

I gulped at his words and hated how close they brought me to tears.

I'd been crying way too much recently, and the tears were always close at hand.

I wasn't sure if I was grieving my mom's death or Steel's absence in my life, but either way, I was hurting.

Being here was bittersweet though.

I knew he was across the way, knew that I could see him any time I happened to venture outside or into the clubhouse for food, and even though my heart was eager for the opportunity, I knew I wasn't going to like what I saw.

He'd ignored a thousand calls and messages from me in the past six weeks, making a liar out of Mav.

Who could do that to someone?

Just cut them out so harshly when their entire world was collapsing around them?

Who could hit 'ignore' on a call when the woman they supposedly loved, even if it was only as a friend and not a girlfriend, was going through tough times? Trying to recalibrate her life, make sense out of the shit her mom had left her in?

If I didn't know him as well as I thought I did, I'd wonder if he'd had some kind of personality transplant. But I did know him.

I knew him well.

So I knew something was going on, something that he didn't think he could share with me.

I just didn't understand why he couldn't.

I'd been tagging along with him and the other guys since I was six years old, for God's sake. Ten years, I'd been in his life and he'd been in mine, close range. Before that? I'd known him from around the clubhouse, because his ma and mine were buddies.

"What's got that pretty smile hiding away like the sun behind the clouds?"

My lips twitched at Bear's poetic turn of phrase. He was the kind of man a girl like me would have a crush on, if she wasn't already in love with someone else.

He was protective, handsome, and I'd been reading way too many older guy romances...

My cheeks didn't burn with heat though. After the life I'd led, even though I was only sixteen, and barely at that, I'd seen more pussies and dicks than I'd had hot dinners.

That was how it rolled when you lived life the way we did.

It was all I knew, but that didn't mean it was all I wanted to know either.

"I'm just..." I hitched a shoulder, unsure what to say that wouldn't sound trite. Wouldn't make me sound like the kid I actually was.

He strolled over to me, curved an arm over my shoulder, and as he bopped a kiss on my head, I got the scent of Old Spice and leather up my nose which, in all honesty, was a pretty nice frickin' scent.

"You need anything, you come to me, okay?"

"I will."

He heaved a sigh. "I know you've seen it all before, but call me first, yeah? Don't go into the clubhouse unless you have to."

My brows rose at that, even as I answered, "Of course."

Bear was hiding something.

He'd said it exactly how it was.

I had seen it all. Had seen everything there was to see. Brothers going down on the snatch, bunnies bouncing away with no clothes on as they fucked three, four, five brothers at a time.

I'd seen everything I shouldn't have, so what the hell was Bear hiding?

And then it hit me.

And I got it.

I got it at long last.

Steel.

He was doing some of those things. Doing them, and Bear was trying to protect me...

I let him go, not really encouraging him to stay with my lack of talkativeness, and as he wandered out, I grabbed my cell and dialed Indy.

She was the only kid I knew who understood me, and while it wasn't technically cool for someone my age to be talking to a twelve-year-old, what choice did I have?

The bikers produced very few female spawn, and she was the only girl around my age. Plus, she needed me as much as I needed her, and I wasn't about to throw her friendship in her face just because she was still in middle school.

"How is it?" Indy asked by way of a greeting.

"It's fine." And it was. Sure, the place was old-fashioned, but hell, my old house hadn't been exactly modern.

It was clean, didn't stink of piss, had a door that locked well, and I was on a compound full of bikers who'd kill to keep me safe.

The only danger I was in was from the DEA or FBI if they decided to raid the place, and even then, it wasn't like they could arrest me for anything.

Sure, I knew more than most because of how openly the guys spoke in front of me, but they wouldn't know that, would they?

"What's wrong?" she pressed, when my tone was lackluster. "I thought you'd love being independent. I mean, I know I shouldn't say it, S, but your ma was a bitch. It must be nice not to have to wait on her hand and foot like you were her slave—"

"Indy! That's unfair. She was sick and in a lot of pain."

She sniffed. "You and I both know that she'd have done the same whether she was sick or not. At least this way, you get to enjoy some of your frickin' youth not being her butler."

My lips twitched, and I couldn't stop my laugh. Most people thought I should be glad Mom was dead, and maybe a little part of me was. It was definitely a relief not to have to worry about her Johns breaking into my room, and it was nice that any money I earned wasn't going to be snorted up her nose.

Still, she was my mom. I wasn't going to get another one, was I?

"Steel still hasn't called."

She heaved a sigh. "Want me to ask Nyx?"

I knew she would, even though she and her brother didn't see eye to eye. "I don't think he'd tell you even if he knew."

Mrs. Biggins swiped at my feet, making me realize she was there. I'd almost forgotten about her, and that made me feel bad. She was Steel's premature birthday gift to me, and I wasn't used to having a pet. She was cool though. She didn't mind being left alone while I worked, so long as I gave her attention when I was home.

I leaned down, picked her up, and kissed the top of her head. She squirmed a little, but by the end, she was purring as she settled into my hold as I moved over to the window that faced the clubhouse, unsure what I'd find when I looked over there.

"Bear said something that's made me wonder about what's going down around here."

"What like?"

"He told me that he was here for me, but to call first and not go into the clubhouse."

She fell silent at that, then questioned, "So when are you going to the clubhouse?"

I snickered, amused because she knew me so well. Amused because, in the same circumstances, she'd be heading straight for the clubhouse too. Pressing my forehead to the glass pane that was cool to the touch, I muttered, "He did it for my benefit."

"You think Steel is—"

Her hesitation told me our minds were on the same track.

"Yeah. I do."

"What did that bitch say to him?" she ground out, sounding anything other than thirteen frickin' years old. "How did he go from being all kissy-kissy with you, and then doing whatever the fuck this is?"

I bit my lip, wondering what the answer to that was, if there even was an answer.

"I don't know."

"Do you want to find out?"

"No."

"Then don't go to the clubhouse."

"Is it as easy as that?"

"You know it is. If you called for me to talk you out of it, then you called the wrong person. Living in a dream world won't do you any good, Stone."

"I know you're right."

"Want me to come over? We can head in together?"

"No." I sucked in a breath. "I'll go over there now."

She hummed. "It's seven. Things should be picking up at the bar now. Nyx left the house a short while ago, so you know where he's at."

I ran a hand through my hair. "I'm nervous."

"I would be too."

That didn't ease my nerves any, but I appreciated her lack of bullshit.

If I could rely on anyone for the truth, it was her.

"Call me after? I'll be waiting."

"I might send a text."

She knew why I was hedging. "Got my fingers crossed for you, S."

I sighed. "Me too."

When we disconnected the call, I put Mrs. Biggins on the sofa and, cell in hand, drew in a deep, fortifying breath.

Licking my lips, I braced myself as I headed on out the door, and even as I approached the front of the clubhouse, I could hear the jeers and the chanting.

My stomach was in my throat at the sound, a sense of foreboding hitting me, and I shuffled inside the clubhouse, careful to stick to corners, not wanting to be seen.

Of course, everyone was focused elsewhere. It didn't take me but a minute to see what.

There was a brother on the pool table, splayed like a star, with three women sucking him down as they all started one big tongue swap. The jeers were for the show, I figured, because the only thing that was interesting about the act was the fact that Steel was the one being sucked off.

He looked like he was drunk. His head was knocked to the side, not like he was watching the women suck him down, but like he was asleep.

My heart pounded as I began to back away, but at least I knew what I was dealing with. Or what I *wouldn't* be dealing with in future.

It would be easy to harden my heart to what I'd seen, to—

I closed my eyes the second I was outside, grateful I hadn't been caught.

When I dashed over to my bunkhouse, I puked up my guts, splashing the small bushes beside the door with my stomach contents.

As the rush in my ears subsided, I wiped the back of my hand over my mouth and propped my clean one on my knee.

This was what brothers did.

Did I think Steel was a virgin? No.

But here I was, on the compound, and he hadn't come to see me, hadn't been the one to bring me here. No, Bear had done that.

Steel was just shit-faced getting sucked off on a pool table.

Where was the man I knew?

Another wave of nausea hit me, making me think that if I didn't get off the compound, I'd go insane.

I headed into the bunkhouse, grabbed my running shoes from the rucksack, and switched my flip-flops out.

I usually wore a supportive bra because my tits were big, and with my stretchy leggings and tee, I knew I could run the couple of miles into town with no problem.

Where I'd go after was another matter entirely.

But getting away was imperative.

I'd only been in my new home for under an hour, and I already wanted out.

That didn't bode well, did it?

Neither did what I'd seen.

Steel was mine. Not those bunnies'. Mine.

Or...was he?

From what I'd just seen, he wasn't, but after that conversation with Mav, my hopes had definitely been high.

Stupid, stupid, stupid me.

Hadn't I learned by now that hoping was the only way to get your heart broken?

I'd hoped Steel would kiss me.

I'd hoped we'd start dating.

I'd hoped he'd claim me.

But here I was, alone in a bunkhouse because Mom had left me in a ton of debt, my arms bruised thanks to the debt collectors who'd come around, all the while, the love of my life was being sucked off by club snatch, and...

I closed my eyes.

I needed to run far and fast away from here, away from him.

He'd been the only hope I'd dared have, and he'd proven to me, yet again, that hoping was a fool's game.

Of course, that didn't stop my heart from hurting even more. I just needed to outrun the pain. I could do that, couldn't I? I had to try at least.

TWENTY

STONE
TODAY

"WE THINK she used a cocktail of drugs to sedate you, Stone," my physician explained, as I tried not to fall asleep, "and that's why the results are lingering as each one has a different length of time for it to leave the bloodstream." The guy blew out a breath. "To be completely frank, you're lucky you're alive with the levels she used of some of them." His eyes flared wide as he checked my charts, and though a part of me wanted to look and read over them, I also didn't want to know.

I guessed that was strange, but I was in a weird half-life at the moment. More passive than usual, more accepting of things I couldn't change.

One of those things was being taken hostage by a nutcase who wanted to hide her killing spree, so what was the point in worrying about the cocktail I'd been fed? All relative, no?

It didn't take a genius to figure out the specifics. For the mix to have hit my bloodstream the way it had, and with the way my heart had been pounding at first, I knew I'd been dosed up with adrenaline. For the instant knockout, there had to be diazepam or something else in there, and with the way I was feeling like I was high? Maybe some morphine in there too.

With that combination, I had more than God on my side for me to still be alive long enough to walk around on this Earth. Now that they knew what I'd been dosed with, I knew they'd treat me appropriately.

My biggest concern were the cops, who I knew were waiting outside my room to speak with me.

Indy had been bitching at them for the past few hours, and I knew that was because they'd been wanting to question me while I was asleep.

Some of that time, I'd genuinely been resting, some other parts, I hadn't. I'd just been playing dead—oh, the irony—because I couldn't face them.

Couldn't face their questions.

I knew what it was like to be suspected of everything because of my background, and I knew that, in this instance, the cops might not believe my side of the story.

I bit my lip, wishing like hell that Steel was here, but before the doctor could finish speaking, someone knocked on the door, then barged in.

My eyes flared wide at the sight of Rachel Laker storming in with a briefcase in hand that I knew cost a small fortune, dressed in a bright red pantsuit that made her look like a butterfly in this shitty room.

I already felt like crap, but to see her looking so pristine just made me feel even shittier.

When the doctor started eying her up, I almost wanted him to give me the breakdown on the drugs, but doubted that would have uncleaved his tongue from the roof of his mouth. So, I stuck my own tongue out at him, then rolled my eyes when he didn't even notice.

Though Rachel was a year older than me, and though she'd always been Rex's, we'd never been all that close.

Why would we be?

Everything about us was opposite, even if we were both professional women who'd worked hard while relying on the MC to get us where we were today.

That wasn't enough to base a friendship on.

Rachel was also stuck up, slightly snooty, a severe pain in the ass, and more argumentative than Judge Judy. In fact, she made Judge Judy look wicked chill.

The thought made my lips curve, and when I cast Indy a look and spotted the disgusted glare she was aiming at the doctor, I had to smile, even as I gazed at the other woman, and asked, "What are you doing here, Rachel?"

She placed her briefcase on the bed beside my feet. "What do you think? Rex brought me in." Her eyes scanned over me with a coolness that didn't surprise me. What did? The warmth in her voice as she inquired, "Are you doing okay?"

I blinked, taken aback by how nice she sounded, and I felt Indy's surprise too.

The doctor cleared his throat. "I-I'll be on my way now, Stone."

I cast him a disinterested glance but nodded my thanks.

He slipped out of the room, his gaze trained totally on Rachel as he almost collided with the door.

Rachel, of course, didn't notice. With her chic bob, perfect makeup, and a figure that was to kill for in the bright scarlet pantsuit? She was above most peons.

I always wondered, whenever I saw her, what Rex found appealing.

Sure, she was beautiful. I wasn't gay, but I'd fuck her, for God's sake. She was that kind of gorgeous. Like she belonged in an artsy-fartsy Italian movie. She was what poets dreamed of having as a muse.

But Rex?

My bud? The head of an MC? Who castrated pedophiles before breakfast and had no issues with engaging in some of the worst crimes imaginable?

With Rachel, who had a stick up her ass? Who believed in the law?

It was more than a match made in hell.

"She's lucky to be alive," Indy ground out on my behalf, and I wanted to smile at her, soothe her, but there was no soothing the truth. "The cops want to talk to her, even though she's just been through a traumatic event and is exhausted and apparently still drugged up!"

Rachel narrowed her eyes. "I passed them on the way in. You haven't said a word to them?"

I shook my head. "No. I've been resting. I've been too tired to say anything."

Her gaze softened. "I'm sorry, Stone. This is a terrible situation to be in."

I blew out a breath. "Thank you, Rachel."

She smiled gently at me. "Okay, we need to get the story straight."

"There is no story," Indy snapped, and I reached out and pressed a hand to her shoulder.

"Calm down, love."

Rachel's gaze drifted to my wrist. "She tied you up?"

"Badly," I admitted. "I don't think she was a hardened killer."

"The police have been through her things. She had detailed notes on patients who recently died. Indy told us your suspicions. I passed them onto the cops, who were wondering why someone like Annie Young would do such a thing as kidnap you."

"Annie," I muttered. "That was her name." I winced then. "Fuck, I feel bad for killing her and not knowing her name."

"What actually happened?" Rachel asked carefully, so I told her.

I explained how I'd been tied down but not effectively, how I'd managed to get myself out of the tape's bindings, then how I'd slashed at her throat as she'd been entering the room.

I bit my lip as she processed all that without a word. "It's self-defense, isn't it?"

I could feel Indy's nerves, and I didn't blame her, considering Caleb had been sent up for a crime where, with a more lenient and less prejudiced judge, he'd have only served a month's sentence in jail. And that was with this shark on his side. Rachel would make a great white quiver in the water.

Rachel nodded. "Without a shadow of a doubt. Rex wanted me here because he said you were concerned about how some things might be perceived because of your ties to the club. I understand that fear, so I came over as soon as I could."

"You don't think they'll twist things around?"

Rachel shrugged. "Just let them try."

It was clear to me, however, that Rachel hadn't been sure if I'd had some more involvement in Annie Young's death. After all, why would she ask me for my story if that wasn't what she expected to hear?

Fiction? I wished.

Christ, I wished this entire nightmare was nothing more than something I dreamed up in an exhausted sleep.

I sucked in a breath as she questioned, "You ready for the police? They're not going to go away, and you might be able to rest easier knowing that particular conversation is over." Seemed like she was asking, but wasn't giving me a choice as she carried on, steamrolling over anything I had to say, "I'll keep things off you, since there's no reason for them to interrogate you, but they'll want to hear the facts as you just told them to me." She pointed to the corner of the room, and murmured, "I'll be standing over here so I can hear everything without being a distraction."

Before I could say a word, she turned around, grabbed the doorknob, twisted it, and then pulled it open. As it opened, she slipped to the side and headed into the corner where she'd pointed.

The police were standing near the doorway, and I smiled wanly at them.

One of the two detectives was a woman, and she cast me a soft smile as I stared at her with concern.

They both wore the requisite bland suits, but the guy had a paunch the size of Long Island, and the woman was as trim as Indy.

She held out her hand as she approached me, and I shook it, feeling the pain in my arms and shoulders from where I'd fallen on my side yesterday.

God, yesterday. How did that feel like a lifetime ago?

I sighed, trying to process that and failing.

"I'm Detective Wandsworth and this is Detective Granger. We're with the fourteenth precinct, ma'am, and we're investigating the incident that occurred yesterday. Are you well enough to speak with us?"

"Would you care if she said no?" Indy muttered, and I shot her a sharp look.

"Indy," I groused, watching as she hunched her shoulders. Though the move was defensive, I ignored it and her, and said, "I'm just very tired."

"The doctors confirmed that you were drugged by Annie Young. The cocktail of medications was most unusual."

"Well, she worked as a pharmacy tech," I replied warily. "I guess it makes sense that she could mix stuff together that shouldn't necessarily be combined."

Detective Wandsworth hummed at that. "What do you remember about the attack?"

"Very little. I was on the phone with my friend, Indy," I replied, pointing to her. "Then, out of nowhere, I felt a prick in my throat, something was shoved over my face that I figure was chloroform, and after that, I felt nothing else. I was out for the count."

"You woke up in Ms. Young's apartment?"

I swallowed. "I was alone, and I knew that I had to get out of there." I released a shaky breath. "I've never been so scared in all my life."

"Understandable," the detective murmured, her smile sympathetic.

"How did you free yourself?"

I stared at Granger, who'd asked the question, and raised my hands. "She tied me up with regular tape, like the stuff you'd use on packing boxes. Not duct tape. She didn't even tape down my feet or anything.

"I knew I had to get loose, otherwise I'd be screwed, so I managed to work free of the ties, and then I escaped by crawling over to a dresser, grabbing one of her vases, and smashing it over her head. When she came for me again, I had no alternative but to —" I dipped my chin, my throat growing tight as I thought about how easy it had been to kill Annie.

Fuck, there hadn't been a second's hesitation on my part either. I'd just slashed at her like I was some kind of pro, and lo and behold, she'd bled out.

I'd seen blood before, for fuck's sake. But that blood was different.

That blood had been shed because of me, and I wasn't sure if I'd ever get over that.

Even if it had been for self-defense.

Do no harm... That was the promise I'd made when I took the Hippocratic Oath, yet I'd broken it. Ruptured it in two.

A hand reached out and patted my arm. I flinched at the touch, then blinked when I realized it was the cop.

Was this the good cop, bad cop shit going down in front of my eyes?

Wandsworth looked sympathetic, empathetic even. Granger looked like he'd sat on a beehive.

While he was wearing no clothes.

I gulped. "Sorry. It was a hard thing to experience."

"Hard thing to see," Granger retorted, his sneer evident. "That was a great hit for your first time, but then, I have to wonder with your ties if it is indeed your first time slicing someone up."

Rachel barked, "Detective, I'll gladly ask you not to bait my client after what was clearly a traumatic experience. My client is doctor, she's an honest, hard-working, decent citizen, who does have a past, because who doesn't? But aside from that past, it has not infringed upon her future.

"Just by looking at her wrists, at the drugs in her system, which her blood tests have confirmed, and the marks on her throat where the injection site was, you can see that she isn't faking this story."

Granger just sniffed, and even though he was talking about shit that was my nightmare come to life, I didn't bother looking at him. Instead, I looked at Rachel.

She'd come alive in a way I'd never seen before, which was interesting because everyone knew she was an ice princess, yet here she was, burning so brightly, it was a wonder moths didn't come out of hiding and start flying around her.

I rubbed at the bandages on my wrists, rubbed at them because they were sore, but they were also a little itchy from the tape I guessed, and I sighed as I wondered if I came alive like that in the ER.

Maybe I did.

If this was her passion, why wouldn't I come alive when I was able to do something that was mine?

I pursed my lips before I muttered, "I had no idea who she was. No idea what her name was or anything. I recognized her face from around the wards, but that's it. I never imagined she'd be the one—"

"The angel of death?"

I nodded but didn't bother to look at Wandsworth.

"How long did you know someone was killing patients at the hospital?"

Nausea only added to my dizziness. "I had my suspicions for ten or so weeks. Three distinct patients who died out of the blue were three people too many, but in those instances, there wasn't much I could do aside from suggest an autopsy, and let's face it, that wasn't going to happen.

"End-stage cancer patients who die with no warning? Yeah, that's exactly how it works. Even if I'd gone to a superior, I was pretty sure it would be hushed up."

"There are protocols in place."

Rachel surprised me by snorting at that—seemed she had as much faith in protocols as I did—but I just shook my head. "The truth is, if I'd gone to a superior, they'd have laughed me out of their office, and I'd probably have found myself on administrative leave for some trumped up BS reason.

"Then, if I'd gone to the cops, you would have laughed me out of the station because I had no evidence, no solid proof to back up the facts I had."

"And what facts were they?"

"Louis Hunt could eat orange Jell-O until it started coming out of his ears. He had eight cups the day before he died."

Wandsworth frowned. "I don't understand."

"Exactly. You don't. You don't get it, and you wouldn't have believed me if I'd come to you back then with my explanations. I had no means of getting retribution for any of my patients who died, and the only thing I could do was try to keep them safe.

"The truth is, I've been working double shifts trying to keep an eye on everyone, but I'm only one person."

"Is that why you've been so busy recently?" Indy asked, astonishment lacing her tone.

I shrugged. "Yeah. It wasn't like I had much of a say in it, Indy. I wasn't about to let them be unprotected, and even then, it didn't work, did it? Angela still fucking died."

"Angela Corburton?"

"Yeah," I answered Granger. "Is it true you found files on patients she 'helped'?"

"It's true. But there are far more than three patients."

My throat grew tight. "How many were there?"

Wandsworth's grimace turned further down at the edges. "Forty-one."

I gasped, and the pain that triggered in my body was enough to make the dizziness hit me full-on in the face.

"Forty-one?" I repeated, unable to believe it. Not *willing* to believe it.

How had forty-one people died, and no one had questioned their deaths?

"How did Annie Young suspect you were aware of her activities?" Granger barked.

For a second, I was so dazed that I didn't even hear his question. "I was talking about it with Harriet, a patient on my rotation. She must have overheard, and when I went outside and talked about it with Indy, she was there then. She must have followed me."

"Harriet Kundy?"

I grew still at that question. "Please tell me she didn't die!"

"I'm afraid she did, Dr. Walker."

My heart twisted in my chest as pain splintered through me.

"She'd believed me when I lied to her. She said she saw someone in Angela's room the night she died, when everyone should have left. I said it was a nurse. There was no reason for Annie Young to believe she was a threat."

"As far as we can see, Young was derailing. She started off with meticulous notes on each patient, everything from their diagnoses to their prognoses, how the doctors were giving them the wrong treatments, and why they needed her help. On her early victims, there were upwards of thirty pages, and in the latter stages of her..." Wandsworth struggled to find a word. "*Work*, she was reduced to four or five."

I rubbed my brow where the ache from the drugs had morphed into a migraine that made it painful to open my eyes.

"As you can see, my client is in severe discomfort. If that's all?"

Rachel's professional tone didn't appease Granger. Instead, he asked, "You want to tell me why when you went missing, a horde of MC bikers overtook your hospital? And you want to tell me why when one of those bikers was riding back to Jersey, he was shot? All around the same time as your kidnapping? I think there's something you're not telling us, Dr. Walker, and I can assure you that we'll figure it out."

I flinched at his words, cast Indy a look, and saw she was just as in the dark over who had been shot as me.

But when I looked at Rachel, I saw she knew, and from her face?

There was pity there.

"No," I moaned.

She winced. "He's stable."

Rachel's reply had me tunneling back into my pillows.

How many times had I used that word to get cops or patients' families off my back while I tried to do my job and save their detainee or loved one?

How many times had someone *not* been stable when we struggled to make them that way?

My mouth worked, no words fell from my lips, but I just found myself in an utter state of despair as I recognized that Steel, the love of my goddamn life, had been shot, and when it boiled down to it, he wouldn't want me at his bedside.

Wouldn't want me there to hold his hand.

And that was a knife to my heart that Annie Young might as well have wielded.

TWENTY-ONE

LODESTAR

WHEN I HEARD the giggle around the back of the clubhouse, I hid a smirk because, all told, I found the sex amusing at this place.

For someone like myself, who was incredibly repressed, it was like watching a show. In fact, it was better than a show. It was like having access to porn twenty-four seven, and here, they actually came.

I'd admit to being fascinated by sex, even if I wasn't very good at it personally. Even if I never really had much desire to do it myself.

But I loved how open they were at the compound—and not just the Sinners' either. Most MC's clubhouses were like this— orgies at night, sleepy and slumberous through the day.

That was why hearing that kind of giggle *now* surprised me. It was far too early for that type of hijinks.

When I peered around the corner, trying to spot who it was, my brows rose when I recognized the two faces.

I tutted under my breath as North slid his hand up the skirt of a woman who was definitely his stepmother, and I arched a brow as I leaned back, content to watch the show of a son cheating on his father.

I swear, this was better than *Maury*.

I mean, come on! This had all the thrill of a soap but with real life action.

Fascinating, I thought. *Fascinating*.

Not as fascinating as what I was going to do, however.

I grinned at North as he moaned into his stepmomma's lips, then I let out a soft wolf whistle that disturbed neither of them when I watched her start to fumble with his fly.

Tipping my head to the side as she slipped her hand around his cock, I registered that this wasn't the first time this had happened.

At least, I didn't think so.

There was no hesitation in the woman's touch, in her grip. And the way North sank his forehead onto hers as he shuddered through his pleasure at her touch told me that this wasn't a one and done kind of thing.

All the better!

I hummed under my breath, and when they didn't hear that, I clucked my tongue.

I'd come out here just to clear my brain.

After trying to find Stone, and failing, and being pissed at the lack of resources that would have enabled me to get her back without any police involvement, I needed a break.

Then I'd heard the giggle, and as I watched a family episode of *Jerry Springer* unfold, I knew that I could use this to my own gain.

Of course, gain was such a hard way of phrasing it.

It wasn't like I was going to blackmail them into doing *stuff*.

At least, not stuff that wouldn't be happening in the long run anyway.

My tongue cluck, surprisingly, did the job, and the woman stiffened. I couldn't, in all honesty, remember her name because

I'd only ever seen her around this place twice, I just knew she was always glued to Dog's side, and Dog was related to Giulia, and therefore, was of interest to me.

When she saw me, terror lit her eyes, and I smiled at her. That didn't soothe her fears, however, so quickly, I muttered, "I'm not going to tell Dog."

My words had North jerking back, and when I saw his dick flop between them, something he hurriedly tried to hide, I whistled between my teeth.

Jesus, he was a big boy.

Eyes on his dick until he got it zipped up, I grinned at him and saw he was scowling at me.

I shrugged, utterly unapologetically. "You'd stare at my tits if I flashed them, wouldn't you?" I winked at him. "Can't blame a girl for looking."

North huffed. "What the fuck are you doing watching us?"

"Watching you make out with your stepmomma?" I grinned at them both. "Don't worry," I repeated. "I won't tell Dog, but I want you to help me with something first."

His brow crumpled. "You're blackmailing me?"

"Clever boy. But we don't have to put a name to it. I only want one thing—"

"All fucking blackmailers say that," the woman interrupted with a huff. Was it Jenny? Charlie? I wasn't sure.

Didn't matter.

"Nope, I actually mean it. I just want to know where the crate Steel brought with him was stored."

North narrowed his eyes at me. "Why would you want to know that?"

The woman elbowed him in the side. "Shut up and tell her, North. If that's all she wants to know."

He tugged at his cut like it was impeding his throat, like it was a uniform or a fucking shirt collar, and I rolled my eyes at the gesture.

"Look, you tell me where it is, I won't say shit."

"I can't tell you where it is. I'm already in the crapper for what went down with Lily and Tiffany."

"What harm can it do?" the woman cooed, placing her hand on his stomach as she batted her lashes up at him.

'What harm?' Well, that was a question worth asking.

I thought about whether my intentions would put North in danger, and I didn't think so. I could probably find my way there myself, but it was easier to ask than to spend the next day hacking into a satellite that would help me pinpoint where this particular bunkhouse was at.

I knew it was called the Fridge, had overheard them talking about it, but the truth was, I'd never been able to find it when I'd visited, so now that there was a treasure trove of goodies in there, it was time that I started working on Lancaster.

I had questions that the Sinners wouldn't ask, and I had means they wouldn't resort to in order to get to him.

North might get into shit, but I wasn't going to hurt Donavan to get my answers.

I was just going to fuck with his head.

The best kind of torture.

I hummed and stated, "I just need to know where it is."

"You can't access it without a truck or an ATV."

"Well, I have an SUV. Remember?" He'd been the one to greet me at the gate when I'd arrived here that first day. It was such a shame North was so pretty yet so dumb. Unlike his brother.

Hawk was a very tasty piece of ass, who very rarely smiled and was usually miserable, but he had a face like a marble statue and apparently the brains of someone who knew how to add two and two together without coming up with eight.

North?

Hmm, I wasn't so sure.

It was clear that the council favored Hawk over North from the tasks they gave each brother. It would make an interesting psychological experiment on twins to see which one fared better with approval from their peers and the opposite, but I wasn't that mean.

Not anymore.

That was another Lodestar. From another time and another place.

The woman patted his belly again. "Okay, North, I know you don't want to, but if your father finds out, you know he'll beat the crap out of me."

He tensed at that, but her words had me narrowing my eyes. "He beats you?"

She flinched at my question and gaped at me. "What the fuck do you care?"

"I care a lot actually." I hummed. "Do you want him out of the picture?"

Her mouth gaped wide. "Huh?"

"You heard me. Is he a danger to you?"

"Only when he's drunk." Her answer didn't fill me with confidence.

"And apparently now. Do you fear for your life?"

I could tell she'd never expected me to ask that question, but also, I wasn't your average blackmailer.

Sure, motive and opportunity were two things, but I wasn't a bitch.

And to my core, I was a feminist.

In fact, I wasn't just a feminist, I was a *fucking* feminist.

No way in hell was I going to let this woman have the shit kicked out of her with no recourse.

"I don't think he'll kill me."

"Not even for cheating on him with his son?" I asked, my tone softer.

When she winced, then shot North a look that I could only classify as puppy love, I heaved a sigh.

"I'm surprised. Nyx usually takes care of the wife beaters."

"Only if they tell him."

North's mutter had me huffing under my breath. "Well, yeah, the man ain't a mind reader. You got to cut him *some* slack."

The woman shook her head. "I don't want no trouble. If I do as I'm told, Dog is good as gold."

Every part of me shuddered at those words.

If I do as I'm told?

What was she?

A Labrador retriever?

I hissed out a breath, unable to deal with a woman undervaluing herself to that extent, and I mumbled, "North, you're going to tell me where the Fridge is, not because I caught you cheating on your dad, but because I'm going to kill the motherfucker and you're going to thank me for it."

His mouth dropped wide open at that. "I don't want him to die. I love him!"

"You love him?" I sneered. "If you loved him, you wouldn't be boning his missus around the fucking corner of the clubhouse where anyone could see. It's not like I had to travel far and wide to find you fucking, was it?" I rolled my eyes. Jesus, were the pair of these numbskulls sharing brain cells?

The woman grunted at that, but I saw a flash of guilt in her eyes.

A flash that made me wonder if she was trying to force a scene.

I wouldn't blame her.

North was a cutie. He wanted her, and if she wanted out of her relationship with Dog, then…

I definitely didn't blame her for preferring the son over the father.

I rubbed my chin as I pondered what that look could mean in its entirety.

Was she manipulating North, or was she genuinely scared of her partner?

Then, I thought about that phrase.

Do as I'm told...

Nah, something wasn't right this side of Kansas.

"If I find out he isn't beating you, and I take him out, then I will come for you and haunt you," I growled, watching her eyes widen with terror.

She gulped, her throat bobbing as she shook her head and whispered, "No. I swear. But it's only when he's drunk."

I hummed under my breath, trusting her fear. Then I beamed at her. "Well, you got your wish. One partner out of the picture."

"I didn't ask for that," she whispered, her mouth quivering with panic and her hands clutching at North like he could keep her safe from me.

Like I was a danger to her.

Puh-lease.

"No, but I'm not about to let him threaten your life." I smirked at her. "Or any woman's life." I was the superhero for my gender that no one knew existed. It was why I dedicated years of my life, my time, my money, all to causes that no one else gave a shit about except for me.

Well, this woman had just gone to the top of my list.

After Donavan Lancaster, of course.

Rex had given me permission to speak with the bastard, but I knew that was for after they'd dealt with him.

Men, they preferred to think that fists and blunt objects could achieve more than the accurate slice of a scalpel.

Fools.

North licked his lips as he cut a look at his stepmother. "I don't want my father to die."

"You should. He beats the woman you evidently care for..." I arched a brow at him, then enjoyed his blush. "And I imagine that he hurt your momma and your sister too."

He winced. "It was their fault."

I snorted at that. "You're working your way onto my list too, buster, if you don't watch your fucking mouth." I huffed. "Their fault, my ass." I shot her a pointed look. "You sure you want this charmer?"

She made some more goo-goo eyes at him. "He's good to me."

I hummed again. "Gotcha. If you say so."

In my opinion, she needed some self-worth, but who was I to judge? Most women needed it. Letting men run them around, breaking their heart left, right, and center?

Fuck that.

I was fine in my ivory tower. No one could touch me.

Well, no one except for that aCooooig cunt.

He'd gotten into my servers and had managed to attack me from the inside.

Bastard.

I huffed as I thought about how much hardware I'd had to toss because of that prick, and prompted, "North, the Fridge? I ain't got all day, sweetheart."

He gulped. "I can take you there."

I smiled. "Good answer!"

Apparently, kiddo wasn't as averse to patricide as it first seemed.

Twenty minutes later, tucked into my SUV, we were riding across a side of the compound that was entirely off road. It irked me that I'd have to have my car cleaned, but fuck, it was worth it for the cause.

As we rolled over grassland—something that was like peat because the wheels almost sunk into the ground—and drifted farther and farther away from civilization, I saw it. Humming at the sight, I muttered, "There you are."

"Why do you always hum?"

"Because I like the song," I replied.

"What song is it?" he inquired when I fell silent, just staring at the Fridge, a barely eighteen foot by eighteen foot box that housed a man I'd been seeking for far too long.

"'Firestarter' by Prodigy," I answered absentmindedly.

He laughed. "I know that one. It's a banging tune."

My lips twitched.

Banging was the word.

"You've got two choices, I can leave you here and you can walk back, or you can stay in the car and not say shit if you hear someone scream. And by someone, I mean the man who's inside the crate in there."

He gulped. "There's a man in that crate Hawk drove back yesterday?"

Jesus. How out of the loop was this kid?

Wary now because Rex was smart and wouldn't have kept him in the dark unless he was a dumb fuck, I wanted to smack myself for running my mouth, but North, apparently, wasn't a total dick.

He swallowed and whispered, "I won't say anything. I'll stay here. Just in case you need a hand with something."

I arched a brow, surprised by his comment.

"The offer is kind, but you don't have to—"

He shook his head. "If Donavan gets away, then I'm fucked."

I snorted. "Trust me, bubba, he ain't going nowhere." I winked at him, unsurprised when he shuddered. "I ain't your average woman."

His gulp said it all, but he confirmed it with, "Yeah, I can see that."

TWENTY-TWO

STONE

IT WAS LATE when Indy wheeled me in. Late because I knew that he'd be asleep, high on drugs, and that this would be the last chance I had to see him before I started the process of being discharged.

He looked ill.

He looked like death warmed over, and from the color of his skin alone, I knew the fight for his life had been a hard-won thing.

As Indy wheeled me over to him, feeling shaky and all kinds of nauseated when I glanced at the bandages on his chest, I whispered, "He nearly died."

Indy sighed. "I told you they didn't tell me how it went down."

"It wasn't a question. I'm telling you that he did."

"And how can you tell? Because of the bandages?" She snorted. "That doesn't make any sense. I got a bandage that size on my arm, and I wasn't shot."

"No, you got a tattoo." I rolled my eyes, but then I realized I was joking while I was at Steel's bedside.

His hospital bedside.

Where he was fighting for his life.

Apparently sensing how inappropriate our conversation was, Indy whispered, "Do you think he'll recover?"

"I hope so." I gulped at the thought of him *not* recovering, and even as I was surprised at him being alone, without one of the MC here, requested, "Do you think you could pass me his charts?"

She did as I asked, even though she warned, "If you get upset, we're out of here."

"I know." I made a 'gimme' motion with my fingers, then started reading through the information on his stats.

He was stable. *Now.*

I flinched as I recalled the treatment he must have gone through, and I knew if I didn't compose my features, then Indy really would make good on her threat.

Trouble was, I wasn't supposed to be here.

Trouble was, it was only a twist of fate that we ended up in the same ICU and that I got to see him like this.

Vulnerable.

I wasn't sure if I'd ever known him to appear this way.

I'd seen him sleep, and I'd seen him sick before, but not like this.

He was sedated, and would be for a few days to keep him still so his body could heal.

But the truth was, just looking at him made my heart ache.

"You're never not going to love him, are you?" Indy rasped.

I glanced at her over my shoulder with sadness in my eyes, a matching one in hers as I shook my head.

"It's too deep inside me."

"Like cancer." She huffed. "Anyway, we need to get you out of here before we get into shit. I mean, some of the nurses here are cuties, but I don't want to get kicked out and get the one who helped us sneak in here into trouble."

I didn't disagree, but being wheeled away from him left a physical pain in my being.

I wasn't sure if I could sustain that pain and all the rest of the aches that were going down in my body at that moment, but I'd deal with it. I had to.

Just as I'd deal with the distance I was going to put between us.

Even if we were going to be in the same town once more, that didn't mean he'd catch sight of me again.

I bit the inside of my lip then whispered, "I'm ready to go."

She sighed. "Okay."

When she wheeled me out of the ICU and toward the department where I was staying, I pointed at the nurses' station as we passed it. "I want to go there."

"Why?"

"Because I'm going to get out of here. I want to go home. There's nothing more they can do for me. I've been here thirty-six hours, I've had more fluids put in me than I know what to do with, and I'm ready to go home."

Indy, knowing better than to argue, just grumbled, "I'll warn the guys."

"Why?"

"Because they're packing up your apartment, *chica*. That's why no one was sitting with Steel. They're all busy right now."

"What?" I burst out, and my declaration was really fucking loud in the silence of the night ward.

"Yeah, *what*. I told you they were intent on getting you out of the city and back to West Orange. Rachel had to strong arm the police, too, because they wanted to keep you nearby, but you're only a person of interest, not a suspect."

My eyes widened at that. "Well, that really makes me feel better," I grumbled. "*Only* a person of interest? Great!"

She snickered. "If you could see your feathers all ruffled right now, you'd have a giggle."

I squinted at her. "Bitch."

She smirked back. "Cow."

We both snickered until the amusement waned, and I was left dealing with the fact that Steel was back in a room I wanted to be in, and my apartment was no longer my own.

I gulped, wondering what was happening, how my life had taken a turn for the worse, and then I decided not to think about it, and just get things moving along.

"To the nurses' station, MacDuff," I rasped, and Indy, thankfully, didn't argue.

When I got there, I smiled at the harried night team, and told them, "In the morning, I'd like to begin the process of being released."

I'd been transferred out of ICU, and only speaking with a nurse who was friends with Raina, a nurse back at High Lidren Hospital, had helped get me back in after hours.

I'd needed to see Steel before I left.

When he didn't know I was visiting.

At a moment where I could let my love for him show, before I tucked it back in the deep-freeze of my chest, and moved on for good.

All these years, I hadn't been pining for him. I'd lived my life, had tried to find someone else, but it had just never panned out.

It was time to let him go though, because I'd evidently been clinging onto him, and I shouldn't have. I'd been in love with Robin, the boy I'd known since I was a child, and that love *was* a cancer. But it was time for chemo.

The nurse's grumble brought me back to the here and now. "You're still under observation."

"The drugs are either going to fade out of my system, or they'll kill me." At this point, it wasn't like being here would do much else.

"You're comfortable with the latter being an option?"

"I'm not comfortable with being in a hospital right now."

Her gaze softened. "Well, I can understand that. The news has been going crazy with what happened at HL."

I nodded, understanding her wide eyes because I'd been watching it all day too.

Wincing as a sudden pain in my side speared me to the quick, I muttered, "I just want some quiet, that's all."

"Understandable. The second I can, I'll get a doctor in there to sign you out, but it will probably be around seven or eight AM."

"I know how it works," I replied quietly. "Don't worry."

She smiled at me as Indy rolled me away, and I heard their whispers as the team discussed what had gone down, what had happened to me, and all the other crazy shit that my life had developed into.

"What about Mrs. Biggins?" I inquired.

"What about her?" Indy asked.

"They're packing her up, aren't they?"

She snorted. "No, Stone. They're not. They're going to leave your eighteen-year-old cat in the apartment you rent here." She hissed out a sigh. "I swear, you come out with the craziest shit."

"I try," I mumbled, but still, the prospect of having my hands on Mrs. Biggins made me want to be signed out even sooner than I already was.

My eyes grew wet with tears as we entered my room again, and I stared at the mess of the sheets I'd left behind with blurry vision.

"Did she mean that?"

Indy's question had me arching a brow. "Mean what?"

"What she said about you dying?"

I shrugged. "We can all die."

"That's not helpful, Stone," she countered.

"No, it wasn't, but it's true nonetheless." I arched my brow back at her. "Do you want to hear the damage the drugs did to me?"

"No. Not if I'm not going to be able to convince you to stay in here."

My lips twisted. "If I had to stay in here, I would. I'm not stupid. But I want to go home, and then, after, I want to get my life back on track."

The second I said that, of course, was the second I felt something in my body snap.

Swallowing through the pain, I winced as I stared up at Indy, who was talking to me, saying shit I just couldn't understand.

Her words weren't penetrating the sudden fuzz that surrounded my brain, and when I looked at her, trying to translate that to her, I registered that she got my predicament.

A horrified gasp escaped her, and when I looked down, I figured out why.

My head plopped forward, showing me a lap that was stained with blood I'd just puked up.

Before I knew it, I didn't even see that.

I saw shit.

Just knew that my overconfidence had led me to push it, but if this was my last night on Earth, then I was grateful I'd seen Steel.

He was the last thing I thought of before I passed out, unsure if I'd ever wake up again.

TWENTY-THREE

NYX

"ARE YOU FUCKING KIDDING ME?"

"Look, marriage hasn't changed me that much. When do you know me to joke? Especially about shit like this?"

Because he wasn't wrong, I rolled my eyes, even as I reached up to rub them—fuck, I was tired. "She did what?"

"Some torture maneuvers that are definitely illegal in most civilized countries."

Fuck if the bastard didn't sound impressed.

I grunted. "Is he alive?"

That was the priority.

After all, I knew Rex had some plans for him, and I couldn't blame him.

The bastard had cost us a lot of money, and it was an investment worth spending if we could get him to sing like a bird.

Our beef with Lancaster wasn't just personal. That would end things, but every ending had a beginning, and Lancaster's involved ratting out his allies. As I thought about the repercussions of what Lodestar had done, I asked, "Did she say what she discovered?"

"No." Mav huffed. "The bitch of it is that she didn't even make him bleed! I swear, you could hear him screaming all the way over at the compound! Jesus. When we rolled over there, I wasn't sure what I'd see, and to find her standing there smiling at him as she tortured the shit out of him wasn't what I thought I'd be looking at today."

"What did she do?"

"What didn't she do?" Mav hissed. "Broke him. Utterly broke him." He heaved another sigh. "On the good side, he's talking like a kookaburra on cocaine. If you want to get Rex over here, if he has questions to ask, you let him know that now's the time to do it. All you have to do is mention Lodestar's name, and he starts squealing like a shit-covered baby."

My nose crinkled at that. Fuckers always had to shit and piss themselves.

Didn't they realize it was unhygienic?

Grumbling to myself, I questioned, "You're getting involved, or are you staying out of it?"

There was a little white noise on the end of the line, then Maverick slowly muttered, "I haven't been getting involved. Someone needed to calm the women down, and for some reason, they listen to me. When he started screaming, I swear to fuck he scared the shit out of me, never mind them."

My lips curved. "I highly doubt that's true," I rumbled. I knew it took a lot to 'scare' Maverick, and I knew it wouldn't be the torture of a man he loathed.

I rubbed my chin as I watched Rex conferring with one of our allies in the city.

Five Points were our main crew, but we had some allegiances with the *Demonios Bandidos*.

Juan Alonso wasn't as much of a prick as might be expected, even if the fuck had most of his face covered in godawful tats— because I was covered in tats too, but fuck, they were on my back— he was actually a shrewd businessman.

I tuned out of that side of things, not really interested because I knew Rex and the Bolivian were discussing the cops that were involved in the investigation of Stone's kidnapping.

After Rachel had told Rex what a prick one of the officers had been to Stone, he had decided to get in the bastard's face.

Not that I could blame him for getting angry.

I didn't like the idea of Stone being interrogated either, especially not when she was ill and still on her sick bed.

That was the pigs for you. Never knew when to shut their traps.

We'd accepted the need for an investigation, but to treat our girl like she was a piece of shit?

He definitely had some bad juju coming his way.

Knowing all was well with my Prez, I retuned into the conversation with Maverick, but as I did, I felt my cell buzz in my hand, and I muttered, "Hang on a sec, Mav."

"Sure," he told me, and I lowered my cell to read the message.

The text from Indy had my heart sinking.

"Gotta go, Mav. Stone's heading into surgery. I need to key Rex in."

"Fuck. Surgery? Yeah." He sighed. "Speak later, brother."

"Yeah, later. I'll keep you in the loop." Cutting the call, I strode over to Rex, nodding at Juan as I did so, then I leaned down and muttered in his ear, "Stone needs us. She's going into surgery."

He flinched, and to be honest, I could understand why Steel had lost his shit the other day.

Rex was a closed book a lot of the time, and even though I'd known he stayed in touch with Stone, I hadn't realized how close they were.

But then, I'd been learning all kinds of shit these past few days.

Like Indy... Apparently, she and Stone were a lot closer than I'd thought.

Places like the MC were a dysfunctional sort of family, a

hotbed of lies and truths, some out in the open, some tucked under the surface. A volcano waiting to erupt.

I was pissed that Steel had been dealing with his own Yellowstone and hadn't told us. I considered the men in the council to be more than just brothers. They were family. By choice. I'd elected each and every one as my kin, and that was a powerful choice to have made.

Especially for someone like me.

Saying I had trust issues was like saying Betty White was an old bitch.

Although, I'd probably say that shit quietly around Giulia because she loved the old cow.

My family was being shaken at its core, and the truth was, I didn't fucking like it.

Not one bit.

Rex's tension had Juan raising a brow at me when I glanced over at him.

"Bad news?" he inquired softly, his tone faintly tinged with a Spanish accent.

In contrast to the face that looked like it belonged in a cartoon, his two thousand dollar suit was sharp as fuck. He could head into a meeting at the White House in that slick outfit.

That was why I didn't understand his tats.

When you made it that far up the ladder, there was no hiding in plain sight.

I wasn't sure if that made me trust him more or less.

There was no evading what he was, no hiding from it, and that meant he was as much of an open book as someone in our position could be.

"Our brother's Old Lady," Rex rasped, "she's taken a turn for the worse."

Juan's mouth tightened. "I'm sorry to hear that."

He sounded it too.

These fuckers—so genuine where family was concerned. It was surreal.

I'd dealt with the *Demonios Bandidos* only twice in my tenure as Enforcer, and I was glad I was passing that shit off onto Sin. He'd be the liaison, just like he would be with the Five Points, and because I couldn't exactly be called a people person, I figured that was all for the good.

"I need to get going, Juan," Rex muttered, his tone a little strained, like he was stoned or something.

"Of course, *mi amigo*. Family first."

Rex dipped his chin, then he questioned, "You gonna make that Granger bastard pay?"

"I already promised I would, but if he exacerbated the...Old Lady's illness, then I'll be more than happy to make a visit to him myself."

Rex gritted his teeth. "I think we can safely say that he didn't help matters. I'd appreciate you showing your face, letting him know how the land lies. In the next couple of weeks, I'll have some shit for you if you want to ride over to Jersey."

I arched a brow, but decided to ask what he was talking about later. I figured it had to do with our laundering operation. We helped the *Demonios* launder their cash, they helped us launder ours.

Juan grinned, revealing a bottom row of gold teeth, then he held out his hand and shook Rex's, then mine.

As we left the garage, I glanced up at the sky, squinting at it with strained eyes.

We'd been in the black hole of Calcutta for a few hours as the two leaders talked business, and I was ready to get out of there, ready to get on with shit.

As we moved out toward our bikes, I told Rex, "Lodestar jumped the gun. She's spoken with Donavan, managed to break him by the sounds of it."

Rex froze at my words, his back stiffened with tension as he hissed out a breath. "Fucking woman." His hands balled into fists. "What is it with the bitches at the compound and following orders?"

I snorted. "You know Lodestar is a loose cannon. Fuck, she's a bomb just waiting to explode."

He heaved a sigh. "Truer words, brother, truer words." He pinched the bridge of his nose, then mumbled, "I want to go to Stone."

I shrugged. "Never thought you wouldn't. That's why I brought it up. Shall I go home, take point on the interrogation?"

He blew out a breath. "The last person I wanted in charge of that was you, Nyx."

I grinned, unoffended because I got it, but also, I didn't... Honest to the last, especially with him, I informed him, "You have no reason to worry where he's concerned. Physically, he didn't hurt Giulia. If he had, it would be another matter entirely."

He hummed. "True. I don't want him dead."

The finality to that statement had my brows rising. "How long do you intend on keeping him alive?"

"As long as we can keep pumping information from him."

"That could be a long time," I murmured. "I don't think Link will sign on for that."

"When isn't there a method to my madness, Nyx?"

"I know, Rex, but fuck, it ain't me whose woman was raped since she was a kid. And that isn't taking into account that Mav is gonna want blood too."

Rex snorted. "Oh, they'll get their fucking blood, but it will be slower than he expects is all."

"What do you think he can tell us?" I whispered, turning into him as we entered the street and a cluster of people headed our way.

Because they were smart, they filed into a straight line to avoid us, and we went on our merry way without them getting into our space.

"I'm hoping he'll be able to dish on the *Famiglia's* compound."

"He wasn't *Famiglia*," I reminded him. "Just affiliated."

"That's what I want to know. Their affiliations and ours, are they similar? Different? I want to know the inner workings of the business, and the one way to learn that is to get an inside look on things."

Slowly, I nodded, and thought about news from the prison where my dick of a baby bro was locked up. "Fieri is dead, so that means the leader is without a son."

Rex shot me a look. "Exactly, that means we have an unknown primed for the top when Benito kicks the bucket. I want to know who might be the next man in line for the throne, and if that's going to cause Tiffany any issues.

"If we waste him, if we end his miserable life now? Then that's our *Famiglia* Google gone forever."

I heaved a sigh. "I get it, brother, I do, but you're not taking into account Link or Mav."

"They're brothers first. We're at war. We need to remember that. Look at what happened yesterday," he rumbled, not pleased with my raising that question to him. "Steel got shot thanks to this stupid fucking game that's going on between factions. I don't want this to carry on longer than it has to. If Donavan Lancaster is the key to ending shit sooner, I ain't going to get rid of him until we've pumped him for all he's worth, and in the meantime, we can make him miserable. Make the place he kept Ghost and the other girls look like the fucking Ritz by comparison. I'm down with that. But we keep him alive, Nyx. You hear me?"

I grunted. "I hear you, bro."

"Good." He sucked in a breath as he made it to his bike. While I walked the few steps to mine, he asked, "What's going on with Stone?"

"I don't know. Indy just said that she spewed up some blood."

Rex's mouth tightened. "Any news on Steel?"

I shook my head. "Rex?"

"Yeah?" he replied, putting his helmet on and fastening it as I spoke.

"Why are you so obsessed with getting them together?"

He tensed just long enough for me to wonder if he'd answer, then he muttered, "Because I was the one who found Steel when he tried to kill himself. I was there when Stone overdosed. All this shit because that fucker was his father..." He shook his head. "You know the rules of chess, Nyx, right? I know you don't play it, but do you know them?"

I shrugged. "The basics."

Rex tapped his forehead. "The truth is, a long time ago, Bear taught me those rules and tied them to the MC and its council. He said that as important as the pawns are in this world, it's the key players who will make or break the MC's future.

"But the MC is different than how it was in his day. Truth is, we're more of a family than ever because of the ties that bind the council."

"I can see that," I agreed.

Before Rex had been Prez, when his father had ruled the roost, the council had been tight, and even had blood ties on there, but that was nothing compared to how it was with me, Rex, Steel, Link, Mav, and Storm. Now Sin too. Even though he was a later addition, he'd fit right in from the start, once he'd returned from his stint as a Marine and had killed his fucker of a father.

"My key players and his are completely different. He wanted his under wraps, always under his thumb because that would help him figure out where he was going, but me? You guys aren't just pieces to move. You're my fucking family. The entire place is. I worry about you all like a goddamn mother hen, and when I see the shit you all go through..." He shook his head. "Of all of you, I was the luckiest. Dad might not have stayed true to Ma, but at least he did in some ways. He never beat me, she never beat me. There was never any bad blood between them. She was loyal, and she raised me to be a good kid, probably too good for an MC—"

We all knew that.

That was one of the issues he had with Rachel. She knew he had potential, and in her mind, he'd wasted that potential on running a band of brothers that did more illegal shit than was on the rap sheet of West Orange's county jail's population combined.

"So when I see you fuckers suffering, it gets to me. It really fucking does. Stone and Steel? They were meant for each other. Just like me and Rachel are. Sometimes, I call it in advance, and the truth is, I get why Steel stayed away from her."

"Because it's for a similar reason that you stay away from Rachel?"

Rex dipped his chin. "Yeah. Not because my father was a scum-sucking cunt, but because I want what's best for her. Now you have Giulia, I know you'll get this more, but sometimes, even though it fucking hurts, you just have to admit you're not the best thing for the woman who owns you." He shook his head. "Kills me to be around Rachel. Fucking slays me every goddamn time, and maybe someday, I'll make shit right between us and I'll claim her, but we got a lot of bad blood between us, a lot of differences that can't be overcome. But Steel and Stone don't."

I nodded. "I get it."

His lips twisted. "You sure?"

"Yeah, I do. Even before Giules, I saw what they should have together. I never envied it because I didn't want it, but I thought he was an ass for not claiming what was his."

Rex grunted. "Stone was that the second she turned into a woman. Steel just got fucked along the way." His jaw tensed. "You okay with who his father is?"

I snorted. "No, I'm fucking not, but it isn't my brother's fault, is it?"

"Your cousin," he corrected, making me pull a face.

"Shit, we've got more incestuous ties going on in our clubhouse than an episode of *The Bold and the Beautiful*."

He snickered at that. "When you have people fucking as much as we do, it's a wonder we don't have an army of brats roaming around the place."

"We do," I said dryly, then I muttered, "Anyway, I get it, and I don't want to keep you. I'll head for the clubhouse, you keep in touch and let me know how they both get along."

Rex nodded. "Will do."

He kicked off his kickstand, and I watched him drive off as I did the same, both of us heading opposite ways.

I wasn't exactly ecstatic at the notion of traveling on the same road as my brother had, a road that had seen him get shot, so I took a different route out of the city and on to West Orange that added an extra hour to my time.

NYC was a smorgasbord of crossed boundaries and territories that were nearly impossible to identify. I did my best to stick to lines where we had affiliations, like with the *Demonios Bandidos*.

We were safe on their territory, and I took advantage of that to make it over the bridge and back into our land.

As I rolled home, the wind in my face, my body buffered on all sides as I slammed into it, needing to get back to the compound ASAP, I felt like a part of me was liberated while another was tethered.

I knew what Rex meant.

The MC *was* like a game of chess or, at any rate, the people were like the pieces on a chess board, and even though I didn't think of it that way, I knew how fucking smart Rex was. Mostly, I knew that Bear had recognized what his son was capable of.

If anyone could think twelve steps ahead, it was Rex. I trusted his judgment in all things, but I'd admit that I wasn't happy that when, eventually, I had to open the door to the Fridge and was faced with Lancaster, I'd have to hold back my brothers who wanted blood while Rex had something else in mind.

Strategy meant nothing when bloodlust was high, and I couldn't blame them. Either of them.

If I had my say, I'd kill Luke Lancaster a thousand times over. And that would never be enough.

My entire body could be inked with a million skulls, each one representing his passing, and it'd never sufficiently cover how I wanted to maim him.

Lily, Ghost, Tatána, Amara, and all the other women Donavan Lancaster had abused in his time deserved justice.

But they weren't going to get it yet.

Which fucking sucked.

When I made it back to the compound, I wasn't altogether surprised to see Giulia was there waiting on me.

She had a bit of an inbuilt radar where I was concerned, and every time it pinged to life, I had this feeling of rightness settle in my heart.

I'd die for her.

I'd kill for her.

But I'd make sure to live for her, because I knew that without me in her world, just like it would be the same if the roles were reversed, she would be living a shadow of an existence.

And the truth was, I'd lived that way for too long.

She'd been in my orbit for months now, a quantity of time that I could still count with my fingers, yet somehow, it was like she'd never not been there.

It was as if she'd always been cemented into my soul.

I hadn't texted her that I was on my way back, but that she knew had me smiling anyway as I rolled to a stop, climbed off my hog, then twisted around just in time to catch her.

Her legs hooked around my waist, her stomach slammed against mine, and her arms went around my neck.

I held her tightly, securely, and loved the feel of all her lush curves against me.

Knowing she was mine and having proof of that resting against my dick was always enough to make me want to blow my load, but when our mouths collided?

Fuck, that was the real welcome a man needed.

She tongue fucked me, proud and unashamed of showing what she felt for me, and I ground my cock into her pussy, holding fast to her ass as I urged her into rocking against me.

I was a private man where sex was concerned, and I knew she was too, but shit had changed since the attack in the bar that had started this entire labyrinth the MC was wading through.

She'd began pushing boundaries, trying to find her limitations, and I'd go with her all the way, wherever she needed to go.

She pulled back, biting my bottom lip hard enough to sting, and I smirked at her for that.

"That's mine."

"I can steal a signature move, can't I?" she murmured, her voice low and husky, making me think of the way she'd cry out tonight when I pounded into her.

It had been too long since I'd been inside her, too long since I'd had her in my arms.

Fuck, I knew I was turning into a pussy, but I just didn't have it in me to give a shit.

I was living. For the first time in my life, I was actually doing more than existing, and I wasn't about to apologize for that.

A huff sounded from the doorway, snatching my attention, and I saw a couple of the club sluts were watching us with misery, jealousy, and bitterness etched onto their features.

I figured that trifecta came from a few things.

One, they were jealous because they'd all, at some point, tried to get their hooks into me. Two, because they wanted an Old Man as badly as some of them needed a meal. And three? They were wearing grimy clothes with dirt marks on them, and from the shit in their hands and the yellow gloves covering them, I just knew that Giulia had taken Rex's edict before we'd left for the city to heart.

"You making them clean at this time of the night?" I asked on a soft laugh as I turned away from them and started toward the side entrance of the clubhouse.

"Course I am," she replied with a beaming smile. "You didn't think I was going to make their lives pleasant, did you?"

I rolled my eyes. "Rex has created a monster."

She winked at me. "No, my darling, you did that." I snickered, knowing she was half right, then she said, "Nyx?"

"Yeah, baby."

"What's going on?"

"With Stone and Steel? They're both under obs right now."

She shook her head. "The screams from the Fridge," she whispered, releasing a sharp breath that told me how bad they'd been if they shook her. She was a tough little nut to crack, but I could see those screams would probably haunt her dreams for a while. "What was going on in there? I didn't think anything would be happening while you guys were all in the city."

"It wasn't supposed to," I grumbled. "It's why I'm back sooner than expected though."

"Oh? Why?"

"Because Lodestar got in and made Lancaster squeal." I heaved a sigh. "Stone's just gone into surgery, and I split off with Rex because I needed to come here and make sure the Fridge is locked down." My nose crinkled. "You ain't even supposed to know about that fucking place, babe."

She waved a hand. "Tiff accidentally found out from Sin."

"And she just had to tell you, huh?"

Her lips twisted. "Women talk, baby."

I rolled my eyes as I finally made it around the side of the building and toward the entrance that would take me straight into the corridor that led to Rex's office.

I wanted nothing more than to take her to our room, but I had shit I needed to do, and I knew Mav would be in there.

I kissed her before we strolled down the hall, then when we made it to the office, I squeezed her ass cheeks and muttered, "I need to sort this shit out, babe. You gonna be okay?"

"Of course," she told me brightly, but I saw the shadows in her eyes and knew she'd have nightmares tonight.

Even if Lodestar was behind them, even though I was here and not Rex because Stone was sick, I was just fucking glad I would be with her tonight.

She needed me more than she'd probably accept. I knew how that felt. I was still coming to terms with how much I needed her.

Just like the white and the black pieces on Rex's chess board were born to fight forever, me and Giules?

We were born to see this life through together.

With her the queen to my king.

TWENTY-FOUR
MAVERICK

I KNEW I should be mad at Lodestar for changing shit up, but I couldn't be. I knew her too well, knew the way she worked, and had figured she'd manage to get to Donavan Lancaster before the rest of us had a shot.

The second I'd watched her wheedle her way into the interrogation with Rex, just before Tiff and Lily had been kidnapped, I'd known that whether or not he agreed to it, she'd do her own thing.

As it stood, in her mind, she wasn't doing anything wrong because she'd gotten permission.

Didn't matter that Rex was a control freak, that he liked to keep his hands on all the strings and pulled them every way he wanted.

She didn't give a fuck.

She had her own agenda, had been following it for a long time.

Not that I blamed her.

She might look normal on the outside, but on the inside? She was a hot mess.

Me?

I was scarred and broken at first glance.

You saw the wars I'd been through, the battles I'd fought. It was clear in the body that was still too skinny, even though Giulia made it a point to fatten me up, and it was obvious from my drawn face.

Lodestar just looked like a regular woman.

I looked like a soldier.

You'd never tell that we'd served at the same time. You'd never know that we'd been on the same unit.

Somehow, even though she was three years younger than me, even though we'd seen the same shit and done worse together, she looked a lot younger than me.

I wasn't jealous, but I knew how devious that could be.

I studied her as she studied me.

A little like we were playing a game with each other, trying to find the other's weaknesses, but the trouble was, we both knew the other's weaknesses too well.

I sat behind Rex's desk, even though this wasn't my position, and she sat facing me, opposite it.

Not once had she apologized for going behind our backs and seeing Lancaster when she wasn't supposed to. Not once had she shown any contrition at the noises he'd made that had Ghost, Amara, and Tatána screaming from their bunkhouse in horror.

I wasn't even sure what she'd done to the bastard to make him holler like that. The walls of the Fridge were more than just soundproof. Men had been beaten to death there, tortured to within an inch of their lives, given fucking transfusions to bring them back to life, just so we could start the torture some more.

Nothing and no one had ever made them scream like that.

She'd barely had twenty-four hours with the guy, and I knew that because that was the last time I'd seen her. Four o'clock yesterday.

Breaking into our stare off, the door opened, and I glanced

across the room, spying Nyx who was just tapping Giulia on the tush.

She shot him a wicked look that made me smile, because if anyone could keep Nyx on his toes, it was that little minx, and she dashed off, evidently enjoying her task of making the clubwhores miserable.

The men had yet to notice that her war against the club sluts had commenced, but when they figured it out, I doubted they'd complain that much. They loved her food, and weren't going to argue with someone who would easily dope a batch of green chilli to get her own way.

The Old Ladies were not a fan of the men's preferences of fucking any of the bunnies whenever and wherever they wanted. Only the fact that Giulia was heading the campaign to make the club snatches' lives miserable stopped the snatch from spreading complaints back to the council, because everyone, even the bunnies, was scared of Nyx.

Hell, sometimes, even I was when he was in a rage.

It wasn't like a regular fear, more like I was fearful *for* him, but still, it was true nonetheless.

As Nyx watched her sashay on her way, he turned to us, then glowered at Lodestar.

"I always knew you were a pain in the ass, but I never recognized just how big of a one you were, Lodestar."

She shrugged. "It's a talent, Nyx. You have to know that."

"Causing mayhem and chaos since 1986," I muttered under my breath, laughing when she grinned at me.

"You remember my birthdate."

I arched a brow at her. "As if I could forget."

When we grinned at each other, Nyx muttered, "Less of the powwow. Mav, what the fuck?"

I rolled my eyes. "Don't be dense. You can't be mad at her. It's impossible. Especially when you know the fucker deserved to be crying like a pig."

He grunted. "Lodestar, you're fucking lucky that I'm the one dealing with you and not Rex."

She shrugged. "I could handle him."

She could too.

Remember that whole deceptive thing I was talking about?

She might look like she was angelic, but she definitely wasn't.

That was what the secret training we'd gone through did to a person. Made you look normal when, really, you were armed without carrying a single weapon.

And I wasn't even talking Krav Maga shit. Our training went deeper.

It was one of the reasons why my back was fucked up, that was the extent of the somersaults we'd been pulling with the shit we'd been trained to do. Evidently, she'd had some extra lessons because even I was in the dark as to what she'd done to make Lancaster respond that way.

I rubbed my chin as I muttered, "Lodestar always has a plan, Nyx. You know that."

"I know that you sound like you're admiring her."

My lips twitched. "I don't *not* admire her," I countered.

"Yeah, well, she broke rank. That's out of order."

Lodestar heaved a sigh, like she was bored with the conversation.

She probably was.

Me and her could have a chat without uttering a word. We could just look at each other, like we'd been doing for the past forty minutes, and somehow, an entire argument could go down.

Once upon a time, I'd felt sure she was the woman for me. Life had changed us both, though, the war had fucked us over, and even if we'd been right together back then, we weren't right now. Essentially because we were both fucked up in the head, and while some types of crazy fit well together—as was the case with Nyx and Giulia—me and Star?

Nope.

"What did you find out?" Nyx asked, after heaving a sigh and sitting on the edge of Rex's desk.

He folded his arms across his chest as he stared at her, totally expecting her to reply.

Dumbass.

My lips twitched as I rocked back in my wheelchair, just waiting on the show that would be her stonewalling him.

I was curious if he'd get anything out of her, or if she'd share whatever her reason for being here was.

Sure, she'd been on the hunt for Ghost ever since Katina had come into her life, but how exactly Katina had come to her awareness was another matter entirely.

She hadn't told me, so I doubted she'd tell Nyx.

Of course, that was when you knew she'd always surprise you because she explained.

Fully.

"About eight years ago, I came across a circle of men who were into buying men and women."

"Men and women?" Nyx echoed. "Like with Ghost?"

She dipped her chin.

"How did you come across them?" I questioned, not trusting her tone.

"I was one of them." Her lips twisted, but her face, her eyes remained blank. "A mission went bad, I was sent offshore, and my contact screwed me over. Suddenly, I was in a worse hell than before. I'd have preferred to be in the fucking sandbox, getting my ass blown up over what I went through, but I eventually got sold, and that was how I escaped."

Nyx's eyes flared wide, but that was nothing compared to the crushing pain in my chest at her easy acceptance of what had happened to her.

"Why the hell didn't you tell me?"

"What was the point? By the time I could get in touch with you, I was out and free to move again. There's no point in dwelling on it, Mav. That's something you never figured out how to do. Shut shit off."

"You really shut shit off," I mocked, "didn't you? You're still coming after them, even if you don't focus on the why."

She shrugged. "I had to make them pay. Not for what I went through." She lifted her head, the move loaded with pride that wasn't feigned. "I'm a soldier. I was born to deal with worse. But the women there? They weren't. Women like Ghost, Tatána, and Amara...easily broken. Easily sold and forgotten and left behind.

"They fucked up when they took me though. I wasn't the average captive, and I made them pay for that mistake."

"You killed the man who bought you?"

She smiled, and that smile would have sent shivers down my spine if I was an ordinary man.

Luckily for her, Nyx wasn't ordinary either, and we both just stared at her, aghast and captivated by the story she was telling.

Not because it was a nice one, but because we were finally getting answers.

She'd been here a little over a month, but when you dealt with someone like her, someone with her skills, not knowing their motives was a weakness in our defenses.

That was how she'd gotten to Lancaster before us.

We didn't know her motivations, so we didn't know how to predict her movements.

Some people you could figure it out, but as she'd already said, Lodestar wasn't 'some people.'

"He paid, don't you worry, but it wasn't enough. I was very angry toward the end," she murmured, like it was a shopping trip that had gone awry. "I needed to make them all suffer, so I started doing some digging—"

"How?"

Her lips twisted into a grin that held no humor. "I had a fortune by that point."

I knew she'd earned a lot of money with her hacking, but the way she smiled revealed a secret she wasn't sharing yet.

"I used every cent to figure out how to dismantle the ring, and to break it apart from the inside out, I needed to annihilate the major players. I'm so close, guys. So fucking close." She released a breath, and when she stared at us, she was alive with a vibrant energy that made me feel like she was the sun beaming at me.

"I convinced my buyer to marry me," she continued, and on anyone else, I wouldn't have believed it, but with Lodestar, I could totally see it happening. "When he died, *accidentally*, I inherited it all. When it put me into some circles that would enable me to figure out who ran things, Donavan Lancaster's name kept popping up, and I was left with no alternative other than to find him.

"When I did, I came across the Fieris, then a son, and all these women's names of purchases they'd made along the way. I figured that the Fieri *Famiglia* were the ones behind the ring, a circle that spanned the globe, and I knew I needed to get closer." She scrubbed a hand over her face. "When I was still hunting down names, I found out I'd been looking in the wrong area, and it tripped some wires that brought me here."

"How did you find Katina?" Nyx asked.

She nodded at me. "Already shared that with the class. Through her mom. She was like me. One of the lucky ones."

I wasn't sure how being married to your purchaser made you lucky, but if she hadn't been stored in the pit that gave Ghost nightmares, I could easily accept how a woman might consider herself fortunate.

Pondering her words, I inquired, "What did Lancaster tell you?"

"Essentially, that the Fieris are behind the ring. I have confirmation at long last."

"What's the end game?"

"Making them burn, and everyone who's associated with their skin trade."

"I can dig that," I rasped. "I'll help too."

She smirked at me. "You have been helping, you just didn't know it."

I grinned. "True."

Nyx shook his head. "Why not tell us that from the start?"

"Because your interests and mine aren't aligned. Sure, you want the *Famiglia* gone, but when I came here, I had to see for myself that you weren't allied with them. It's only a quirk of fate that you're friendly with the Five Points and not the Fieris, after all."

"She has a point," I conceded.

Nyx shuddered. "We'd never be a part of anything that involves the skin trade."

"True, but she couldn't know that, could she?"

Nyx sniffed. "Lodestar, do you know about the tattoos on my back?"

She beamed at him. "I do, and I think they're the best part about you."

He twisted around to arch a brow at me. "There you go—she should have known all along we'd never be involved in anything like that.

"Lodestar, I'll share this with Rex, and it will make him soften up on you, but if you want to speak with Donavan again, then you need to wait until Rex okays it."

"Of course. But don't worry about it," she replied calmly, her shoulder hitching. "I got what I needed, and anything you find out, I know I'll be able to access—"

"How will you be able to do that?"

She waved a hand. "I figured out the key to Mav's coding a long time ago."

I scoffed at her arrogant statement. "What if I upgraded shit a year or two ago?"

She smiled at me, but it was a beatific one, not even smug, almost loving. "Oh, Mav, don't be silly."

I had to laugh, even if she pissed me off by dismissing my skills. Nyx's brow furrowed at me, and I rolled my eyes.

"Mav's coding is solid," she assured Nyx, sensing his doubt, "but I just know him too well, that's all. It will be more than sufficient to defend against some of the best hackers in the world."

"But you're the best, huh?" Nyx queried drolly.

She beamed a smile at him. "Yes. I am."

"Until someone whooped your ass and sent you running," I pointed out smugly—hey, even if she wasn't, didn't mean I couldn't be.

She blew a raspberry at me, but that alone told me I was speaking true.

I let it go, let her go, in fact, and when she drifted out of the office, leaving Nyx and me to discuss what he had to say, I arched a brow at him when he muttered, "She's not lying, is she?"

"No. Lodestar rarely lies. She'll hedge, but never outright lie."

He snorted. "She's a tricky bitch."

I shrugged, because that wasn't a lie.

"I wish she had been lying," Nyx rumbled, his mouth tightening.

"Honestly, I wish so too, but she wasn't. She just processes things differently. She can switch stuff off in a way I've never come across before."

"She's probably a psychopath," Nyx muttered, which made me laugh.

"Well, she's in the right place then, isn't she?"

His lips formed a reluctant smile. "Did you secure Lancaster?"

I nodded. "Of course. Had a couple of brothers go over the Fridge with a fine-tooth comb, made sure he was caged in nice and neat."

"Good. I have no desire to go there tonight." He stood up, stretched, then rubbed the back of his neck. "It's been a fucking bastard of a few days, Mav."

"When ain't it that way?"

He rolled his eyes. "True."

When he yawned, I told him, "You should get some rest. Things will start early in the morning."

"What kind of things?"

"The screams."

My words had him tensing. "Huh?"

I shrugged. "Whatever she did to him, it doesn't stop. Every now and then, he bursts into sporadic screams, so after a long night of being left on his lonesome, it will only get worse."

Nyx frowned. "Can they hear him on the road?"

I shook my head. "No. I checked. But if anyone goes behind the cabin, maybe they can."

"That's our land too though."

I nodded. "Yeah, they'd be trespassing."

"And trespassers will be shot," he muttered on a low growl.

"Exactly. I'm not worried." I laughed when he sniffed. "But yeah, get some rest because the fun will start again in the morning."

He sighed, then muttered, "Night, brother. It's good to be home."

As he made it to the door, I asked, "Any updates?"

"Would have told you if there were any."

I let him go, accepting that answer, even as I pulled out my phone and scanned the records that were being updated into the system at the hospital where Stone and Steel were being treated.

He wasn't wrong.

Nothing had been updated in the past forty minutes, and I'd been checking since I'd learned that Steel was stable and that Stone's emergency surgery was about to begin.

I tensed up, hating the lack of news, and instead of getting mad like I was inclined, I sighed and decided to do as I'd told Nyx—get some rest.

It wasn't that late, only eleven, but our days and nights were all fucked up here. We slept when we could, got the rest when we needed it, and right now, I needed it.

After rubbing my eyes, I stuck my hands on the wheels and rolled out from behind the desk and toward the door.

I yanked it open, irritated as always that Rex hadn't replaced it with a swing door years ago, but it hit me then that I hadn't been using my crutches for a good long while.

Hell, I didn't even know where the fuckers were.

Pondering their fate, I made it into the hall, only scraping two of my knuckles rather than all of them like usual, and made my way to the ramp that led down to the basement.

It was long, about the length of the building, but it was the only way I could access that part of the clubhouse. I slept in the attic, which I reached through the elevator that had been installed in the basement.

By the time I was there, my heart was pumping because it was like a fucking maze.

I knew the brothers had done it on purpose, trying to force me into moving, into rehab, but I was a stubborn bastard and I did what I wanted when I wanted it.

When I was in my room, I hauled my ass out of the chair and onto my bed.

The room was hot, but then it always was, thanks to the many computers I had running. Even constant AC didn't do shit, but I was used to it. I even liked it.

As much as I liked the glow from the screens as they ran their tests, constantly processing, so that the hum of the machines was as much of a lullaby to me as a song from my mother's lips.

Not that she'd sang for me often, but when she had? I'd always drifted off to sleep as restful as I ever had been.

The memory of her, that long blonde hair that had always made me think she was an angel, the blue eyes that always seemed to know when I was lying, the smile that could make my heart quicken with happiness, I felt my eyes drift closed, happy, for once, as I realized that my mom and Ghost were kind of similar in appearance.

Not in a way that was creepy, just in that angelic way.

Looking at Ghost was like looking at someone with a pure soul. Just touching her made me feel like I was staining her, but she never seemed to mind, and I wasn't about to argue with her over it. I never pushed shit, never would, because I didn't need to, but hell, I loved just holding her hand, letting my fingers clasp her wrist.

The touches were innocent, but each one was proof of a growing trust between us, and that meant more to me than her spreading her legs.

After I fell asleep, a while later, the slight crick of my door opening warned me that someone had come in.

I always slept light, had ever since my time overseas, and though I tensed up, I played opossum, wanting to know who'd sneaked in before I let my anger loose.

All the snatch knew to stay out of my room. At first, when I'd made it back home, they'd all thought they could cure my PTSD with fucking blowjobs, and it had been a rough time in getting them to realize that sex did not heal mental breakdowns.

So, that someone was stealing into my room, sneaking into my space when they knew they were supposed to back the fuck off?

Well, it didn't make me a happy man. Let's put it that fucking way.

I waited to see what they were doing, wondered even if they were going to try and check out the work I had open on my computer, then I felt the whisper of a hand on the bed sheets, and the scent hit me square in the nose.

Ghost.

I wanted to tense up, wanted to ask her what the fuck she was doing, but my heart was pounding with excitement.

This was the first time she'd come to me, ever, at night, and even though I knew not to get excited, my dick started to ache.

For a second, I didn't even recognize that burn of need.

It had been so long since I'd felt it, and even though it came in sporadic waves when she did something that managed to break through the fog that disconnected me from my sexuality, this time?

It hurt.

So badly that it stole my breath away.

My heart pounded, roughly and unevenly, making me feel like I'd been working out, and how I managed not to utter a sound, I'd never fucking know, but I did it.

I managed it.

Then she was there.

Her body lying against mine.

She moved as softly as a church mouse, drifting against me in a way that, with any other man, they'd never have known that she'd sneaked into their room, but I wasn't a regular man.

I was anything but ordinary.

When her hand came to rest on my abs, I felt my cock twitch into an erection that, again, hurt so badly, it was more painful than pleasurable.

I gulped when she settled into me, her body relaxing against mine in a way that told me she was trying to see if she could do this. Testing if she could be near me.

When her breathing evened out, I figured her nerves had died, even if she wasn't asleep yet.

"Why are you here, Ghost?" I inquired softly, so softly that it rivaled even her whispery voice.

She didn't tense, which told me she knew I'd awoken at her arrival, but she mumbled tiredly, "I didn't want to be alone tonight."

I wasn't averse to being used as a mattress, but I needed answers. Sometimes, making her talk was the only way I knew how to bridge the gap between us. A little like with Lodestar, I could look at her, communicate with her without having to utter a word, but I didn't know her as well as Star. I hadn't served with her overseas, seen her broken, seen her victorious with a mission's success. I didn't know all her weaknesses and her strengths, didn't know how to balance those with my own flaws and qualities.

She was a stranger, essentially, but she was mine.

I'd known that pretty much since the first time I'd gone into her room in the bunkhouse across the way and she had peered at me through those long lashes, catching me in a chokehold with a single glance.

I'd never believed in love at first sight until her, but now I did.

I knew what she was, knew I'd be patient for thirty years if it meant getting her close to me, making her accept that she was mine without fear.

"Maverick?" she murmured softly, her voice soothing me just like my momma's had when she talked me to sleep.

"Yes, Ghost."

"Why was he screaming?"

"You mean, is he dead?"

She tensed up a little. "Yeah. I guess that's what I mean."

"Because Lodestar hurt him. He isn't dead. He might wish he was."

She sighed. "I'm glad."

My lips twitched. "You are, huh?"

"Yes. Does that make me a bad person?"

"No, I think it makes you fucking normal."

She snickered a little. "Normal? Me?"

"Yes, well, remember who's telling you that," I said dryly.

"True. But I prefer to be your kind of normal. Your normal makes me happy."

My throat felt thick. "It does?"

"Yes. It does." She sighed. "Do you mind if I stay here?"

"Please do," I rasped, even as she stunned the hell out of me by gently lifting her leg and resting it on my calves.

It wasn't a play, if it was, she'd have nudged my dick with her knee, pressing the heat of her pussy to my thigh.

Instead, it was just her way of getting closer.

I felt like a human teddy bear, and I'd never been happier about my fate.

When she sighed against me, the soft sound hitting me keenly, I whispered, "You can stay here every night if you want, Ghost."

Her lips moved into a smile—I felt them against my arm. "I would like that."

No more than I would.

I pressed a kiss to her temple, then murmured, "Go to sleep. Tomorrow will be here sooner than you like."

She sighed. "That is a sad truth."

Wasn't it just?

But tonight, it was that much sweeter because she was here, and in the morning, it would be brighter still, because she was tucked against me, and I was more than happy to wake up with her at my side for the rest of my fucked-up life.

TWENTY-FIVE

STEEL

WHEN I WOKE UP, it was like every part of me flashed into 'on' mode.

I'd been shot before, had been put in comas before too, so I knew what it felt like to come awake after that.

This time, however, it was different.

Why?

My brain, some part of it, was aware that I'd been shot while being a coward as I turned tail and ran home, rather than go to my woman who'd been kidnapped by a whacked serial killer.

Shame hit me, and it was followed by the thought that, for some reason, I was waking up again.

Was it weird to know that you'd almost died?

I knew I had.

When I'd felt the bullet's trajectory, as it tore into my body like a stray tennis ball on a court, I'd known that death was likely.

Sure, I'd been pissed about it, but you went into this life knowing that it would probably end early.

What I couldn't forget, though, was the last thought that had brushed my consciousness before I'd snuffed it.

Unto death, I'd vowed to protect Stone from myself, and I'd fulfilled that vow.

I'd died.

That meant I could have her now, didn't it?

Nineteen-year-old me was shaking his head. But the guy who'd spent nearly two decades avoiding the woman he loved? Desperate to lose his principles, to accept that, finally, he could have Stone in his arms, in his bed.

Fuck, that man would settle for having her just in his life.

I reached up with my good arm and scrubbed a hand over my face.

"Thank fuck."

The mutter had me squinting as I peered over the side of the bed to find Link watching me.

He yawned when I caught his eye, and I slurred, "How's Stone?"

His brow furrowed. "What do you care?"

Anger flashed through me, and though I was definitely awake and aware, I was still very much sluggish. Too sluggish to be dealing with Link when he was in a mood, to be handling the temper he usually triggered.

I loved the fucker, he was my brother in more ways than just the bonds of the MC, but Christ, he did my head in.

I spent most of the time wanting to break his nose, but unfortunately for me, I was tethered to the fucking bed with all kinds of wires and shit.

"I care."

Two words, simple, but his eyes flashed wide in surprise—not at the admission, I figured, but that I was admitting it.

"She had a turn for the worse," he said, and his tone was cautious now, like he sensed he'd baited the bear and knew to back the fuck up.

My jaw clenched. "Is she okay?"

"She's been better."

More of the messing around with words.

I growled at him, then as I moved my hand, I brushed the remote thing they gave you and pressed the nurses' call button.

When someone dropped by a few minutes later, I ground out, "I need to be in a wheelchair."

"Mr. Pringle, you have to stay in bed!"

"Don't call me Pringle," I ground out. "The name is Steel."

The woman, in her late fifties, just arched a disapproving brow at me as Link sniggered beside me. "Mr. Pringle," she enunciated, "we use 'please' and 'thank you' in this hospital. You need to stay in bed."

"I need to visit my woman."

The nurse's crinkled brow crumpled further at that. "Your woman?"

"Stone Walker," Link clarified, evidently sensing that I was about to get into a fight with a woman who was close to retirement.

That wouldn't look good for my street cred, that was for sure. But if she called me fucking Pringle again, I wouldn't be held responsible for my actions.

"Oh," the nurse muttered, then she winced and conceded, "I'll get a wheelchair, but you have to do as I say and must return here when I tell you to."

That she was compassionate told me what Link hadn't—Stone had been in a bad way.

I blew out a breath, feeling like death warmed over twice now, and carefully began to raise the bed.

I needed to do that when she wasn't watching, because if she did, she wouldn't let me off the mattress.

"I'm surprised you're not knocked out," Link muttered, watching me before he started helping me sit up.

My body was totally asleep, but I was making it move. Will alone would bring things back into full working order, because every part of me wanted to see her. I just needed to bring my limbs up to par.

Fucking drugs.

Hated them.

I grunted. "I need to see her."

"What's changed?" Link asked softly, even as he propped me up when I sat upright, panting like a dog who'd been left in a car in the summer heat with the windows up.

I swallowed. "Timing."

"Timing?" I felt his confusion. "What's that got to do with it?"

"It has everything to do with it," I rumbled. "I nearly died. You don't have to tell me for me to know it's true. How my head wasn't rolled over by the trucks on the road with me was sheer fucking luck."

"You flew into the median and, lucky for you, you landed in a flower bed," Link informed me, ever helpful when I didn't actually need him to spell it out for me. "Plus you had some help from a Five Points' man."

I rolled my eyes at him, then muttered, "You're a pain in the ass, do you know that?"

"Exactly how I like it," he teased, smacking his lips.

I shoved him away. "How Lily puts up with you is beyond me."

He laughed, like I'd intended, and my lips were twitching too as Nurse Ratched made an appearance, wheeling in a chair for me.

"I wouldn't ordinarily do this, but everyone knows that Stone has been through a rough couple of days. If you're her boyfriend, then my goodness, it's even worse than I first thought."

I wasn't about to correct her, and Link, smart fuck that he was, didn't correct her either.

With a lot of grunts, groans, and my head turning light to the point where I legit thought I was going to pass out, I finally made it into the wheelchair.

Every part of me screamed that it was too soon to be moving around, and I felt it in every inch of me, but you'd never have gotten me back into my bed. Not even with a shotgun at my back.

As I was rolled down the corridor to the end, I sucked in a breath, preparing myself for when the door opened and I could see her.

I didn't expect to see Rex, snoring away, first, but I was glad to see that she'd had someone sitting with her.

Wasn't it weird how it would never occur to me that one of my brothers wouldn't be in here, keeping her company?

Just like Link had been here for me.

That was what we did. How we rolled.

We were never alone in a crisis. That was the joy of the MC.

As I squeaked in, feeling weak and pissy, he woke up, but my eyes weren't on him at that point. They were on her.

She looked…

Fuck.

She looked sick.

Her face was kind of yellow, in a weird way that looked like she'd been colored in with a yellow felt pen, and then she was a lot thinner than she'd been the last time I'd seen her.

How long had I been out of it?

It figured Rex would know the foremost thought on my mind. "You've been unconscious for four days."

Jesus. That was why my body was wrecked.

I really had pushed it by coming in here after being still for that length of time.

"She's been like this for three."

"What's wrong with her?" I rasped, reaching over so I could curl my fingers in hers.

Whatever I'd expected when I woke up, it wasn't this.

Truth be told, I'd thought she'd be back home in West Orange, setting up her life, getting things back on track.

But she wasn't.

Couldn't.

She was here.

Looking even sicker than I felt.

My throat was thick, choked, as I turned to look at Rex, who appeared to be as exhausted as Link, the same as usual, a bit pale, maybe, with his black eye having faded into a khaki green.

I couldn't blame them for being tired. We'd been sleeping away on comfortable beds, while they'd been on those godawful chairs that seemed to be the standard in all hospitals.

"She's got jaundice at the moment," the nurse explained softly, her gaze flickering between me and Stone. "Then we had a major complication when a peptic ulcer that was previously undiagnosed burst."

I winced. "She always did live on her nerves."

"Well, her stomach told the tale of that particular truth. She'll need a dramatic change of pace if the ulcers are to be kept at bay."

Oh, she'd have a change of pace, all right.

The whole point of me fucking off out of her life was for her to live a good one.

For her to attain everything she ever wanted, to grab the goals that kept her up at night. For her to be a better woman than her momma had been.

Mostly, it had been a certainty that I could never give her what she needed. That, with my twisted blood, somehow, I'd poison the one pure thing in my life.

But as I stared at her, realizing that she hadn't been living her best life, I knew I could have her anyway, and make her see the woods for the trees.

"What else is wrong with her?" I mumbled, because that wasn't enough to explain why she looked like a ragdoll.

"She had some complications from the drugs she was poisoned with," the nurse explained. Then, she whistled. "I'm not going to lie, Mr. Pringle—" I gritted my teeth at that. Fucking Pringle, my ass. "I've never seen quite a concoction of drugs. It's had us all a little bewildered by what the intention behind the draft was."

I frowned. "What do you mean?"

"The angel of death in her hospital was a pharmacy tech, and she had access to a lot of meds which she evidently used liberally when she was making up the medication she used on her—" She winced. "Victims. It appears that she gave Stone a smaller dosage than what she ordinarily would have done, but thanks to the potency of the poison, it's still done a lot of damage."

"Will she recover?" I questioned in a soft voice.

"Yes, in time," was the cautious reply. "If she doesn't have any further complications."

My brow puckered, and I curved my fingers about hers. "I'll make sure she doesn't have any."

"Unfortunately, that's not how it works," she said dryly. "As it stands, we've managed to treat every issue she had, some of which were pre-existing, just undiagnosed. The truth is, Mr. Pringle, she was a little like a walking time bomb anyway."

My mouth tightened. "In what way?"

"She has heart issues."

I gaped at her. "What?"

The nurse winced. "The irony is, the dose of drugs she was given contained a large amount of aspirin. It caused the peptic ulcer to explode, but it stopped her from having a heart attack. She'll need some real R and R once she wakes up from the coma we have her in."

I rubbed my brow, then I muttered, "I'm surprised you're telling us any of this."

From out of nowhere, she grinned at me, and as she wandered out, making my eyes widen, she called, "Tell Ripley I said hi."

Rex laughed as the door closed behind her. "Yeah, apparently Nurse Ratched was a clubwhore back in the day. Ripley told me about her, and I had things arranged so that she was working on our girl and you."

"Thanks, man."

My voice was hoarse with emotion, husky with fucking fear.

I could deal with bullets. They were in and out—well, hopefully. But illnesses? Heart conditions? Fuck. What the hell had Stone been doing with herself?

"You don't have to thank me. I feel like I fucking failed her. You heard what she said. A goddamn time bomb. She's not even thirty-five yet, for fuck's sake."

Link rumbled, "She takes too much onto herself."

"You got that right." Rex pinched the bridge of his nose. "Truth is, I was proud of her when she graduated early, but I never thought about the health repercussions—"

I bit my bottom lip. "Where's Mrs. Biggins?"

Rex shook his head at my question. "Tiff's looking after her."

"Must be fucking love if you remember her cat," Link muttered.

I ignored them both, relieved to know the cat from hell was cared for, and demanded, "Is she covered? Insurance wise?"

"She's on the MC's plan," Rex assured me.

Catching his eye, I stared him down. "Whatever it costs, it comes out of my cut."

He scowled at me. "That's stupid. You don't need to—"

"It's from my cut," I ground out, unwilling to accept anything else.

She was my woman.

Her debts were mine too.

Rex grunted, but Link just snorted out a laugh. "And they say romance is dead."

"It is in capitalist America," I grumbled, then I squeezed her fingers and muttered, "Does that mean the old bitch knew my name all along and called me fucking Pringle anyway?"

Rex chuckled. "Yeah."

I rolled my eyes. "Figures."

TWENTY-SIX
STONE

HE WAS the first thing I saw when I woke up, and I knew, if I had my way, he'd be the last thing I ever saw.

Truth was, I hadn't been sure if I was going to live or die that last night I'd passed out, and to wake up and for him to be here?

I couldn't say it was a dream come true, because from all the pain in my body, this was definitely more of a nightmare, but still... having him here was wonderful.

That he was sitting in a wheelchair gave me the stark reminder that he'd been hurt too. His head was tipped forward at an awkward angle, meaning I couldn't see his face to judge how he was doing, but he was snoring like a trooper which had my lips twitching at the sight, even as I devoured every other part of him.

Having the ability to watch him without feeling like a creep, while being able to feast on him like my eyes truly wanted, was heaven.

I'd never allowed myself that treat before, because I never wanted him to see the hurt in my eyes, the need and the want in my soul.

My name was Stone, and I had a rep for being a stone in

temperament, but I wasn't like that. Not really. He was the reason I'd changed, shifting from someone who was open and loving to cold and hard with everyone except my patients.

I knew what it was like to hurt because of this man, but I also knew what it was to feel. And the love in my heart for him was so large that sometimes, some days, I felt sure it would explode out of me.

I'd been dumb to think that I could just wash this man right out of my hair, by thinking it was as simple as that...

Nothing was simple. Nothing at all. Not when love came to mind, and a love this old? This pure? This untouched? Nothing could tear it asunder.

So that was why I feasted. Because I accepted that I would always love him, and accepted that even though he was here, and that he was sitting with me, it probably didn't change anything on his end.

He would be here because of who I was to the club. That was it.

They never left anyone out in the cold, and certainly not someone like me, who'd been one of the tagalongs back when I was a kid and they were teens.

The MC was a family, and even though I'd left and they were mad at me, they were still mine. So his presence was just a courtesy. He could come here while Link and Rex or Nyx could head to a hotel and nap, get some rest.

Even as my body was slow to respond to wakefulness, my brain ticked over, accepting that even if I wanted to waste a million wishes on his opening his eyes and looking at me with love, I knew that wouldn't happen.

Because he was asleep and I'd evidently been unconscious for a while, I took my sweet time about waking up properly.

My legs and arms ached from lack of movement, and my back?

Jesus, fuck. That killed. There was a knot down the middle of my spine that was probably the size of Greenland.

I had a lot of other shit going down too, shit that told me I'd been in a lot of trouble for a while, but I didn't bother to waste time thinking on that.

Not when Steel was here.

I could think about my health later, when he'd gone. Now?

I just enjoyed his presence.

When the nurse bustled in, I wanted to scream at her to get out, but I didn't. Nurses got a lot of shit from doctors and patients, and I would never treat them so badly, even if this one *had* just woken up Steel.

He blinked blearily for a second, then when they were focused, his eyes widened as they caught mine.

My heart leaped as he rolled forward, eagerness in his gaze as he grabbed my hand. I winced when it pulled a shit ton of IV lines, but I didn't care. He was holding my hand, sitting close to me, not wheeling out like I'd thought he would.

"Thank fuck."

Two words. Not the most romantic, but for Steel? He might as well have written me a sonnet that was dedicated to my hair.

I blinked at him, and I realized my tongue was a little fuzzy, thick too—why couldn't I speak?

Jesus. I'd been intubated!

Panic hit me, and then, before I could let it consume me, his hand was on my forehead and he hushed me. "Calm down, sweetheart. Calm down. I'm here. I won't go anywhere."

And that was everything I needed to hear, because with that, I drifted back into unconsciousness, somehow knowing that he meant it, that he wouldn't leave me, and that he was going to stay by my side.

TWENTY-SEVEN
STEEL

SHE WOKE up four times over the next three weeks, and each time, when she saw me and checked in, she checked out again.

She wasn't the only one living on her fucking nerves.

As I grew stronger, she never seemed to change as the doctors worked hard to rectify the damage the poison she'd been given had done to her body.

If I had a say in things, I'd have asked her to do more than fucking slice the bitch's throat. I thought her attacker deserved a good kick between the fucking legs and a knife in the back too.

I rubbed my eyes, tiredness in them as I yawned through one of Nyx's stories.

There was a mini rotation going down so I could return to my hotel room, which was just down the block, and get some rest every now and then.

I'd been allowed out on an outpatient basis, and though my shoulder still ached like a bitch, things were mending in the healing department.

I'd had an infection that had slowed shit down, but thankfully, someone had been on my side, because as soon as it had started, it had faded pretty quickly with the high dose of antibiotics I'd been fed. I'd only missed two days of sitting at Stone's side, and I'd begrudged every fucking minute of it.

Ever since then, I'd been getting better, and when I'd moved into a hotel, the rotation had begun.

Brothers waded in and out through her door like troops on a battlefield, some to keep me company, some to bring me food. Even the Old Ladies had been by, and I'd watched them, studied their brands, all along wondering what it felt like to own a woman in truth.

I was owned by one, but I didn't own her, and the urge was strong just to get a tattoo artist in and have her branded as mine, even if she rejected me after so many years of rejecting her.

I deserved it if she asked me to leave her room the second she was lucid. I deserved it if she never wanted to see me ever again.

After something like this, something where her life was forever veered off course, it brought decisions to a head, and choices and options changed and ricocheted in completely different directions.

I knew that was how Nyx and Giulia had ended up together. Sure, they'd been fucking, but her being attacked in our bar had led to Nyx claiming her ahead of schedule.

Jesus, all my brothers had claimed their women in the face of tragedy. So, that led me to the conclusion that tragedy was a trigger.

But Stone wasn't a regular woman.

I wouldn't be surprised if she decided that she wanted to dedicate herself to her career in the aftermath of this, as a thanks to medical science for saving her.

"You listening?"

I blinked, surprised when Nyx's voice softened, even as he'd broken into my jarred thoughts.

"No, sorry, man."

He grimaced, then muttered, "Don't worry about it." He cut her a look. "So glad that intubation has been taken out."

"Me too. Every time she drifted into awareness with it in, I could feel her panic. It made me feel claustrophobic."

"They're waking her up now, aren't they?"

"Yeah."

He hummed at that. "That's good news, isn't it?"

"It is unless something else goes wrong."

She'd had two other surgeries since the last one, and that had been to cut out part of her fucking kidney and some of her liver.

That bitch had done a real number on her. As it stood, she was healing, but she was loaded down with scars from the surgeries she'd had. They were saying it might be difficult to have kids for her now, which fucked with my head because she deserved to have children. But those kids should be mine, and I didn't want any—not when they'd share my demon DNA.

Confused, a little irate, I rubbed a hand over my chin as I walked away from her bedside and moved over to the window.

From here, it was hard to see much of the city, but what I could see was how it was bustling away, busy with life. In here, it was silent except for the beeps and the humming of the machines that helped keep her going, and it was beyond bewildering to me to be sitting here, at her bedside.

Things had changed, deviating off course so dramatically that I was still reeling with it.

"You doing okay, brother?"

I shot Nyx a look, then snorted. "You've probably talked more today than you have in years."

His grin was sheepish. "It's hard not to talk. You look like you're about to kill someone."

"I wish I could."

Nyx grunted. "I know how that feels."

"I get it now," I muttered, understanding his outrage that Giulia had killed her attacker.

Even while I was grateful Stone had done the same with that bitch, I wish I'd had a chance to go over her.

"Fuck, I'd give my left kidney to run that bitch over and tear her into a thousand pieces for what she's put my woman through."

Nyx hummed, then queried, "Your woman, huh?"

I glanced at him from the corner of my eye and shrugged. "Just an expression."

He snickered. "Yeah. Some expression." His mouth quirked into a smirk. "You forget, I've seen your back."

That shut me the hell up. "She needs me."

I hated that there was a plea in my voice at that. I didn't need his approval or his permission to do shit, but somehow, I wanted it.

Nyx... He didn't know it, but we were family. His opinion mattered to me more than anyone else's in the world. It always had, even before Lana Jane had ruined my life by telling me something I wished could have remained a secret forever.

"I want you to claim her the second she's well enough to be claimed."

I snorted. "She might ask me to get the hell out of here."

"Doubt it. She loved you before, and she'll love you when she wakes up."

When.

Not if.

We'd all been very careful to use that word, because for so long, it had been touch and go. With every day that had passed, each twenty-four-hour period had felt like a lifetime, one in which we could lose her on a frequent basis.

I'd never imagined the terror that came from sitting at someone's bedside, never imagined that I'd be more scared about Stone losing her life than I was when those bullets had torn into me...

Maybe that was love though? Caring more about whether someone lived or died than whether you yourself did?

Uneasily, I rubbed my chin. "I only hope that's true. I'm not sure I could deal with shit without her now."

"Funny how it's like a switch in your mind, no?" Nyx mused softly.

A tap sounded at the door, and though it broke into our conversation, I stared straight at him, nodded in agreement, then turned to the doorway where Indy waded in with three pizza boxes.

At first, I'd felt bad about eating in here. I mean, technically, I wasn't even supposed to be in the room period, not for as long as I was occupying it, but then, it had just become normal.

I hated that this was the new normal.

My old normal was Stone hating on me, bitching at me, scowling at me like she hated me when we both knew she didn't.

That, if anything, she loved me as much as I fucking loved her.

Fuck.

So much wasted time.

So many goddamn moments lost.

All of them my fault.

And here we were, I'd almost died, she'd almost died, and fuck, if she didn't keep on having these scares that frightened the shit out of me and made me wonder if I'd left it just that little bit too long.

Regrets were like a lead weight in my gut, and the only thing that made me eat was the fact that my family kept bringing food in.

I'd seen that shit Marilyn Monroe had once said. That you should have no regrets, because at the time, it was exactly what you wanted.

But what if you didn't want what you'd done?

What if you'd done it for a specific reason, and that reason, at the end of your life, suddenly made no fucking sense?

Truth was, it didn't matter who'd given me my DNA. It didn't matter if I was related to that evil cunt.

I was me.

Steel.

My own level of evil, my own level of cunt, but it had nothing to do with being a kid fucker.

I was just me.

Not a saint, definitely a sinner, but even through all that, there was something in there that Stone found lovable. Or if she didn't, whenever she opened her eyes and looked at me like I was the one who'd put the Earth on Atlas's shoulders, she was lying to herself.

That look?

It was the only thing that made waking up easier right now. Knowing that she might open her eyes for a longer time, that today might be the day she woke up for good.

Indy's hand came to my shoulder, and when she stroked me there then ran her hand over my head, I turned my face into her belly as she bent down to give me a hug.

I felt like a pussy for wanting to cry, but I wasn't about to do that in front of Nyx.

So much wasted time.

That was the litany at the moment.

"She'll be okay."

"She better be," Nyx grumbled, and I rolled my eyes because he was grousing around a slice of fucking pie.

"You got your hands on my man, Indiana?"

The slow drawl, the mumbled words, each one half-laced with sleep, but fuck if I hadn't heard sweeter threats come from any woman's lips.

We all froze, even Nyx, because he didn't have a shit thing to say, and then, Indy twisted around and whispered, "Stone? Are you really awake?"

She was.

She looked wrecked. Her eyes were exhausted, and I could see from those depths that she'd woken up because she was in pain.

I bit my lip, tempted to call the nurse in just to see to her management. They'd been weaning her off IV meds, and this was the intended result. Her waking up. She was still foggy from the morphine, that much was clear, but the sight of her like this was sheer magic.

Sleep-rumpled, face creased by the pillows, and her body a mass of scars?

Beautiful.

I'd never seen a more beautiful woman in all my life.

For real, my throat clogged up. This time, there was no escaping the need to cry, and I just wiped my face on my good shoulder, because she was here and she was talking, and I had to believe that this time, the doctors had done everything in their power to make her right.

I surged forward, moving away from Indy to the other side of her bed, and I carefully took a seat.

My woman was ripe with curves, rich with them, a butt that wouldn't quit and tits and hips that rolled for days.

She wasn't right now. Her weight had shrunk dramatically, and I hated that because she looked emaciated, and I knew the second she was back on solids, that was something I was going to fix.

Fuck, I'd have MickyDs on speed dial because I knew that was her weakness. Although, with her heart condition, maybe not...but I'd figure something out. No way was she doing without, not now she was here with me again.

"Hey," I rasped softly as I took a seat, careful not to shift the weight of the bed too much and have her roll toward me.

She gulped. "You're really here?"

I frowned, a little taken aback by that first comment. "Yeah, I'm here."

Her eyelashes fluttered shut. "Thought you were a dream."

They stayed closed, and I barked, "Stone!"

They fluttered open again.

I sucked in a breath and muttered, "Stay awake, Stone. Come on, it's time for you to return to the land of the living."

She whimpered as she wriggled slightly, like she was trying to move her body and was failing. "Why does everything hurt?"

She'd gone through a lot while she'd been unconscious, and ordinarily, the person who explained this shit to us was the person in bed now. Each time we'd had an accident, Giulia, then Tiff and Lily in the hospital—Stone had been called, and she'd explained the situation to Rex.

I knew I could call in the doctors, and I would in a minute, but also, I didn't want her finding out everything that had gone on. It would probably depress her and set back her healing.

I pursed my lips as I stared at her, and entwining my fingers with hers, I murmured, "We'll get you some meds soon."

She sighed, her pupils blowing as she turned to look at Nyx and Indy, who were standing over in the light. "Why are you guys here?"

"You've been asleep for a while, Stone," I rasped. "They keep me company and bring me food."

Indy pouted. "Steel won't let me spend much time here, because the nurses don't like having one of us in your room, never mind all three of us. We're technically only allowed in because it's visiting hours."

She blew a raspberry at me, but I shrugged. "Wasn't about to leave your side, Stone."

She swallowed at that, her throat working. "You say that now."

"No, not now. I say it and mean it. Ain't leaving your side again, Stone."

She squeezed my fingers. "Am I dying?"

I blinked. "Huh?"

"Are you saying that because you think I'll die soon?" She licked her lips, and they were so dry, even though her words froze me, I had to reach over to grab the small cup with the ice chips the nurses kept refilling.

They were mostly melted, just water, but there were a few still big enough to dampen her mouth.

"No, you're not dying," I grumbled, "you'd better not die either. I'll get really fucking mad if you do."

"You're always mad at me," she said with a sigh, as the water made the pale pink of her dry lips bloom into fuchsia with the liquid sinking into it.

"I used to be." I tipped my chin up. "Then you nearly died, and I nearly died, and I figured that was too much fucking dying for one day. For one lifetime."

"What are you saying?" she whispered.

"He's saying that he's got you booked in at my studio the second you're out of this place."

Indy's comment had me glowering at her. "Shut up, Indy. You'll piss her off!"

But Stone didn't look angry, she just looked confused. "I'm tired," she mumbled.

"Get a doctor, Indy," Nyx rasped, and his sister, who, during Stone's hospitalization, had revealed how close she and Stone were, like sisters themselves, darted off and went to do as directed.

"Do we keep her awake or let her rest?" I asked, worry bleeding into my tone as her eyelids kept flickering to a close.

"I think we keep her awake until the doctors can see her."

Moments later, two doctors came in, and just in time, because I could feel her slipping away.

They shooed us outside, and I almost disobeyed, needing to know what was going on, but Indy grabbed me, and Nurse Ratched, a pretty nice woman who was actually called Sandra, squeezed my arm and muttered, "Let them do their job. You want her out of here as much as she wants to be out of here, Pringle. Let them do their thing."

It grated on me, but I did as she asked, and I didn't even fucking notice that she called me Pringle, that was how out of it I was.

I rubbed my brow with my thumb and forefingers, then started to pace in the corridor. I'd never been in a hospital as much as I had been in this one, and the truth was, I hated it. I wasn't sure how Stone could stand it, being in here all day and all night, the endless beeps, the scents, and the noises that came from quiet whispers and the hushed sobs of someone grieving or in pain.

I knew I'd go insane if I stayed here much longer, but stay I would because I'd already run out on her when she needed me once before. I didn't think she'd have fared much better with me at her side, but maybe she would've.

Maybe she'd have been stronger with me at her back.

Instead, she had almost died, and all while I was in recovery for a surgery that should never have happened, because if I'd stayed at that diner with my brothers, then I'd never have been fucking shot.

I gritted my teeth when Nyx came for me, his hand on my good shoulder as he stopped me from striding back and forth.

"I have a gift for you if you want it."

I scowled at him. "How about you make my woman better, Nyx?"

He scoffed, then muttered, "She's in the right place, and this will do you some good. You need some fresh air. Worse, you need to make someone pay."

I gulped and registered how fucking right he was.

"I promised myself I wouldn't leave the hospital until I really needed to."

"You were about to wear out the lino, Steel. I think you need to get out and get some different stimuli going on. This is like white torture, for fuck's sake. You're the one who's worse off. Let Indy stay, she'll sit with Stone because she was already falling back to sleep, so I don't see why she wouldn't be resting when we got back anyway.

"It won't take long. Maybe even an hour. Tops."

"It had better not be to take me to a fucking restaurant—"

"No," Nyx said with a laugh. "I wasn't about to bring your skinny ass any food. This is something good."

I gritted my teeth, but when I tried to peer into the room where Stone was being tested, a room that Sandra had lowered the blinds on, I bit my tongue, knowing I needed to do something before I lost my mind.

I turned to him and rumbled, "I need to be back here before she wakes up."

Nyx shot Indy a look, who turned to me and reached to pull me into a one-armed hug. She wasn't tactile by nature, none of their family was, with Quin being the most affectionate of the bunch—of course, that was before he'd been sent up—but still, that she was hugging me so much told me she was scared.

I didn't blame her.

I was scared too.

The one person who could clarify this fucking situation was in the bed, terrifying the shit out of us. Sandra tried, but she just wasn't explaining it how we were used to.

Stone gave us our answers with 'fuck yous' and 'get over yourself' thrown in.

I squeezed her back, knowing that we were both going through this, and that, if anything, she was being kind because she let me in with Stone when she had more right to be there than anyone else.

I was the one who'd abandoned Stone, and Indy was the one who'd picked up the slack.

I whispered in her ear, "Thank you," and she squeezed me tighter.

"She loves you," she rasped. "Just don't break her fucking heart again. After all this, I don't think she'll make it. And you wouldn't, because I'd come and make you pay."

I wanted to call bullshit on that, but I didn't. Couldn't. I knew she was right.

And the truth was, I had no desire to turn my back on Stone. If anything, I was just terrified that she'd turn her back on *me*.

"Don't be long," she warned Nyx, who grabbed my arm and tossed something at me. I blinked at the cut, new and squeaky clean, but with my 'Secretary' patch on. I hadn't worn one in the hospital since this entire fuck up had started, and I shrugged into it, feeling like I was settling into my second skin.

It was stupid, but that saying, 'clothes maketh man'? It was true.

This was me.

My cut made me the man I was, and with it on, I felt stronger. More invincible.

I wanted the old cut, but that had gone in the trash without my fucking say so. I'd have worn it with the bullet holes, covered in blood, and snipped to shit by the EMTs when they worked on me, because they were my badges of honor.

This new one would have to do, but even as I was grateful for Nyx's foresight, I resented the loss of my old one. I should have been buried with it—of course, there was no more time to think about death.

I had to move on and so did Stone.

Together.

I followed Nyx once I felt my temperament right itself, and as we strolled through the hospital, I clicked my neck, working at the crick there. I hadn't worked out much since the shooting, and I totally needed to get back in the gym, but until the wounds weren't pulling anymore, I was fucked, and I refused to only do leg days and end up with Schwarzenegger thighs and a stick man's torso.

Vanity, thy name is biker.

The thought made my lips twitch, especially when I thought about Stone's reaction. She'd probably laugh if I was little and large all in one body, and it would be worth it just to have her smile at me again. Just to see her laughter, to watch it in her eyes as well as the joy unravelling from her.

Throat thick, *again*, I grunted under my breath as we headed underground to the parking lot.

Our bikes were clustered together in a single space. It wasn't Baby, which had been totalled in the aftermath of my shooting, and I missed the bright orange bitch like a motherfucker, but as Nyx rolled his out, I did the same with mine. Grateful, in a way, that I had a ride at all.

My brothers rocked for bringing me my wings on the back of a cage.

Without a word, we set off, and I followed him as he took me out of the hospital parking garage and through the mean streets of New York.

And fuck, they *were* mean too.

Christ, he sure knew how to show a friend a good fucking time.

Rolling my eyes, I followed him as he eventually led me to a small, beat-up building that looked like, once upon a time, it had served as an office, but was now a shady place where drug deals went down.

Maybe they fucking did. This neighborhood wasn't exactly pretty.

When he pulled up, I parked behind him, and as I climbed off the bike, I grabbed a hold of his shoulder and hissed, "Where the fuck are we?"

He tapped his nose. "It's a surprise."

"Fucking hate surprises," I ground out.

His lips twitched. "You'll like this one."

I scowled at him. "Nyx," I growled in warning.

He heaved a sigh. "You're a fucking killjoy." He wafted a hand at the building. "You want to know who shot you?"

My eyes flared wide. "The *Famiglia* fucker is in there?"

His wink had my heart roaring. "Sure is."

"Then what the fuck are we waiting for?"

Adrenaline high as we stalked down to the office, which was wall-to-wall shitty, dirty windows, we approached a door. When Nyx shoved a gun at me, then another, I stuck one in the back of my jeans and watched as, armed himself, he shot off the lock on the door.

With the noise of the traffic going on in the distance, and a train that rumbled by at that precise moment—which made me wonder if the fucker had planned this, and if he had, how the hell he'd planned it to a T—I didn't know if the occupants of the office were aware of what he'd just done.

When I heard no noise from the inside, I grabbed my other pistol after I twisted the doorknob, opened it up then kept it that way with my boot, and then waited for whatever it was Nyx had planned.

Before I could go inside, Nyx tugged my arm, stopped me, then shoved a bandana at me.

I grinned, covered up my face, and then we strolled in, both guns high. He entered first, like he didn't have a care in the world, which we both knew was bullshit, and as we carried on into the darkened hallway, me wondering what the fuck was going on but knowing to keep my trap shut, we approached another door.

When someone burst out of the shadows toward us, I didn't even fucking hesitate.

Bang.

My aim was renowned in the club, even if I wasn't as good of a shot as Maverick, and when the guy who'd come at us fell to the ground as a dead weight, Nyx just chuckled.

I didn't blame him for chuckling, because suddenly, I wanted to laugh as well.

Fuck, this felt good. Putting down *Famiglia* cunts? Talk about a natural mood booster.

My heartbeat settled, and I waited for the adrenaline to die off as we carried on walking, me still following Nyx as we headed toward a cluster of shadows.

Another door was there, but this time, when he shot off the lock and I kicked it open, four guys surged forward.

Security.

Bang. Bang. Bang. Bang.

Four shots from Nyx and me, taking each one out a piece, and they only managed to get one off before we had them on their knees. I pistol-whipped one who still went for his gun, even though he was quivering and gasping like a dying fish, and as he sank to the floor, I stepped over him and peered into the doorway.

What I saw didn't necessarily surprise me.

It was early, too early even for an underground casino like this one to be that busy.

The roulette tables had three or four people around them a piece, the blackjack stands were empty except for the dealer, and where there were a few craps tables, they had barely anyone manning them either.

No one registered us at first, which clued me into the fact we'd come in the back way, but then someone screamed—I thought it was a blackjack dealer—and Nyx blew a bullet into the ceiling and shouted, "We don't want your money, we don't want to hurt you. We want Jacob Russo."

My brows rose at that, and when a woman squeaked, "He's over there," which granted her a backhander from the guy she'd pointed to, someone who I assumed was her fucking date, I grinned as I strolled forward, knowing Nyx had my back, even as Russo pulled out his weapon.

Sure, I knew I was getting myself into shit, but for this motherfucker, the fucker who'd shot me, who, according to Lancaster's intel, was one of the few snipers they had on the payroll—as the others took jobs as payment for favors owed—and who was a *lot* reckless when it came time to disobey his orders, I was more than ready to put myself in the line of fire.

As I reached for him, he fingered the trigger, but I was faster. The next second, the gun spun out of his hand, rolling onto the floor, as did a couple of fingers.

While he howled out his pain, some of his crew decided to play dumb and swarmed toward me, but Nyx had the situation under control.

They sank to the ground like the sacks of shit they were, and when I strolled over to Russo, who was crying like a baby, I kicked his legs out from under him, watched as he dropped to his knees, then I moved around behind him, bent low, and whispered, "You're getting a faster death than you deserve."

I pressed the muzzle to the soft flesh under his chin and let my bullet loose before he could struggle too much.

When his brain splattered everywhere, I didn't even give a fuck, was just glad that it hadn't splattered me.

I just rolled out of there, as calm as how we'd come in, and while the women screamed, the dealers were quiet, watchful, evidently used to this level of violence in their establishment.

With Nyx at my back, the pair of us headed on out, and as we made it outside with no one else surging forward, the security evidently shit at this place if they thought they only needed five men to keep the underground casino safe, I asked, seeking confirmation for something I pretty much knew, "*Famiglia* owned, right?"

Nyx grinned. "Yep. The Five Points want their illegal gambling dens. I knew about this one because of Lancaster, and thought I'd make some calls, see if this was one of Russo's hang outs. Dumb fuck has a lot of markers out on him."

"Not anymore." I smirked at my brother, and just before I gunned my bike, I declared, "You're right, that *was* a gift. Thanks, bro. I feel a hell of a lot better."

TWENTY-EIGHT

STEEL

BEFORE

"WAKE UP, DUMB FUCK."

Someone shook my shoulder, roughly jerking me to wakefulness.

"Huh? What's wrong?"

Rex's scowl was suddenly up close and person. "Stone. That's what's wrong."

Pain flashed inside me. "Huh?"

"You heard me. She's not in the bunkhouse."

I blinked, totally out of it as I tried to figure out what the fuck he was talking about. But he wouldn't let me flop back onto the pool table, didn't let me do shit. He hauled me off and shoved my clothes at me.

"About fucking time. I wanted to play a game of pool—"

I growled at Grizzly, uncaring that the fucker was a mean dick, and just dragged on my jeans, even though my head was swimming.

When I was covered, Rex hauled me across the room, out of the bar, and from the clubhouse onto the driveway. When we made it to the end bunkhouse, I staggered inside, then immediately hissed when Mrs. Biggins, the cat I'd bought Stone, attacked me.

She was little, but her claws were nasty, especially when she managed to pull some kind of judo cat shit and flew at me. The claws scraped up my chest as she slid down me, the little points digging in.

I hissed, but even though the nasty fucker was hurting me, I grabbed her before she could fall, then tossed her spitting, hissing, snarling self onto the sofa before she could bite me again.

Talk about a rude fucking awakening.

Still bleary-eyed, even though I was feeling a bit more awake after being shredded by a kitten, I blurted out, "What are we doing here?"

"She was supposed to come over for breakfast, and when she didn't, Mom sent me over to find her. Her shit was unpacked, the bed not slept in." Rex ground his teeth. "What the fuck did you do now, dipshit?"

I squinted at him. "Ain't done fuck. I've been away from her this entire time."

He shook his head. "There's no fucking hope for you." He grabbed my shoulder, twisted me around, and muttered, "You're not exactly living up to this, are you?"

I shrugged out of his hold, not wanting to think about the brand I'd had done a few months ago so that it would be ready for my time to claim her.

My mouth tightened. "Why did you bring me here?"

"Because she's your woman. Don't you give a shit where she is?" he snarled.

"Of course I fucking do, but she's probably working. You know what she's like."

Rex hissed at me, much like the fucking cat, and ground out, "How is it you're turning into a cunt, doing cunt things, when you're more scared than ever of being like your fucking father?"

I felt my skin blanch at that, every part of me turning white-hot with rage as I snapped, "Don't you dare compare me to him—"

"If you act like a piece of shit, I will. In the blood, isn't it?" When he hit out at me, I grabbed his fist, then snapped a firm hold on it as I slammed mine into his face.

Blood spurted, spraying over me, mingling with the fine rivers of blood dripping down my chest, but I ignored it as the two of us got into a brawl that saw us tipping over half the furniture and nearly crashing into the window.

What stopped us?

Mrs. Biggins attacked again. Her claws went to my face, scratching me up real good as she bit and hissed, her paws getting tangled up in my already tangled hair.

When she nearly sliced my eye, I raised my hands to fend her off, and she only stopped when Rex grabbed a hold of her, cuddling her to his chest.

I hissed at her, wondering what this was all about, then grimaced when I saw how she'd managed to bloody me up.

"She's got it in for you, and I can't fucking blame her," Rex snapped. "You gonna come with me to find her?"

Though I knew I should, I just—fuck, I couldn't.

I needed to stay strong, to stand firm. She didn't need me in her life, tainting it. Making everything so much worse for her.

She needed the chance at a fresh start. The chance for more than this compound had to offer.

Before he could curse me out for being a coward, his cell buzzed. When he frowned at the screen, I tensed up, and as he answered it, the tension soared in me even more.

"She's in the hospital?" he barked. "Nyx, what the fuck?"

He glowered at me before he spun around and spat, "Where did she even get that shit?" He hissed. "Fuck. Just fuck. Dipshit is here, pissed out of his brains as usual. I can get us there in twenty minutes. She's being treated?" A pause. "Good, yeah. Make sure everything's copacetic, brother. Jesus, I never thought she was into drugs—"

"She isn't," I rumbled, earning myself a glare.

"Then what the fuck was she doing overdosing on coke?" he snarled at me, but deep in his eyes, we both knew the answer.

Somehow, I was to blame for this. And the 'somehow' wasn't all that hard to figure out.

She'd just lost her mom, and even though she wasn't much of a mom, there was still grief to be dealing with. And beyond that, she'd lost me. Her closest confidante.

I'd been AWOL ever since—

My mouth suddenly tasted like vomit, and I dashed to my feet, faster than I could manage so I almost fell over, before I slammed myself down in front of the porcelain throne and puked my guts out.

When I was done, I felt like shit, shittier than ever before, and Rex, deciding to hammer the nail in my coffin, rumbled behind me, "You're coming with me."

"No," I snapped weakly, my head hanging low over the toilet bowl. "I'm not."

"She needs you, fuckwit. You can't just abandon her."

"I'm doing what needs to be done."

He kicked my ass, pushing me into the toilet, and I let him, relieved only when he stormed out of the bunkhouse, leaving me in my misery.

I loved her. There was no avoiding that.

But I loved her enough that I knew ripping off the Band-Aid now would be a thousand times more bearable than it would be in the future.

Rene, Rex's mom, would bring her under her wing, and she'd make sure Stone stayed on the straight and narrow, and the truth was, I was anything but straight or narrow.

I was a path that led to danger. A path that led to misery, and I'd been that even before Lana Jane had told me who I was.

What I was.

I sucked in a breath, grimacing at the sour scent of vodka-laced vomit. Reaching over to flush the toilet, I sank back on my heels, then nearly screamed when I felt the ninja cat come at me again.

This time, I was a little meaner, because fuck, she was hurting me! I managed to grab a hold of her, then quickly tossed her out into the living room before closing myself into the bathroom.

Then I passed out on the floor, where thoughts of Stone, bastard fathers, and broken promises couldn't reach me.

TWENTY-NINE

STONE
TODAY

I WOKE UP TO, what for me, were the sweetest sounds ever.

Bickering.

I was well aware that was strange, but then, it wasn't to me. I'd grown up with this low-level noise from the men who were like brothers to me, and to hear them all shooting the shit in my room was probably the best way I could have woken up.

"You remember that time she beat the shit out of Candy?"

I opened my eyes at that, because Storm's voice wasn't one I'd anticipated hearing. I knew he was in another chapter now, but hearing him sent another wave of homesickness through me.

Even though my family was here, all around me, being in a hospital room was the last place I wanted to be.

"Storm?" I rasped, and my words had all the guys rushing to stand beside my bed.

In their cuts, with all their scraggly hair, stubbled cheeks, and the beginnings of a beard, they epitomized the roughness of a bunch of bikers. Some women might be scared of them, but I wasn't 'some women.'

These were brothers.

This was family.

Sure, they'd let me down along the way, but that was family too, wasn't it?

Tied and linked in ways that didn't have to make sense to just be.

I smiled at them, feeling sleepy still while dealing with a level of pain that took my breath away.

"What's going on?" Storm complained, and my lips curved at his grousing.

"Ever the whiner," I mumbled, appreciating the lightening of the faces around me as they backed down some.

I didn't have to be told that I'd gone through some rough patches, because not only did I feel like death warmed over, but their expressions were grim. And that grimness was overlaid with a certain light of relief that told me how bad things had gotten.

While it was stupid, I made a point of not looking at Steel. I knew he was there. To my right... I wanted so fucking badly to grab his hand, to cling to it, but I didn't.

Along the way, I'd learned that I couldn't rely on him, so I wasn't about to start doing that now.

"I'm not a whiner," Storm protested.

"Isn't that you whining now?" Link teased, grinning at me from the foot of the bed. His hands were tight around the railing, like he was fighting himself and almost losing—I knew he wanted to hug me, because he was an affectionate bear, and damn if I didn't want a hug too.

But I was aching. I had shit going into me and shit going out in more places than I wanted to think about, so moving my head was about all I could manage right now.

I grinned weakly at him, feeling much better when his eyes sparkled with delight at connecting with him.

"I'm not whining. I'm in buttfuck—"

"You know that isn't a nice way to talk about your new home, don't you?" Nyx mocked, his arms folded across his chest. He had a few more lines on his forehead, and since he was the brother that was the most cut off, it warmed me, even as it made me feel a bit weepy to see his concern etched straight onto his brow.

"Coshocton might be nice if you work for an accountant or something, but fuck, I ain't no corporate—" He groaned under his breath. "The only good thing is I'm Prez. The rest is just shit."

"Always knew you coveted my spot," Rex joked, but his grin was amused. "Should have kept an eye out for you sticking a knife in my back to grab it."

"If I'd known the only way I could be Prez was to move down here, you bet your ass I'd have stuck one in there. Maybe twisted it too."

"You're all fucking heart," Rex retorted.

Joy filled me at the teasing, and I sighed happily until Steel rumbled, "You need anything, baby doll?"

I gulped, and even though I wanted to look at him, I didn't.

Couldn't.

Biting my lip, I shook my head. "No, thank you."

The look in Link's eyes told me that he knew my game. There was a kind of resignation as well as frustration that came across in his knotted brow and grumpy smile, too, but I ignored both.

"You don't even need any water?" Nyx questioned.

I caught his eye, saw from the tic in his jaw that he was mad at me as well.

Fuck!

What was I supposed to do?

Crumble to Steel's feet in gratitude for his being here? When he'd been absent for close to two decades? And when I said absent, I meant it.

No, he hadn't gone anywhere, but neither had he been present.

I'd gone from having one of the most loving, tactile, affectionate people as a friend, to someone who made Casper look fucking tangible.

Where the others were concerned, they'd each let me down in ways they wouldn't even realize, but I could look at them without breaking down, because I loved them, but I hadn't been *in* love with them.

There was a massive difference.

Plus, the guy I'd been in love with had boned every chick in the Tristate area, *literally*, so I didn't owe him shit.

Because their disapproval rankled, I grunted, "No, thank you." Then I closed my eyes.

"You in pain?" Rex asked, and his calm voice told me he understood as much as the others, but he wasn't going to judge me. He was the best kind of friend, because he never judged. No matter the circumstances.

"A little."

"I'll get the doctor."

That was Steel.

Which had my eyes popping open when I heard his boots thumping on the floor as he left the room.

"You gonna give him shit—"

I scowled at Nyx. "I beg your pardon?"

He glowered back at me. "Been at your bedside since you took a turn for the worse, Stone."

"So? What do you want me to do? Suck his dick in thanks?" My jaw tensed. "He's got a half-dozen bitches back at the compound who can do that for him."

Rex heaved a sigh. "If you two are going to knock heads, then I can make him go home."

I shrugged. "Why shouldn't he be here? I'd be here for him too."

That had them gaping at me.

"What?" I groused.

"You're going to be mean to him but still want him to stay?" Link inquired warily.

"I'm not going to be mean, I'm not going to do all that much to him," I retorted, my tone a little wearier as I closed my eyes. "I just want to sleep."

"Think they'll argue?" Sin asked in a soft voice a few minutes later, telling me he thought I'd fallen back asleep.

"Probably," Rex said on a yawn. "Not sure that's a bad thing. This is probably what they both need. Not like he can go far anyway. Not yet. Still has stitches that need taking out, and that's even if I could get him to go home, which isn't going to happen." His cut rustled as he shrugged. "Anyway, he deserves this. Maybe if she'd stopped letting him get away with shit, they'd be over this already."

"Fuck you, Rex," I snarled, my eyes popping wide open and coming face to face with a smug smile that, if I had been more mobile, I'd have smacked his goddamn teeth in.

"That any way to speak to a lifelong friend?" he retorted, but his smile was still fucking smug.

"Yeah, it's exactly how I should speak to you. How dare you even suggest that I—"

"What? That you what? Put up with his shit when you should have just shaken him the fuck out of what he was going through? You never pushed back, babe. Ever."

"He's right, you didn't," Nyx agreed.

"No, you didn't."

I had the same answer from the circle of motherfuckers as they went around and around my past, delving into shit they could never understand.

Even Storm got in on it, for fuck's sake.

"You were talking about that time I beat the shit out of Candy before I woke up, weren't you?" When they all nodded, I ground out, "Know why I beat her up?"

Rex shrugged. "You never liked the snatch."

"No, the bunnies make my blood boil," I agreed. "But that wasn't why. I'm not violent by nature—"

Nyx snorted. "Say that to the woman whose throat you sliced."

I glared at him. "That was in self-defense."

Nyx shrugged. "Could have just whacked her over the head."

"I did. It dazed her, but she was still coming after me. I did what I had to do to survive."

"Plenty of things you could have done. You went for the carotid." He shrugged again. "Not saying I blame you. Wish you'd done more to the cunt after the shit she's put you through, but, Stone, if you think you're not violent, then you're the one who's deluded, not me."

My mouth tightened. "Since when were you all a bunch of shrinks? Pricks, sure, but shrinks? Nope." When they didn't answer me, I just glared at them some more. "I'm a survivor. That's what I do. I survived Steel, and I'll carry the fuck on. But the reason I beat the shit out of Candy is because I was back there to get over pneumonia. Remember? I came home to recuperate.

"Every fucking time she screwed him, she came to me. She'd fucking tell me every single piece of shit that I didn't need to know. They all knew he was mine and that I was his, but it never fucking stopped them," I ground out, and in my anger, I grabbed the remote to the bed and forced it upright.

As the bed surged, I winced as my body protested the abrupt movement, but I dealt with it as I'd dealt with every ounce of pain over the years.

I shoved a finger in Rex's face, and carried on, "They took joy out of it." I could feel my expression turning feral. "They reveled in shoving what they did in my face, when they did it, and how they did it. I never did shit because I thought it would encourage them, but it only encouraged them to continue. I took it. Because I take everything. I'm stupid, that's what I am. I just deal with it like I deal with all the shit you throw my way.

"But that day, enough was enough."

Rex ground his teeth for a second before he snapped, "What did she do?"

I stared at him, and I hated the tears that began to prick my eyes. A wave of fatigue hit me, and I sank back into the pillows, wondering why I was getting so mad over old news. "Christ, what does it matter?"

"It fucking matters," Rex snarled as he grabbed my hand and carefully bridged my fingers with his. "Tell me."

It took me longer than I'd like to get the words out. "She was his flavor of the month, and she fucked him outside the bunkhouse where I was sleeping. I know everywhere is free game on the compound, but she did it on purpose." Old, remembered pain had me grimacing. "You know what the fucker did?"

"What?" Link rasped.

"He was shit-faced. Wasted on whatever you dicks had been drinking, but when he came? He moaned my name."

Silence fell at that bombshell, and I clenched my jaw, growling, "That's why I beat the shit out of her the next day, because she had to know he'd do that. Because she wanted me to hear it. Wanted me to fucking know he still loved me, and that even though he did, he'd fuck her. Just like he'd fuck anything with a pussy because he's a slut.

"And when I'd done that, if you remember, you didn't see me around for a couple of years because that was the moment when I actually started to hate him. When I just left because it was easier." My mouth twisted into a snarl. "You say I didn't push back? I was fifteen years old when Mom died. When my world was torn apart. When he fucked off and abandoned me. When he repeatedly fucked everything in a skirt. I didn't push back because there was *nothing* to push back against. He didn't give a shit about me and carried on showing me that every single time he let me catch him fucking someone else.

"So I stopped giving a shit too. None of you backed me up. Not one of you. That was when I got the bro code. It finally stuck in my head, and I realized you were always going to back him over me." I tipped my chin up. "We're family. I know you'll kill for me, but you didn't give a shit that *he* was killing me from the inside out.

"I stopped giving a shit too, then. I moved on. From all of you, and though I stayed true to the club, I knew you never realized that I'd checked out. I made my own life, took my own path, and I got laid at long goddamn last. You know what? I discovered orgasms. They fucking rock," I snapped, completely pissed off. "I had boyfriends and lovers, and sure, I pined for him a little, but one thing you didn't see me doing was hovering around him like some whiny bitch. I got on with things, did my shit, and did it fucking well, all while boning whoever the fuck I wanted just like he did.

"You say I didn't push back, but I *did*. I lived my goddamn life exactly how I wanted to, and I'm a doctor. I'm fulfilling one of my dreams. I don't live *for* him, you fuckers. I live for me. And he's the one who's too fucking stupid to realize that he pushed away the one person who truly loved him, but that's on him. Not me. You get me?"

There was the sound of a throat clearing, and the men around the bed dispersed, revealing a doctor who was blushing at my words, and Steel, whose face looked like he'd seen a ghost.

My mouth pursed at the sight of him before I turned away and stared straight ahead.

"I'll need you gentlemen to leave the room," the doctor practically whispered.

"You heard her. Fuck off," I growled, backing her up, even though I knew they were only hovering around out of shock.

When they stormed out, their boots clomping like thunder, I

turned to the doctor the second the door was shut, and asked, "How many times did I almost die?"

Her brows arched. "I know you're a doctor, but that's the first thing you want to know?"

My smile was tight. "Figured it would calm you down. All that man meat in here is enough to muddle anyone's brain."

A laugh escaped her, but her smile was rueful as she muttered, "Yeah. Muddled is the word. Got everyone from the nurses who are newlywed to the grandmas drooling over them. The administration is having a seizure over it."

"I'll just bet," I replied dryly.

"My name's Dr. Sugden, but you can call me Mallory."

I nodded in thanks. "I'm Stone. But you knew that already."

"Sure did. Anyway, you really want to know the answer to that question?"

I shook my head. "No. I can feel each 'almost' like it's still happening."

"The drugs certainly put you through the wringer—"

The door burst open, making us both jolt, which had me wincing with pain because fuck, that hurt!

Steel was there, his face still pale, but there was a fire in his eyes I hadn't seen in years.

The doctor started to speak, but Steel glared at her, then stormed into the room, moving around so he was beside me and opposite her. Then he grabbed my hand, laced his fingers with mine, even when I tried to fight him, and ground out, "Carry on."

"The fuck are you doing here?" I spat, but it was his turn to ignore me.

"Wasn't there before. Was a dick before. You're right. Now I'm here. Now you can call me a dick but for a million different reasons." His smile was tight. "She's mine, Doc. You can say whatever shit you need while I'm in the room."

"This is most unorthodox—"

I stared at him, stared at a face that haunted me, that was turned away from me. Then I looked at our hands. Fingers knotted together. Skin to skin. Close, like we hadn't been in years.

Though everything inside me wanted to shove him away, I didn't.

She's mine, Doc.

I wanted that to be true. Dumb bitch that I was. I wanted that to be so fucking true it hurt. So even though he hadn't earned the right to call me his, I didn't shove him away. Instead, I clung to his hand, well aware that whatever the doctor was going to tell me about my condition wasn't going to be cheerful as I said, "Go ahead, Mallory. Hit me with it."

And together, for however long it took before he fucked off back to the compound and screwed anything in a skirt, we faced the storm.

THIRTY

STEEL

"RACHEL'S BEEN ON THE LINE."

My shoulders bunched up at that as I turned to stare out the window, tilted away from Stone, who was sleepily playing a game on her phone. "What'd she say?"

"DA says he's dropping the investigation against her. They agreed it was self-defense."

"Thank God for that," I muttered, staring down as a member of the hospital staff pushed a massive trash container across the asphalt lot toward an eighteen-wheeler.

My jaw worked as I thought about the repercussions of that, then I asked, "So, no more visits from the cops?"

She'd only seen them once, and I'd dealt with them every time they'd skunked around, monitoring if she was really unconscious or not.

Like we'd lie about that.

Fuckers.

I was tired of it though, which was why Rex had called Rachel in. Knowing our resident shark, she'd probably threatened them with a lawsuit over discrimination.

"Nope. No more visits," he confirmed.

"Good."

"The investigation into your shooting is still pending, by the way," he said with a snort.

I rolled my eyes at that—justice. Ha. "Someone's gotten a nice fat pay packet this week, then, huh?"

"Yeah. Can't see it going much further than the unsolved case room. But for Stone, at least, it's over."

"Shame it's only just fucking beginning here." I rubbed my eyes, trying not to think about her sobbing herself to sleep at night when she thought I wasn't listening. Sobbing from the fucking pain.

"How's our girl doing?" Rex questioned, his concern clear.

"Sleeps a lot." *Cries a lot.*

"She cut you some slack?"

"Well, she hasn't asked me to leave," I replied dryly. "So I'm thinking that's for the good."

"Yeah. You probably deserve it."

"I know." And I did.

I knew that.

I'd shoved so much distance between us, there was more space between me and her than the Atlantic Ocean, but she hadn't given me too much shit since two days ago when she'd told Rex and my brothers about what Candy had done.

Was I aware that I moaned her name when I climaxed?

Nope.

But it rammed shit home to me in a way that only confirmed what I'd been thinking since I'd woken up with my shoulder ripped to shreds.

It was our time.

What I hadn't expected to hear was her talking about her getting hers.

I knew it was hypocritical, but fuck...*I could whore around,* but she couldn't. It made every possessive bone in my body stand at attention.

I couldn't say that I'd ever really thought about her having boyfriends and shit, but now that I knew about it? It fucked with my head.

"You there, dickwad?"

I grunted. "Yeah. Thinking."

"I know that must hurt."

"Yeah, yeah, prick." I rubbed the back of my neck.

"You know what sucks?"

"What?"

"Only realized it when she said it, but we did back you up. Every time. Sure, I stayed close, kept in touch, and I know the others did too. Texts and shit. But I always took your side. *We* always did. Never even occurred to me that I was doing that, because that's what we do. Bros before hos. Only, Stone ain't a ho."

"No, she's not," I rasped, guilt sucker-punching me in the gut. "You think I don't feel like a shower of shit about that? That she lost all her family because of me?"

"Just proves that you gotta make it up to her. Don't fuck her around, Steel."

"I won't," I vowed grimly, then, because I couldn't talk about this anymore without wanting to smash my fist into the wall, I ground out, "I'll tell her about the investigation."

"She probably doesn't even remember being visited by the cops."

"Maybe not, but if she does, at least she knows what's what." I grunted. "I'll be in touch."

"Yeah. I wanna know about every update."

"Course. Bye, bro."

"Speak later, Steel."

When I twisted around to face her once more, it didn't surprise me to see she was watching me. She did that a lot.

When I thought about before, at the compound, all the various times she'd been around, I realized she'd never really looked at me before. She hadn't ignored me or avoided me, she'd just never *looked* at me.

Sometimes, when I caught her staring, I wondered if she was making up for lost time, and while in another time, another place, I might have teased her over it, watching her watch me was a relief.

Apparently, I hadn't pushed her away enough for her to be sickened by the sight of me.

Unless, of course, she was shoring up every detail on this fucking mug that was loathsome.

"Do you know why I fell in love with you?"

The question blindsided me.

My mouth worked until I finally regained muscular control and muttered, "No. Why?"

"Because you were sweet." Her lips curved. "You were so kind to me, letting me read your poems and things. While the others loved me and did shit for me, you were always there. Always. You made me feel safe, and you were the only one who made me feel that way." The soft smile disappeared. "It was different than how I felt with the others. I knew they'd get into shit for me, but start a war? No."

"They would," I told her, wanting her to know that, no matter what, she was one of us.

"They would now. But things are different now. Back then, I was a teenage girl. A bit of a pain." She grimaced. "A lot of it, probably. I wasn't in the MC, not for real, anyway, and I knew about the life but wasn't a part of it.

"I think that changed when I started living with Bear and Rene. I saw shit that I'd never normally see or hear, and it changed things."

"We always used to talk about business around you."

"Hearing it and understanding it are two separate things entirely. You know that."

I shrugged. "I guess."

"Now they'd go to war for me. I know that. I'm valuable to them—"

My ire sparked at that. "Shut the fuck up, Stone. Don't you dare carry on talking shit like that."

"I didn't mean it in a bad way." She shrugged. "I really didn't. You're valuable to the MC, aren't you? Rex is, Storm is. We all have an inherent value."

"Yeah, we do, but what they feel for you goes beyond that. You're one of us."

Her lips twisted, and a shyness appeared in her eyes that I hadn't seen in years. "Thank you for that."

I scowled. "You don't have to thank me for telling you the truth."

"Sure I do." She sighed and settled a little deeper into the covers. Her dark hair was longer than normal, having grown out some during her time here, and it tangled over the pillows. I was used to seeing a gleam that wasn't there at the moment. Like her health issues were draining it of life.

The notion put me on edge, especially after the doctor had explained about some of the issues she was going to be dealing with for the next few weeks.

"What did Rex have to say?" she asked when I didn't say anything, didn't even move, just looked at her. Taking in the sallow cheeks, the shadows under her eyes. Shit that shouldn't have been there but was.

Every sign of illness was something worth starting a war over, but there was no one to rage against.

"He told me that the DA isn't going to be pressing charges against you."

Stone winced. "Shit, I dodged a bullet, didn't I?"

"Better than I did," I countered ruefully, reaching up and gently motioning to my shoulder.

"What's the prognosis?" she queried in doctor mode.

"It's okay. Tore through muscle, luckily, not bone."

"Did some damage or they wouldn't have put you under."

I waved a hand. "I'm made of strong stuff."

Her lips pursed. "You know I read your charts, don't you?"

I hissed under my breath. "When?"

"The night you were brought in. Before this all started." She tipped her head to the side. "You'll need rehab."

"Fuck that," I groused.

"Then you'll never regain full mobility—" When I just grunted, she shrugged. "You could work on the exercises while you're here with me. You've got nothing better to do."

I sniffed. "Says you. I have plenty of work." I pointed to my laptop. "Plenty."

"Yeah? Well, you might as well give the nurses a show. They walk past the window often enough to see you."

Was I a jerk if I wanted her to be jealous?

Probably.

She didn't sound it though, just weary. Like she couldn't be bothered to argue with me, and I suddenly wanted that.

I was tired of our status quo. I wanted her to be annoyed. I wanted her to give a shit again.

"I'll give you a show," I retorted. "No other bitch."

She huffed. "That makes a change."

I shrugged, taking that on the chin with barely a wince. "That was then."

"And this is now? What changed?"

"Both of us almost died."

Her mouth tightened. "Can't argue with that. Not sure if that means—" Her cell buzzed and she grinned, her face lighting up as she answered, "Raina! It's so good to hear from you. I've been dying to find out what's going on there. Have the cops been crawling all over the place?"

As she started a discussion about the police inquiries into Annie Young's murder spree at the hospital, I'd admit I was pissed at the interruption, but also, I was glad. She'd had a dozen phone calls since she'd sent a text to her friends yesterday, one that explained how she was doing and what was going down, and each call just confirmed exactly what she'd said to the guys.

She had moved on.

So why was I still stuck in the past?

Why was I still fucking any passing woman that moved just to get her out of my head?

I grabbed my laptop and switched it on to give her some semblance of privacy in that I wasn't just listening to her conversation, but it was hard to focus. I wanted to listen. Wanted to know about everything and everyone in her life.

A life I should have been a part of.

A life that I'd torn myself out of.

That I'd done it to protect her was a given, but it was getting harder and harder to figure out what exactly that was.

It had made sense at the time. Not so much anymore.

Sure, I'd kept tabs on her, but apparently, they hadn't been good enough for me to see the men she was boning.

As I stared at the screen, staring at a jumble of figures that I needed to piece together for Mav so he could work on the books, I ignored the tension headache that was growing like a tornado in my mind.

She had a life.

My life was her.

Why was I only just seeing that now?

THIRTY-ONE

STONE

WHEN I PEERED at the IV site on my hand, I felt like shit had come full circle.

"It's infected," I told the nurse, thinking back to Harriet and that morning when my entire world had changed.

She smiled at me. "It's under control."

It was hard not to micromanage. These guys knew their jobs, who was I to say that I knew better?

But I'd told them two days ago it was getting infected, and I knew they'd only started me on a course of antibiotics this morning.

When she'd finished poking and prodding me, I turned to see Steel was still snoozing in the chair. He'd pulled it over to the corner so that it was no longer always at my bedside, and it was amazing how that little pocket of space did wonders for the pair of us.

That was his part of the room, and this was mine. When he was over there, he usually slept or worked and we didn't talk. When he slept, I let him rest because though he had a hotel room, he didn't use it often.

I was glad for that.

I'd thought he'd have left for West Orange by now, figured he'd have left me on my own and would have stopped terrorizing the doctors and nurses when they worked through yet another diagnosis that would turn out to be a misdiagnosis.

But he hadn't.

He'd stayed. In fact, he stayed to the point of stinking, and only when he was sick of his own smell did he head to his hotel room and shower. Even then, he'd reappear a few hours later. He wouldn't look rested, but I knew he'd take a nap in a full-size bed, and that he'd head out for some food that wasn't in cartons.

Indy and the rest of the fam visited daily, bringing us both food, but I knew he had to be sick of eating takeout. Often, he'd bring me something back. Something that wasn't chicken wings or burgers—I mean, I loved McDonalds, but there was only so much I could stomach, and with my current health issues, they weren't the best for me. So the stuff he brought back were dishes he knew I loved. Casserole and spaghetti marinara.

Drool alert.

The hospital food was bleugh, as usual, so what he brought back was always appreciated. More than that, though, I was just glad he got some rest. Even as I was grateful he didn't leave me alone for long.

I was struggling.

I'd admit it.

I didn't want to get used to him being here, because I knew he'd leave me alone again when this was over, but it was harder and harder not to see the Steel I'd once known.

He was strong, caring. Affectionate. *Interested.* He listened to me. He didn't look through me anymore. He wanted to help. Wanted to scream when I was in pain, and wanted to fight for me when I was crying because I hurt so badly and the doctors wouldn't listen.

He was my rough and ready knight in shining armor when I'd long since dropped him from that role.

I bit my lip at the thought, watching him shuffle in his chair as my phone rang. He didn't wake up, but then I didn't let it ring long enough.

I needed the distraction.

"Harry, hi!" I said softly, warmly. Harry was an ex who'd almost gotten through my wall of indifference.

The only thing that had stopped things from progressing was when he'd transferred to the West Coast after a position in a cardiology unit opened up, one that would have him overseeing the department.

"How are you doing, Stone?" Harry asked, his tone sincere, his concern clear.

"Rough. They're not fucking listening to me. I swear, once this shit is done, and I'm back on the rounds, I'm going to make sure I listen to patients."

He snorted. "Like you didn't already? You've always been conscientious."

"Well, I need to be more. I told them two days ago my IV site was getting infected. They only gave me antibiotics today."

"You don't know every aspect of your treatment, do you?"

"No. But still, doesn't take a damn genius."

"What if they were waiting to see a change in your blood report?"

I heaved a sigh. "Don't be rational."

"Or logical, hmm?" He laughed. "Okay, I agree. They're bastards. Absolute bastards. Want me to come and visit and knock heads?"

I grinned. "You'd take the red-eye flight for little old me?"

"Nothing little or old about you, Stone," he said dryly, making my nose crinkle.

"Thanks, I think." I rolled my eyes. "You always were a charmer."

"My British charm at play."

"You're about as British as I'm French."

He snorted. "Third gen, baby."

"Exactly," I told him smugly. "My grandma was French. At least I speak it."

"I speak English. At least, I think I do."

I scoffed, "Only because you didn't have to learn it. If anything, I'm more French than you're a Brit."

"I had one of those bloodwork tests done, you know the DNA tests? Where you find out your heritage?"

"What did yours tell you?"

"That I have Asian descent."

I had to laugh because Harry was a red head with bright green eyes. "Did your granddad get down and dirty with one of the locals when he was stationed overseas?"

"Only if they had Asian ladies in France, and I don't think immigration was as widespread back then."

"Never say never." I grinned. "How are things, anyway?"

"Since the last time I called?" He hummed. "I guess…I figured out I miss you."

My lips curved into a soft smile. "I miss you too."

"We always got on well together, didn't we?"

"Yeah," I admitted. "We did."

"So, what are you wearing?"

I burst out laughing, just like he'd intended. "I look really sexy right now," I teased. "I'm wearing a light gray backless number. I'm ready to head out for a party—"

"Who the fuck are you talking to?"

I jerked in surprise at Steel's angry snarl, then glowering at him, muttered, "Harry, I'd better go."

"Who was that I heard?" he asked roughly.

I heaved a sigh. "No one."

"I'm not no fucking one," Steel growled.

"Doesn't sound like it," Harry grumbled. "Are you okay?"

"Yeah, of course. It's just..." I pursed my lips. *It was just, what?* "A friend. He's watching over me while I'm in the hospital."

"While you're in the ICU?"

I cleared my throat. "I had to pull some favors."

"To breach basic rules of the ward? Those are more than some rules."

I didn't want to know who Rex had bribed to make it happen, just was glad he had.

"I guess." I sighed. "I'll talk to you later, Harry. Thanks for calling."

When I cut the call after his farewell, I glared at Steel. "What the hell is your problem?"

"You were going to talk dirty to someone while I was in the fucking room?" he snapped, making me aware of just how big he was. His shoulders were bunched up, his biceps like rocks, and he was *throbbing* with outrage.

I narrowed my eyes at him. "If I wanted to, I could. Just like that time you fucked Hattie while I was in the bar."

His nostrils flared, but he took a shaky step back.

"Or how about the time you screwed Erin on the pool table while I was there, or the fuck against the wall I caught with JoJo... or how about—"

"Enough," he snapped, his face drawn.

"Yeah, I think so too." I narrowed my eyes at him. "Harry and I were joking around. That's what we do when things get awkward."

"Awkward?" He scowled at me. "What kind of awkward?"

"He said he missed me." I jerked my chin up. "We were almost dating when he got a new position in California."

That had him gulping.

He raised a hand, and I was astonished to see that it was almost shaking. "I don't need to know this."

Maybe he didn't, maybe he did. I just knew I hadn't seen Steel this shaken since—

Fuck.

Since that first and only kiss. When I'd found him coming out of Mom's room, looking like he was going through a heart attack.

When he stormed out ten seconds later, I just watched him go, unsure what had happened but not altogether sad about it.

I'd had a life. One that went by without him. I'd been happy. I had men friends. I was an adult.

Seemed like Steel was the one who was forgetting all those things, and he'd just had the reminder he needed.

Of course, the second he was gone, I stared around the empty room and heaved a sigh.

He took up so much space that I instantly felt alone. My lungs started to burn when I realized just how alone I was, and the walls felt like they were closing in on me.

No, this wasn't the first time he'd left, but it was the first time he'd gone in anger.

Would he—

He'd come back, wouldn't he?

Shit, why had I riled him up? Made him angry?

Why—

I heard the thundering of boots once more and was stunned when he made a reappearance. His face was still white, his jaw like stone, but his head was wet. Like he'd splashed water on his face.

He sat back down in his chair, pulled his laptop onto his knee, and began working.

Neither of us said a word. Not for a good six hours. He worked, I watched him, letting my breath regulate, my panic die down—what the hell had that been about?—until I recognized he wasn't going to leave again and that I didn't have to watch him at all times to know he was staying put.

That he hadn't gone mattered.

That he'd come back meant more to me than he'd ever know.

And that I was coming to depend on him, his presence, was a fact I could no longer ignore. But it was something to worry about at another time, another place. For right now, I was just glad he was here.

THIRTY-TWO
STEEL

IT WAS hard to accept that I was jealous.

I wasn't sure of what though.

Of the men she'd fucked? Of the kisses they'd shared? Of the secrets they had together? Of the lives they'd had as a pair?

How many had she fucked? How many kisses, secrets? How had they been together?

Harry.

That was his name.

Fucking Harry.

I wanted to kill him, throttle him.

How dare he kiss her?

How dare he—

Of course, that was when I knew I was being irrational. But I was often irrational around her, and I recognized that she was the same around me. From her never arguing with me, suddenly things had shifted.

We bickered. A lot.

Fought. A lot.

And we both simmered down, watching each other warily, wondering what the other was thinking but not asking.

Each time, I'd storm off and head to the bathroom to splash my face, to calm down.

Each time I returned, she'd watch me with big eyes, registering the whole, hard truth.

No matter how many times she pissed me off—and she did that a lot—I'd come back.

I was going to be a fucking boomerang.

Heaving a sigh as I stared at my face in the mirror, at the tired lines under my eyes and the weariness that made me look gray, I rubbed a hand over it to slough off the excess water, and then grabbed a paper towel.

When I was dry, I headed out of the bathroom and back down the hall to her room. I wasn't surprised when she wasn't alone. It was visiting hours, but the people there weren't anyone I knew.

She'd had a lot of guests visiting her. From coworkers to old colleagues and friends from med school. Each new face was a reminder of how much I'd missed out on, and I didn't appreciate the goddamn prompt.

Seeing the bunch of dudes sitting on her bed, guys that weren't my brothers, immediately got my back up.

I'd been in the bathroom for twenty minutes. Each one had been used to cool off. To calm down. Whenever she threw the shit I'd done in my face, it always sparked up into an inferno, and we always ended up snarling at each other.

Once, I'd almost gotten kicked out over an argument, so we always made sure to argue in whispers.

Truth was, much as I wished we didn't argue so fucking much, I knew what it meant.

These angry words were healing words.

Each time she pulled off a scab, exposed it to the air, it allowed it to heal without bitterness infecting it.

Seemed like I'd done a lot of shit in my life, shit I couldn't fucking remember anymore.

I nodded at the guys, received some nods in return, but I ignored her and went over to my laptop. She didn't mention me to them, and though I sensed their curious looks, they didn't ask.

They shot the breeze with her, talking about people I didn't know, about things I didn't understand. Each reference was a smack in the face I needed to get over, and I did.

Barely.

Until they started to leave. Three of the four guys just waved at her, told her they'd visit again soon.

The fourth?

Leaned down and kissed her.

Kissed her.

In front of me.

Sure, my head was turned to the side and I had my boots on the wall as I faced the window, but I saw everything.

The fucking kiss, the way he touched his lips to her temple. The soft whisper in her ear, the way she smiled at him with affection in her eyes.

Each one was a death knell.

For him.

Whoever the fuck he was.

But I let him go and stayed silent until the door was closed, then she threw gas on the fire. "Aren't you going to say something?"

I could hear the taunt in her voice, and fuck me, she was working up to getting her ass spanked. I could almost imagine the way her butt would bounce with how hard I paddled it, but I cracked my knuckles instead.

If anyone had ever needed to be spanked, it was her.

Sweet fuck.

Because the only shit I could say was going to cause another argument, I stayed silent. I heard her huff, but I ignored it.

Then, when she was playing a game—I knew because she kept cursing it out—I rasped, "You kiss another man again, and I'll gut him."

She fell silent. "You have no right to say that," she said eventually.

I cut her a look. "I have every fucking right. And you know it."

Her jaw tensed, but though she looked mutinous, I saw something she didn't.

Hope.

It made her eyes gleam.

And that made the itch in my palm lessen some.

Where there was hope, there was a promise for more, and that was something I could handle.

I just needed to prove to her that I wasn't the dumbass she'd come to know. I was the same guy she'd fallen in love with all those years ago.

She was bitter, even a little twisted over what had gone down during those years, but I could deal with that.

They'd forged a woman who was worthy of being my Old Lady. Who could deal with any of the shit the life threw at her, and fuck knew, there was plenty of that.

Before, she was so young, she wouldn't have been ready. Even with as much as she knew about our world, she didn't know it all—the bad or the ugly, because there was barely any good. But after a lifetime without me in it, stitching up people who'd been torn apart from GSWs to car accidents, I knew she could handle anything.

Everything.

And she'd have to.

Because once she was better, I was making her mine.

She could hiss and kick at me, bitch about it, but that wouldn't change the unrelenting, undeniable, tireless truth.

She was my woman.

My future.

I just needed to make her realize that.

And, five days later, when the same guy who'd kissed her before visited again, she didn't let him kiss her. I felt like that was a huge leap forward.

Because maybe, at last, she was starting to see the lay of the land.

THIRTY-THREE

STONE

THREE WEEKS LATER

I WAS GRUMPY, grouchy, cranky, and every other -y word that could describe—no, that could *define* just how pissed off I was.

Short-tempered wasn't the word.

I was itchy too. My stomach was on the mend, the surgical sites having healed and, in doing so, were itching up a storm, even though they weren't infected, just getting fucking better.

Nothing hurt as bad as it once did, but I was still stiff and sore, and the last thing I wanted was to be driving in a cage today of all days.

I wriggled my shoulders, well aware that I was in a mood and that only one person could handle me like this—Indy.

Only, Indy wasn't here. She was at my new apartment in West Orange, setting shit up for me so that when I got home, I could essentially curl up in bed and do shit until I was in a better frame of mind.

I had another six weeks to lie around and do nothing, and that was way too much in my opinion.

I wasn't made for stillness, and the only consolation was the fact that, at last, I was getting better, and the only other time I'd tried to push it in the hospital, I'd almost passed out from the acute agony it had caused when I'd pulled a muscle in my torn up stomach.

The memory alone was enough to make me crabbier, and I glowered at nothing, fuck, I glowered at how high the sun was and how it glinted off cars' bodywork, because yeah, that was enough to piss me off.

"What the hell are you huffing about now?"

And here was the crux of my biggest problem.

Steel.

I ground my teeth at his question, then huffed again as I turned my face to the window.

The bastard was still here, hadn't gone anywhere through the long weeks at the hospital, and here I was, wondering when the other shoe would drop, when he'd fuck off like he always did, because now that I was out, the rules of the game had changed.

Now I was on my way to my new home, he'd probably leave me alone again, alone after months in his company, and I just couldn't deal with that right now.

And my huffing? Because I was scared.

Terrified.

Not of being by myself, but of being *without him.*

I sucked in a breath, released it, tried not to be angry with him for being who he was, even though that was damn hard, and then I bit off, "I'm in pain, all right?"

I wasn't lying, because I was. I was more than in pain. I was uncomfortable, felt like a thousand mosquitos had bitten my stomach, and I wasn't that enamored about being in the truck for an hour in busy traffic.

I knew he'd planned it so that we were supposed to be driving around during a non-rush hour period, but a pile up had fucked us in the butt, and here we were, in a truck, stuck together, when I both wanted to be stuck with him forever, all while being unsure if I could handle it when we were torn apart.

Trust, that was what it boiled down to.

I could love the man, I could want him with enough of a fever that it distracted me from my body's woes, but trust him?

Nope.

I didn't have that, and I was finding it interesting that trust outran love. Before I woke up, he'd been there for three weeks. Watching over me. Then, for five weeks, he'd been at my side.

For five weeks, he'd been there when the doctors talked shop with me as I learned the repercussions of the strange doses of drugs Annie Young had used on me—a lesser form of the poison she'd used to kill her patients, a clever concoction of OTC medicine as well as some drugs used in cancer treatment so that, if an autopsy did go down, nothing appeared to be totally irregular—and as I went through the aftercare of surgery that kept throwing complications my way. Whether it was fever or infections, if it could go wrong, it had.

But today, I was better than I'd been yesterday, and the day before that, and I was well enough to go home.

I just wasn't sure if I wanted him or Indy sitting here, because though I wanted him to be driving me there, though I wanted us to be going into a house we both shared and for him to be there all the rest of my fucking natural life, I didn't think he would.

And that was why I was grouchy.

Why I was huffing.

Because I got the feeling that as soon as I was home, wherever home fucking was—Indy had just told me she'd found me a nice place close to the hospital—he'd be out of the picture, back to the clubhouse, and I felt sure it would be like nothing had changed.

My throat thickened with tears at just the thought. I wanted to cling on to him, wanted to glue myself to him and beg him not to leave me, but I had some self-respect. Something that was forged in lessons that I'd learned from being around so many bikers.

A woman who had no self-respect was a woman to be used and abused.

That was why I was a bitch to him. That was why I didn't let him get away with shit.

I wanted to. I fucking wanted that so badly. I wanted to just sink into him and allow myself to relax, not to give him shit, just for us to be at peace together, but I knew how he'd take that.

He'd see it as a weakness, and while I was pathetically weak where he was concerned, he'd never know just how rotten I was to the core because of my love for him.

It had never felt like that before, but I was different now. I was ill, coming off of months in a hospital bed, and the Stone of before was not the Stone of now.

My time in my hospital room had changed me in ways I was only just starting to see, and I wasn't sure if I'd ever return to normal. Sure, when I was back on my feet, I felt certain there'd be an improvement, but equally, an improvement wasn't how I'd been before, was it? Even if I'd been in denial, because that didn't take into account the lifestyle changes I'd need to make to ensure my heart condition didn't flare up or that my stomach ulcers didn't give me crap.

The upcoming days, the stress and strain, the physical and the emotional pain, all of it had me feeling the tears dampening the upper curves of my cheeks, and I was grateful for the sunglasses I wore, just because they covered them up.

We had NOFX playing on repeat, one of my favorite CDs, and I even had a paper bag of MickyDs that he'd grabbed for me which I was picking at. I had a favorite pillow from home, a blanket that I knew Indy had to have given him because he wouldn't know the difference between a blanket and a comforter, and even though he'd done everything he could for me, none of it would make up for him leaving me when we got to my new place.

So I stayed sullen and silent and probably gave him every excuse in the book to make him be grateful he could fuck off to the clubhouse and get some pussy at long last.

The journey took place in that grim silence for the entirety of the drive back to West Orange. I half expected him to dump me there and then, but he didn't. He carried on driving past the area where the hospital was located, where I thought I was staying, and we rolled on up the large hill to where the compound was situated.

My brows rose with each mile we took, and when we made it to the gates, which opened instantly, and we drove on through, I wasn't sure what to expect.

The compound was quiet. Deadly so. It was weird, in fact, because I was used to it being busy, rippling with life and energy from so many people living together, but it wasn't like that today.

He didn't stop driving until he drove over to one of the bunkhouses that was farthest away from the clubhouse and pulled up outside.

"Just so you know," he said softly, a low threat in his voice that shouldn't have made my aching body feverish but totally did anyway, "if you pull this attitude on me again when you're better, I'll spank you until you're sweet again, and then I'll fuck you until you're purring."

My heart skipped a beat with hope. *Hope.* Dangerous, toxic hope.

He rolled his shades down his nose, stared at me pointedly, and said, "Now, you gonna stop being as sour as that fucking cat of yours?"

I gaped at him over that, even as excitement flushed through me. "Mrs. Biggins is not sour!"

He snorted. "Trust you to bitch about that, but not the idea of being spanked."

I shrugged. "If I need a spanking, then I need a spanking."

He hissed, his head jerking to the side like I'd slapped him. His response stunned me, but what he said next?

Floored me.

"You can't say shit like that, baby doll, when you ain't in fighting form."

He reached over, cupped my chin, and pinched the tip between his forefinger and thumb. The move knocked my shades a little, and with his free hand, he reached over and tugged them up so they were lodged in my hair, which made me squint because it was really bright out, and after so long at the hospital, I wasn't used to it.

However, when he let out another hiss, and his thumb traced over my cheeks, I knew he saw them.

Tear tracks.

They'd probably dried and messed up the minimal mascara Indy had insisted I wear before she'd left my hospital room this morning to come back here and help set up the place for me.

It was clear to see why now.

If I was staying in one of the bunkhouses, they hadn't been renovated since the sixties.

Not that I was about to complain.

Maybe if I was here, and with his words still buzzing in my ears, he wouldn't forget about me. He'd come and visit, maybe?

I bit my lip at the thought, and he muttered, "Why you crying, baby doll? You hurting that much?"

I shook my head. "No."

I was honest about that, because I couldn't lie about pain and the management that came with it.

Sure, I'd lie to him about a hell of a lot of stuff, but not that.

A girl had to have principles, didn't she?

He rustled around in the paper bag that my burger and fries had come in, grabbed a napkin, and tugged it over my still sweating

Coke. He wiped the now wet tissue over my cheeks, cleaning me up some, the gesture both unexpected and somehow charming, even if I probably stank of McDonalds' fries.

I mean, in all honesty, was there a better scent in all the known universe?

I bit my lip as he cleaned me up, then, as he started to move back, I caught his hand, my fingers sliding around his wrist as I held him there.

"Do you mean it?"

"Do I mean what?" he asked, his brow puckering as he stared at me.

"About the spanking?"

He laughed. "Baby doll, I ain't never gonna lie to you about spanking."

That wasn't the answer I wanted to hear, but it gave me an idea.

Fuck, if being spanked was all it took for him to stick around, I'd get spanked. It was my favorite thing anyway, and I'd had only one boyfriend who ever enjoyed doing that. Everyone else just thought I was weird.

Of course, I should have invited them to an orgy at the clubhouse, because if they thought spanking was kinky, they'd have had their eyes opened for real.

Inwardly, I wanted to laugh, but I didn't. Hope fluttered inside me, and that was a dangerous ass thing, but hell, I'd been in danger ever since that bitch had done what she had to me. Why shouldn't I up things a notch and reclaim the man who should have always been mine in the process?

When he helped me out of the truck, I muttered, "Don't think I've ever seen you riding in a cage before."

He snickered, then made me squeal when, in a smooth move, he bent down and scooped me up into his arms so he was carrying me.

Call me a sucker, and I'd allow it—just this once—but it made my heart melt. Ugh, it did more than that! It was totally *An Officer and a Gentleman* moment. Where Richard Gere had swooped in and swept Debra Winger out of her shitty job at a factory and taken her to another life... I wasn't a romantic, not really, but who the hell didn't love that film when they were in possession of a pair of ovaries?

I sighed inwardly as he carried me to the door. I didn't worry about his back or his shoulder because I'd lost a lot of weight in the hospital, and to be honest, I was looking forward to getting my curves back.

Even if it was handy when it came time to being hauled around by a strong, handsome man who I just happened to fucking love.

The door opened on a squeal, and I smiled when I saw Indy bouncing around, more effusive than I'd seen her since she was a kid. Behind her, the place had been completely renovated, but even as I noticed that, I also saw that the small, self-contained 'apartment' was full of people.

I didn't even have it in me to moan, because I was tired and ready for bed again, but the sight of all the people I loved?

Jesus.

It hit me square in the feels.

My heart in my throat, I grinned, wide and happy, for the first time feeling like maybe this was reality.

I'd gone from being so alone, inhabiting a tiny apartment in Manhattan, barely connecting with anyone from my old life, to suddenly being here.

With everyone who mattered.

With men I loved like brothers, a woman who was my sister, and in the arms of a guy who should be my Old Man by now but wasn't.

I guessed now that I was here, I could admit I was happy to be on the compound, and that the idea of being tucked away in an apartment in West Orange had been another reason for my misery.

I was tired of being lonely. I loved Mrs. Biggins, but she wasn't a replacement for all the people I'd left behind when Steel had broken my heart.

I'd missed them all, and I missed Storm, too, who was in fucking Ohio of all places, even though he should be here, welcoming me back. I didn't doubt there'd be a strong reason. Still, I figured I couldn't sulk when all my fam, apart from him and Keira, was cramped into my new place, just for me, just to welcome me home.

I felt like my face was gonna crack with how happy I was.

Seriously, I felt so ecstatic that it was such a stark contrast to how miserable I'd been on the ride over.

Amazing what this place, the people, and the thought of a spanking would do for a girl.

I wasn't sure in which order those had cheered me up, but hey, I didn't care. I'd take it.

And all the while, Steel carried me.

He took me through the bunkhouse, letting me greet people in his arms, as he showed me around the new layout which, if I remembered from before, had been on two levels, a low level, granted, but in my current state, that was too much.

The kitchen and dining room led into a small living room that had an L-seater couch long enough for me to lie on in front of a wide TV. Then at the back, there was a bedroom and a large bathroom, which was actually one of those washrooms where the shower head was in the center of the ceiling and everything just got wet through.

Impractical for real life, but for me, now? Very helpful, especially since I could sit on a chair and get washed up. There was even one of those—the white and silver seats that would let me have some independence—in the bathroom.

The hard thing about being a doctor was knowing exactly what I had to go through to heal. I'd told people the rules of aftercare a thousand times, and still, it had hit me hard when I'd broken the rules myself. But I was back on the bandwagon, making sure I was following every protocol, because I didn't want to be stuck on my ass, in bed, for much longer.

I wanted nothing more than to finish up my education and finally be out on the open road as a practicing physician. I couldn't do that if I kept pushing myself, and now that I was here? Home? I didn't have the random things to worry about that I ordinarily would.

When you lived on the compound, it was a free meal ticket. Well, sort of. In my position, it would be. I didn't have to worry about rent or bills, food or anything like that.

If I'd come home, without being injured, I'd have to pull my weight, and that was only fair, but now? I could get the R and R I needed with no anxiety over covering rent and things like that.

Pride would have stopped me from asking the MC for help if I'd been staying in West Orange, but they weren't letting me be prideful. Which, all told, was pretty smart.

They knew me, and they were taking away my objections.

When I'd been shown around, Steel took me over to the sofa, and he slid me down onto it. Out of nowhere, Mrs. Biggins sprang up, fangs bared, her mottled tortoise shell fur on edge, and I laughed because she always reacted like that to Steel, and he always muttered under his breath, "Fucking pussy."

It was like their thing, and I loved it, even if its origins were actually kind of sad.

Mrs. Biggins had learned as a kitten that Steel always hurt me, so she was defending me, and that was just one of the reasons I loved her miserable self.

When I curled up on the sofa, Indy pressed the blanket to my knees, and Mrs. Biggins kneaded my lap for a little while, somehow aware that I was hurting, knowing which parts to avoid, all while staying close to me and not leaving my side.

Someone else who didn't?

Steel.

He got up to use the bathroom once, and when he returned, he came back with juice for me, a container of meds, and some open-faced sandwiches that Giulia had made and were the bomb.com.

I took the meds with the juice, ate the sandwich, ate half of his too, and then settled with his arm over my shoulder, Indy by my feet, sitting on the L of the sofa as we just shot the shit.

I didn't say much, because I didn't have the energy to get involved. Just doing what I'd done today had taken it out of me, but the others spoke, and it reminded me of old times.

Made me think of when I was younger and things had been less complicated.

I wanted those days back again, I wanted Steel always at my side like he'd been before.

I'd known where things were heading, even if I hadn't felt sure about it.

Steel was always unpredictable, but the way he'd looked at me back then was impossible for even naïve me to misunderstand. Until it had seemed like I misunderstood everything.

I hadn't misread things, I just knew that something had changed that first night when we'd kissed. I'd always known Momma had said something to him, something that had set him off, but I'd never asked him what.

Maybe now was the time to ask him, to talk about what had changed things between us.

Well, maybe not right now.

With the women slowly drifting away as the hours passed, the guys were talking about club business—something else that hadn't changed. They'd always talked in front of me, even though they shouldn't have.

I knew that was because Indy had popped off to open the tattoo studio, and Giulia had gone back to the clubhouse to make some clubwhores' lives miserable.

Man, I was so beyond down for that, it was unreal.

I couldn't wait to watch her make them scrub the floors and shit. Talk about a popcorn-worthy event.

So it was just me and the guys—and Mrs. Biggins, of course—and I was content to listen to them speak of someone called Lancaster who was, apparently, being tortured in the Fridge, and to learn that Granger, the cop who'd been a prick to me back in the hospital, was now sporting a cast and his jaw had been wired shut after a 'mugging' that had gone wrong.

If anything, words that should have given me nightmares soothed me to the point of sleep, and when I relaxed into Steel and finally allowed myself to rest, I did so praying that when I woke up, he was there.

THIRTY-FOUR

BEAR
BEFORE

I WATCHED her rub cream into her face, smoothing the different serums and shit into her skin, with a fascination that wasn't feigned.

Rene always transfixed me. It was why my various mistakes along the way perplexed me. Why I let myself betray her, I'd never know. Not when just watching her at the end of the night was transfixing.

"What are you looking at?" she teased, her lips quirking because she knew.

She always knew.

A love like this was hard to find. I was lucky that I'd found mine, and even luckier that she forgave me for being a dumb fuck.

"You're beautiful," I told her softly, watching as she twisted around, eyes gleaming as she did so.

"Thank you," she replied primly, but there was a flush to her cheeks that didn't surprise me.

Twenty-four years, and that blush still got to me.

Twenty-four years, a kid, one lost kid, and a lifetime of mistakes, and she was still the only person who got me.

She climbed onto the bed, straddling my hips. I put my hands there, keeping her in place as she carried on smoothing the cream into her skin, and I watched her, now with a perfect view, feeling all the stress of the moment wash away as she went about her nightly routine.

My Old Lady was like no other. Capable of calm amid an ocean of stress... I wished I had that ability.

"What are you thinking?" she asked, her skin gleaming now she'd finished, before she began to unravel her hair from the strange wrap she wore it in after her evening shower, and started to braid it.

"I'm thinking that Stone's a good girl." And it was a damn shame she was in the hospital tonight... I'd need to set her on the straight and narrow, which wasn't easy, considering my path was anything but that.

But the cries for help had to stop. Two more overdoses were two too many, and now she'd lost her college scholarship because her grades had started suffering. It was time for me to meddle, even if, rightly, it wasn't my place... I was gonna make it my goddamn place. Someone had to take the girl in hand. She had too much potential to just let things go to waste.

Over my dead body would she be a clubwhore like her momma. I knew Rex felt the same way too...

Her brows rose at my pensiveness. "You gonna start matchmaking?"

My lips curved. "Stop knowing me so well, girl."

"After twenty-four years? If I didn't know you well by now, then there'd be no hope for either of us."

"True." I gnawed on my bottom lip. "Thought I knew Steel better."

"He's going through a phase," she soothed.

"He's hurting the girl." I shook my head. "Never thought I'd see that come to pass."

"No. He's always been ga-ga over her. But before you get your hopes up, Rex isn't going to fall for her. She's a sister to him. You know that." She leaned down, hair now braided, and pressed her lips to mine. "She's Steel's, and he's Rachel's."

My nose crinkled at that. "Rachel and him will eat each other alive."

"Ain't that part of the fun?"

I grinned as I reached down and grabbed her ass. "That's part of it, sure. But what about the peace at night? Just watching your woman smooth cream on her face and feeling like all is right with the world, huh?"

"They'll find their balance," she told me softly, reaching over and cupping my chin, smoothing her greasy fingers over my skin. "They all will."

"They will if I set them on the right path."

My grumble had her laughing. "You're not Solomon."

"Feels like it, some days anyway."

She tapped her thumb against the divot in my chin. "You took care of Lana Jane, didn't you?"

I crinkled my nose. "Bet your sweet ass I did."

"You did the right thing. Stone will be okay once she's here with us. We can pick her up tomorrow, get her settled in."

"Thank you, sweetheart."

Rene shrugged, downplaying her generosity like she always did. My woman, the fucking saint. God love her. "My pleasure. She's a good girl, and with a mother like she had, she needs all the help she can get."

"I want her and Steel together."

"Why?"

"Because he's a good kid too, and she's the best. She's what he'll need. But if he's gonna fuck it up, I'd like her for Rex. Can you imagine her as the Prez's Old Lady?" I whistled under my breath. "They'd be ferocious together."

"Stop plotting people's lives for them," she chided, but her lips came to mine to soften the blow of her reprimand. "I know you like to think of the world as one big giant game of chess, but I can tell you now, our boy ain't gonna be happy unless Rachel is his queen.

"As for Steel? Finding out that evil bastard was his father was bound to mess with him. I told you you should have told him when Kevin died. Where did your Grand Master brain go then, huh?"

I tapped her on the tush. "It's not sexy to say 'I told you so.'"

"Shame I know all your weaknesses then, isn't it?" she teased, her hand sliding down between us to grab my dick.

I let her, even as I rasped, "Rene?"

"Yep?"

"I love you, you know that?"

Her eyes softened. "I do."

"I'm sorry."

She shook her head. "I forgave you."

"Won't forgive myself."

"Good." She shrugged. "Means you won't do it again."

And I wouldn't.

Because it had taken me too fucking long to realize that without my Old Lady riding bitch on my bike, there was no freedom to be found in this life.

No freedom whatsoever.

And for the kids who were like my own flesh and blood, I wanted the same for them. Freedom and love.

Shame none of them were making it easy on me by accepting what anyone with eyes could see.

THIRTY-FIVE

STONE
TODAY

HE WASN'T there when I woke up.

That was my first thought.

The next was misery, then came heartache, and then came anger—at myself. Not him.

I was a stupid bitch for hoping.

Then, a couple of things resonated with me.

One, I wasn't on the sofa anymore.

Two, the bed I was in smelled new, the sheets were perfumed with my favorite softener—*thank you, Indy*—and beside me, where it should have been cold, it was warm.

Really warm.

So warm that I knew the person who'd been lying there moments before had only just left the bed.

When I strained my ears to figure out why, I heard him in the bathroom.

Sure, it wasn't the nicest serenade in the world to hear a man pissing, but I'd take it because that meant he was here.

Even better, it meant he'd slept with me.

Steel had actually slept with me.

I wasn't sure I could stand it. Every part of this tired, thirty-four-year-old body suddenly felt like it was fifteen again.

I was almost vibrating when the door squeaked and I heard his footsteps, before I followed his path through the dim lights from the compound behind us pouring through the open blinds.

When he moved into the bed, I happened to see he was naked, and while my eyes widened in surprise, my belly burned in a way that had nothing to do with the surgical scars, and everything to do with the excitement that came from being with the man I loved who was as naked as the day he was born.

If I'd been whole and healthy, I'd have fist pumped the air, done a fucking rain dance in thanks, but I wasn't well, and it sucked, but that was the only reason he was here.

Still, I wasn't going to rain on my parade. If anything, I was just going to savor these unexpected moments.

When he settled at my side, cautious about disturbing me, he muttered, "Know you're awake, baby doll."

I bit my lip, loving how that endearment sounded on his lips, an endearment that I'd been hearing more and more regularly. But it was different here. Different now.

We were in bed together.

Sharing a fucking bed, with him naked in it!

Jesus, that was sending a pretty strong message my way, wasn't it? Talk about ramming it home! There was no misreading this, no thinking that him calling me 'baby doll' was just because he pitied me.

"How do you know I'm awake?" I complained.

He snorted. "The fact you answered when I asked a question?"

My lips twitched. "Smarty-pants."

"Always was a genius," he agreed.

I didn't tease him about that as he'd had a sore spot about his intelligence since forever. That boggled my mind every time it cropped up, because he was really clever and what he could do with words, making poetry so beautiful it made me melt, was something no dumbass was capable of. But I had no desire to annoy him. Not when he was in my bed.

Naked.

Priorities, ya know?

So I just muttered, "Didn't expect you to be here when I woke up."

"That's what had your panties in a wad all day?" he rumbled, and I shot him a surprised look, saw that he was glowering at me from his side of the bed.

I knew the distance between us was because of my situation, but fuck, I'd have given my left tit to roll astride him and to know what that cock felt like sliding into me.

I'd been waiting eighteen years to feel it. I think I deserved to be a little curious.

I shrugged at his question, and murmured, "Why wouldn't I think it?"

"Because I keep on telling you I'm going nowhere?"

Had he?

I mean, he'd been glued to my side throughout my stay in the hospital, but I couldn't remember any heartfelt vows and promises of love and adoration.

No 'in sickness and in health' talks.

He heaved a sigh. "Woman, I swear you just don't listen."

I laughed a little. "And you do?"

"True." He scraped a hand over his face. "Don't you remember what Indy told you?"

"Told me about what?" I asked, not feigning my confusion. "Indy tells me a lot. What in particular?"

"About the appointment at her studio?"

"What appointment?"

He sighed. "Your appointment."

"I'm not getting a tattoo," I retorted. "I don't fucking want one."

"You want this one." His hand was suddenly in my hair, and how he'd moved on the bed without knocking me or making the mattress shift, I'd never know.

But his hold on my hair was absolute, and the way he arched my neck, all without making me uncomfortable, was like weaving the lyrics of a song and singing them in my ear.

He tipped my head back, made sure I was staring straight at him, and muttered, "You're mine. About time the world knew it."

I narrowed my eyes at him. "And what about vice versa? Hmm? I've seen Nyx's and Link's brands. Sin's too." I huffed. "If you think I'm getting a tattoo, then you're nuts if you think you aren't adding to your collection—"

He took the wind out of my sails by moving away from me and twisting around to reach over the nightstand, and when a light flickered on, I winced as it made my eyes ache.

When the pain ebbed away, the glow too, I stared at him, scowling at the jerk move, then I saw his back.

Oh.

God.

It was old.

Fucking ancient.

Well, as ancient as a thirty-eight-year-old man could be.

But there it was.

My name.

His brand.

My brand on *him*.

Pierre in massive letters. The French word for stone. The name that was on my birth certificate.

Fuck.

I started crying. I had no choice. No freaking alternative.

I sobbed, and it hurt and felt so good all at the same fucking time, but the poison of years' worth of misery and heartache just wouldn't abate.

I cried until I was in pain, and cried some more whenever I opened my eyes, which were on the same line as him now he was sitting slouched over the side of the bed, where I could catch a glimpse of that massive fucking tat that declared to all the fucking world that he was mine.

Without me even knowing it.

"Why?"

The question didn't slip from my lips. Oh, no. It roared from me.

I was hurting in more ways than just physically. But even though I wanted to strangle him, I urged myself into a sitting position, sore stomach be damned, so I could trace the lines of my name.

It spanned the width of his shoulders, a long, cursive slant that spewed from the 'hot lips' logo for which my name had been granted—my mom was a Rolling Stone superfan.

I stared at it, tracing the letters, unable to believe, unable to credit what I was seeing.

It felt like a dream, which was slowly turning into a nightmare. Because if this was as ancient as it looked, the ink old and slightly faded, not fresh, then he'd put us through decades of misery, and for what?

Because he didn't want to be tied down?

That was the only thing I could think of.

My brain was a buzz, a blur of sounds and images, flashbacks of all the shit he'd done over the years.

From fucking clubwhores, to ignoring me, to shoving me away, to being absent when he'd been the one constant in my fucking life.

I was sure, at that moment, that I hated him.

I hated him so fucking much in a way that could only ever be the flip side of love, because this hatred went so deep, it funneled into me, tunneling into my heart.

But I couldn't stop touching him.

He was here.

He was naked.

He was showing me this.

He'd been with me for months, sitting with me through my recovery, and I knew something had changed in his mind, something that had been like a light switch flipping on, morphing into a 'yes' we can be together, from a 'no' this can never be.

He'd tensed at my touch, and I got the feeling he thought I was going to hit him.

But I didn't.

Even if he deserved a knife in his fucking back.

Shit, he deserved for me to carve out my name and to throw it at his fucking feet.

Years of misery, and for what?

Beneath my touch, his shoulders were bunched, and it took a second for me to realize that he was speaking through the white noise in my head.

"I made myself a vow to you, that I'd protect you from me until I died. Well, I died," he said simply. "And I was tired of being a hero. Tired of being away from you. What's the point in living if I can't have you at my side?"

For a second, I wasn't sure what I was hearing. Steel wasn't poetic anymore, wasn't even that sentimental. At least, not the man I'd come to know. And not with me.

As a kid, he'd been gentle with me, and he'd said sweet things, made me feel like I was lucky when he'd scrawl something with a Sharpie on the front of my notepad. Something that would make my teen heart melt.

But this was different.

Steel was harder now. He'd done shit that I would never know about, killed people, done bad business, and I just knew that the MC was likely helping Nyx purge his soul with the rash of vigilante murders that were happening around the Northeast.

I pressed my face into his shoulders, ignoring the ache in my stomach, the way I felt all rattled up inside, and instead, I breathed him in deep.

"You died?"

"It's a miracle I'm alive," he rasped. "I knew the second the bullets hit I was gonna die. When I woke up, I knew it was a gift. Knew not to waste shit a second time over."

I felt like an orange had lodged itself in my throat. "Why did you waste it the first time?"

He inhaled, and it was more of a rasp than a smooth sound. "I know I have to tell you, but I've been keeping this shit bottled up inside for so long that I don't know if I can."

The pain in his voice, the sheer agony in the words?

I believed him.

I couldn't not.

Whatever it was, whatever goddamn motherfucking reason he'd been using to keep us apart for all this wasted time, it hurt him.

Maybe as much as the poison I'd been given had been hurting me.

"My mom told you something that day, didn't she?" I asked softly as I moved to lie down, suddenly feeling way more fatigued than I ought to after basically just sitting up.

Fuck, this recovery was going to be a bitch.

Sweat had popped up on my brow, beading at the back of my neck, and it was with relief that I cascaded into the pillows.

When he joined me after switching off the light, he curled into me, his body curving so I was as close to him as we could be together.

This was so beyond surreal. To have the heat of him scorching along one side of me, to have his breath brushing my lips. The scent of him in my nose, the essence of him burrowing into the sheets.

I'd had boyfriends over the years, because I wasn't a nun, but I'd never moved in with any, never let them stay over at my place.

We'd always split up because they wanted more, and I was happy with being close fuck buddies, and it was because of this man.

Not because I was holding out for him, although maybe I was, but because I'd been burned once, and there was no way I was going to be burned again.

So why was I willing to listen to this? Why had my mood been so down today at the thought of him just dumping me at my digs and then heading home?

He'd torn me up, ripped me into shreds, and him pasting me back together again was going to take a long time. Trust? Fuck. We had so much shit to make up for, but I felt like...

Christ.

I'd learned a long time ago that hoping was for fools.

I didn't hope for shit. It might as well have been a wish.

I worked hard. I studied hard. I fought for everything I got, and nobody could say that wishing or dreaming or hoping was how I'd done it.

No.

I'd fucking strived for every miserable inch of ground I'd broken.

But Steel made me hope again.

And that was dangerous, because I wanted to hope. I wanted to trust. I was just scared of being hurt again.

His hand came over to cup my cheek, and I shuddered as the callused thumb rubbed along my jawline.

But the callused thumb made me think of what I'd overheard

today. "Hard to think of you breaking up shit in a chop shop. You always hated the auto shop class in school."

He tensed at my words, then his lips twitched. "Fuck, we did it again, didn't we?"

"What? Talked club business in front of me?" I laughed softly. "Yeah. You did. But I bet Rex knows."

"Rex knows all and sees all. He always loved you."

"I always loved him. He must know that I'd never do anything to hurt the MC."

"Probably knew that the first time I tore out your heart and danced on it." He gritted his teeth, then he lowered his forehead to my shoulder. "I'm so fucking sorry, Stone."

I gulped, because it wasn't enough. The words weren't enough.

"Just tell me why you did it."

"Lana Jane was...fuck, she was a bitch."

His insult didn't offend me. I'd never liked my mom all that much while she was alive, and in the aftermath of her death, when I'd been left to handle a lot of her affairs, some that had seen me taking a beating meant for her because she was in debt to some nasty people, I'd liked her even less.

"I know she was."

"Yeah, you think you do," he rasped. "But you don't." He sucked in another shaky breath. "That kiss has kept me going, Stone. I swear to fuck. Every morning, it's the first thing I think of, and at night, it haunts my dreams."

I scoffed, "I'm sure, what with all the snatch you've been fucking to screw me out of your system—"

He shook his head. "Never that. Not possible. To get through the agony of being away from you, sure. But it's like a heroin junkie just derailing and using to take the pain away. I probably fucked more women than you can even imagine" —ouch, that didn't hurt much, did it?— "and not a single one ever counted. It was like scratching an itch. It never meant anything to me, and no, that isn't supposed to sound good. I know how shitty it sounds. But your mom, she fucked me up. She fucked me up real good, and I couldn't deal with what she told me."

"How about you start with telling me what she actually said?" I questioned, my tone deliriously calm.

"Her first thing was, 'If I'd known you were into kids like your daddy, Steel, I'd have sold Stone to you when she was younger.'"

Whatever I'd expected him to say, it wasn't that.

It was never, ever, in a million *lightyears*, that.

I froze. Unable to compute all the different things he was saying. Then, when I was just as mind-blown, unable to process it, he murmured, "Yeah. That was pretty much my reaction, and to be completely frank, even all these years later, even reliving that afternoon a million times, I still can't get over how she said it. Just so fucking blasé that it was surreal."

I gulped, unable to believe it, but also able to accept it too.

I'd always known—

Hadn't I?

I sucked in a breath. "I got the vibe that if I'd been thinner, or prettier, she'd have tried to sell me, so I guess it doesn't come as much of a surprise."

My words were a husky rumble that had him tensing. "I'd have fucking killed any bastard who touched you. You have to know that—"

"I do. I did. You guys kept me safe a lot of the time, especially with all the shit she pulled."

His hand moved to my other arm, so that his forearm rested on my chest. It was a heavy weight, but it made me feel closer to him. He couldn't hold my stomach, not with the surgical sites still a mess, but this was how he could hold me, and I'd take it.

"Her Johns would wiggle the handle on my door some nights

—" I released another shaky breath. "I never slept so well as I did at Rene and Bear's place."

"I can imagine," he murmured. His lips went to the curve of my shoulder, to the ball, and he whispered, "But you missed something crucial in her words, Stone."

Had I?

"You mean you didn't break things off because you thought she'd been whoring me out—"

He sat up in an explosive move that had me yelping as it jolted my body. Even as he was hissing, his hands snapping out to stabilize me, he ground out, "Fuck, I'm sorry, baby doll. No! That wasn't why I broke things off! Fuck, Stone. Fuck! How could you even think that?"

My mouth trembled. "Well, something tore you away—"

"Yeah, what she was saying. What she was enjoying telling me." He gritted his teeth. "My father... Do you remember Kevin? Nyx's uncle?"

I tensed.

How couldn't I remember Kevin?

That weird time when I was, like, nine, when Mom had brought him over to the house? And he'd been looking at me...

I wrinkled my nose at the memory, because it had ended with me throwing a tantrum to get out of the room and being grounded for a month for 'showing Mom up in front of guests.'

When Carly, Nyx's sister, had killed herself, when Kevin had died a little while later, it had come out then exactly what Kevin was. And after that, when he was long since dead, Indy had confessed that he'd visited her room at night. That was why she had nightmares now. That was why she had insomnia.

"Of course I remember him." If I sounded like I was wheezing, then that was because I was. "The sick fuck."

"She told me he was my dad, Stone. She told me Mom had told *her*."

My mouth trembled. "Oh, Steel," I whispered. "You couldn't believe a word she said! You know she was a liar!"

"I did, but the way she said it, Stone, just fuck... I knew it was true. She got a kick out of it. She enjoyed telling me. So I got out of there, and I made sure I went and asked the one person who I knew would *know*."

My throat tightened. "Bear?"

"Yeah."

He scrubbed a hand over his face. "Kevin is my biological father."

For a second, the revelation hovered between us like a bomb that was just waiting to explode.

I could feel the seconds ticking down as I tried to figure out what to say, what to do.

Then, he rasped, "I'll go if you want me to."

I shook my head, but he didn't see it, and when he started to get off the bed, I groaned as I shot up and snapped my hand around his arm.

"You're going nowhere," I growled.

"I can't stand to look at myself in the mirror, Stone, I can't fucking bear it. So why the fuck should you want me anywhere close to you?"

I didn't know what to say, I truly didn't. I never could have anticipated this, but I figured I was just mad.

"You slept your way through the population of Sweden and pushed me away because of who your sperm donor was?" I whispered, just wanting to make sure I saw things the way he saw them.

"No, I stayed away from you because you were young, and I realized I was just like him."

My mouth dropped open. "Huh?" I let my hand slip away. "You like..." For a second, I couldn't even say it. "Kids?"

"No!" he ground out. "I liked you. When you were young."

"But you were young too!" I reasoned, totally perplexed.

"There's a four year age gap between us. My God, it creeps me out now just thinking about it."

I felt like I'd been tossed down the rabbit hole headfirst.

All I knew was that soon, my brain was going to reach a melting point, and when that happened, steam was going to be coming out of my ears. Especially as it was more like three years considering how close to his birthday mine fell.

"You didn't so much as kiss me until that night, and that was a month before my sixteenth birthday," I pointed out softly.

"The second you got tits and an ass, I wanted you—"

"Isn't that the exact opposite of what a pedophile would want, Steel?"

He froze at my question. "What?"

This was the most disturbing conversation I'd ever had, but trying to convince the love of my life he wasn't a deviant pervert really topped the fucking list of weird shit I'd had to do.

Ever.

I gulped, then reasoned, "Pedophiles groom young children for a long time, and then, when they start to sexually mature, they... ummm...well, they don't want that, do they? If anything, when I grew a set of tits and a butt, you should have been turned off. If you were like your father, I mean."

A ragged, explosive sigh escaped him, and suddenly, I was flat on my back and he had a leg curved over my thighs, his face was tucked into my throat, and even though he'd hurt me so many fucking times, even though he'd broken me, that was nothing compared to feeling this strong, powerful man break down against me.

His sobs of relief as he accepted my truth made my own eyes burn, and I curved my arms about him, because this, I realized, was mental torture.

He'd been in a prison since he'd found out, a jail of his own making, sure, but a jail that he hadn't known how to escape from.

His every betrayal I wore like a scar on my heart, but this?

Living proof that he'd endured an agony far worse than mine.

So I held him as he sobbed, and I knew that somehow, we'd move on from this. We'd make it work.

Because just like the brand on his back declared to the world, Steel was mine.

It was about time the rest of the world knew that I was his.

THIRTY-SIX

STEEL

SIX WEEKS LATER

"SHE'S SUCH A FUCKING CUNT," I heard a whiny voice mutter.

My lips curved as I peered out of the open window and saw who exactly the fucking cunt was.

Although, to be fair, it was definitely plural.

With Giulia in charge of cleaning up the MC, at Rex's behest, Stone, who was the original club snatch hater—and gee, it didn't take much to wonder why—had taken to the task as her sergeant at arms. The two of them were sitting outside the front stoop on deckchairs with a bag of popcorn in each of their laps as they directed the sweetbutts on how to tidy up the yard.

All along the line of the driveway, there was a column of white pebbles that gleamed an unholy white in the sun. The bunnies were having to clean each of them with soap, and I had to admit, it was amusing watching the little generals directing the snatch to go back to ones they didn't deem clean enough.

I shook my head at the sight, then grunted when Rex ground out, "I'm sorry if church is disturbing you, Steel."

"Not disturbing me, but I can multitask."

He strode over to me, his clomping boots echoing over the floor as he pulled up behind me.

When he saw what I did?

He laughed.

I just grinned.

"Getting those two together was a bad thing, huh?"

Not unsurprisingly, Nyx, recognizing that Giulia was involved somehow—because when trouble was down, it was either Giulia or Lodestar who was in the middle of it now—moved over to the window too, which, of course, led to Mav wheeling over, and Link and Sin joining us to see what was going on as well.

We all snickered at the sight of two mini Hitlers giving their soldiers orders, and Rex clapped me on the back and told me, "She's looking brighter."

I nodded, even though I wanted to hiss out the pain of him clapping me right where my bullet wounds were nearly healed but still sensitive. "Been making fucking sure of it. She wanted to go back to work too early, so getting into this tiny torture session with Giulia was exactly what I needed if I wasn't going to throttle her. I swear to fuck, she pushes herself harder than she pushes me."

"It's good to have her back," Nyx admitted, his voice gruff.

"Yeah, it is," Link agreed. "Missed the shit out of her. Didn't even realize it until we got her ass back home."

Guilt hit me at the same time as, I knew, it hit us all. We shared looks, hunched our shoulders at the reminder of how badly we'd let her down, then turned our attention back to the women-folk. It was either that or start singing 'Kumbaya,' and we weren't no saints. Sinners to the core, but that didn't mean we left a brother behind.

Stone was a brother too, but we'd forgotten that along the way —every last one of us. I knew we'd all spend a long time working to make up for the lost years, the wasted moments, and the lack of loyalty we'd shown her. Me, more than anyone, I knew. But family first was our creed, and we'd fucked up on that score.

She'd checked out on us, stopped caring as much, and that was because of how we'd treated her. Sure, she'd stayed loyal to the MC, and I didn't doubt Rex wasn't the only one she'd checked in with on a regular basis, but that didn't mean she was close to us. She'd done as she said she had, back when she was in the hospital —she'd made her own life.

Now, we had to prove that we deserved for her to choose us. For her to choose to let us be in her life once more.

"She's okay to work now, isn't she?" Link asked, clearing his throat.

"As of today, yeah."

My body tightened up at what that meant.

For six weeks, we'd shared a bed. For six fucking weeks, I'd been in both heaven and hell. Holding her, being close to her, reveling in her snark, loving her moods and her, and enjoying the way she never let me get away with shit, but I'd only kissed her once.

Once, because that one time? She'd started bleeding, and because that was my idea of hell, I'd nipped that in the bud.

For six weeks, that heaven and hell had kept me going, inspiring me to make her life miserable as I controlled every fucking thing she did to ensure her rehabilitation. I'd driven her to the hospital and helped her with her physical therapy. I'd groaned with her when she had the staples in her stomach removed, and had sat with her, hands folded together, as she dealt with blood test after blood test as they made sure her kidneys and liver were working back to capacity.

There'd been a spot where they feared she might need dialysis, but it hadn't come to pass, and her kidneys had kicked in after some meds they'd given her finally fucking worked.

The last six weeks hadn't been easy, but she'd been with me, we'd been together, and I figured that whatever hurdle was thrown our way, we could deal with it.

In that time, the officer from Cambodia had been in touch, the guy whose sister had been snatched, and we'd managed to torture some info of the Asian operations from Donavan, but we'd found no solid leads, even though Link's fists had been bloody for over a week as he pounded out his fury on the man who'd tortured his Old Lady throughout her childhood.

That didn't mean we would stop trying, of course.

Lodestar was on it, and she was determined to make sure that every woman who'd been lost was found. A fight that the MC was wholeheartedly behind, even if it was impossible to make that kind of promise.

Still, we had to try, and we were all on board.

I narrowed my eyes at the glare from the sun as I saw Keira, Storm's Old Lady, wandering over to Giulia and Stone.

I grinned when I saw why the glare had appeared.

The metal of her deckchair had caught the sun's rays, and she took a seat beside them, snagged Giulia's bag of popcorn from her lap, and took a handful.

The two had a little tussle over the bag before Giulia relinquished it with a huff.

"Never thought the three of them would get along," Nyx muttered.

"They have a common hatred," I said dryly. "Always make alliances over mutual enemies," I intoned, like this was a history class and I was the teacher.

Nyx snorted. "True."

Keira had had trouble making rent, and as her boss at the diner, I'd urged her to come and stay at the compound with Cyan, because she'd been working double shifts and literally couldn't work any more because there weren't enough hours in the day.

I understood pride, I did, but she wouldn't ask Storm for shit other than what he had to pay in alimony—and I knew he paid more than double what he was supposed to—and I knew he'd have lost his rag if he learned how things were for her, without us telling him, but a woman had her pride. Especially when she was trying to make a go of it on her own.

I had no idea why she needed so much money, but who was I to ask?

I'd given her as many shifts as I thought she could handle before I'd insisted she stay at the compound.

Rex had been on board because most of us had liked Keira, we'd especially liked her for Storm until he'd fucked up.

I'd fucked up years before he had, and I was lucky Stone let me anywhere near her, never mind had started to look at me like I mattered again.

The past six weeks had been hard on my dick. But they hadn't been hard on *us*.

I knew she was starting to trust me again, and that was sweeter than I could have ever imagined.

I gnawed on my bottom lip when Rex muttered, "We have business to discuss, fuckers."

I sniffed, twisted around, then, because I knew he was right, muttered, "Get on with it then."

We had one dead brother and two people missing from the clubhouse. Shit like that required my full attention, but even though I couldn't focus totally, I had to try.

His lips twitched. "Someone's got plans for tonight?"

Wryly, I admitted, "I got two plans."

"What are they?"

I eyed Link. "Getting her branded at long fucking last, because if I have to reschedule that appointment one more time, I'll lose my mind. Then after, I'm not coming out of that bunkhouse for at least three days."

Nyx snickered. "You taken some Viagra?"

"No. Just never had to fuck my fist this long in my life." My grin was sheepish, but they didn't give me shit.

I knew why too.

This was Stone.

Stone mattered.

They all left me alone, trudging back to the table where we sat around for church, but I stayed standing at the window with my attention averted from the only person I wanted to look at.

"So, do we need to hunt them down?"

I tuned in, because hunting always got my attention.

"Nah, they didn't do it."

Link's surety had me shaking my head, and Nyx grumbled, "I'd prefer not to have to kill my brother-in-law, but Dog's dead, and they ran off the next fucking day, Link. It looks shady as fuck."

"Katy wouldn't have hurt Dog. She wasn't like that."

"So who the fuck did?"

"Me."

The voice came from the doorway, and I rolled my eyes, unsurprised to see Lodestar standing there, her arms folded as she leaned against the doorjamb.

"Huh?" Sin muttered.

Mav rolled his eyes. "What the fuck did you do, Star?"

He wheeled toward her, but she shrugged. "He was beating her. I wasn't about to allow that to continue."

Rex pinched the bridge of his nose. "Star, for fuck's sake, you can't go around killing men because they—"

"What? Beat their Old Ladies? Make them scared of them?" She tipped her head to the side as she tapped her chin with her pointer finger. "I think if someone decided to beat the shit out of Rachel, or Giulia, or Tiff, or Lily, or Stone, or—" Her smile was false. "I think you'd be shedding more than blood. I think you'd be stringing them up by their dicks," she sneered at us. "So, yeah, sell your bullshit to someone else."

I cleared my throat. "She isn't wrong."

Nyx exhaled noisily through his nose. "She isn't, Rex."

The Prez looked like his jaw was made of stone, and I didn't blame him. He didn't like being handed his ass, and Lodestar had a habit of doing that to a man.

"We need to organize the funeral," was all he said, surprising me by not giving her any more shit than that.

"I'm on it," I rasped. As Secretary, it fell to me to organize that kind of thing.

"What about Sarah?" Lodestar rumbled.

Ghost, Amara, and Tatána had survived the Lancasters, but Sarah hadn't.

"I haven't forgotten," I soothed her, because it was only as I looked at her then that I saw how highly strung she actually was.

Jesus, she practically vibrated with emotion.

"The cops only just released her body from the morgue," I assured her softly.

Her chin jerked back and in, like I'd put it back into joint, and the tension in her lips lessened some.

"I'll cover her funeral," she stated.

"Not necessary."

She glowered at Rex. "Very necessary. I'll cover it."

He rolled his eyes. "Knock yourself out."

She huffed. "I will."

"How the fuck did you open the door without us knowing?" Link groused.

Unsurprisingly, she and Mav both sniffed, which prompted us all to grunt.

Sneaky spy shit, that was how.

We'd never actually found out what the fuck Mav and Star had done for Uncle Sam, but their time served had sure as hell sent them out into the real world with a lot of skills that had little to no real-world applications.

Unless, of course, they were involved in crime.

I rubbed my chin, discounting the idea that the government was training soldiers to be top criminal masterminds, as she turned on her heel, sniffed at us once more, then wandered out.

I shook my head, muttering, "Why the fuck do we put up with her?"

Mav snorted. "Why do you put up with me?"

"You're a brother," Nyx answered instantly, stalwart to the last.

Mav's grin was sheepish, and it was so disconcerting to see a grin like that on his face that you could have knocked me down with a fucking feather.

The sight of him even smiling was such a fucking change of pace that, I had to admit, it was pretty epic to behold. He'd been so miserable for so fucking long that we were all just used to his misery.

Sure, we wanted to help, but he wouldn't help himself.

He refused rehab classes, scoffed at the idea of physical therapy, and getting him to talk to a frickin' shrink? We might as well have asked him to talk to a fucking demon.

Ghost had to be behind this.

Shit, it was always a woman, wasn't it?

I wanted to shake my head at us all. Fucking tough bikers, killers the lot of us, all melting because we suddenly had the right pussy in our beds.

A laugh sounded behind me, reaffirming exactly who was pussy whipped, and you know what?

I wouldn't change a fucking thing.

Decades of misery suddenly felt like they were on the road to changing into contented ones, and I could no more stop myself from turning around to watch my woman than I could stop my lungs from needing another gulp of air a second later.

"We put up with her because she's a fucking genius," Rex

muttered grimly, telling me he believed every word he said but he didn't damn well like it. "Even if she's a severe pain in my ass."

"All our asses," Link corrected. "And not in the way I like either. The fuck? She can't go around killing brothers."

"Dog was a schmuck," Nyx said unapologetically as he traced shapes on the beat-up dining room table we used as a conference table. "He was on my shit list a long ass time, and the truth was, if I'd seen him beat his Old Lady, I'd probably have strangled him myself. Especially after watching him go for Giulia. A dick that handy with his fists is no brother of mine," he finished grimly.

I rubbed my chin at his statement, accepting it as fact, even as I accepted that murdering brothers wasn't the best way to go about business.

"A shit-kicking," I concurred. "But to kill him? Seems a bit...extreme."

"Lodestar is a woman of extremes," Mav rasped. "And she must have seen something that told her it was needed. Anyway, you saw Dog and Lizzie back in the day. They were always bruised and beaten from pounding on each other."

"We can't sanction Dog's killing," Sin muttered uneasily. "We can sanction a lot, but that ain't one of them."

"What do you want to do? Kick her out when she's helping us?" Mav scoffed.

Rex shook his head. "No. I don't want that. She's safe here, and we need her to stay that way, as well as for Katina's sake. I don't think Ghost is ready to be dealing with her sister full time, and I can't blame her. Katina is a lot to handle, but also, she loves Star—anyone with eyes can see that.

"We just need to make sure she's contained."

"Like Ebola?"

Rex grimaced at Link's snarky retort. "Yeah. Like Ebola." He blew out a breath. "We need to make sure if there are any brothers beating their Old Ladies—" He grunted. "I can't even believe I'm going to say this, but fuck. We need to strike preemptively. You hear of an Old Lady even complaining about a bruise, you go to the brother, you give him the shit-kicking of his life, and then you warn him because, fuck, if she does it one time, she'll do it again, and we're seriously short of brothers. The last thing we need is to limit our numbers at a time like this.

"Evidently, Star doesn't believe in fucking rehabilitation, and that's fine, *once*. Now we know she's a psycho, we can adapt."

"Good thing she's fucking worth it," Nyx rumbled.

"She is," Mav confirmed, and I wasn't sure if that was loyalty to a brother-in-arms or if that was him being sentimental—if that was even possible.

I ran a hand over my chin, pondering that.

Lodestar might look put together, but she was definitely on the edge. I'd never seen that before.

Mav wore his broken scars on his face, in his body. They were clear to see, clear for everyone to behold because he did it on purpose. He wanted you to know he'd been to war so that you'd leave him the fuck alone. And the truth was, I was used to that.

Because Star looked so goddamn normal, it was easy to think she was exactly that.

Ordinary.

Except she was anything but ordinary, which was dangerous.

I already knew how far her machinations had helped us, and while I was cleared to know every aspect of her input into our work, I'd been out of it the past six weeks as I focused on making my girl better.

Somehow, though, Lodestar had managed to tear down a *Famiglia*-owned drug ring in Chicago by cracking some firewalls that even had Mav sporting wood, and I was well aware that the gambling operations the *Famiglia* managed in NYC, where Nyx and I had made a real splash? She was on the cusp of tearing them down too, which was putting us in the Five Points' good books.

Always a plus.

Especially when we'd had two runs in the past eight weeks, and had another coming up next week. The money was really rolling in.

"While we're talking about crazy women," Link muttered a few minutes after we all agreed to monitor the men, make sure there was no domestic violence going down in their homes, "I have a suggestion."

"What kind of suggestion?" Rex asked, eying him warily. "If it has to do with your ass, Link, then you can just go fuck—"

"No, it isn't." He grunted. "I don't know how much you want the women getting involved in shit, but Lily is going to go insane soon. She needs to do something. Anything. To keep her mind off what's going down." He pursed his lips. "They're all staying close to the clubhouse, and she understands that and agrees with it, but I can see it's killing her—"

"We can't kill Lancaster yet, Link," Rex muttered tiredly.

I knew why too. Link argued for the bastard's death every church.

"I know that, and I get it. After seeing what he's letting us in on? I totally understand now." He sucked in a breath. "With Maverick and Lodestar focused on tearing down the *Famiglia's* operations from the inside out, I figured we might need a hand with the books. Lily's an economy major. If anyone could handle it, she could."

Silence fell at his words, then Nyx muttered, "I'm down for that. She's a smart little thing, and it seems a shame to waste brains like that."

Rex scowled. "I don't know—"

"What's not to know?" Nyx argued. "You use Rachel and Stone—"

"They're home grown."

"Lily might be new to the MC," Link argued, his ears growing pink with his annoyance. "But she has more reasons to be loyal to us than anyone. We kept her safe, and we brought home her bastard father. She owes us a blood debt, if you even need to phrase it like that."

Rex grunted, and seeing his dubiousness, I decided to help. Link was right—Lily was solid—so I murmured, "He's right, Rex. Maverick has a lot going on."

I cut my brother a look and saw that he wasn't freaking out, which told me he wasn't averse to the idea.

That was a good sign.

For a long time, the books and keeping the MC's financial records straight had been the only thing keeping Mav going. But now?

It seemed he had more to live for than facts and figures.

"I think she can do it," Mav said slowly. "And I'll help her, apprentice her, see if she can handle everything."

"She ain't a brother," Rex countered wearily. "You know that will sow distrust among the men."

Mav shrugged. "Then don't tell them." He cut Link a look. "Does she know you're asking this?"

"No." He sighed. "I didn't want to get her hopes up."

Mav grunted. "If she does it, she has to know that if she so much as squeals once, we'll kill her."

His hard tone didn't even make Link flinch. "She won't let us down," he rasped. "She's loyal. To the MC, but even more so to me. She'd never do that to me."

"Relationships break down," Rex grumbled.

"No. This is a loyalty that goes past that."

"She ain't married to you yet—" Rex added.

Link's mouth firmed at that. "It's just a matter of time."

Nyx heaved a sigh. "What the fuck are you waiting for?"

"There's no rush now, is there? Fieri is fucking dead!"

Rex rubbed his forehead. "I don't want to know what's going

on in your head, Link, but this is on your shoulders. You'll be the one who has to pay the price if she fucks up and goes squealing to the pigs."

He straightened said shoulders and ground out, "I trust her with my life. Even more importantly, I trust her with my family's life."

Rex stared at him long enough for any sane man to squirm, but like most of the council, Link wasn't exactly *sane*.

Eventually, Rex muttered, "Okay. Mav, get her started on the ropes. She shouldn't find it too hard, but we juggle a lot of pies. Start her with the legit stuff first. The West Orange businesses. Get her interested in the micro-brewery and managing the investments. She'd probably get a kick out of that. Then, when she proves herself, get her involved in the other stuff."

Mav dipped his chin in agreement. "Got it."

Rex grunted. "Is that everything? Or do you fuckers want a pussy to sit in on the council next? Already got more bitches running around my home than ever before—"

I snorted. "Just wait until Stone hears you called her a bitch."

Rex bunched his shoulders. "If you fucking tell her—"

I grinned at him. "You'll what?"

When he just glowered at me, I smirked.

My ball buster had a rep, and I was fucking proud of it.

THIRTY-SEVEN

KEIRA

STONE SNORTED when Jingles did her thing—jingled—as she flew ass over tits on her back.

I guessed it was mean to laugh, but the woman was so busy trying to get her T-shirt wet so one of the brothers would sweep her away to a bedroom to fuck rather than have to do her chores, that it was just satisfying to see her felled.

God, I hated the club snatch, and I loved that Giulia was making them do all the miserable shit. Loved even more that Rex had given her power over them.

Sure, she was lording it over them. Or I guessed, in this instance, ladying it was more fitting, but damn, it was wonderful to behold.

These bitches had ruined my marriage.

They had.

Storm, too, but I wasn't going to attribute none of the blame to these sluts.

I'd seen how hard they worked to get the men to cheat. I'd seen what they'd do to brothers who were trying to stay loyal to their girlfriends... Anything and everything was on offer.

Sure, the men should resist temptation, but even I'd cave in if I was that way inclined when I was given access to all fucking areas.

Every single one of them, ironically enough, wanted to be us.

And us?

We just hated the ground they walked on.

When Jingles glowered at us for snickering at her tumble, I didn't even care about the malice prevalent in her eyes. What could she do to me?

Ruin my marriage?

Oh, wait, she'd already done that, along with all the other sluts who worked here.

"You look pretty evil right now, K."

My lips curved at Giulia's comment, and I shrugged at her. "Feeling that way."

I loved Giulia. God, I wished I'd been like her back when I was her age. Maybe things would have worked out differently.

Maybe my Old Man would still be my Old Man, and maybe my daughter wouldn't hate me because her daddy was hundreds of miles away in a different state.

I bit down on my lip and confirmed, "I feel evil."

She snorted. "You're too good to be really evil."

Stone nodded, but her gaze was kinder when I caught her eye. Giulia was gutsy and brash, unafraid of anything, but Stone was in possession of a warm heart, and she was usually careful with what she said, unless she was blurting something out and reaming the brothers a new one.

I wasn't saying Giulia didn't have a kind heart too, because she did. She just didn't wear her heart on her sleeve like Stone did.

Giulia had helped nurse three women back to health, while Stone was a healer, empathetic to her core. Was it any wonder I liked both of them? They were Florence Nightingales just like me.

Because I liked them both, my mind wandered. I pursed my

lips, wondering if their men would stay true to them, and I hoped against hope that they would.

I truly wanted no one to go through what I was dealing with right now. I never wanted that for any woman.

"You okay, darlin'?" Stone asked me softly.

Again with the warm heart... My eyes blurred with tears, and I shook my head. "Another argument with Cyan." Ever since we'd moved into the bunkhouse, sharing it with a woman called Lodestar and her foster daughter, Katina, things had been hard going between Cyan and me.

Giulia hissed out a breath. "Oh, sugar, I'm sorry. I was glad when Mom took us away from Dad, it was just the club I missed." She winced. "It'll get better with time."

It was clear she wasn't about to start wearing funeral blacks for Dog's death. The news of his mugging had been all around the kitchen this morning, and she'd looked bored by most of the whispers.

"He's a really great dad," I said mournfully. "I don't think she'll ever forgive me for not agreeing to go down there with him."

"She will. Giulia's right. It just takes time."

"I don't know if I have time. She's never been so moody or so unhappy. I know she was being bullied at school, but I thought I had that under wraps, but all this—it's just a lot to deal with right now."

Stone peered at me. "Steel mentioned money was tight."

I heaved a sigh. "He said he wouldn't talk about that with anyone."

She shrugged. "I'm not anyone, and he was worried about you."

"You don't think he'll tell Storm, do you?" I whispered fiercely. "I don't want him to know!"

"To know what?" Giulia asked.

I grimaced. "It doesn't matter."

She sniffed. "I smell secrets, and that means it's juicy. Come on. Give it up."

I bit my lip. "I-I'm saving up to go back to school."

Stone's brows rose. "That's why you're working so hard?"

I nodded. "I know that it will be tough at first, so I was doing all the work now so I'd have a cushion when I was in school."

Giulia blew out a breath. "Well, that's a lot less fun than I expected."

I snickered. "Sorry to disappoint." When she blew me a raspberry, I just grinned at her.

"What do you want to study?"

I ducked my head, feeling embarrassed when Stone was a doctor. What did my stupid dreams matter to someone like her?

"I want to be a nurse."

Her eyes widened. "You do?"

I nodded.

"That's brilliant. Hell, you should tell Rex! He'll help fund your studies."

Whatever I'd expected her to say, it wasn't that. My mouth dropped open. "Huh?"

But Stone was nodding at me, her enthusiasm clear as she sat up, leaning toward me with barely a grimace as she explained, "He paid for me to go through school. If it'll help the MC along the way, he'll invest in you."

"But how can a nurse be an investment for the MC?"

She shrugged. "You know how many times these fools get shot up."

I grimaced. "True."

Giulia hummed. "That really true? He paid for your education?"

Stone nodded. "He did. Rachel Laker's too."

Giulia's surprise was clear. "Rex paid for her to become a lawyer?"

"No way!" I sputtered.

"Yes way." Stone looked amused. "With me, and Rachel too, his dad had a lot of say in it because he was Prez back then, but Rex was the one who finally convinced Bear for us both. Instead of running yourself ragged, go and ask him for help. I bet he'll give it to you." She winked at me. "And if he doesn't, tell me and I'll have a word. Every doctor needs a nurse."

Giulia laughed. "Didn't know you swung for the same team," she cackled.

"She doesn't," Steel muttered grumpily, striding out from the clubhouse, his focus pinpointed on Stone.

His hand slid over Stone's shoulder, and I wanted to sigh at how happy she was, how the tension on Steel's face lightened just a tad as their fingers tangled, bridging and settling close to her throat.

Storm and I had been like that once upon a time.

What the fuck had gone wrong?

Why had things gone downhill all the way until they were in the crapper?

In my defense, I'd tried. I'd never wanted Cyan to be apart from her daddy, but also, I wasn't about to stand for him treating me like dirt. I had to make her see that she was worth more. That no man, not even her daddy, could treat a woman like he did me.

In all honesty, I'd only left him with the hope he'd wise up. I never wanted them to be apart for long. But he'd just gone back to his old ways, and here we were, me at the clubhouse and him at the chapter in Ohio.

I bit my lip as Giulia asked, "Steel?"

"What?"

"Is it true that if you want a career that might help the MC, Rex'll fund it?"

He snorted. "I dunno if I'd call it the Satan's Sinners' Grant, but yeah, if he thinks it's needed, he'll invest in you. Why?"

"Keira wants to be a nurse?"

His gaze dropped to me, and instantly, I hunched my shoulders.

I'd never had the relationship with Storm's brothers that Giulia, Lily, Tiff, and Stone appeared to have, and to be honest, I was jealous.

It was like they would all go to bat for them, go on a rampage to keep them safe. While me? I just felt like a hindrance sleeping in one of their bunkhouses.

But his eyes were kind as he looked at me, and he murmured, "I don't see why he wouldn't help with that. You could help Stone."

"That's what I said."

I cut her a grateful look, muttering, "I might not be any good at it."

Giulia sniffed. "Well, you'll never get anywhere with that attitude, will you?"

I chuckled despite myself, appreciating how she always knew what to say to help me get over any shyness. I didn't used to be timid, but something had changed, and I was annoying myself. Giulia didn't exactly allow for that, and even though she was younger than me, and though Stone was older, the pair of them always seemed to level me out after another fight with my eleven-year-old.

"You should ask him," Steel prompted. "Is this why you've been so short on cash? You're going to school?"

"No, she's smarter than that," Stone replied proudly. "She's been saving up for school."

"Running yourself ragged isn't exactly smart, Stone," he grumbled.

"I wasn't. I—" My nose crinkled, ashamed to admit what I'd been about to say.

"What is it?" Giulia questioned.

"Cyan's happy with Jenna." I shrugged, talking about one of the Old Ladies who minded some of the brothers' kids for a little money on the side. "She's happier with her than she is with me right now, so I might as well work."

Giulia grunted. "I think that kid needs a talking to."

My eyes flashed wide. "No!" And I had to laugh because Stone and Steel bellowed that at the same time.

Giulia huffed. "I wouldn't scare her. Not too much anyway."

"She doesn't need to be scared," Stone grumbled.

"Fuck, scare her if you want Storm riding up from Ohio to come and tear you a new one," Steel retorted. "Jesus. Giulia, leave it to her mom."

"She's being mean to her," Giulia argued, like I wasn't here. "I hate that shit. It wasn't like Keira asked her Old Man to fuck that bunch of *skanks*!"

She yelled the last word so that each of said skanks could hear her opinion on them, but before anyone could say shit back to her, Nyx appeared, perfect timing for Giulia's sake, and the bunnies instantly ducked their heads and got on with the job at hand.

The irony was, in all the years I'd been around the MC, in all the years the snatch was supposed to be cooking and cleaning as well as boning the brothers in exchange for board and lodging, I didn't think I'd ever seen them clean stuff.

Not once.

That was pretty fucking gross now that I thought about it, nose crinkling.

I guessed Giulia was being mean to the women, maybe even bullying them, but they were just as cruel with any amount of power they thought they might have in their grasp, and I knew they'd cut her in an instant.

They weren't weak. They were snide bitches who would wreck a man's life just for the chance to wear a brand before they were too old to be the bikers' cum sluts anymore and were tossed out.

I gnawed on my lip, wondering what Storm was doing, if he'd broken in all the new sweetbutts down at the Ohio chapter, and even as the thought speared me with pain, I was filled with a joy I couldn't describe when I saw Steel help Stone onto her feet.

She was much stronger now, a lot healthier, but still a little wobbly when she was standing.

I'd never thought Steel could be so devoted to a woman, and I was happy for Stone. Happy because when these brothers loved, they loved hard.

Which meant Storm had just never loved me.

The bitterest pill of all to swallow.

"Where you going?" Giulia inquired as she grabbed Nyx's hand when he strode past her, moving to her back before he bent over and pressed a kiss to her throat.

My stomach churned at the intimate kiss, and I tried not to get turned on by such a blatant display of possession.

If wishes were horses...then Storm would have done that to me.

Showed the club who owned me.

"Indy's branding Stone," Steel declared, and I could sense his pride.

Stone's cheeks burned, and I giggled a little. "Have fun."

Her nose crinkled. "Fun? Being stabbed with a needle? That's what I have people pissing themselves over when it's time for a shot."

Though Giulia and I laughed, Nyx shook his head. "How the fuck you and Indy were so close for so long and she didn't ink you yet—"

"I'm strong willed," was her retort.

Steel and Nyx laughed. "Understatement of the year."

"You know it, boys. You know it."

Her wink had me grinning, and I waved her off as she leaned on Steel, grinning back at me as they walked toward where his bike was parked.

"Is it wise for her to ride his bike?"

"Probably not," Nyx replied, his tone bored. "But you heard her. She has her own mind, and she wants to ride bitch. Says it's only right she's on his hog as her inaugural ride as his Old Lady."

Giulia laughed. "She ain't the first lady."

"You tell her that," Nyx said wryly. "Anyway, to Steel, she's definitely the first lady. Fuck, she's his only lady. It's about time he claimed her. Been wearing her brand all this time, it's fucked up that she hasn't been wearing his."

Giulia twisted around to peer up at her Old Man. "Huh?"

He waved a hand. "Got a big ass tat on his back with her name on it. Only right she wears his name too."

Giulia arched a brow at me, but this was news to both of us.

I shrugged, wondering at that. Stone didn't share that much about her relationship. About the brothers, sure. Stories about when they were kids, definitely. I'd loved hearing about Storm, but the truth was, they were stories I should have heard from his lips.

Being back at the clubhouse was bittersweet because I shouldn't need to be here, surrounded by Storm's family, and yet, they were mine too, by proxy.

They were the family who'd caused me pain along the way by being loyal to him when he was being disloyal to me, and yet, the women had taken me in.

Not just Giulia and Stone, but Tiff and Lily as well.

For the first time, I had friends who actively hung around the compound. Most Old Ladies didn't, not liking the club life and the animals their men turned into in the clubhouse, but it was different now.

Maybe so dissimilar that if it had been like that when I was with Storm, things might have been different.

But crap, there was no point in even thinking of that.

Was there?

THIRTY-EIGHT

STONE

I LET LOOSE a holler as we rolled onto the highway that would take us over to Verona.

My joy was unconfined at being on the back of Steel's bike. It hurt, sure, but I was getting used to the pain, getting used to minimal discomfort, and I knew, eventually, it would just become a part of my day. And there was no way I was missing out on this.

I was going for my brand, and I refused to not be riding bitch when I came back from the studio.

It was my right.

The last time I'd been on the back of his bike was when I was fifteen frickin' years old. I had a lot to make up for.

And so did he.

With every swoop and curve on the road, I let loose another holler because I was thrilled to be flying again. That was how it felt. Like I was rolling through the clouds, wings akimbo.

Of course, I didn't have a death wish. My arms were tucked tightly around his waist, and hell if that wasn't more fun than I remembered.

The last six weeks had been hard. I'd suffered, a lot, and the treatment had been arduous, making me wish I'd done something worse to Annie Young when I'd had the chance.

Slicing her throat wasn't enough for what she'd put me through with her poison concoction, but though I could regret I hadn't stood on her tits or kicked her in the cunt, mostly, I was just amazed at how Steel had stood by me through it all.

Then, oddly enough, as amazed as I was, I wasn't.

He'd always been loyal. That was why he'd broken me when he'd cut that off from me.

Once I'd seen his brand, I'd known we'd been heading this way, and I figured it was perfect timing, because when I was wearing his name on my skin, that was when shit would be official in the club.

It was almost terrifying, but also exciting.

For so long, I'd been a part of the MC, but somehow, an outsider too. This was like the cherry on the cake.

When we made it to Indiana Ink, I winced as I climbed off, and I'd admit to the spell of dizziness as my body protested the movement required to climb off the back of the hog.

He knew, of course, grunted at me, but held me still as I got my shit together.

When the door burst open, I laughed when, from behind, I was embraced and squeezed to the point of pain, but I was okay with that.

It felt good.

My man on one side, my best friend on the other.

Bliss!

I reached around and patted her back, laughing as I said, "You happy to see me, Indy?"

"Fuck, you only saw her yesterday," Steel groused, making my lips twitch.

"Do you know how long I've been waiting to break ground on her virgin skin?"

My nose crinkled. "Could you make it sound any creepier?"

She laughed, but I knew she didn't care. "Years," she replied, answering her own question and aiming it not at me, but at Steel. "I'm excited."

"It's only a little one."

"I know, but we're planning a doozy, aren't we?"

I rolled my eyes, but she didn't see that.

I was getting his name scrolled on me behind my ear, just until the scarring on my abdomen was fully healed.

I didn't know if I'd ever be having kids, and I knew tattoo artists advised against having tats on the belly when you were a woman, but I couldn't deal with the scars and wanted them covered up.

That was where my brand would go. Eventually. And I knew Indy had big plans for it.

She'd made a name for herself by donating tattoos to mastectomy patients, and her generosity and kindness had seen her name travel far and wide—exactly what she deserved.

She was used to dealing with scar tissue, so I was excited to know what she'd come up with because, according to her, she'd been planning this design since she was sixteen.

Yeah, my best friend was definitely a weirdo.

When we walked in, I was faced with another weirdo. I'd never liked her assistant, but she thought he was harmless. I knew David kept her organized, and considering that was a miracle, I wasn't surprised that she loved him. Still, I greeted him cordially, as was my way with people I didn't particularly like, and he smiled at me warmly after asking how I was doing.

I wasn't going to be honest, because if I told the truth every time someone asked me how I was feeling, they'd just break down and sob.

And I had too much to be happy about.

The pain was definitely rough, and sometimes, I just stood there and cried, but what made it all better? Knowing Steel would appear, like my white knight, and he'd take me in his arms and tell me that soon, things would change. That I'd be better *soon*. And even though I was the doctor and understood that recovery was a bitch, I believed him.

In his arms? My life had changed.

I knew that sounded pathetic, but I'd deal with that.

I *was* pathetic for this man, and the best part? He was pathetic over me!

When Indy guided me into her studio, I eyed the equipment warily. She knew I hated this shit, but for Steel, for the man who'd been by my side throughout this entire ordeal, I'd wear his name with pride, so I let her set me up.

She got to work, preparing the area, and Steel hummed his approval as she inked his name down the tender skin.

When it was done, the official act of his claiming me sealed, I grinned at him, excited to see the heat in his eyes.

Even though the last few weeks hadn't exactly been lust central in our bunkhouse, somehow, the fire in his gaze never seemed to abate, and I'd never been happier about that.

Fuck, how he could feel that way when we'd been dealing with a lot of gross shit that came as part of what I'd been through, I didn't know.

To be honest, that was how I knew he loved me.

How I knew what he felt for me was real and honest and true.

If he could look at me with need and lust, all while he'd helped me when I puked, while he'd helped change the bandages on my stomach, and had held my hand at the doctor's office…yeah, it was love.

I didn't care what any naysayer could throw at us. I knew it.

She put a little gauze over the small tat and taped it up, but warned me, "It'll be irritating as hell, and your hair will catch on it. But make sure you apply Aquaphor on it, okay?"

I nodded. "I probably know the aftercare better than you do, Indy."

She stuck out her tongue at me, reminding me of Giulia with the move—fitting that Nyx was surrounded by two women who weren't afraid to flip him the bird and shoot him raspberries—and queried, "Okay, are you ready to see the tattoo I've been designing for, like, ever?"

I shot her a half grin. "I'm ready."

I wasn't.

I was actually nervous. What if I hated it?

What if—

Then the tracing paper was there, and the outline was in front of me. Beyond that, she passed me a sketch, and my eyes widened at the color image.

"Oh my God."

"Jesus, Indy, that's spectacular."

That Steel was impressed was a given. I knew her talent was renowned, but holy shit...the tattoo was beyond epic, and it would fit on my stomach to perfection.

It blew my mind how perfectly it would sit there, and I gaped at it, then gaped at her some, gaping harder when she laughed, clearly sensing that I loved it.

The tattoo depicted a cat, Mrs. Biggins of course, who was sitting proud and straight behind the light of a strawberry moon. It was high and full in the sky, illuminating the ocean that gleamed a silvery navy blue. The moon was made up of mandalas, and inside the lines, Steel's name was intertwined.

What made the ink so spectacular was the shading on Mrs. Biggins, who had her face twisted toward me in a perfect likeness. It was as though she was sitting there, right in front of me.

Miserable and grumpy and beautiful.

She'd be on my belly forever.

And even more epic? On Mrs. Biggins' tiny shoulder? A small bird.

Robin.

For Steel.

"I love it," I whispered, my eyes gleaming wet with tears.

"I knew you would," she muttered, her tone cocky, but I saw her joy at my pleasure, at my appreciation, and I reached for her hand and squeezed it.

"Thank you, Indy."

She hitched a shoulder, but her grin was shy. "You're welcome!"

Then, being Indy, she changed shit up and muttered, "Steel, I got a forty-minute slot...you want some new ink or a touch up?"

Steel winked at me. "Yeah, I got some ink that needs freshening up."

And when Indy saw which tattoo needed the fresh ink, and when I muttered that *pierre* meant stone in French? She gaped at me as much as I'd gaped at her over her drawing. I couldn't blame her either. Only a handful of people knew I'd been assigned a boy's name at birth by my off-her-head mother, and they were all on the Sinners' council.

When I winked, she just shook her head, then muttered, "Steel, you're insane."

His grumbled, "I know," warmed my heart.

At least the man could accept he was crazy for putting us through what he had.

I appreciated a man who owned up to his mistakes.

THIRTY-NINE
STEEL

WHEN SHE CAME out of the bedroom later that night, the little gauze still taped behind her ear somehow, just visible on the side of her throat, I watched her with a desire I couldn't hide.

She wore a pair of panties and a slim cami to bed, and the clothes were a lot different than what she'd been wearing before—my tees, usually, with a pair of boxers.

I knew why.

She wanted me, and her body was ready for it.

Well, I could argue over that with her for days. I didn't think, even if the doctor agreed, that she was on the mend and ready to work soon, but to be honest, Stone did whatever the fuck she wanted.

And right now?

I was whatever the fuck she wanted.

Thank God.

Her cami hid her stomach, which pissed me off. I knew why, but I didn't like it, only I wasn't about to push it. Not when her banging tits were peeping out of the V-neck, and the panties were high on the leg, revealing long limbs that I wanted around my waist.

Her gait was smoother than it had been in weeks, and I watched her stroll toward me, loving the healthier look to her.

She'd gained weight since I'd been shoving food in her mouth, and the rounded hips, the swell of her tits, and the strength in her thighs all made me want to attack her, but yeah, that wasn't going to happen.

I needed to take this slow, even though I was feeling anything but *slow*.

I sucked in a breath, well aware that my cock was hard, but as she approached me, I had no choice but to slide my hand down to grab my dick. As I jacked off, she stopped, paused, and watched me, her gaze glued to my crotch so I put on a little show, loving how she moaned, loving how she bit her bottom lip.

I groaned when she reached down and cupped herself between her legs, over her panties, and as we stood there watching each other touch ourselves, I knew sex had never been this weird before.

And it wasn't even fucking weird.

Christ.

But...

I could touch her. Yet she was touching herself.

She could touch me. But I was touching myself.

Stupid, but fuck, it was hot.

I'd waited for her hands to be on me for a lifetime, and here she was, a few feet away, but knowing that she loved the show got me harder, and I watched as she finally slipped her hand through the side of her panties and began touching the good stuff.

"Get rid of them, baby doll," I rasped, loving that she bit her lip, that she sucked on it as she shucked out of them with her spare hand, leaving her fingers tucked between the lips of that beautiful pussy I couldn't wait to see.

My mouth watered as she moved them down to her knees, and when she reached up, popping both her tits out of the neckline, even knowing she was self-conscious enough about her scars to do that, it didn't stop me from feeling like I was going to explode.

I grunted as I reached down and grabbed my balls. Rolling them in my fist, I watched as she moaned, her gaze glued to them, and suddenly, I realized she was watching me like she probably watched porn, and that made shit a thousand times hotter.

Fuck.

I began to jack off, quicker, harder, giving her more of the show so that she'd never need fucking porn again—that was why I was here.

I was her personal fucking BOB.

And the thought was enough to have me leaping off the bed, possessiveness zapping through me like electricity as I surged toward her.

She yelped as I dragged her panties down her legs until they were puddling at her feet, then I picked her up about the thighs, ignoring the pinch of my shoulder as it protested the move, and hauled her high so she was clinging to me, her feet digging into my ass.

When my dick settled in the notch of her pussy, I wanted to congratulate it on a job well done, but hell, talking to my penis wasn't going to win any awards with my woman.

I grabbed her ass and ground her into me as I joined our mouths together.

She sighed into the kiss, and I sighed into her, loving the taste of her, savoring it, and savoring the fact that she was mine.

In the eyes of the club—the only laws that mattered to me—she was mine, and no one could ever change that.

She wore my brand, and the second I could, I was getting her a fucking cut with my patch on.

I grunted as I slipped my tongue into her mouth, then felt like cursing when she thrust against me, fucking me as much as I was fucking her.

Her cunt was slick around my dick, wet and juicy, making me want to pound into her, but I fucking couldn't.

I had to be careful with her, and in all honesty, I'd never fucked with care before in my life.

But for her, I'd figure it out, it was just where to start.

I pulled back after I nipped at her pouty top lip, then asked, "How, baby doll? How do I take you?"

She groaned, arched her back, then rubbed her pussy against me. I saw the little flashes of pain on her face, flashes she couldn't hide, but I knew she was too into it to care about them.

It killed me that she was acclimating to low levels of pain, but she was strong-willed, more so than an ass, and I wasn't gonna start complaining about that, not after her obstinacy had seen her survive what that bitch had done to her.

"Can I ride you?" That surprised me. My brows rose high, making her laugh. "If you didn't want that, then why ask?"

I snorted. "Not complaining, baby doll, just surprised. Won't that hurt your stomach?"

Her nose crinkled. "Fuck! Do you know how many times I've jilled off to thoughts of riding you?"

I laughed, leaned down, and kissed her. "We've got all the time in the world, baby doll. Let's not put you back in the hospital. I'd hate for you to face your new colleagues with a sex-related injury on your record."

She snorted. "At least I'd be fucking cool." That had her snickering before she muttered, "I-I think maybe on our sides?"

"Our sides?"

Her nose crinkled, and I sensed her disappointment. "I want nothing more than for you to pound into me, Steel, but..." She grunted, then rested her forehead against mine. "This isn't going how I wanted it to."

I shrugged. "As long as my dick ends up home tonight, I don't care."

She gulped, and I knew my statement had affected her.

"You mean that?"

"You know I don't say shit I don't mean."

She gnawed on her bottom lip. "I do."

"Good." When she gnawed on her lip some more, I growled. "You better stop doing that. Got things I want that mouth to be doing—"

"Have you been tested for STDs?" she blurted out.

"Think I'd sit by your bedside for as long as I have, then put you in danger the second you're on the mend?" I arched a brow at her, pleased when she ducked her head and rounded her shoulders. "Exactly. I'm clean."

"You can't blame me for asking," she argued. "You were a skank."

I had to hide a smile at that, but I squeezed her ass cheeks and warned, "You earned two sets of spanks for this conversation. When you're ready."

Her pout was even more amusing, because I wasn't sure if it was for the timing or the fact that I was gonna spank her until it hurt to sit down for even daring to think I'd come to her disease-ridden.

Sure, I'd fucked a lot of bitches in my time, but all with rubbers.

"Tut tut, baby doll," I rumbled, as I walked us over to the bed and carefully sat down. I was carrying precious cargo, more precious than even the cargo herself fucking knew, and I gripped her tightly, holding on close as I carefully reclined so she was on top of me.

When she moved, I leaned up and sneakily tugged her nipple between my lips, flicking it with my tongue so I could tease her some.

Her high-pitched moan was like the sweetest song, and it was music I'd been longing to hear all my fucking life.

I grunted as I rolled us over so she was on her side. At first, I thought she meant for my front to be touching her back, but she didn't. She hitched her leg up, reached between us, and though it was awkward, she dragged my dick up and down the length of her sex.

I grunted, pushing my forehead into hers again, loving that she was confident, loving that she knew what she wanted from me.

She took her pleasure, her breath hitching as she nudged her clit, massaging it every time she passed by, and when I felt her hips rock from side to side and not just from back to front, I rumbled, "You ready for me to fill you up, baby doll?"

She gulped. "God, Steel, so fucking ready."

"Do it then," I ordered, letting her own this moment.

I maneuvered us a little, helping her, and when she pressed the tip to her gate, I wanted to roar out my relief as the head of my dick finally started to slide home.

Skin to skin.

Fuck, it was phenomenal.

Epic.

Heaven.

Paradise.

Every fucking magical word in existence as, slowly, my dick tunneled its way inside the place it had been craving for a lifetime.

I was panting, out of breath by the time I was all the way in, but she stunned me by clamping down on me, her pussy pulsing and her breathing hitching—the panicked throb to her heart told me she was close to coming, and while I felt the same way, that she was ready to explode stunned the shit out of me.

"Christ, Stone, you're gonna fucking kill me," I muttered, taken aback that she didn't need a fuck ton of foreplay.

"Been waiting on this a long time," she moaned, and I felt her hand between us, working on her clit, getting herself off.

Was there anything more fucking powerful than a woman who knew what she wanted and wasn't afraid to take it?

I peered down in the meager light, watching her touch her clit, seeing the evidence of my cock deep inside her pussy, and I let out a rumble. My growl made her moan, and slowly, I began to pull back.

It was a little awkward, I wouldn't lie.

Fuck, I'd give my left nut to roll her over onto her front, and plow into her from behind, but the moment was a thousand times more intimate for all that I couldn't move away from her, for all that my eyes were on her at all times. Knowing I wasn't causing her any pain was orgasm worthy in and of itself, but seeing her joy, her fucking pleasure, owning it, and being so close to her while I gave it to her, as she took it, I knew there'd never be anything as special to me as this ever again.

Our first time together should be memorable, and it was.

It would be seared into my memory, along with the weight of her tits on my chest, the way her nipples dragged against my pecs. How her skin cleaved to mine, the silk of the cami brushing up against me, making the hairs at the back of my neck stand on edge. How her lips were plump and pouty, gliding against my neck, my throat, sucking down here and there as her slick juices flooded from her, slipping onto my dick as I carefully made love to her.

I felt her hand working frantically, and the gentle noises of her fingers as they moved in her juices were a music of their own. I loved how her breath hitched, how, when I grabbed her hair, tugging on her ponytail, she let me tip her head back and plunder her mouth.

I fucked her there like I couldn't fuck her body, but that was enough. Jesus, it was more than enough.

It was everything I'd never known I needed, and it took Stone to another level in my mind.

She wasn't a hole to fuck.

She was my woman. My Old Lady. Branded as mine.

The thoughts were like electric shocks to the back of my eyes, and I sped up some, trying to stay careful, but needing everything she had to give. When her cunt clenched down around my dick, when she shrieked out her joy, I moved faster, my tongue thrusting against her harder, hotter, needing her to fuck me back.

Her moans and squeaks came around my invading tongue, and when her fingers, ever frantic, tried to get her to another level again, I let her, making sure I held back long enough for her to get off twice before I exploded inside her.

When she pulled back, her face burrowing into my throat, biting down hard enough to hurt, I roared my own pleasure as my cum slalomed into her.

She groaned, long and low as her orgasm overwhelmed her, and that was nothing compared to how I felt as her pussy swallowed every fucking drop I had to give.

We lay there, panting, wrecked, destroyed, and reborn in each other's arms, and even though I'd spent the night in her bed for weeks, never once had it felt righter than it did now.

At this moment, the world we lived in was up in the air. Families were at war, we had a captive a few miles down the road who was going insane, an even more insane hacker who was going homicidal on wife beaters in the club, and that was nothing compared to what was happening to women the *Famiglia* captured and sold.

But none of that mattered at that moment. Sure, it would later, but now?

She was my entire universe, and I was hers.

And my life, everything in it, had never been sweeter for her simply being there.

For the breath she took that was mingled with mine, for the heart that beat hard enough for me to feel it against my chest.

She was mine, but more importantly, I was hers.

And tonight was a night neither of us would forget. Which, in the coming days, was exactly what both of us needed.

FORTY

STONE

"ALWAYS DID KNOW how to show you a good time."

His whispered joke had my nose crinkling, and I slapped him on the gut. "Hush," I chided, biting my lip as the reverend moved from one rectangular hole in the ground to another.

This was not a good day, but it wasn't a bad one either. We were in the Sinners' cemetery, a private graveyard on the east of the property. It was only now I realized how, with my mom buried in the cemetery in West Orange, that she'd been disrespected.

And I couldn't find it in myself to be unhappy about that. Not after what she'd done to Steel.

But today wasn't about her. It was about two other people who'd died ahead of their time. I'd never liked Dog. I'd always thought he was a prick. Especially when I'd accidentally learned how he got his road name—because he was a *dawg*.

Bleugh.

Still, though I'd always disliked him, I didn't like that he was dead either. Such a fucking waste.

I knew Giulia had problems with him, and there was definitely something shady going on as one of his sons and his Old Lady weren't attending the funeral—

In Steel's ear, I asked, "Think something was going on between North and Katy?"

He caught my eye. "Wouldn't put it past either of them."

I hummed at that, my suspicions confirmed, and thought about whether or not I found that icky.

I reckoned the MC life had corrupted me because I actually didn't.

Stepmom and stepson...definitely a porn movie in the making, but I didn't find it all that taboo.

What actually saddened me today was the other burial.

Sarah.

I'd tended to Amara, Tatána, and Ghost, all while their friend had been left to rot in the prison they'd been kept in, and as much as I knew that it hurt them to be here, to watch her be buried now that the authorities had relinquished her body, I figured it would give them some closure.

Closure—what we all needed.

Sometimes, people were luckier than others though. I'd pay to have closure after my mom's death, but I wouldn't like what I got either. So what was the point?

Regrets in these instances were so fucking pointless that I wasn't even sure why I was thinking that shit.

Mostly, a little like with Annie Young, I just wished I'd hurt them more before they died.

I included my mom in that too.

Did that make me horrible?

That I'd have done something to make her suffer for the decades of misery she put me and Steel through?

There were a thousand ways to tell someone who their father was, and Lana Jane Walker was not the best person to be imparting such news.

Not on a good day, and certainly not on a day where she was dying of cancer.

Her bitterness skewed everything, and the truth was, I hoped she rotted in hell for what she'd put Steel through.

The mental anguish—it was a wonder he hadn't tried to kill himself.

The thought froze me up inside, and I rasped, "Steel?"

"Yeah, baby doll?"

"Did you try something stupid after Mom—"

He tensed, and that tension in the face of how relaxed we were together said it all.

I gripped his arm, tightened my fingers around it until I knew I had to be hurting him, and I whispered, "If you ever keep any shit like that from me in the future, I will—"

"What?" he replied, but his tone was light, his eyes amused at my anger at his past self. "What will you do?"

"Spank you."

That was as much of a threat as I could come up with right now, and whether or not it actually constituted as a threat, period, was another matter entirely.

I prodded him in the chest, making sure I didn't aim for the still tender spots on his shoulder, then muttered, "Promise me."

"Ain't going nowhere now, baby doll. You're stuck with me." He pressed a kiss to my forehead.

"Good. Nowhere else I wanna be stuck," I admitted, hearing him sigh and smiling because he was a softie sometimes.

The irony, right?

Steel the softy?

I'd never tease him about that, because I loved it too fucking much when he revealed that gooey side to his nature, and I'd hoard it zealously as my own. But I loved that he melted when I told him how I felt. I loved that it mattered to him.

It was what gave me hope, what made me believe we had a strong chance of surviving together for a long time to come.

And I said surviving because he was still steel-headed, and I was still as stubborn as a rock...we'd butt heads, but I was pretty sure we'd fuck to make things right.

When we finally made it to the other side of the private cemetery which was on Sinner land, a place where Ghost had requested Sarah be buried, and I quote, "Because here, she can lie near the wildflowers, and she can see the city, have the sky overhead, and the sun on her, and the rain and the wind. She needs that after where she died."

Even Giulia, who was hard as fucking nails sometimes, had started weeping at that request.

Steel, as Secretary, had come to us to ask about the funeral proceedings, which I'd figured was unusual at the time, until I'd learned about the release of Sarah's body too.

Bitches weren't involved in the ceremony of a brother's funeral, so this time, it was different.

Ghost had helped him pick Sarah's coffin and some flowers, and I'd watched on, touched that he could be so gentle with her.

Sure, he could be gentle with me, but I wasn't as fragile. Even sick, even almost dying, I was made of stronger stuff than Ghost.

I wasn't saying she wasn't strong in her own way, because she fucking was. To be honest, I'd have been dead a lot earlier than Sarah because I'd have been killed. I'd have bitten off a dick or tried to escape and gotten shot in the interim.

There were different kinds of strengths, and Ghost, Tatána, and Amara had it in spades—the strength to survive.

Inspiring shit.

So, here we were at a plot in the corner of the graveyard that was on higher ground, that looked over the city slightly, that watched over the compound, and which would be battered by all the elements, thanks to its open terrain when the seasons changed.

It had touched me then to hear Ghost's logic behind it, and it touched me now when she gave a short speech in Ukrainian, something that had Tatána and Amara nodding. She proceeded to start a song, that I swear to God, would haunt me until the day I died. It had shivers whispering down my spine and back up again, because the notes were haunting. Absolutely haunting.

When she finished her solo, I'd admit that my eyes weren't even just wet anymore—they were drenched.

I bit my lip as I reached into the casket to scatter dirt onto the coffin, and when we were on the brink of walking away, Steel's phone buzzed. As did Sin's.

I eyed them both, then muttered, "That bodes well, doesn't it?"

Steel grunted as he read the screen, then spat, "Shit." To me, he muttered, "Can you make sure the wake goes down okay? I'll be in touch if I can't make it."

I nodded, a little surprised when he started walking off without a backward glance. Then he froze, like he'd been stuck with a cattle prod, and quickly shifted around. When he was back at my side in less than five seconds, I grinned at him as he cupped my cheeks and kissed me.

In front of the entire congregation.

Everyone knew who I was to him.

The snatch included.

They'd seen the long reach of the cursive 'S' that drifted down my throat, so they were well aware I was branded, but this confirmed it.

And I'd never felt more like crowing with delight in my life.

When he pecked me on the lips after that too fast tongue fuck and muttered, "Be good," I pouted at him, which made him laugh, the somber expression lightening some before he shook his head.

When he bopped me on the nose, just the tip, my brows lifted, but I'd admit to appreciating the little touch.

This time, when he stalked off, I sighed, watching that fine butt of his as he walked across the way, back to the compound where whatever the fuck was going down was apparently happening.

A few minutes later, I heard an unusual sound, and when the council saw what was happening, it snagged their attention almost immediately.

The ATVs were out.

Sin and Steel on one each.

That meant they were going to the Fridge.

I knew about who was in there, knew about why, and I had to figure that either Lancaster had broken or he was ill.

I strode over to Rex, feeling only a slight twinge in my body as I did so, and when he saw me, he wasn't scowling, just appeared a little surprised.

"You need me?" I asked him.

Rex shrugged. "Don't think so, babe."

I jerked my thumb at the direction in which my man had gone. "He'd only take off like that, him and the Enforcer, if something had gone wrong."

He sighed. "Fuck. Can't we even have a fucking funeral in peace?"

"You don't exactly live a peaceful life, Rex," I told him dryly. "Peace comes to those who earn it."

He rolled his eyes. "If I wanted to be preached at, I'd talk to the reverend."

I grinned. "Who you'd promptly try to convert—"

He scowled at me. "I only did that once."

"Did what once?" Giulia inquired, her eyes pink after the service and that haunting song of Ghost's.

Rex heaved a sigh. "Nothing."

"Not nothing," I joked. "You know how Jehovah's Witnesses come knocking door to door?"

She pulled a face. "I do."

"Well, this kid comes around, a little older than Rex at the time, maybe twenty-four? Anyway, Rex invites him in and only proceeds to convert him."

"Convert him to what?" she asked with a laugh.

"Non-Jehovah's Witness-ism?" Rex replied warily. "It was a shitty thing to do. I actually regret it."

It was proof of just how fucking clever he was, and I knew he didn't like to be reminded of that time.

There was a big chunk of Rex's life that had been spent with him at war with himself.

A war, I knew, Rachel Laker didn't help him with.

Giulia arched a brow at me as Rex twisted around when Nyx caught his attention. "You okay?" she questioned, surprising me because I thought she'd bring up Rex and how I knew that story.

They were used to my little tidbits though, accustomed to me doling out stories about the brothers at random moments.

Hey, it was the perk of being the little sister to most of the council. I got to embarrass the shit out of them.

"That song, fuck, right?"

Giulia nodded. "Never been much of a crier, but damn."

Before we could get into it, a hand grabbed me, and I peered over to look at Rex.

"You sure you're ready?"

I cast Nyx a glance, saw he made the Grim Reaper look cheery, and shrugged. "Sure."

The next twenty minutes were a blur, and I'd admit that I never expected to start my journey back into medicine after my unintentional sabbatical in a torture chamber, but that was how the cookie crumbled sometimes, no?

Being in the SUV as we drove across the rough terrain wasn't pleasant, mostly because it made me nauseated. It was so fucking bumpy on this stretch of land that I was grateful I'd only had a piece of toast this morning to down my meds.

I peered at Rex, who was behind the wheel, and muttered, "I hope you ride your bike better than you're driving this."

He sniffed at me but didn't bother to comment.

That was enough to make me realize that all was not well.

I mean, I figured that, but he actually looked concerned.

When we made it to the Fridge—a shitty little building that I knew had a weird roof so that, from a satellite view, it just looked like a big bush, especially with the way it was shielded by a lot of trees the way it was—the tension in the SUV became even more palpable. I'd been in triple heart bypasses that were less tense, and that was really saying something.

I'd never been here before, even though I knew what happened within those four walls, and while my physician's heart wasn't happy about it, I knew how this world worked.

I'd been touched by it myself, hadn't I?

Had dealt with the clusterfuck of crime in my own small way.

Some people deserved to die.

I'd work myself to the bone helping those who needed my healing hands, and I'd do what I could, work every last hour as I strived to help people live out every moment of their life to capacity, but I was a little like the angel of death.

Annie Young had wanted to save people by giving them peace.

Me? I felt like making the people who deserved it die with a little dash of hell on the side.

Not exactly the best ethos for a doctor, but fuck it. Who'd know except for the MC?

When I took the few steps toward the structure, the door opened, and the stench that hit me had me blurting out, "Jesus Christ. You torturing his nose as well?"

Rex huffed, but Steel ground out, "What the fuck are you doing here, Stone?"

I grinned at him, even though that smell was no small thing to smile through. Christ, I could feel it in the back of my mouth, that was how pungent it was. "I'm the doctor. Aren't you lucky?"

"You shouldn't have brought her here." he growled at Rex. "She might catch an infection or something."

That wasn't exactly how this kind of thing worked, but I wasn't going to tell him that.

I liked that he was trying to protect me, and after a lifetime of him ignoring me, I'd deal with moments of him being overbearing... just until the novelty wore off.

Taking a few more steps toward him, I was cautious as I climbed the wooden stairs to the outer walkway which led to the door, because they were rickety.

"I can deal with whatever you've got going on in there."

Sadly, it wasn't a lie, even if it was gross as fuck.

I'd seen worse during my time in the ER, but this was definitely a close second.

The man in the Fridge didn't actually resemble a man anymore. They'd kept him here for...fuck, I couldn't even guess. His face was one big swollen mass, and his body wasn't much better.

He was naked except for a pair of grimy, bloodstained boxers, making me wonder if he had a dick behind them or not, and on the floor, there was a dog bowl with a water bowl beside it.

My stomach twisted at that, even if I got it.

Somehow, though, understanding wasn't enough to deal with the evidence of psychological and physical torture ahead of me.

The state of him was one thing, but knowing my brothers could do this to someone?

Another matter entirely.

I flinched when Steel touched the small of my back, and he stiffened in return, but I shook my head and muttered, "It's okay."

It was the opposite of okay.

The guy on the floor was barely breathing, and though the

space was black, pitch-black in fact, so dark that the corners of the room were covered in shadows, he didn't even flinch at the sight of the light coming in from the door.

Light which enabled me to see maggots—

Okay.

I breathed in slowly. Exhaled deeply. Figuring out where the stench came from wasn't a pleasant discovery.

"Where do I fucking start?" I rasped.

"Just keep him alive," Rex ordered, and I cut him a look, shaking my head at him as I saw the stoniness on his face.

He knew I was disgusted, knew what I was thinking, but he didn't care.

I wasn't used to that from him, was used to my opinion mattering, even if he'd sometimes give me shit for it.

"Why? He's nearly dead," I muttered.

"Because Lily needs the chance to end his life," Link rasped.

He popped up out of nowhere, like Link usually did, and I tilted my head to the side.

"You think Lily could end her father's life?"

"That was her goal before we got together." He shrugged. "I at least want to give her the opportunity."

"The opportunity to vomit," I muttered.

Nyx grabbed my arm at that, then twisted me to face him. I was used to him looking glum, used to him looking as though the four horsemen of the Apocalypse were riding across the Earth for him and him alone, but this?

It was nothing like how he usually was.

I could see the cold in his eyes, the sheer block of ice that he'd turned into as he snapped, "That bastard raped Lily for years. Throughout her childhood. When she was little. He psychologically tortured her just as badly as what we've done to him.

"He's singlehandedly behind one of the largest human trafficking rings in Asia because he's the money man, and without him, every single one of those circles dies. He's done shit that makes how we treated him seem like a benediction, so don't fucking judge—"

I snapped at that, shaking off his hold on my arm and grinding out, "I'm a healer. It's what I do. You can't bring me here, expect me to look at a still breathing corpse that's being eaten a-fucking-live by maggots, and expect me to just click my tongue and tell you I'll heal him up in a jiffy.

"I get that you don't want my opinion, and I understand that you don't care what I think. But don't tell me to be a fucking robot, Nyx. Don't you fucking dare."

Steel cleared his throat. "She's right, Nyx."

"I know she fucking is," was his reply, but he was still scowling at me. "Can you keep him alive or not?"

I rolled my eyes. "I can do my best."

"It needs to look like he's fucked up, but that her killing him is the final stroke."

"You got a goddamn makeup trailer out here to pretty him up? Maybe you can get the fucking funeral home onto him, get some formaldehyde to make him beautiful," I snapped. "If you want to hide most of the shit you've done to him, then you cover him up. No way can I heal some of this with a first aid kit."

"More extensive than that." Rex shoved something at me, and my brows rose when I saw he had, somehow, purloined a fucking paramedic's kit.

Before I could grumble and wonder at his connections, Lancaster started seizing.

And that was the tip of the iceberg for this bastard.

He was being granted his living hell, and while I was glad for it —this was just a lot more than I'd anticipated.

FORTY-ONE
STEEL

WHEN SHE STORMED out an hour later, having loaded Lancaster up with more drugs than a pharmacy, she didn't look back, didn't try to connect with me in any way, shape, or form.

I'd admit that hurt.

It hurt because I knew she was judging us for what we'd done, and to be honest, I couldn't blame her.

I hadn't been involved this time, but I had in the past. It wasn't the first time we'd used techniques Mav had learned in his days overseas to our benefit, and it wouldn't be the last.

But the way she'd looked at him, then us, and I'd seen her opinion of her brothers fall?

It had gutted me.

But I didn't have time to be gutted.

At the same time as Stone was being rolled out in an SUV, another was incoming.

I could see Lily's white face through the windshield, saw Link's lips moving a mile a minute as he tried to shore her up.

I wasn't sure if she'd be able to do it, even if he was most definitely on his deathbed right now. I hoped for her sake that she had the strength to do what she needed to for herself.

Closure came in many ways. I had to figure she'd know which option was the best for her.

When she climbed out of the SUV without waiting on Link to open the door for her—because, unlike Stone, she was a lady, a thought that had my lips twitching—then strode over to us without waiting on him?

I was surprised by the fire in her eyes.

"Is it true?" she demanded, staring Rex down.

He peered up from his cell phone, then shrugged. "I don't know what Link has been telling you."

Her Old Man cleared his throat. "Been telling her that he's come to the end of the road. His usefulness has reached its limits."

Rex cut Link a look, then arched a brow at Lily. "Have at him, honey."

She licked her lips, then surprised me by taking a shaky step back.

Her gaze flickered over to the Fridge, fixated on the door, and the rest of us just stayed there, not moving, watching as she reached her decision.

When she began to move, acting like she'd been instantly defrosted, I watched her climb the same stairs Stone had stormed up before she flung open the door.

The next few minutes were passed with her puking up her guts as she dealt with the stench and the sight of her father. Twice she vomited, twice Link had to hold her as she trembled like a leaf.

It was a testament to how much we respected Link, how much we knew he loved her, that we stuck around, waiting on her to make a decision.

She didn't know it yet, but she didn't have only the one knight in rusty armor.

We kept our backs to her, letting her do what she had to do, but when she stopped puking and made her way through the door, I wasn't the only one to peer over my shoulder to see how things were going to take shape.

She headed inside, eying him like a puma that was caught in a bear trap, one that was ready and willing to snap at the slightest provocation, then she surprised me—she let her leg fly back and she kicked him.

Hard.

Enough for Donavan to start coughing, loud enough for me almost to miss her words, "That was for me."

He rolled over, thanks to the drugs Stone had pumped him with, and lay curled on his side as she did it again.

"That one is for Ghost."

And again.

"For Amara."

"For Tatána."

She kicked him until I knew her leg had to hurt. "This one is for Sarah." Then she snapped, "Give me a knife, Link."

Her voice, however, this time, triggered something in Donavan.

A snort escaped him, and a laugh followed it. "Lily, Lily, Lily," he rumbled, before he started slurring, "Should have known you were a treacherous little cunt. Just as bad as your mother."

His words were barely audible, and I was used to translating the nonsense torture victims came out with, but somehow, she knew what he was talking about and she hissed at him.

"You're the treacherous bastard. I can't wait until you're dead. Until you're not even a memory."

"Dead or not, alive or not, I'll always haunt your nightmares." Lancaster cackled. "I hope I do. I hope I make your life miserable—"

She kicked him again, this time harder than before, so hard

that my eyes flared as I watched him lift up with the momentum and sail away across the room.

"That was for Mom."

When he landed and started sputtering, it was clear he had a death wish.

I couldn't blame him, not after what he'd been through. He could see the end was in sight, had been forced back to the land of the living just for this moment, and I knew the fear that Stone would work to keep him alive just for us to carry on pumping him for information had to be a strong one.

Maybe there was more to learn, but when Jaxson had contacted us, telling us that Lancaster was nonresponsive—and when he said that, we all knew he meant nearly dead, because nonresponsive was pretty much how it worked when you were as badly beaten as Lancaster—we'd known the writing was on the wall.

"You don't have the guts to do it," Lancaster sneered. "Always was a pussy, just like your mom. I want your soul to be stained with me," he said with a gasping laugh. "I want my blood on your hands, Lily—it's the one thing you can do that will ever make me proud of my cunt of a child."

Lily gasped at his words, but my brows rose as Link stormed forward, gun high as he took a single shot at Lancaster's head.

At this close of a range, it wasn't pretty. Lily gasped, then whipped around to spy who had done the job for her, and though it blew my mind that we'd gone to all this effort to keep the fucker alive just so that she could kill him…I got it.

I did.

No way was he going to have that power over her, not if Link could help it, and he'd made damn sure she'd have nothing to repent or to regret.

Even if she wished she'd been the one to fire that gun, she could never regret not taking the killing blow because a few more kicks like that, and the already damaged body would have likely given out.

She didn't rail at him, didn't even wail at him making the kill on her behalf.

Instead, she peered down at herself, at the blood that spattered her, at the way her father's brains decorated the wall, then rasped, "Is there a hose anywhere?"

I arched my brow, but I muttered, "Yeah, but there's a bathroom too." A tiny outhouse attached to the back, nothing fancy...

She shuddered. "I have no desire to know what a bathroom in this place would even look like, never mind smell like."

I snickered, unable to stop myself, and wasn't surprised when a few of the others joined in too. Wasn't like we could blame her. There was a shitter and a sink, even a bath! But the tub was definitely forged in hell. While it was pearly white at the moment, soon enough, it would contain the pink gunk of Donavan's rotting corpse as we melted it down with boiling lye and water.

Ah, chemistry. It hadn't been my favorite subject back in school, but it sure as fuck was now.

She straightened her back, shoved her nose in the air, and swanned out of the torture chamber as though she was wandering into a ball in a fancy gown.

I had to give her points for that—she had goddamn gumption.

When she was outside, she allowed herself to be sprayed down with a hose. The blood disappeared into the soil, and later on, one of the Prospects would be out here, destroying any potential evidence, but she watched it go, watched it leave her body as we got her clean.

When she was standing there like a soaked rat, Link approached her, his arm coming around her shoulders. She didn't tense up, didn't say shit, just stated, "I'd like to go home now."

He nodded, but I sensed his worry. Even though I knew he

was concerned about her and her response, I knew he wouldn't have changed a thing.

Deep in his eyes, I saw his resolve.

And a happiness that was impossible to feign.

Yeah, a happiness.

He'd saved her soul, and if that wasn't the end of a romance book right there? I didn't know what fucking was.

As they drove off, I turned to Rex and muttered, "That didn't go down how I expected."

Rex just smiled at me, a tiny half smile that was cocky as fuck, while also just telling the tale of how well he knew us... "I knew that was how it would go down all along. Link's a fixer, Steel. Always was, always will be."

And like always where we were concerned—he wasn't wrong about that.

FORTY-TWO

STONE

THE WAKE WAS LOUD, raucous, and contained way too many naked bodies for my liking.

For *any* of the Old Ladies' liking.

Lily had disappeared, and I had to think that Lancaster was dead now and she was at home, mopping up her life as she came to terms with what had just happened. As for the rest of us, we were sitting around just shooting the shit.

What else could we do?

It wasn't like any of us were going to get on the pool table and start an impromptu striptease like Peach, was it?

Or that we'd decide that it was an appropriate time for us to be eaten out on the counter of the bar like Jingles.

I'd always hated those two more than most, especially because Peach was Rex's favorite, and that meant she got away with a lot more than the others.

I couldn't wait for her to turn thirty-three, which was when club sluts were 'retired.' I had one more year to wait, one more fucking year, and I'd be happy as shit.

With the bottle of beer in my hand, one that I'd been nursing all night because I had no desire to get lit with the meds I was on, even though what I'd done today would probably weigh me down for a good long while, mostly, I was watching shit.

Keira had turned her back on the bar so she couldn't see what the women were doing, and Giulia kept eying them up. I knew she was formulating a million different jobs for them to have to do tomorrow—I'd be along for the fucking ride.

It was hard to believe this was the celebration of someone's life, and the brothers were just okay with destroying that.

I felt bad for Sarah, felt even worse for Ghost. Amara and Tatána had returned to the bunkhouse the second a set of tits had popped out, but Ghost was sitting here, watching everything unfold like she was watching porn for the first time in her life.

She wasn't exactly disgusted, nor was she reviled or upset, mostly, I sensed she was curious.

A thought she confirmed with her question, "They have little respect for themselves, don't they?"

My lips twitched, and I shot Giulia a look. The pair of us started snickering, but it was Tiff who muttered, "Self-esteem issues, the lot of them. Sin's already warned me off trying to get them to change. Says the MC likes their daddy issues just fine."

My nose curled in disgust at that answer. "Fucking pigs. The lot of them."

Giulia sighed. "As venomous as that sounded, Stone, and I don't think they're *that* bad, I agree with ya."

If she'd seen what I had, she'd think the same way, but I wasn't about to tarnish her view of the family she had here.

To be honest, my own opinion wasn't all that tarnished. I knew what they were capable of, I'd just never seen it in the flesh before.

Or, I guessed, the *rotting* flesh.

Bleugh.

My stomach churned at that, just a little, but I quickly gulped down a sip of beer.

When the door to the clubhouse opened and the council walked in, a raucous cheer echoed around the bar, and I shook my head at the sight of them.

They were all wet through, all drenched, and I wasn't surprised when they raised a hand in greeting and trudged off to their respective quarters.

Earlier on, if I hadn't mopped up gangrenous sores and necrotic tissue, I'd have joined Steel, just like Tiff and Giulia were doing as they wandered over to their men, evidently wanting to help clean them up, but I wasn't in the mood for that.

I didn't even know what I was in the mood for.

"He's dead, isn't he?"

Ghost's tone was conversational, and I cut her a look. "Do you really want to know the answer to that?"

"Yes. Of course."

I glanced at Keira, saw she was on her phone, not really interested in our conversation, and though I felt bad for not including her in this, because she was as much of an Old Lady as the rest of us, I just wanted to be careful.

She had a lot of reasons to hate Storm and the MC, and I didn't need my man suddenly getting his ass tossed in jail when I'd been forced apart from him since forever.

"Why do you ask that?" I hedged.

She smiled, her shoulder hitching as she replied, "I can just feel it. The air is lighter somehow."

I didn't roll my eyes, because if that made her feel better, then I was all for that. I'd seen the state the women were in, I knew exactly what Lancaster Sr. and Jr. had done to them, but still, I wasn't about to impart—

Or maybe she'd be happy about it.

Maybe she wanted to know that he'd suffered as much as they had, that he'd shared a similar death as Sarah.

I cleared my throat, went to speak, then her hand came over to cup my knee. It was an intimate touch, but it wasn't sexual. More like she was bracing herself as she stated, "I hope his pain was worse than ours, and I know the brothers are violent enough to have given him that kind of end."

Because she'd confirmed my suspicion, as well as affirming that she was a bloodthirsty little thing, I set my hand on hers, and knotted our fingers together. "I can promise you he died a nasty death."

She met my eyes, a plea in them. I understood what she was asking, and I nodded. "I promise. You wouldn't wish that kind of death on an enemy," I told her, tongue in cheek.

Her soft smile was as angelic as her request had been devilish, but I'd admit it eased some of the strain on me, made it a little easier to accept what they'd done to him.

Ghost hadn't had to deal with the aftermath of weeks, maybe months of torture, but still, if she had seen the state of him, maybe it would have made her smile.

A grim thought, but true nonetheless.

Her acceptance made it easier for me to find a resolution—one that made me need to be with my Old Man.

"I'm gonna go see Steel," I told her, squeezing her fingers before I got to my feet and muttered, "You can sleep well tonight, Ghost."

Like a curtain was pulled over her face, she stared up at me, revealing a fatigue she often concealed. "I hope so, Stone. I hope so."

I left her, suddenly needing to be with Steel. Needing him to hold me, to take away the shit I'd done today, the things that had happened.

It took me longer than I'd like to make it up the stairs, and I passed way too much squealing and moaning as I made it to his room.

His door was open, which came as a surprise, and what else came as a surprise?

The underwear and the short shorts on the floor.

My temper surged, and rage filtered through me. If the fucker had—

I sucked in a calming breath, feeling my heart start to pump, the anger sending adrenaline whirling around me so I felt like Wonder Woman as I stormed inside. I saw that cunt Tink with her hand on the bathroom door, just on the brink of tiptoeing in.

"The hell do you think you're doing?" I asked from the doorway.

She spun around, not even having the decency to cover herself up—why would she? Unfortunately for me, I'd seen this shit a hundred times, probably a thousand.

"Steel asked me to join him," she informed me, a smug sneer on her face. "You should have known you weren't enough for him, Stone." She tutted. "I mean, come on, what would he want with a cripple like you when he could have this?"

"This? You mean every chlamydia-tainted piece of you? Hell, if that was true, and he wanted you over this cripple" —did she even know what that meant? Figured she didn't— "then I'd let him have your skanky ass," I told her with a sniff. "But you're a fucking liar, like all the snatch."

Her eyes narrowed, gleaming with hatred, but I was used to that. The bunnies never liked me, mostly because they were jealous.

I had the brothers' respect, even though Steel had always made it a point to avoid me, and they'd used that as a way to get back at me. Over the years, I'd had it all. Everything from my car being egged to getting into bitch fights. I was sick of their shit, and to be honest, I was too fucking old to be dealing with these bitches.

The brothers wanted their clubhouse to be a fucking brothel?

Then they could take that shit to another room in the fucking house.

I wasn't sure how Giulia and I would do it, how we'd make that happen, but I knew she was as tired of it as me.

Seeing pussies left and right when I wasn't at my goddamn day job?

No more.

When she came for me, like some kind of fucking cat with her arms high, intent to hurt me, I merely braced myself. I knew she was going to go for my stomach, and the truth was, I kind of hoped she did.

It would kill me not to fight back. And when I said *killed*, I meant it.

Instead, I knew of one way to bring about this bitch's time at the compound. Maybe all the sluts...

I let her hit me.

And though it stung, I wasn't a girl. I knew how to fight as nasty as this bitch did.

So when her fist hurdled into my belly? I howled.

I howled and dropped to the floor so fast that she gaped at me. My response stunned the shit out of her just long enough for Steel to come storming out of the shower and for him to see me curled up in a ball on the floor.

When his face turned bright red, his expression livid, I watched him rush over to me, shoving her out of the way and deeper into the bedroom, uncaring if she fell. When he was on his knees at my side, helping me unfurl as he supported me from the back, I shot her a smile.

It was filled with as much malice as she'd sent my way, and was a hell of a lot smugger too.

Old Lady: 1

Snatch: 0

She sobbed, "Steel! I didn't do anything!" But there wasn't a cat in hell's chance that Steel was going to believe her. Especially when I knew she'd hit me with enough force to bruise, but he didn't even look at her, just snarled, "Tink, pack your fucking bags and leave before the night is out."

A shocked gasp escaped her, and my smug smile turned into a gleeful one. Sure, my belly ached like a bitch, but hell, it was so worth it.

"I only slapped her—"

"You raised a hand to an Old Lady?"

Oh, boy.

Rex.

The big guns were here.

His voice was like gravel, mean and nasty, and to be honest, I'd never, ever in a million years want to face him down, and I loved him like a brother.

Instantly, Tink started sobbing, but it was no good.

Rex snapped, "Stop the crocodile tears. Get the fuck out before I drag you out of here by your hair."

And that was that.

Steel's word was backed up by Rex, and that meant she was fucked.

And not in the way she usually was.

Ha.

Make that, Old Lady: 2

Club snatch: -1

The day, though it had felt like it was going to end shittily, actually ended in a way that made me smile.

And later on that night, when Steel tucked me into bed like I was a priceless possession? I let him. I also let him go down on me by way of apology for what had happened.

It was a hard life, but sometimes? You just had to make it your bitch.

FORTY-THREE

STEEL

WHEN HER MOUTH slipped around my dick, my eyelashes fluttered. Fuck, what she could do with her mouth was insane.

I groaned, unable to stop myself, unable, also, to refrain from letting my fingers slide through her hair so I could grip the base of her skull.

She raised her eyes, peering up at me in a way that would forever blow my mind, because this was Stone sucking my dick.

Stone.

I'd never thought I'd get inside her once, never mind as many times as we'd fucked since that first night, and to be honest, I was still stunned by that.

She was sore, and after what that cunt had done to her a few days before, and after what she'd seen in the Fridge, I'd figured I wouldn't be getting any anymore.

I'd almost thought that she'd be on her way out of here, a finger in my face and hatred in her eyes, because I knew she'd been repulsed by the sight of Lancaster, and I couldn't blame her.

He'd been gross.

Simple as.

But here she was, still at my side, in my bed, and hell, sucking me off.

I groaned again when she did this thing with her tongue that sent the tip fluttering up along the vein at the back, and I moaned as she sank down deeper onto me, sucking harder, faster, until I knew I was going to come, hard.

I groaned, whispering, "Gonna come, baby doll."

She didn't stop. Just carried on. Working me faster, harder, letting me tug on her hair, letting me grip her so I could shove my cock down those extra few inches.

Then she was deep throating me, and my head tipped back as I hissed out some curses as I came.

Fuck, it was almost painful.

It felt so fucking good, and it hurt so fucking bad, that I was pretty sure I'd gone blind in the aftermath.

I felt my cock jerking around in her mouth as the aftershocks hit me hard, and I growled when she carried on swallowing, the motion drawing every last bead of cum from my poor cock.

When my hands were urging her off my dick rather than onto it, she obeyed, for once, and sat up, grinning as she wiped her mouth with the back of her hand.

I squinted at her. "You trying to kill me?"

"Death by blowjob?" She tapped her chin. "Thought that would be the best way for a man to die?"

"Best way for a man to die is not to die at all," I said dryly, glancing down at my spent cock and muttering, "She hasn't broken you, buddy. You'll be back in full working order soon enough."

She snorted, but didn't say shit, just stunned me further by straddling me and setting her pussy right on top of my cock.

I groaned at the slick heat of her connecting with me, and I worked my jaw as she used me to get herself off.

Her breasts jiggled over the soft cami's neckline, and the sight of them made me reach up and pinch the tips.

"You feel like getting these pierced?"

She snickered. "I told you, whatever I get, you get."

I pondered that. "Best not ask for a clit ring then, huh?"

A grin cracked her cheeks. "From what I hear from Giulia, piercings are the best way to go."

I rolled my eyes, because everyone knew about Nyx's dick. It was a wonder the astronauts on the ISS didn't fucking know about how much metal he had down there.

"Girl talk, that's all we need."

She let out a breathy gasp as she rocked her hips, and I took the moment to grab the V of her neckline and swiftly tear it from her.

She froze, her hands coming up to keep the covering on her belly, but I wouldn't let her. I grabbed her wrists, holding them in one of mine, and when she got in my face, anger making her skin flush, I twisted us around, so she was on the bottom and I was on top.

I nipped one of her nipples, then with her arms under her, which I knew had to be awkward but was tough shit, I went to work on kissing her stomach.

The scars were bad. I wasn't going to lie. They were centered at the sides where the surgeons had aimed for keyhole surgery, but had to extend the operating site into more exploratory operations, and while the front of her stomach wasn't too bad, it wasn't the best.

But she was mine.

If all my scars belonged to her, then that worked the same way.

Because that thought hit home, I reared up, and twisted slightly so she could see my shoulder. "You aren't repulsed by this, are you?" I demanded.

She was heaving, her breath heavy, her skin pink and flushed with exertion. I knew she was angry, so angry she could damn well spit, but I was okay with that. I could handle her anger, what

I wanted was her awareness that I didn't give a fuck about her scars.

They belonged to her, and that was all that mattered to me.

She sneered, "I know what you're doing."

"Good. If you know, then you'll know that you covering this shit up only makes me want to take it off you."

Her throat bobbed as she gulped. "They're ugly."

"They're perfect. They helped keep you alive. Let's not add necrophilia to my list of issues, Stone, because even when we're dead, I'll want to fuck you."

Her nose crinkled. "Let's not do that."

"No?" I pretended to ponder that for a second. "You don't think that would look great on a Hallmark greeting card? 'I love you to necrophilia and back'?"

She hissed out a breath, but I knew she was trying to stop herself from laughing. Shit, if that wasn't what I loved about her— she got my weird sense of humor.

"The second you start eying corpses funny, I'm gonna blow your brains out."

"You don't have to use a gun for that, just those lips of yours." I let my mouth go lax. "I didn't know you could deep throat. I guess I should be jealous, but fuck—"

"Don't be, I practiced on a zucchini with Indy," she said with a giggle, and my eyes flared wide as I tried to imagine Indy and her going down on a fucking zucchini.

I hooted with laughter, and I had no choice but to roll off her, to land flat on my back as I chuckled my ass off.

I swear to fuck, I rolled around like a lunatic, and all the while, she was watching me, laughing too.

How this had happened, I had no idea. How we'd gone from pissing each other off to laughing about it? I didn't have a clue, but it made me happy. So goddamn happy.

When, eventually, the thought of her and innocent produce

didn't make me laugh so hard my belly ached with it, I turned to her and saw she was watching me with warm eyes.

But her stomach?

Bare.

She hadn't used my attack of the giggles as a means of grabbing the tatters of her shirt and covering herself up.

Nope, she lay there. Naked. Bare. And I sighed at her beauty.

I placed a hand on her stomach, making sure I traced over the scars, even though I knew they were sensitive—but I was careful. I let the tips trail over the bruise where that bitch had hit her, and I murmured, "If you got any more perfect, I'd think you were spiking my drinks with Viagra."

"You wish."

She reached down, though, and jacked me off. As predicted, I got hard, and I saw the relief in her eyes and was really grateful for my dick because, after she'd sucked me dry, somehow, it had decided that now was the best moment to come back on board.

I grunted as she carried on working me, and this time, when she rolled onto me, I let her. She didn't stop as she had before. She rocked until she was wet, slippery with it, and when she slid down onto my length, taking all of me, I let my eyes close as I enjoyed the fucking moment.

Coming in her mouth *and* her pussy? Talk about the best way to start a day.

Better than fucking breakfast, that was for sure.

I groaned when she reached down, one hand between her thighs as she touched her clit, and one aiming for my hand. She bridged our fingers, then used that to hold herself steady.

Her hips rocked and rolled, and I just enjoyed the view. Her tits jiggled, unimpeded now by the fabric that had kept them taut like they were on a shelf. I didn't like that, and I loved this more. The way they bounced and swayed, how her stomach tensed and tautened as she rode me hard and wet.

When she came around me, her cunt clenching down harder than she'd sucked me dry earlier, I saw fucking stars too. And the best part?

I knew she was flying around the solar system with me, because there was no way that orgasm hadn't been as cataclysmic for her as it had been for me.

FORTY-FOUR

STONE

BY THE TENTH hour of my twelve-hour shift, I'd admit—to myself only—it was too soon to be back here.

Every part of me was aching, and before the entire shit show—i.e when I'd been poisoned—I'd grown used to the aching. It was part of being a doctor. Of being on your feet so fucking long, trying to stay awake and aware, even though you were running on no sleep, all while buzzing around like a fly trying to get everything done as you made sure you didn't drop one of the ten plates you were spinning and generally being a superhero.

Seriously, people didn't give enough credit to the doctors or nurses who tended to them.

Batman and Superman wouldn't be able to pull the shifts we did, that was for fucking sure.

Regardless, pre-shit show, I'd ached.

This ache?

Wow.

Just...wow.

I mean every bone felt like it needed a massage. Not just my back or my legs, but every single frickin' bone. And my head was pounding like a mofo, all while I had to try to help some kid pull a marble out of his nose.

It wasn't my first marble, but it might as well have been. Patience definitely hadn't been my virtue today, so much so, I'd made the kid cry when I'd told him off for fidgeting and had ended up bribing him with a bag of Skittles from the vending machine by way of apology.

Learning the ropes in the new hospital sucked as well. I didn't know where anything was, the staff on shift were friendly but distant because they knew who I was and didn't like it—my rep with the MC preceded me, and not in a good way—and on the whole, I wished my day could have been improved by tasting the fucking rainbow.

Only, it didn't.

When I cringed as I bent down to grab some gauze from the bottom drawer of the medical cart that I kept kicking around, my patient, a woman who'd come in with a nasty cut on her palm, murmured, "I think you need some ibuprofen. You look like you're in as much pain as me."

I cut her a wry look and was on the brink of joking, when I remembered I couldn't do that shit anymore.

Sigh.

It sucked having to be PC after weeks of being so non-PC, but I'd get used to it.

Joking that I needed a bed and a bath would probably open me up to a damn lawsuit if I skipped a stitch on her palm, so it was better just to politely smile at her and hope she'd shut up.

She did.

Thankfully.

We walked out together, where I wrote her a prescription for antibiotics and pain meds at the nurses' station, then I let her walk on her merry way while I returned to the cubicle I'd tended her in.

Thankfully, it wasn't as busy as it was at High Lidren, and the ER here was practically a ghost town by comparison.

So when I returned to the cubicle, and found it clean, I sank into the uncomfortable visitor's chair and closed my eyes for a second.

I was pooped.

When I heard the rustle of the curtain open, my eyes popped open though, and I stared at the face of a man I hadn't seen in too long.

"José!" I cried, then, when getting up felt like too much of a pain in the butt, I muttered, "Excuse me for not hugging you, but I'm aching like a son of a bitch."

His lips twitched, and the handsome jerk pulled off his hat, pressed it to his chest as he came in, and leaned back against the gurney.

I'd been in the same class as the town's sheriff, and I fully admitted that if I hadn't been head over heels for Steel, I'd totally have had moon eyes for José.

"Joseph now, Stone," he corrected me. "The white folk don't like to be reminded that I'm Mexican."

His crinkled nose told me what he thought about that, but I just scoffed, "Surprised you give a shit."

"I don't, but unfortunately I need to get re-elected to sit in my office, and I quite like my job." Then, he patted his hat, and I realized I hadn't seen the yellow envelope beneath it that he had tucked to his chest. "Even if, some days, it's not so pleasant."

I cocked a brow at him, and asked, "Huh, I should have guessed this wasn't a social visit. I haven't seen you in years," I complained, "and you're here to talk about the club?"

His lips twitched. "It's handy that you're home," he replied dryly. "It's fucking hard getting to talk to Rex, but me popping in here and chatting with you makes shit a lot easier."

I rolled my eyes. "Just what I always wanted to be—a telegram."

His lips twitched again, but his gaze remained somber. "Got some bad shit in here," he muttered, wiggling the envelope before he passed it over.

If I was going to be the telegram, then I was going to have a look and see what information I was passing around.

When I popped the seal, he didn't chide me, just cocked a brow at me when I studied him, then the envelope.

As I pulled out some pictures, I didn't gasp, because after Lancaster, I was pretty sure I was impossible to stun, but seeing Lodestar with her hand around Dog's neck in a grainy CCTV picture definitely got my heart pounding.

She'd been the one to kill him?

I'd never thought Star would give that much of a damn about Dog. I'd figured it was North and that stepmom of his, some kind of weird star-crossed lovers shit they were both pulling since they wanted to get away from her Old Man—there had to be a reason, after all, why they'd taken off together. Dog was definitely vindictive enough to go chasing after her so he could haul her back by her hair. And even though they'd asked Hawk if he knew anything, Steel said Hawk was making a virgin asshole look slack.

Back in the day, the Old Ladies had surmised that Lizzie Fontaine, Giulia's mom, had taken her kids somewhere Dog couldn't officially go—to territory that the Sinners weren't allowed to enter. Figured that was why she'd stayed gone too, and he hadn't been able to do shit about it.

The question on my lips was one I'd never get an answer to—why? Why on earth had Lodestar decided that Dog needed to be put down?

But before I could even process what I was looking at, José muttered, "Shit's changing around here, Stone. I never signed up for this."

I grunted at that, because it didn't take a fucking genius to figure out that he hadn't signed up to be covering up murders for the club.

I stared him square in the eye, not making him say anything, as I told him, "I'll talk to Rex. Make sure you get something nice for your assistance."

He dipped his chin, and his smile was pleasant—he liked my answer. "That's great to hear."

"I'll bet." I peered at the pictures again, but her face was easy to see.

It stunned me, knowing what she was doing for the club, that she'd let herself be caught on CCTV, but also, Lodestar was difficult to read.

Who the hell knew why she did what she did?

I stared at her, then at José, and questioned, "Is she going to be all right?"

He grunted. "Made sure of it."

"Thank you. She's good people."

His head tipped to the side. "Figured you'd be angry. He's a brother."

"She's involved with the MC," was all I said, even as I wondered if Steel knew about this. I raised my legs, wincing as I let them rest on the gurney, and he watched me with a curiosity that was impossible to deny.

"It's true then?"

"What?"

He tapped his ear, telling me he'd spotted the tat. "You're branded?"

I grinned at him. "Yeah."

"About time. Wondered when he'd get his head out of his ass."

I shrugged. "My mother fucked him up."

That had him snorting. "Lana Jane would fuck anyone up."

"Me included," I retorted brightly, before I waggled the envelope and continued, "Appreciate you coming to me with this, José. I'm not working tomorrow, but I am in two days' time. Come and visit me then?"

"Will do."

He nodded at me with a politeness that was weird, considering we'd been in school together, but I watched him go, even as I returned my attention to the pics.

Pursing my lips, I grabbed my cell, grateful that Steel had replaced it with a burner that Mav had secured, and I took some pics of the grainy images, then sent them to him, Nyx, and Rex in a group text.

Me: *We have a problem.*

Steel: *Shit!*

Rex: *Where the fuck did you get those from?*

Nyx added Sin to the conversation

Sin: *Christ. You couldn't wake me up with good news?*

Nyx: *Where did you get them from?*

Me: *Joseph, the sheriff, just walked in.*

Rex: *Fuck.*

Nyx: *Nah, he went to Stone. It's all good.*

Me: *It is, so long as you make it worth his while. I'm on shift in two days. I told him to come and visit me again.*

Steel: *You shouldn't be involved in this shit.*

Me: *He involved me, and hey, if it works out well, then it's all good. I don't want Lodestar going down for this.*

Me: *Dog was a creep anyway. I figure he did something to deserve it.*

Nyx: *You really are one of us, aren't you? Lol.*

Me: *Bloodthirsty? No. Not so much, but as weird as she is, she doesn't strike me as someone who'd get her hands dirty unless she thought it was necessary.*

Rex: *Truer words. Fuck. Thanks, Stone. I'm sorry he involved you, even if it will make it easier to deal with him.*

Me: *No problem. GTG.*

The soft tread of someone outside the cubicle had me quickly lowering my legs, and when a nurse popped her head around the curtain, I was sitting there, staring at her curiously as I checked a clipboard I had on my lap, one I'd just grabbed from the side.

"Everything okay, Marla?"

She'd been in my class at school too. I'd never liked her. At least she wasn't looking down on me now, more like she eyed me as if I was some kind of freak...

It was a testament to how much of a bitch she'd been when I was a kid that I preferred the 'freak' treatment than the bully shit.

"You ready to see another patient, doctor?"

I smiled at her, inwardly crowing at her calling me by my title. Something I'd insisted on earlier when she kept calling me Stone. "Yes, Marla. I'm ready."

I wasn't.

But hell, I had just under seventy minutes to kill—unless they killed me first.

FORTY-FIVE
STEEL

WHEN SHE ROLLED IN NEARLY two hours later, looking like death warmed over, I hustled her into the shower and watched as, for the first time in a while, she grabbed the waterproof stool and sat on it to clean up.

I kept an eye on her, even though I knew she hated that, before I left her right at the end to go and make her a hot drink.

It was eight AM, because she'd worked the night shift since it was quieter and she said that it was best to start then rather than during the day, but she looked exhausted, and I didn't like it. Not one fucking bit.

She had circles under her eyes and a stoop to her shoulders. She was drawn and weary—by choice. Christ, sometimes she was too stubborn for anyone's good.

Heading out to make her some toast and a cup of the herbal tea I knew she liked, which tasted like piss to me, I waited on the kettle to boil and the bread to toast under the grill. Reaching for my phone, I eyed the few messages I'd received in the short time since she'd returned home, and my brow furrowed at the group text chat the council had going on.

We'd already been discussing the sheriff and Lodestar, but shit had evidently heated up in my absence.

Sin: *It's going to be one of those fucking days. Just had a warning from Brennan O'Donnelly.*

Rex: *What kind of warning?*

Sin: *Brennan didn't say, only hinted at the fact Benito Fieri might have figured out who went gunning for his sons.*

Me: *Shit.*

Sin: *Yeah.*

Nyx: *He had to figure it out at some point.*

Rex: *Preferably never, but I agree. Okay, we need to meet for emergency church.*

Nyx: *What we NEED, Rex, is to up our game. It's time Jaxson and Hawk became brothers.*

Link: *Hawk's hardly prospected.*

Me: *He's good as gold. You know he's solid.*

Sin: *Unlike his brother.*

Me: *Figures that North would be more interested in the pussy than the club.*

Nyx: *Hawk bounty hunted for a while. That tells you the mindset he has.*

Rex: *What about the drive for new Prospects?*

Link: *Got four interested.*

Nyx: *You know I hate making hangers-on Prospects.*

Rex: *We ain't got a choice right now, Nyx. Even if they're just glorified watchdogs, I don't give a fuck.*

Nyx: *You say that now.*

Rex: *If you've got a workable solution, you tell me what the fuck we should do. We can't use private security, but the council's Old Ladies have fucking crosshairs on them.*

Me: *Not all of them.*

Rex: *No. But they're targets because they belong to the council.*

We need to make sure they're protected so you pussy whipped fuckers don't lose your heads.

Link: *Fuck off. Like you don't want a brother protecting Rachel.*
Nyx: *She'd never let him.*
Rex: *This isn't about me.*
Me: *Isn't it?*
Rex: *No! Get your asses to church in the next half hour. We got shit to discuss.*

As I thought about what the repercussions were of Benito Fieri figuring out we were gunning for his family—none of them were great—I fixed Stone's toast, clutched the dish and the mug, and walked into the bedroom and placed them on the nightstand.

Heading for the closet, I grabbed her robe, which we had to keep in there because everything got soaked through otherwise when we showered, and wandered back into the bathroom.

She was staring in the mirror, naked as the day she was born, and though I had no idea what she was looking at, she was fine as fuck, even if she was exhausted.

"You checking out my ass back there?" she rumbled, catching my eye in the mirror.

I gave her a sheepish grin for an answer, then held open the robe for her.

She sighed, twisted around, then dragged her feet over to me. If I'd needed proof that she was exhausted, then I just got it.

She let me tuck her into the robe, and when she leaned on me, fuck, I wasn't sure if I wanted to holler with glee or get pissed.

I'd known it was too fucking soon, but she always had to push it.

Grumbling under my breath though, because she didn't need me moaning at her right now, I walked her to the bed and helped her beneath the comforter.

When she'd settled, I passed her the mug and then, after she'd taken a sip of hot tea, passed her the plate.

She took a bite of toast just the way she liked it, almost charred, lots of butter, and just a smidgen of jelly on the left corner—yeah, precise, but she could be weirdly precise when she wanted to be. She swallowed her bite, bit her lip, then muttered, "I can't believe you get my toast right every time."

"I'm good with details when it's for someone I care about." I eyed the envelope she'd dumped in here before she'd gone for a shower, and asked, "You doing okay?"

She shrugged. "Not my monkey, not my circus."

That had me grimacing. "It kind of is."

"Yeah, to a point, but even though you boys let me listen in on club business, it's not like I have any say in shit. But I think you're a fucking fool if you don't encourage Rex to up whatever it is you're giving Joseph. He didn't look happy."

"Can't blame him." I scraped a hand over my jaw. "Paid him to keep his eyes and ears open for us, not to cover up murders." I grunted. "We'll make it right."

"Did you know Lodestar was the one behind it?"

He sighed. "Sadly, yeah. She said he was beating on his Old Lady."

Her brows lifted. "As much of a feminist as I am, I don't know if that was a good enough reason for murder."

"I think she's more on edge than we ever realized. Mav is defending her, but she's volatile."

She snorted. "Volatile isn't the word. You need to watch her."

"We are. Well, Mav is. Mostly, we're making sure that any of the brothers who get a little handsy with their Old Ladies—the ones that Nyx hasn't already dealt with—get the shit kicked out of them and are encouraged to straighten themselves out."

That had her snickering around another piece of toast. "Well, that's one way to clean up the place."

"If that was her intention, then it worked," I agreed, leaning back against the bed, resting my elbow close to her feet.

I was dressed for the day and she was ready for sleep, but it was nice just sitting here with her, talking shit over as she settled down.

I'd hated last night. I knew that made me sound like a pussy, but I was going to heavily suggest to whichever coordinator Rex had bribed to get Stone a place at the hospital that she only work the day shifts. I didn't give a fuck if it was fair or not.

After a lifetime's worth of being in an empty bed, I was pretty fucking used to having Stone beside me, and I didn't want to get *un*used to it either.

When she finished her toast, I grabbed the dish, watched her drink her tea, then asked, "You think you'll sleep?"

"I'm exhausted," she admitted, surprising me.

Not that she was tired, but that she was *actually* confessing to it.

Apparently sensing my shock, she rolled her eyes. "I may have pushed it."

"Ya think?"

She huffed. "I'll be better in two days."

I rested a hand on her foot and inquired, "Are we good?"

She cut a look to the envelope. "I grew up knowing the shit the MC did. I was well aware you didn't belong to a My Little Pony Club." She shrugged. "Would it be easier if you were a doctor too? Maybe, but I wouldn't get to see you in that sexy cut, plus, you probably wouldn't have a massive tattoo of my name on your back." She winked. "Some you win, some you lose."

I laughed at that. "Them's the cards that fall, huh?"

She grinned. "Exactly." With a final sip of her tea, she shoved it on the nightstand, and I watched her settle down.

"Can you close the curtains please?" she requested softly, tilting her head to the side to look at me.

I nodded, reared up, settled close to her, and pressed a kiss to her lips. "Sleep well, baby doll."

She hummed. "I will." When I moved to get off the bed, she grabbed my cut and asked, "Steel?'

"Yeah?"

"When I'm not the walking wounded, you will spank me, won't you?"

I blinked, taken aback at that, because whatever I'd expected her to say, it wasn't that. So I grinned at her. "Who said I'll wait until you're not the walking wounded?" I teased.

Her cheeks pinkened. "Oh."

"Yeah. Oh." My grin morphed into a smirk. "But not today, baby doll."

She heaved a sigh. "No. Not today. Maybe tomorrow?" Her eyelashes started to flutter to a close.

"Maybe tomorrow," I confirmed, even though she didn't have a cat in hell's chance of me spanking her when she was so fragile.

If I could wrap her in a blanket and let her walk around in that, I totally would. Instead, I was left handling an independent woman who I knew I'd push away if I didn't let her do what she wanted.

Back when she was fifteen, she'd been pliable. Moldable. I could have probably made her mold to me, bend her to my will, but the truth was, I didn't want that from her.

I liked that she had guts. I liked that she had the balls to deal with law enforcement who was talking about murder and bribery all without batting an eyelash.

I loved that she was strong, that she was a fighter.

I loved that she was my Stone.

And because I was turning into a pussy, for real, and not one as hardcore as Mrs. Biggins, who hissed at me from under the bed but otherwise left me alone—I was almost proud of the fact she hadn't scratched me in over a month—I leaned over before I started out the door, and gave her one more kiss. A tender one. To the forehead. I murmured against her temple, "I love you, baby doll."

She sighed, and sleepily whispered, "I love you too."

I wasn't sure if she'd remember telling me that when she woke up, but it didn't matter. She'd said the words, and they felt like she'd given me the passcode to her heart. Her fucking soul.

I'd made a lot of mistakes along the way, listened to people when I shouldn't have, had allowed my fucked-up brain to fuck itself up even more, and I'd almost ruined my and her life. Yet, here we were.

She'd forgiven me. She loved me.

And I knew I'd count every fucking day we had together as a blessing, because I deserved neither her forgiveness nor her love, but I was selfish. I was greedy. And I'd take it all. All she had to give.

Forever and a day, because Stone was mine. And I was fucking hers.

FORTY-SIX

STONE

MY BODY ACHING with the regular grumbles that came after working a long shift, I squinted at the clock on the nightstand and groaned with relief when I saw it was only one PM. I hummed under my breath and, about to snuggle some more into the covers, I flopped backward, and yelped my ass off when someone was already there. Someone that was definitely not Mrs. Biggins.

Of course, when I twisted around and saw Steel, my heart stopped its pounding, and when I saw him peering at me, all grumpy like, he muttered, "You forget about me, Stone?"

My nose crinkled, then I yawned and twisted around so I could cuddle into him. "In my defense," I muttered back, "I went to bed alone."

He snorted as he settled his hand on my butt as I lifted my leg and rested it on his thighs. A quick tap to the tush was my thanks as he replied, "Yesterday."

"Huh?" I yawned some more as I shoved my face into his throat. "What was yesterday?"

"When you fell asleep," he said dryly.

Jerking upward, I blinked and gaped at him, then shook my head. "No way."

"Yes way. You've been asleep thirty-six hours." His lips twisted. "You almost scared the shit out of me, but you were snoring like a trooper, so I knew I didn't have to worry about you."

I narrowed my eyes at him. "I don't snore."

He raised a hand, stuck one of his fingers up to tell me to wait a minute, then rolled over to grab his phone. When he played my snoring, I huffed at him. "I can't believe you recorded that. Anyway, that could be anyone snoring."

"Carry on listening," he replied dryly.

Grumbling under my breath as I sank back into bed, yawning again, I tensed when I heard a moan. A very feminine moan. Followed by a sleepy-voiced me muttering, "Stop it, Harry."

My eyes flared wide, and I shot him a sheepish look. "Oops."

His eyes were the opposite of wide. He narrowed them at me, and replied, "I think we need to teach your body who owns it."

I bit my bottom lip. "I dream about a lot of things."

He shook his head. "Not anymore. I'm claiming them all."

"Claiming my dreams? My subconscious isn't Greenland!" I sputtered, then shrieked when he rolled me onto him and maneuvered me so I was straddling his hips. The second I was there, my pussy against his dick, his hand sailed through the air and walloped my buttock. "Hey! No fair! I can't be blamed for what my subconscious does or says! Anyway, I have a lot of bad dreams too."

When a giggle sounded next on the recording, I heaved a sigh. "Can we switch that off now?" Especially as yesterday's Stone was intent on getting me into trouble.

"We can in a second," he rumbled, and deep in his eyes, I could see his amusement at my predicament, even if I could also feel his hardness growing against my pussy.

As much as I could tell that he didn't like my mentioning other dudes' names while I was asleep—and I couldn't blame him, because I'd toss him out of bed if he so much as groaned one of the clubwhores' names—he was definitely okay with using it to his advantage.

When he slapped my ass cheek again, it was in time to me moaning, "Steel, right there."

I gaped at his phone, which he'd rested on my pillow, then turned to him, cheeks blazing, "Well."

"Apparently, you've got dreams of a threeway, huh?" he rasped, before he soared up, all those yummy muscles in his abdomen tightening and tautening before he clamped me to him and brought me down so I was resting on his chest. "I ain't never sharing you, baby doll. Neh-vuh. So I think you need to get used to my dick being the only dick that's going in this pussy until kingdom comes."

"What kind of kingdom?" I replied, because that was all I had to say.

Him and me were more than on the same page. We were writing the same frickin' book.

No way in hell did I want to have a threeway. And even though sleepy Stone was apparently down and dirty, I sure as shit wasn't.

He narrowed his eyes at my question, which made me wonder if he'd thought I'd argue with him. Not only was Harry on another coast, in another world, almost, I had no designs on him. If, back in the day, I'd asked him to stay in New York, he probably would have. He wanted more than I wanted to give, as was usually the way with all my relationships.

But I was all in with Steel.

Had been since I was fifteen. Would be until I was a hundred-fifteen.

I tipped my head down to press a kiss to his lips as he slapped my butt, which had me jerking back to glare at him. "What was that for?"

"Moaning another guy's name in your sleep!"

He was huffing now, and my lips twitched as I wriggled my butt. "You gonna keep on spanking me for stuff I can't help?"

"Yeah, I am," he grumbled, spanking me on the other cheek too.

The sting felt so good though, so good.

"Where did my bathrobe go?" I queried as I rocked my hips, rolling my pussy down his dick so that I could get some good friction. When his glans nudged my clit, I sighed with delight.

"Pulled it off you last night. You were all tangled in it," he muttered as he buried his face in my throat, his tongue coming up to trace the letter 'S' of his branding there.

I shivered as he nibbled his way down from that part, which had barely any flesh on it, all the way to the softer part of my neck. When he nipped me, sucking down hard too, and then spanked me, I yelped before I felt my pussy flood with heat.

That had fucking hurt, but in the best possible way.

With his hold on me absolute, the way his arm was banded at the center of my back, with the hand on my shoulder so he was keeping me pinned down, the only thing I could move was my lower body, so I wiggled my ass and loved how that had me nudging my clit too.

"You getting yourself off there, baby doll?"

I squinted up at him, bare and unashamed in the midday light that pierced the blinds and gently pooled around us. "Can I help it you're better than porn at getting me wet?"

His lips twitched at that, before he surprised me yet again, by sitting up, then twisting me around so I was lying flat on his thighs, butt to the air, all my body on the mattress apart from my groin, which was on his lap.

It was a clever way to hold me, actually. The sneaky shit. My scars were resting on the sheets, my pelvis area tipped up, thanks to his legs, and my face was burrowed in the rest of the bedding.

I yelped when he gave me a good lick on one cheek, then I hummed when the burn that instantly came after had me rubbing my face into the sheets.

Maybe some women didn't like being spanked, maybe some liked it during sex. Me? It was an instant pacifier.

I could already feel the buzz in my head as he carried on tanning my ass, turning the skin pink and rosy. Every now and then, he'd pause and ask, "In pain?"

"Nothing I can't handle," I'd reply, drowsy to the last as he somehow gave me what I needed. Without my even having to ask for it.

Unless I'd been talking in my sleep again, of course.

For real, I needed to have a conversation with my subconscious, and make sure it was well aware that I stopped mentioning men in my dreams but definitely talked about spanking and how much I fucking loved it.

When his fingers traced down between my butt cheeks after a couple more spanks, he rumbled, "Someone's wet."

"Someone loves your hands on my ass," I rumbled back, groaning when he speared a finger inside me, coated it in my slickness, then rolled it down to my clit to rub me.

I whined slightly when he carefully touched me, until another finger slipped into my gate and he began dragging the tips down the front wall of my pussy as he played with my clit.

Biting the inside of my cheeks, hips arching high as I groaned, legs splaying wider to encourage him to carry on. His free hand slapped one of my cheeks, and he growled, "You move, I stop."

That had me pouting but freezing mid-movement, and I hissed out a breath when he started to fuck me faster with his hand. I had no idea how he did that, timing it so perfectly so that he could caress my clit too, all I knew was that he had me seeing stars.

I groaned, tensed all the muscles in my stomach to stop myself from rolling my hips, but sweet fuck, it was close to impossible. I needed to move, I felt like all my muscles were juddering with the pleasure I was forced to contain, when that was the last thing I wanted.

When I rocked once, he gave me three slaps, one on each cheek and then a small one on my clit, which had him screwing his fingers into me in a different direction.

Behind my eyelids, my eyes were rolling, and when my thighs trembled with the need to stay still and I sank onto his lap, hoping that would ground me and stop me from wanting to rock, he returned to what he'd been doing.

He finger fucked me until I was screaming, until the need to *move* was painful, and when I did? When I climaxed and was sobbing as I was pummeled with pleasure, he pulled out at the worst possible time as my pussy was clenching down around him, and showered my butt with tiny slaps that burned like a bitch.

Each one made me whimper, and each one made my body jerk like I'd been shocked, and each fucking one had my climax soaring higher and higher, until I was almost goddamn howling with need.

When he maneuvered himself so that he was no longer under me but on top of me, with me flat to the bed and my body still whining from the orgasm he'd stunned me with, he bent over me and whispered, "Pull your ass cheeks apart."

I instantly obeyed, even as everything that made me me was going into meltdown mode, and when his cock landed on my ass, sliding down and coating my skin with his pre-cum, I prepared for his dick to tunnel into me.

When it did, my eyes flickered with the sensation, and I growled as he thrust into me, filling every inch. In this position, he felt so much bigger and thicker, and I loved it. My stomach twinged slightly, but I made sure to stay still as he began to rock into me.

His gentleness, at a moment, where I knew he wanted to pound into me meant more than he could ever know, because I wanted that too. I wanted him to take me roughly, I wanted him to burn off his feelings on me, and while we couldn't do that yet, I loved that we'd found a compromise.

He leaned over me, settling his forearms either side of my head, and rasped, "This pussy is mine."

"This dick is mine," I moaned back.

"No one else's."

I gulped. "No one else's."

"Ever."

"*Ever*." I sighed at that, melting into the sheets which, even though it should have hurt my stomach even more, actually didn't. He sped up, like he sensed it, and as his cock hit me in places no dick ever could, because I was made for him and he was made for me, I snarled, "I love you, Steel."

A sharp cry escaped him, and I felt his body jerk as he came, his dick spurting into me, his seed flooding my pussy. We'd never talked about birth control, but at that moment, I resented my IUD, even though we needed a lot more time together before we were ready for that next step. I wasn't even sure if a kid was possible with my scarred stomach as it was, but I knew, then and there, that I wanted his baby.

I wanted his everything.

I wanted to be *his* everything too.

As he filled me full of his cum, I sighed into the sheets, more than happy that I'd got mine, but what I loved even more? When he pulled out and carefully rearranged me so that I was on my back. He spread my legs, settled his now-softening dick against my pussy, and when he slipped the tip in, my eyes widened some as they caught his, but he didn't try to go deeper, just rocked into me, sliding over my clit with our mingled arousal, before he moved over me, resting so that his forehead was on mine.

"I love you, Steel." I smiled at him, a little sleepy now after that.

He pressed a kiss to my lips, and asked, "You going to make an honest man out of me?"

I felt my heartbeat slow, and everything in me burn with excitement. I knew what he meant. Knew it, and heard it, and wanted *that* so fucking badly that I didn't know what to do with myself. But my answer was, "I don't know. I don't want an honest man. I just want you."

He scoffed at me, lifting slightly so that his eyes were tangled in mine. But his grin? Beatific. Like a kid whose mom had just told him he could eat the full tray of freshly baked chocolate chip cookies.

"You got me, baby doll."

I licked my lips as I reached for his left hand with mine. "Forever?"

"Forever."

"That a vow?"

"It's a vow."

I sighed. "Good." He kissed me. *Softly*. Cherishing me with his gentle touch. Then I whispered, "Wanna nap?"

He snickered. "With you in my bed? What kind of question is that? Course I do."

So we napped.

And it was the best nap ever.

EPILOGUE

STONE

PATCH-IN PARTIES WERE BORING, because they were like frat parties but with bikers.

That meant, of course, that the random shit stupid college kids did in frat houses looked like a bunch of pussies were behind the pranks by comparison.

I remembered Steel's patch-in party and knew he'd had his stomach pumped. As had Nyx. And watching Jaxson and Hawk—who'd grown even grumpier since his brother had gone missing and his Dad had died—be promoted from Prospect to full brother, while four other guys from the local area were patched in as Prospects and treated to the same fate, I realized why.

They were challenging each other to finish a bottle of tequila the fastest.

Dumb fucks.

I caught Giulia's eye, watched her roll hers, and I pointed to the door.

She nodded, and made her way toward me, as did Lily and Tiff, who were evidently as bored as me.

Parties here were actually a lot of fun when you were able to dance and could drink, both of which I couldn't do yet, but this was just stupid. I hated stupid.

It was annoying.

Especially as, tomorrow, I was back in the ER, so I'd probably be the one examining these dicks' stomach contents.

Fun.

Heaving a sigh as I made it outside—a two-day break wasn't enough to make me feel normal again—I took a seat on one of the benches that had made an appearance recently just outside the door. Lots of benches and chairs had suddenly appeared since my return here too, which I knew was for my benefit. A gentle hint to take it easy, to keep my ass on a chair.

When I seated myself, Giulia plopped her butt there too, and Tiff and Lily made an appearance, with Tiff sitting on the bench and Lily leaning against her legs. Unsurprisingly, Ghost and Keira popped up, and they sat cross-legged on the ground in front of us.

We were a real bunch, the new Old Ladies, and it amused me to think that because I'd always thought I'd be here when I was a kid, but as an adult, I'd never been able to imagine it happening.

Funny how life turned out, wasn't it?

I stared up at the sky, grateful to be breathing in fresh air and to be away from the loud music. Sure, it spilled outside, but I could actually hear it over the bass now, and I hummed along to the sick beat as the others started talking.

In the distance, I heard the gate open, and my brows rose because I knew the entire club was on the compound. Which meant those gates should be locked up tight all night.

Giulia evidently heard it too, and she sat up straighter, squinting down the driveway.

When a bike rolled up, coming to a halt halfway to the clubhouse, I sat forward, squinting through the darkness, wishing the damn flood lights would pop on as I tried to figure out who it was.

I guessed it could be Storm, because I knew Keira had been

having trouble with Cyan, and it made sense for him to come and see her.

But when my eyes adjusted, and the spotlights finally blared on when the biker moved into its sensor, I gasped when I registered who it was.

Giulia tensed, and she went to stand, jerking upright for her butt to hover above the bench, but Bear, Rex's dad, shook his head.

My gaze darted between them, trying to figure out the silent communication going down beside me, but I had no idea what was happening. Especially when Giulia, who never obeyed anyone—rarely even Nyx—plunked her ass down.

Confused, I looked around, trying to figure out what was going on, and when the others saw our attention was diverted, they twisted and swiveled to see who we were looking at.

"Who's that?" Tiff queried in surprise.

"Rex's dad," I replied, still bewildered by how Giulia had looked at him. Sure, she'd been raised here, but she hadn't seen him in years. Would she even remember him? I knew Bear hadn't been back home since she'd returned to the clubhouse, because Mav would have kept me in the loop.

So why the long look? Why the weird, silent communication—

"Is it weird that I think he's hot?" Lily questioned, making us all laugh.

Well, apart from me.

I knew Bear too well. Something was going on.

When he stared straight at me, I sensed his urgency, but I didn't get what the fuck was happening.

He was trying to tell me something, and the way he was standing? Not coming toward us? That was a message in and of itself.

Then I saw it.

The little red dot darting and weaving on his chest.

My entire being froze. Every part of me turning to ice at the sniper's target, even as he mouthed, "Warn. Rex."

Adrenaline surged into being, and I screamed, "Run!"

The women figured out I wasn't shitting them, thank God, and they surged to their feet, rushing toward me. I felt someone grab my arm, then someone else grab the other one as they helped me run, dragging me with them, but even as my heart pounded and I groaned in pain at being tossed around, I heard it.

The shot.

It whistled through the air, somehow louder than the blaring music, and then, the music was silent.

Everything was as a blast ripped through the sound barrier, but that was nothing compared to the heat.

Screams billowed around me as the explosion tore through the compound, and even as I felt myself being hurled forward, soaring through the air like I was a feather being picked up in the breeze, I could only think two things.

The man who'd been like a father to me had to be dead.

And someone needed to pay for not only his murder, but for destroying our home.

THE NEXT BOOK IN THE SERIES IS NOW AVAILABLE TO READ ON KU!
www.books2read.com/CruzSerenaAkeroyd

FILTHY

FINN

Obsessive habits weren't alien to me.

They were as much a part of me as my coal-dark hair and my diamond-blue eyes. Ingrained as they were, it didn't mean they weren't irritating as fuck.

As I rifled through the folder on the table in front of me, staring down at the life of one pesky tenant, I wanted to toss it in the trash. I truly did.

I wanted not to be interested in her.

Wanted my focus to return to the matter at hand—business.

But there was something about her.

Something. . .

Irish.

I was a sucker for my own people. When I was a kid, I'd only dated other Irish girls in my class, and though I'd become less discerning about nationality and had grown more interested in tits and ass, I'd thought that desire had died down.

But Aoife Keegan was undeniably, indefatigably Irish.

From her fucking name—I didn't know people still named

their kids in Gaelic over here—to her red goddamn hair and milky-white skin.

To many, she wouldn't be sexy. Too pale, too curvy, too rounded and wholesome. But to me? It was like God had formed a creature that was born to be my downfall.

I could feel the beast inside me roaring to life as I stared at the photos of her. It wanted out. It wanted her.

Fuck.

"I told you not to get those briefs."

My eyes flared wide in surprise at my brother, Aidan O'Donnelly's remark. "What?" I snapped.

"I told you not to get those briefs," he repeated, unoffended. Which was a miracle. Had I been speaking to Aidan Sr., I'd probably have lost a finger, but Aidan Jr. was one of my best friends, as well as a confidant and fellow businessman.

When I said business, it wasn't the kind Valley girls dreamed their future husbands would be involved in. No Manhattan socialite, though we were wealthy as fuck, would want us on their arm if they truly knew what games we were involved in.

My business was forged, unashamedly, in blood, sweat, and tears.

Preferably not my own, although I had taken a few hits for the Family over the years.

"My briefs aren't irritating me," I carried on, blowing out a breath.

"No? You look like you've got something up your ass crack." Aidan cocked a brow at me, but his smirk told me he knew exactly what the fuck was wrong.

I flipped him the bird—the finger that I'd have lost by showing cheek to his father—and he just grinned at me as he leaned over my glass desk and scooped up one of the pictures.

That beast I mentioned earlier?

It roared to life again when his eyes drifted over Aoife's curvy form.

"She's like your kryptonite," he breathed, tilting his head to the side. "Fuck me, Finn."

"I'd rather not," I told him dryly. "Now her? Yeah. I'd fuck her anytime."

He wafted a dismissive hand at my teasing. "I knew from that look in your eye, there was a woman involved. I just didn't know it would be a looker like this."

I snatched the photo from him. "Mine."

My growl had him snickering. "The Old Country ain't where I get my women from, Finn. Simmer down."

Throat tightening, I grated out, "What the fuck am I going to do?"

"Screw her?" he suggested.

"I can't."

He snorted. "You can."

"How the fuck am I supposed to get her in my bed when I'm about to bribe her into selling off her commercial lot?"

Aidan shrugged. "Do the bribing after."

That had me blowing out a breath. "You're a bastard, you know that, right?"

Piously, he murmured, "My parents were well and truly married before I came along. I have the wedding and birth certificates to prove it." He grinned. "Anyway, you're only just figuring that out?"

I shot him a scowl. "You're remarkably cheerful today."

"Is that a question or a statement?"

"Both?" The word sounded far too Irish for my own taste. My mother had come from Ireland, Tipperary to be precise—yeah, like the song. I was American born and bred, my accent that of someone who'd been raised in Hell's Kitchen but, and I hated it, my mother's accent would make an appearance every now and then.

'Both' came out sounding almost like 'boat.'

Aidan, knowing me as well as he did, smirked again—the fucker. "I got laid."

Grunting, I told him, "That doesn't usually make you cheerful."

"It does. I just never see you first thing after I wake up. Da hasn't managed to piss me off today."

Aidan was the heir to the Five Points—an Irish gang who operated out of Hell's Kitchen. It wasn't like being the heir to a candy company or a title. It came with responsibilities that no one really appreciated.

We were tied into the life, though. Had been since the day we were born.

There was no use in whining over it, and Aidan wasn't. But if I had to deal with his father on a daily basis? I'd have been whining to the morgue and back.

Aidan Sr. was the shrewdest man I knew. What the man could do with our clout defied belief. Even if I thought he was a sociopath, he had my respect, and in truth, my love and loyalty.

Bastard or no, he'd taken me in when I was fourteen and had made me one of his family. I'd gone from being his kids' friend, the son of one of his runners, to suddenly being welcome in the main house.

All because Aidan Sr.—though I was sure he was certifiable—believed in family.

I shot Aidan Jr. a look. "Was it that blonde over on Canal Street?"

He rubbed his chin. "Yeah."

Snorting, I told him, "Hope you wore a rubber. I swear that woman has so many men going in and out of her door, it should be on double-action hinges."

He scowled at me. "Are you trying to piss me off?"

"Why? Didn't wear a jimmy?" I grinned at him, my mood soaring in the face of his irritation. "Better get to the clinic before it drops off."

Though he flipped me the bird as easily as I'd done to him—I was his brother, after all—he grumbled, "What are you going to do about little Aoife?"

I squinted at him. "She's not little."

That seemed to restore his humor. "I know. Just how you like them." He shook his head. "You and Conor, I swear. What do you do with them? Drown yourself in their tits?"

Heaving a sigh, I informed him, "My predilection for large tits is none of your business."

"And whether or not I wore a jimmy last night is none of yours."

"If it turns green and looks like a moldy corn on the cob, who you gonna call?"

"Ghostbusters?" he tried.

I shook my head, then pointed a finger at him and back at myself. "No. Me."

Grunting, he got to his feet and pressed his fists to the desk. "We need that building, Finn."

"The business development plan was mine, Aid. I know we need it. Don't worry, I won't do anything stupid."

He snorted. "Your kind of stupid could go one of two ways."

That had me narrowing my eyes at him, but he held up his hands in surrender.

"Fuck her out of your system quickly, and then get started on the deal," he advised. "Best way."

It probably was the best way, but—

He sighed. "That fucking honor of yours."

I had to laugh. Only in the O'Donnelly family would my thoughts be considered honorable.

"If I'm fucking someone over, I want them to know it," was all I said.

"That makes no sense."

"Makes for epic sex, though," I jibed, and he shot me a grin.

"Angry sex is always good." He rubbed his chin, then he reached over again and flipped through the photos. "Who's the old guy to her?"

"To her? Not sure. Sugar daddy?" The thought alone made the beast inside rage. I cleared my throat to get rid of the rasp there. "To us? He's our meal ticket."

Aidan's eyes widened. "He is?"

I nodded. "Just leave it to me."

"I was always going to, *dearthái*r." He tilted his chin at me, honoring me with the Gaelic word for brother. "Be careful out there."

"You, too, brother."

Aidan winked at me and, with a far too cheerful whistle for someone whose dick might soon be 'ribbed for her pleasure' without the need for a condom, walked out of my office leaving me to brood.

The instant his back was to me, I stared at the photos again. Flipping through them, I glowered at the innocent face staring back at me through the photo paper—if only she knew.

Hers was a building in Hell's Kitchen. Five Points Territory. One of many on my hit list.

Back in the 70s, Aidan Sr., following in his father's footsteps, had bought up a shit-ton of property, pre-gentrification, and it was my job to either sell off the portfolio, reconstruct, or 'improve' the current aesthetics of the buildings the Points owned.

This particular one was something I'd taken a personal interest in.

See, I was technically a legitimate businessman.

This office?

I had views of the Hudson. I could see the Empire State Building, and in the evening, I had an epic view of the sunset setting over Manhattan. This office building, also Points' property, was worth a cool hundred million, and I was, again technically, the CEO of it.

On paper?

I looked seamless.

The businessman who sported hundred thousand dollar watches and had a house in the Hamptons. No one save the Points and my CPA knew where the money came from. I liked that because, fuck, I had no intention of switching this pad for a lock-up in Riker's Island.

Still, this project cut close to home, and the reasoning was fucking pathetic.

I'd never admit it to any of the O'Donnellys. The bastards were like family to me, and if I admitted to this, they'd never let me hear the end of it.

Extortion?

I usually doled that out to someone else's to do list. Someone with a far lower paygrade than me, someone expendable. But the minute I'd heard of the troublesome tenant who was refusing to sell her lot to us? After not one, not two, not even three attempts with higher prices?

Five outright refusals?

The challenge to convince her otherwise had overtaken me.

See, I liked stubborn in women.

I liked fucking it out of them.

Throw in the fact the woman's name was Aoife? It had been enough to get me sending someone out to follow her.

If she'd been fifty with as many chins as she had grandchildren, she'd have been safe from me.

But she wasn't.

She was, as Aidan had correctly stated, my kryptonite. All

milky flesh with gleaming auburn hair that I wanted to tie around my clenched fist. Her soft features with those delicate green eyes that sparkled when she smiled and were like wet grass when she was mad, acted like a punch to my gut.

Now?

My interest hadn't just been piqued.

It had fucking imploded.

Yeah, I was thinking with my cock, but what man, at the end of the day, didn't?

I'd just have to be careful. Just have to make sure I put pressure on the right places, make sure she'd bend and not break, and the old bastard in the pictures was my key to just that.

See, every third Tuesday of the month, Aoife Keegan had a habit of traipsing across Manhattan to the Upper East Side. There, at three PM on the dot, she'd enter a discreet little boutique hotel and wouldn't leave until nine PM that night.

Five minutes after she arrived and left, the same man would leave, too.

At first, when Jimmy O'Leary had told me that Senator Alan Davidson was at the hotel, I hadn't thought anything of it.

Why would I?

Senators trawled for donations in fancy hotels every fucking day of the week. It was the true luxury of politics. Sure, they made it look real good for the press. Posing in derelict neighborhoods and shaking hands with people who did the fucking work . . . all while they lived it up large with women half their age in two thousand dollar a night suites.

My mouth firmed at that.

Was Aoife selling herself to the Senator?

The thought pissed me off.

I couldn't see why she'd do such a thing. Not when I'd looked into her finances, had seen just how secure she was. But maybe that was why. Maybe the Senator was funneling money to her.

The only problem was that the lot Aoife owned—did I mention it was owned outright? Yeah, that was enough to chafe my suspicions, too, considering she was only twenty-fucking-five years old—was a teashop in a small building in a questionable area of HK.

I mean, come on. I loved Hell's Kitchen. It was home. But fuck. Where she was? What kind of Senator would put his fancy piece in *that*?

My jaw clenched as I studied the Senator's and Aoife's smiling faces as they left the hotel. Separately, of course. But whatever they'd been doing together, it sure put a Cheshire Cat grin on their chops–that was for fucking sure. Jimmy being a dumbass, hadn't put the two together, had just remarked on the 'coincidence,' but I was no fool.

How did I know they were together in the hotel?

Jimmy had been trailing Aoife for four months—told you I was obsessive—and every third Tuesday, come rain or shine, this little routine had jumped out, and when Jimmy had picked up on the fact Davidson had been there each and every time, I'd gotten my hands dirty, bribed one of the hotel maids myself—and fuck, that had been hard. Turned out that place made even the maids sign NDA agreements, but everyone had a price—and I'd found out that my little obsession shared a suite with the old prick.

My fingers curled into fists as I stared at her. Butter wouldn't fucking melt. She was the epitome of innocence. Like a redheaded angel. Could she really be lifting her skirts for that old fucker? Just so she could own a teashop?

Something didn't make sense, and fuck, if that didn't intrigue me all the more.

Aoife Keegan had snared one of the biggest, nastiest sharks in Manhattan.

She just didn't know it yet.

***

Aoife

"We need more scones for tomorrow. I keep telling you four dozen isn't enough."

Lifting a hand at my waitress and friend, Jenny, I mumbled, "I know, I know."

"If you know, then why the hell don't you listen?" Jenny complained, making me grin.

"Because I'm the one who has to make them? Making half that again is just . . ." I sighed.

I loved my job.

I did.

I adored baking—my butt and hips attested to that fact—and making a career out of my passion was something every twenty-something hoped for. Especially in one of the most expensive cities in the world. But sheesh. There was only so much one person could do, and this was still, essentially, a one-woman-band.

With the threat of Acuig Corp looming over me, I didn't feel safe hiring extra staff. I'd held them off for close to six months now. Six months of them trying to tempt me to leave, to sell up. They'd raised their prices to ten percent above market value, whereas with everyone else in the building, they'd just offered what the apartments were truly worth. Considering this place wasn't the nicest in the block, that wasn't much.

Most people hadn't held out because, hell, why wouldn't they want to live elsewhere?

Those who were landlords hadn't felt any issue in tossing their tenants out on the street. The tenants grumbled, but when did they ever have any rights, anyway?

For myself, this was where my mom and I had worked to—

I brought that thought to a shuddering halt.

Mom was dead now.

I had to remember that. This was on me, not her.

My throat thickened with tears as I turned to Jenny and murmured, "I'll try better tomorrow."

The words had her frowning at me. "Babe, you know I'm not the boss here, right?"

Lips curving, I whispered, "I know. But you're so scary."

She snickered then peered down at herself. "Yeah, I bet I'd make grown men cry."

Maybe for a taste of her. . . .

Jenny was everything I wasn't.

She was slender, didn't dip her hand into the cookie jar at will—the woman had more willpower than I did hips, and my hips seemed to go on forever—and her face looked like it belonged on the cover of a fashion magazine. Even her hair was enough to inspire envy. It was black and straight as a ruler.

Mine?

Bright red and curly like a bitch. I had to straighten it out every morning if I didn't want to look like little orphan Annie.

I'd once read that curly-haired women straightened their hair for special events, and that straight-haired women curled theirs in turn, but I called bullshit.

Curly-haired women lived with their straightening irons surgically attached to their hands.

At least, I did.

My rat's nest was like a ginger afro. Maybe Beyoncé could make that work, but I sure as hell didn't have the bone structure.

"I think grown men would cry," I told her dryly, "if you asked them to."

She pshawed, but there was a twinkle in her eye that I understood. . . . She agreed with me, knew it was true, but wasn't going to admit it. With anyone else, she might have. She had an ego–that was for damn sure. But with me? I think she figured I was zero competition, so she felt no need to rub salt in the wound, too.

I plunked my elbows on the counter and stared around my domain as she bustled off and started clearing the tables. It was her last duty of the day, and my feet were aching so damn bad that I didn't even have it in me to care.

This owning your own business shit?

It wasn't easy.

Not saying I didn't love it, but it was hard.

I slept like four hours a night, and when I wasn't in bed, I was here. All the time.

Baking, cooking, serving, and smiling. Always smiling. Even if I was so sleep-deprived I could sob.

Jenny's actually a life saver.

My mom used to be front of house before. . . .

I sucked down a breath.

I had to get used to thinking about it.

She wasn't here anymore, but just avoiding all thoughts of her period wasn't working for me. It was like I was purposely forgetting her, and, well, fuck that.

She'd always wanted to have a teashop. It had been her one true dream. Back in Ireland, when she was a little girl, her grandmother had owned one in Limerick. Mom had caught the bug and had wanted to have one here in the States. But not only was it too fucking expensive for a woman on her own, it was also impossible with my feckless father at her side.

I didn't want to think about him either, though.

Why?

Because the feckless father who'd pretty much ruined my mother's life, wasn't the only father in my life. My biological dad hadn't exactly cared about her happiness, but once he'd come to know about me, he'd tried. That was more than could be said for the man who'd lived with me throughout my early childhood.

"You look gloomy."

Jenny's statement had me blinking in surprise. She had a ton of dishes piled in her arms, and I'd have worried for the expensive china if I hadn't known she was an old pro at this shit. Just as I was.

We could probably earn a Guinness World Record on how many dishes we could take back and forth to the kitchen of *Ellie's Tea Rooms*. I swear, I had guns because of all that hefting. My biceps were probably the firmest part of my body.

More's the pity.

I'd have preferred an ass you could bounce dimes off of, but, when it boiled down to it, there was no way in this universe I could live without cake.

Just wasn't going to happen.

My big butt wasn't going *anywhere* until scientists could make zero calorie eclairs and pies.

"I'm not glum."

"No? Then why are your eyes sad?"

Were they? I pursed my lips as I let the 'sad eyes' drift around the tea room. I wish I could say it was all forged on my own hard work, but it wasn't. Not really.

"I was just thinking about Mom."

"Oh, honey," Jenny said sadly, and she carefully placed all the dishes on the counter, so she could round it and curve her arm around my waist. "It was only seven months ago. Of course, you were thinking of her."

"I just—" I blew out a breath. "I don't know if I'm doing what she'd want."

"You can't live for her choices, sweetness. You have to do what you think is right for you."

I gnawed at my bottom lip again. "I-I know, but she was always there for me. A guiding light. With Fiona gone and her, too? I don't really know what I'm doing with myself."

This business wasn't something that made me want to get up on a morning. It was my mom's dream, her goal. Every decision I made, I tried to remember how she'd longed for a place like this, but it wasn't my passion. It was hers, and I was trying to keep that dream alive while fretting over the fact my heart wasn't in it.

"I think you're doing a damn fine job. You have a very successful teashop. Your cakes are raved about. Have you visited our TripAdvisor page recently? Or our Yelp?" She squeaked. "I swear, you're making this place a tourist hotspot. I don't think Fiona or Michelle could be more proud of you if they tried."

The baking shit, yeah, that was all on me, but the other stuff? The finances?

I'd caved in.

I'd caved where my mom had always refused in the past.

With the accident had come a lot of medical bills that I just hadn't been able to afford. Without her help, I'd had to take on extra staff, and out of nowhere, my expenses had added up.

Mom had been so proud of this place, so ferociously gleeful that we'd done it by ourselves, and yet, here I was, financially free for the first time in my life, and I still felt like I was drowning because my freedom went entirely against her wishes.

"Is this to do with Acuig? I know they're still pestering you."

Jenny's statement had me wincing. Acuig were the bottom feeders who wanted to snap up this building, demolish it, and then replace it with a skyscraper. Don't get me wrong, the building was foul, but a lot of people lived here, and the minute it morphed into some exclusive condo, no one from around here would be able to afford to live in it.

It would become yuppy central.

I'd rejected all their offers to buy my tea room even though I didn't want the damn thing, not really. Mostly I wanted to keep mom's goals alive and kicking, but also, it pissed me off the way Acuig were changing Hell's Kitchen. Ratcheting up prices, making it unaffordable for the everyday man and woman—the people I'd grown up with—and bringing a shit-ton of banker-wankers and 1%ers to the area.

So, maybe I'd watched Erin Brockovich a time or two as a kid and had a social conscience . . . Wasn't the worst thing to possess, right?

"Aoife?" Jenny stated, making me look over at her. "Is Acuig pressuring you?"

I winced, realizing I hadn't answered—Jenny was my friend, but she also worked here and relied on the paycheck. It wasn't fair of me to keep her hanging like that. "They upped the sales price. I guess that isn't helping," I admitted, frowning down at my hands.

Unlike Jenny who had her nails manicured, mine were cut neatly and plain. I had no rings on my fingers, and wore no watch or bracelets because my wrists were usually deep in flour or sugar bags.

I spent most of my life right where I wanted it—behind the shopfront. That had slowly morphed where I was doing double the work to compensate for Mom's loss.

Was it any wonder I was feeling a little out of my league?

I was coping without Fiona, grieving Mom, working without her, too, and then practically living in the kitchens here. I didn't exactly have that much of a life. I had nothing cheerful on the horizon, either.

Well, nothing except for next Tuesday, and that wasn't enough to turn my frown upside down.

The money was a temptation. I didn't need to sell up and start working on my own goals, but that just loaded me down with more guilt and made me feel like a really shitty daughter.

Jenny squeezed me in a gentle hug. But as I turned to speak to her, the bell above the door rang as it opened. We both jerked in surprise—each of us apparently thinking the other had locked up when neither of us had—and turned to face the entrance.

On the brink of telling the client we were closed for the day, my mouth opened then shut.

Standing there, amid the frilly, lacy curtains, was the most masculine man I'd ever seen in my life.

And I meant that.

It was like a thousand aftershave models had morphed into one handsome creature that had just walked through my door.

At my side, I could feel Jenny's 'hot guy radar' flare to life, and for once, I couldn't damn well blame her.

This guy was . . . well, he was enough to make me choke on my words and splutter to a halt.

The tea room was all girly femininity. It was sophisticated enough to appeal to businesswomen with its mauve, taupe, and cream-toned hues, and the ethereal watercolors that decorated the walls. But the tablecloths were lacy, and the china dishes and cake stands we used were the height of Edwardian elegance.

Moms brought their little girls here for their birthday, and high-powered executives spilled dirt on their lovers with their girlfriends over scones and clotted cream—breaking their diets as they discussed the boyfriends who had broken their hearts.

The man, whoever the hell he was, was dressed to impress in a navy suit with the finest pinstripe. It was close to a silver fleck, and I could see, even from this distance, that it was hand tailored. I'd seen custom tailoring before, and only a trained eye could get a suit cut so perfectly to this man's form.

With wide shoulders that looked like they could take the weight of the world, a long, lean frame that was enhanced by strong muscles evident through the close fit of his pants and jacket, then the silkiness of his shirt which revealed delineated abs when his bright gold and scarlet tie flapped as he moved, the guy was hot.

With a capital H.

"How can we help, sir?" Jenny purred, and despite my own awe, I had to dip my chin to hide my smile.

Even if I wanted to throw my hat into this particular man's game, there was no way he'd choose me over Jenny. Fuck, I'd screw her, and I wasn't even a lesbian. Not even a teensy bit bi. I'd gone shopping with her enough to have seen her ass, and I promise you, it's biteable.

So, nope. I didn't have a snowball's chance in hell of this Adonis seeing *me* when Jenny was in the room.

Yet. . . .

When I'd controlled my smile, I looked over at the man, and his focus was on me.

My breath stuttered to a halt.

Why wasn't his gaze glued to Jenny?

Why weren't those ice-white blue eyes fixated on my best friend's tits, which Jenny helpfully plumped up as she preened at my side?

For a second, I was so close to breaking out into a coughing fit, it was humiliating. Then, more humiliation struck in a quieter manner, but it was nevertheless rotten—I turned pink.

Now, you might think you know what a blush is. You might think you've even experienced it yourself a time or two. But I was a redhead. My skin made fresh milk look yellow, and even my fucking freckles were pale. Everything about me was like I'd been dunked into white wax.

But as the heat crawled over me, taking over my skin as the man looked at me without pause, I knew things had rarely been this dire.

See, with Jenny as a best friend, I was used to the attention going her way. I could hide in the background, hide in her shadow. I liked it there. I was comfortable there. Sometimes, on double dates, she'd drag me along, and even the guy supposed to be dating me would be gaping at Jenny. As pathetic as it was, I was so used to it, it didn't bother me.

But now?

I just wasn't used to being in the spotlight.

Especially not a man like this one's spotlight.

When you're a teenager, practicing with your mom's blush for the first time, you always look like a tomato that's been left out in the sun, right?

I was redder than that.

I could feel it. I could fucking feel the heat turning me tomato red.

When Jenny cleared her throat, I thanked God when it broke the man's attention. He shot her a look, but it wasn't admiring. It wasn't even impressed.

If anything, it was irritated.

Okay, so now both Jenny and I were stunned.

Fuck that, we were floored.

Literally.

Our mouths were doing a pretty good fish impression as the man turned back to look at me.

Shit, was this some kind of joke?

Was it April 1st and I'd just gotten the dates mixed up again?

"Ms. Keegan?"

Oh fuck. His voice.

Oh. My. God.

That voice.

It was....

I had to swallow.

Did men even talk like that?

It was low and husky and raspy and made me think of sex, not just mediocre sex, but the best sex. Toe-curling, nails-breaking-in-the-sheets sex. Sex so fucking good you couldn't walk the next day. Sex so hot that it made my current core temperature look polar in comparison. Sex that I'd never been lucky to have before, so I pined for it in the worst way.

Jenny nudged me in the side when I just carried on gaping at the man. "Y-Yes. That's me." I cleared my throat, feeling nervous and stupid and flustered as I wiped my hands on my apron.

Sweet Jesus.

Was this man really looking for me while I was wearing a goddamn pinafore?

Even as practical as they were, I wanted to beg the patron saint of pinnies to remove it from me. To do something, anything, to make sure that this man didn't see me in the red gingham check that I always wore to cover up stains.

And then I felt it.

Jenny's hand.

Tugging at the knot.

I wanted to kiss her. Seriously. I wanted to give her a fucking raise! As I moved away from the counter and her side, the apron dropped to the floor as I headed for the man whose hand was now held out, ready for me to shake in greeting.

There are those moments in your life when you know you'll never forget them. They can be happy or sad, annoying or exhilarating. This was one of them.

As I slipped my hand into his, I felt the electric shocks down to my core. Meeting his gaze wasn't hard because I was stunned, and I needed to know if he'd felt that, too.

From the way those eyelids were shielding his icy-blue eyes, I figured he was just as surprised.

It was like a satisfied puma was watching me. One that was happy there was plump prey prancing around in front of him.

Shit.

Did I just describe myself as 'plump prey?'

And like that, my house of cards came tumbling down because what the hell would this man want with me?

I was seeing things.

God, I was so stupid sometimes.

I cleared my throat for, like, the fourth damn time, and asked, "I'm Ms. Keegan. You are?"

His smile, when it appeared, was as charming as the rest of him. His teeth were white, but not creepy, reality-TV-star white. They were straight except for one of his canines, which tilted in slightly. In his perfect face, it was one flaw that I almost clung to. Because with that wide brow, the hair so dark it looked like black silk that was cut closely to his head with a faint peak at his forehead, the strong nose, and even stronger jaw, I needed something imperfect to focus on.

Then, I sucked down a breath and remembered what Fiona had told me once upon a time. When I'd been nervous about asking Jamie Winters to homecoming, she'd advised me in her soft Irish lilt, "Lass, that boy takes a dump just like you do. He uses the bathroom twice a day and undoubtedly leaves a puddle on the floor for his ma to clean up. I bet he's puked a time or two as well. Had diarrhea and the good Lord only knows what else. Just you think that the next time you see that boy and want to ask him out."

Yeah. It was gross, but fuck, it had worked. Her advice had worked so well I hadn't asked anyone out because I could only think of them using the damn toilet!

Still, looking at this Adonis, there was no imagining *that*.

Surely, gods didn't use the bathroom.

Did they?

"The name's Finn. Finn O'Grady."

My eyes flared at the name.

No.

It couldn't be.

Finn O'Grady?

No. It wasn't a rare name, but it was a strong one. One that suited him, one that had always suited him.

I frowned up at him wondering, yet again, if this was a joke of some sort, but as he looked at me, *really* looked at me, I saw no recognition. Saw nothing on his features that revealed any ounce of awareness that I'd known him for years.

Well, okay, not *known*. But I'd known his mother. Our mothers had been best friends. And as I looked, I saw the same almond-shaped eyes Fiona had, the stubborn jaw, and that unmistakable butt-indent on his chin.

At the reminder of just how forgettable I was, my heart sank, and hurt whistled through me.

Then, I realized I was *still* holding his hand, and as he squeezed, the flush returned and I almost died of mortification.

CHAPTER 2
FINN

GOD, she was perfect.

And when I said perfect, I meant it.

I'd fucked a lot of women. Redheads, blondes, brunettes, even the rare thing that is a natural head of black hair. None of them, not a single one, lit up like Aoife Keegan.

Her cheeks were cherry red and in the light camisole she wore, a cheerful yellow, I could see how the blush went all the way down to the upper curve of her breasts.

She'd go that color, I knew, when she came.

And fuck, I wanted to see that.

I wanted to see that perfectly pale flesh turn bright pink under my ministrations.

Even as I looked at her, all shy and flustered, I wondered if she was a screamer in bed.

Some of the shyest often were.

Maybe not at first, but after a handful of orgasms, it was a wonder what that could do to a woman's self-confidence, and Jesus, I wanted to *see* that, too. I wanted a seat at center stage.

My suit jacket was open, and I regretted it. Immensely. My

cock was hard, had been since we'd shaken hands, and her fingers had clung to mine like a daughter would to her daddy's at her first visit to the county fair.

Fuck.

Squeezing her fingers wasn't intentional. If anything, I'd just liked the feel of her palm against mine, but when I put faint pressure on her, she jerked back like she'd been scalded.

Her cheeks bloomed with heat again, and she whispered, "Mr. O'Grady, what can I do for you?"

You can get on your fucking knees and sort out the hard-on you just caused.

That's what she could fucking do.

I almost growled at the thought because the image of her on her knees, my cock in her small fist, her dainty mouth opening to take the tip....

Shit.

That had to happen.

Here, too.

In this fancy, frilly, feminine place, I wanted to defile her.

Fuck, I wanted that so goddamn much, it was enough to make me reconsider my demolition plans.

I wanted to screw her against all this goddamn lace, which suited her perfectly. She was made for lace. And silk. Hell, silk would look like heaven against her skin. I wouldn't know where she ended and it began.

When her brow puckered, she dipped her chin, and that gorgeous wave of auburn hair slipped over her shoulder.

If we'd been alone, if that brassy bitch—who was staring at me like I could fuck her over the counter with her friend watching if I was game—wasn't here, I'd have grabbed that rope of hair, twisted it around my fingers, and forced her gaze up.

Some guys liked their women demure. And I was one of them.

I wasn't about to lie. I liked that in her, but I wanted her eyes on me. Always.

It was enough to prompt me to bite out, "Can we speak privately?"

She jerked at my words, then as she licked her bottom lip, turned to look at the waitress. "Jenny, it's okay. I can handle the rest by myself. You get home."

Jenny, her gaze drifting between me and her boss, nodded. She retreated to a door that swung as she moved through the opening, and within seconds, she had her coat and purse over her arm.

As she sashayed past—for my benefit, I was sure—she murmured, "See you tomorrow, Aoife."

Aoife nodded and shot her friend a smile, but I wasn't smiling. There were dishes on every table. Plates and saucers and tea pots. Those fancy stands that made any man wonder if he could touch it without snapping it.

Aoife was going to clear all that herself? Not on my fucking watch.

When the bell rang as the waitress opened the door, I didn't take my eyes off her until it rang once more upon closing.

Aoife swallowed, and I watched her throat work, watched it with a hunger that felt alien to me, because, God, I wanted to see my bites on her. Wanted to see my marks on that pale column of skin and her tits.

Barely withholding a groan, I asked, "Do you often let your staff go when you still have a lot of work to do, so you can speak to a stranger?"

Her cheeks flushed again, and she took a step back. "I-I, you're not—" Flustered once more, she fell silent.

"I'm not what?" Curiosity had me asking the question. Whatever I'd expected her to say, it hadn't been that.

She cleared her throat. "N-Nothing. You wished to speak with me, Mr. O'Grady?"

My other hand tightened around my briefcase, and though seeing her had made my reason for being here all that more necessary, I was almost disappointed. There was a gentle warmth to those bright-green eyes that would die out when I told her my purpose for being here. And her innocent attraction to me would change, morph into something else.

But I could only handle *something else*.

Some men were made for forever.

But those men weren't in my line of business.

I moved away from her, pressing my briefcase to one of the few empty tables. I wasn't happy about her having to do all the clearing up later on, and wondered if Paul, my PA, would know who to call to get her some help.

There was no way I was spending the rest of the night alone in my bed, my only companion my fist wrapped around my cock.

No way, no fucking how.

I paid Paul enough for him to come and clear the fucking place on his own if he couldn't find someone else.

I wanted Aoife on her knees, bent over my goddamn bed, and I was a man who always got what he wanted.

In this jungle, I was the lion, and Aoife? She was my prey.

I keyed in the code and opened my briefcase. The manila envelope was large and thick, well-padded with my documentation of Aoife's every move for the past few months.

It had started off as a legitimate move.

I'd wanted to know her weaknesses, so I could put pressure on her and make her cave to my demands.

Now, my demands had changed. I didn't just want her to sell the tea room we were standing in, I wanted her in my bed.

Fuck, I wanted that more than I wanted to make Aidan Sr. a fucking profit, and Aidan's profit and my balls still being attached to my body ran hand in hand.

Aidan was an evil cunt.

If I failed to deliver, he'd take it out on me. Whether I was his idea of an adopted son or not, he'd have done the same to his blood sons.

Well, he wouldn't have taken their balls. The man, for all his psychotic flaws, was obsessed with the idea of grandchildren, of passing it all on to the next generation. He'd cut his boys though. Without a doubt.

I knew Conor had marks on his back from a beating he refused to speak about. Then there was Brennan. He had a weak wrist because his father had a habit of breaking *that* wrist.

Without speaking, I grabbed the envelope and passed it to her.

She frowned down at it and asked, "For me?"

I smiled at her. "Open it."

"What is it?"

"Leverage."

That had her eyes flaring wide as she pulled out some of the photos. A gasp fell from her lips as she grabbed the photos when she spotted herself in them, jerking so hard the envelope tore. Some of the pictures spilled to the ground, but I didn't care about that.

Leaning back against one of the dainty tables once I was satisfied it would take my weight, I watched her cheeks blanch, all that delicious color dissipating as she took in everything the photos revealed.

"Y-You've been stalking me. Why?"

The question was high-pitched, loaded down with panic. I'd heard it often enough to recognize it easily.

I didn't get involved in wet work anymore. That wasn't my style, but along the way, to reach this point, I'd had no choice but to get my hands dirty. Panic was part of the job when you were collecting debts for the Irish Mob. And the Five Points were notorious for Aidan Sr.'s temper.

He wasn't the first patriarch. If anything, his grandfather was the founder. But Aidan Sr. was the type of guy that if you didn't pay him back, he didn't give a fuck about the money, he cared about the lack of respect.

See, you owed the mob and didn't pay? They'd send heavies around, beat the shit out of you, and threaten to do the same to your family, and usually, that did the trick. You didn't kill the cash cow.

Aidan Sr.?

He didn't give a fuck about the cash cow.

Only the truly desperate thought about borrowing money from Aidan, because if you didn't pay it back, he'd take your teeth, and your fingers and toes as a first warning. Then, if you still didn't pay—and most did—it was death.

Respect meant a lot to Aidan.

And fuck, if it wasn't starting to mean a lot to me. The panic in her voice made my cock throb.

I wanted this woman weak and willing.

I wanted it more than I wanted my next breath.

Ignoring her, I reached for my phone and tapped out a message to Paul.

Need housekeeping crew to clean this place.

I attached my live location, saw the blue ticks as Paul read the message—he knew better than to ignore my texts, whatever time of day they came—and he replied: *Sure thing.*

That was the kind of reply I was used to getting. Not just from Paul, but from everyone.

There were very few people who weren't below me in the strata of Five Points, and I'd worked my ass off to make that so.

The only people who ranked above me included Aidan Jr. and his brothers, Aidan Sr. of course, and then maybe a handful of his advisors that he respected for what they'd done for him and the Points over the years.

But the money I made Aidan Sr.?

That blew most of their 'advice' out of the window.

The reason Aidan had a Dassault Falcon executive private plane?

Because I was, as the City itself called me, a whiz kid.

I'd made my first million—backed by the Points, of course—at twenty-two.

Fifteen years later?

I'd made him hundreds of millions.

My own personal fortune was nothing to sniff at, either.

"W-Why have you done this?" Aoife asked, her voice breathy enough to make me wonder if she sounded like that in the sack.

"Because you've been a very stubborn little girl."

Her eyes flared wide. "Excuse me?"

I reached into the inside pocket of my suit coat and pulled out a business card. "For you," I prompted, offering it to her.

When she turned it over, saw the logo of five points shaped into a star, then read Acuig—in the Gaelic way, ah-coo-ig, not a butchered American way, ah-coo-ch—aloud, I watched her throat work as she swallowed.

"I-I should have realized with the Irish name," she whispered, the muscles in her brow twitching as she took in the chaos of the scattered photos on the floor.

Watching her as she dropped the contents on the ground, so she was surrounded by them, I tilted my head to the side, taking her in as her panic started to crest.

"I-I won't sell." Her first words surprised me.

I should have figured, though. Everything about this woman was surprisingly delicious.

"You have no choice," I purred. "As far as I'm aware, the Senator has a wife. He also has a reputation to protect. I'm not sure he'd be happy if any of those made it onto the *National Enquirer's* front page. Not when he's just trying to shore up his image to take a run for the White House next election."

She reached up and clutched her throat. The self-protective gesture was enough to make me smile at her—I knew what the absence of hope looked like.

There'd been a time when that had been my life, too.

"But, on the bright side," I carried on, "this can all be wiped away if you sell." As her gaze flicked to mine, I added, "As well as if you do something for me."

For a second, she was speechless. I could see she knew what that *something* was. Had my body language given it away? Had there been a certain raspiness to my tone?

I wasn't sure, and frankly, didn't give a fuck.

There was a little hiccoughing sound that escaped her lips, and she frowned at me, then down at herself.

"Is this a joke?"

"Do I look like I'm the kind of guy who jokes, Aoife?" Fuck, I loved saying her name.

The Gaelic notes just drove me insane.

Ee-Fah.

Nothing like the spelling, and all the more complicated and delicious for it.

"N-No," she confirmed, "but . . ."

"But what?" I prompted.

"I mean . . . you just can't be serious."

"Oh, but I am." I grinned. "Deadly. You've wasted a lot of my time, Aoife Keegan. A lot. Do you think I'm normally involved in negotiations of this level?"

Her eyes whispered over me, and I felt the loving caress of her gaze as she took in each and every inch of me. When she licked her lips, I knew she liked what she saw. I didn't really care, but it was helpful for her to be eager in some small way—especially when coercion was involved.

Aidan had called it bribery. I preferred 'coercion'. It sounded far kinder.

"No. That suit alone probably cost the mortgage payment on this place."

I nodded—she wasn't wrong. I knew what she'd been paying as rent, then as a mortgage, before some kind *benefactor* had paid it all off. Free and clear.

"I had to get my hands dirty, and while I might like some things dirty . . .," I trailed off, smirking when she flushed. "So, as I see it, we have a problem. I want this building. You don't want anyone to know you're having an affair with a Senator. Or, should I say, the Senator doesn't want anyone to know he's having an affair with someone young enough to be his daughter . . ."

If my voice turned into a growl at that point, then it was because the notion of her spreading her legs for that old bastard just turned my stomach.

Fuck, this woman, the thoughts she made me think.

Because I was startled at the possessive note to my growl, I ran a hand over my head. I kept my hair short for a reason—ease. I wasn't the kind of man who wasted time primping. It was an expensive cut, so I didn't have to do anything to it. Even mussing it up had it falling back into the same sleek lines as before—a man in my position had to look pristine under pressure. And very few people could even begin to understand the kind of strain I was under.

The formation of igneous rock had less volcanic pressure than Aidan Sr.

She licked her lips as she stared down at the photos, then back up at me. "And you want me to sell the place to you, even though this is my livelihood and the livelihood of all my staff, and then sleep with you?"

Her squeaky voice, putting suspicion into words, had me crossing my legs at the ankle. "We wouldn't be doing much sleeping."

Another shaky breath soughed from her lips, then, those beautiful pillowy morsels that would look good around my cock, quivered.

"This is crazy," she whispered shakily.

"As far as I'm concerned, all of this could be avoided if you'd just sold to me a few months back. Now you have to pay for my time wasted on this project."

"By spreading my legs?"

Another squeak. I tsked at her question, but in truth, I was annoyed at her using those same words I had to describe her with that old hypocrite of a Senator.

I didn't move, though. Didn't even flex my arms in irritation, just murmured, "Small price to pay. And, even though it's ten percent above market price, I'll stick to the last offer Acuig gave you. Can't say anything's fairer than that."

She shook her head, and there was a desperation to the gesture as she cried, "I need this business. You don't understand—"

"I understand that some very powerful and very dangerous businessmen want this building demolished. I understand that those same powerful and dangerous men want a skyscraper taking up this plot of land. I understand that a four hundred million dollar project isn't going to be put on hiatus because one small Irish woman doesn't want to go out of business . . ." I cocked a brow at her. "You think I'm coming in hot and heavy? These kinds of men, Aoife, they're not the sort you fuck around with.

"Take my check, and my other offer, before you or the people you care about are threatened." I got to my feet and straightened my jacket out. "This suit? These shoes? That briefcase and this watch? I own them because I'm damn good at what I do. I'm a financial advisor, Aoife. Take my word for it. You're getting the best deal out of this."

She staggered back, the counter stopping her from crumpling to the floor. "You'd hurt me?"

"Not me," I repudiated. Not in the way she thought, anyway. "But the men I work for?"

Her gaze dropped to the one thing she'd retained in her hand—my card. "Acuig," she whispered. "Five in Gaelic."

My brows twitched in surprise. She knew Gaelic?

"The Five Points." Her eyes flared wide with terror. "They're behind this deal."

I hadn't expected her to put one and one together, but now that she had? It worked to my advantage.

Nodding, I told her, "Any minute now, there'll be a team of housekeepers coming in here to clear up for the night." When she gaped at me, I retrieved the contract from my briefcase, slapped it on the table, and handed her a pen as I carried on, "I suggest you let tonight be your last night of business."

What I didn't tell her, was that my suggestions weren't wasted words. They were like the law.

You didn't break them, and, like any lawmaker, I expected immediate obeisance.

**

Aoife

SO, the beautiful man just happened to be an absolute cocksucker of a bastard.

Still, this couldn't be real, could it?

The dick could have anyone he wanted. Jesus, Jenny was panting after him like a dog in heat. She would have gone out with him if he'd so much as clicked his fingers at her.

But he'd had eyes for me.

Like he wanted me.

He thought he'd bought me. Or, at least, bought my silence, and yeah, to some extent he had. But . . . why buy me, why not just drop the price on the building if he wanted me to pay for the time he'd wasted on me?

The arrogance imbued in those words was enough to make me pull my hair out, but that was inwardly. I was a redhead. I had a temper. But that temper was mostly overshadowed by fear.

Senator Alan Davidson wasn't my boyfriend, my lover, as this dick seemed to believe. He was my father, and as Finn O'Grady had correctly surmised, he was aiming for the White House.

How could I put that in jeopardy?

My dad was a good man. He'd made a mistake one summer when he'd come home from college, one that only some careful digging by his campaign manager had uncovered. Dad himself hadn't known of my existence, not until his CM had gone hunting for any nasty secrets that could come out and bite him in the ass.

This had been five years ago when he'd run for Senator. Now, Dad's goal was the presidential seat, and I wasn't going to be the one who put a wrench in the works.

When Garry Smythe had approached me back then, I'd thought he was joking. I was out on the street, heading home from work. At the side of me, a black car had driven in from the lane of traffic, just to park, or so I'd thought. As he'd held out his hand with a card, one of the car doors had opened up, and I'd been 'invited' inside.

Had I been scared?

At first.

But when Garry had told me my country needed me, I hadn't been sure whether to laugh or tell him to fuck off. He hadn't shuffled me into the car, though, hadn't tried to coerce me. He'd just asked if I'd voted for Senator Alan Davidson in the elections, and because he was one of the only politicians out there who wasn't a complete douche, and that was the name printed on the card in my hand, I'd shuffled into the back of the car.

Where the Senator himself had been sitting.

Now, when I thought about that day, I realized how fucking naive I'd been to get into the back of a limo for such a vague reason. But I'd been fortunate. Alan *had* been waiting for me. Waiting to tell me a story that still shook me to my core.

I'd made a promise to my dad that I wouldn't tell anyone. He'd offered me money, and I hadn't accepted it. I guess I should have, but back then, I'd been haughty and proud, and because the good guy I'd thought him to be hadn't been so good when he tried to buy my silence, I'd told him to fuck off. I'd been disappointed in him, frightened by the lifelong lie I'd been living, and equally hurt that the man who'd sired me was just concerned that I was a threat to his campaign.

I'd walked out of that car never expecting to see my dear old Dad ever again.

Then, the day after he'd been elected, he'd been sitting in the booth of the cafe where I worked part-time to get me through culinary school.

Seeing him, I'd almost handed that table off to one of the other waitresses, but I hadn't. Not when every time I'd passed the table, he'd caught my eye, a patient smile on his lips, one that said he'd wait for me all day if he had to.

Ever since that second meeting, I'd been catching up with him every three weeks.

And this bastard thought he could use our limited time together against my father? The one politician who could make a difference in the White House? One who didn't have Big Oil up his ass, a pharmaceutical company sucking his dick, or any other kind of corporation so far up his rectum that he was a walking, talking lie?

No.

That wasn't going to happen.

Which meant I was going to have to sleep with this stranger.

Before this conversation, hell, that hadn't been too disturbing a prospect. Because, dayum, what woman wouldn't want to sleep with this guy?

Even with an ego as big as his, he was delicious. Better than any cake I could bake, that was for fucking sure.

More than that, I knew him.

And I now knew that the life Fiona would never have wanted for her son was one he'd been drawn into.

The Mob.

The Five Points were notorious in these parts. Everyone was scared of them. I paid protection money to them, for God's sake. I knew to be scared of them, and having been raised in their territory, it was the height of stupidity to think paying them wasn't just a part of business.

Still, Fiona had never wanted that for Finn, and her Finn was the same as the one standing before me here today. In my tea room, which looked far too small to contain the might of this man.

She'd be so disappointed. So heart-sore to know that he was up to his neck in dirty dealings with the Five Points, and as he'd pointed out, the cost of his shoes, his clothes, and his jewelry, was enough to speak for itself.

If he wasn't high up the ladder in the gang, then I wasn't one of the best bakers of scones in the district.

Like Jenny had said, I had five star ratings across most social media platforms for a reason. I was good. But apparently, this man wasn't.

Before I could utter a word, before I could even cringe at how utterly sorrowful Fiona would be about this turn of events—not just about the Five Points but what her son was making me do— the door clattered open.

Like he'd predicted, a team of people swarmed in.

Finn motioned to the floor. "Want anyone to see those?"

With a gasp, I dropped to my knees and collected the shots, stuffing them back into the envelope with a haste that wasn't exactly practical.

Two shiny shoes appeared before me, followed by two expensively clad legs, and I peered up at him, wondering what he was about. He held out his hand, but I clasped the photos to my chest.

"You're making more of a mess than anything else, Aoife." His voice was raspy, his eyes weighted down by heavy lids.

For a second, I wondered why, then I saw *why*.

He had an erection.

An erection?

I peered around at the staff, but they were all men. Not a single woman in sight, well, save for the seventy-year-old with a clipboard who was barking out orders to the guys in what sounded like Russian.

So that meant, what?

The erection was for me?

The blush, the dreaded, hated blush, made another goddamn appearance, and to cover it, I ducked my head, then pushed the photos and the envelope at him.

For whatever reason, I stayed where I was, staring up at him as he calmly, coolly, and so fucking collectedly pushed the photos back into the torn envelope—it was some coverage. Better than none at all, I figured.

Being down here was. . . .

Hell, I don't know what it was.

To be looked at like that?

For his body to respond to me like that?

It was unprecedented.

I'd had one sexual experience with a boy back in college, and that had not gone according to plan. So much so I was still technically a fucking virgin because, and this was no lie, the guy had *zero* understanding of a woman's body.

Craig had spent more time fingering my perineum than my clit, and every time he'd tried to shove his dick into me, he'd somehow managed to drag it down toward my ass.

I'd gotten so sick of him frigging the wrong bits of me, that I'd pushed him off and given him a blowjob. It had been the quickest way to get out of that annoying situation.

Yeah, annoying.

Jenny, when I'd told her, had pissed herself laughing, and ever since, had tried to get me to hook up with randoms, so I could slough off my virginity like it was dead skin and I was a snake. But life had just always gotten in the way, and I'd had no time for men.

Shortly after *that* had happened, we'd lost Fiona. Then, I'd graduated, and after, Mom and I had set up this place thanks to some insurance money she'd come into after her husband had died. It had been crazy building the tea room into an established cafe, and then mom had passed on, too.

So, here I was. Still a virgin. On my knees in front of the sexiest man on Earth, a man I knew, a man whose mother had half raised me, one who wanted me in his bed as some kind of blackmail payment.

Was this a dream?

Seriously?

I mean, I'd been depressed before Finn O'Grady had walked through my doors. Now I wasn't sure whether to be apoplectic or worried as fuck because he wasn't wrong: you didn't mess with the Five Points.

God, if I'd known they'd been behind the development on this building, I'd have probably signed over months ago.

The Points were. . . .

I shuddered.

Vindictive.

Aidan O'Donnelly was half-evil genius and half-twisted sociopath. St. Patrick's Church, two streets away, had the best roof in the neighborhood and the strongest attendance because Aidan, for all he'd cut you into more pieces than a butcher, was a devout Catholic. His men knew better than to avoid Sunday service, and I reckoned that Father Doyle was the busiest priest in the city because of Five Points' attendance.

"I like you down there," he murmured absentmindedly.

The words weren't exactly dirty, but the meaning? They had my temperature soaring.

Shit.

What the hell was I doing?

Enjoying the way this man was victimizing me?

It was so wrong, and yet, what was standing right in front of me? I knew he'd know what to do with that thing tucked behind his pants.

He wouldn't try to penetrate my urethra—yes, you read that right. Craig had tried to fuck my pee-hole! Like, *why?*

Finn?

He oozed sex appeal.

It seemed to seep from every pore, perfuming the air around me with his pheromones.

I hadn't even believed in pheromones until I scented Finn O'Grady's delicious essence.

It reminded me of the one out of town vacation we'd ever had. We'd gone to Cooperstown, and I'd scented a body of water that didn't have corpses floating in it—Otsego Lake. He reminded me of that. So green and earthy. It was an attack on my overwhelmed senses, an attack I didn't need.

With the envelope in his hand, he held out his other for me. When I placed my fingers in his, the size difference between us was noticeable once more.

I was just over five feet, and he was over six. I was round and curvy, and he was hard and lean.

It reminded me of the nursery tale Mom had sung to me as a child—Jack Sprat could eat no fat, and his wife could eat no lean.

Did it say a lot for my confidence that I couldn't seem to take it in that he wanted *me*? Or was it simply that I wasn't understanding how anyone could prefer me over Jenny?

Even my mom had called Jenny beautiful, whereas she'd kissed me on the nose and called me her 'bonny lass.'

Biting my lip, I accepted his help off the floor. My black jeans weren't the smartest thing for the tea room, but I didn't actually serve that many dishes, just bustled around behind the counter, working up the courage to do what Mom had done every day—greet people.

I wasn't a sociable person. I preferred my kitchen to the front of house, hence the jeans, but I regretted not wearing something else today. Something that covered just how big my ass was, how slender my waist *wasn't*.

Ugh.

This man is blackmailing you into his bed, Aoife. For Christ's sake, you're not supposed to be worrying if he likes the goods, too!

Still, no matter how much I tried, years of inadequacy weighed me down as I wiped off my knees.

"Do you have a coat?" he asked, and his voice was raspy again. "A jacket? Or a purse?"

I nodded at him but kept my gaze trained on the floor. "Yes."

"Go get them."

His order had me shuffling my feet toward the kitchen, but as I approached the door, I heard his strong voice speaking with the old woman with the clipboard: "I want this all cleaned up and boxed. Take it to my storage lot in Queens."

With my back to him, I stiffened at his brisk orders. *Was I just going to let him do this? Get away with it?*

My shoulders immediately sagged.

Did I have a choice?

If it was just him, just Acuig, then I'd fight this, as I'd been fighting it since the building had come to the attention of the developer. But this wasn't a regular business deal.

This was mob business, and it seemed like somehow, I'd become a part of that.

FML.

Seriously, FML.

CHAPTER 3
FINN

SHE WASN'T AS fiery as I imagined.

Did that disappoint me?

Maybe.

Then I had to chide myself because, Jesus, the woman had just been *coerced* out of her business. What did I expect? For her to be popping open a champagne bottle after I'd forced her to sign over her building to me?

Sure, she'd made a nice and tidy profit on her investment—I hadn't screwed her that way. But this morning, she'd gone into work with a game plan in mind, and tonight? Well, tonight she was out of a job and knee deep in a deal with the devil.

Of course, she hadn't actually agreed to my other terms, but when I guided her out of the tea room and toward my waiting car, she didn't falter.

Didn't utter a peep.

Just climbed into the vehicle, neatly tucked her knees together, and waited for me to get in beside her.

Like the well-oiled team my chauffeur and car were, they set off the minute I'd clicked my seatbelt.

The privacy screen was up, and I knew how soundproofed it was—not because of technology, but because Samuel knew not to listen to any of the murmurs he might hear back here.

And if he was ever to share the most innocent of those whispers he might have discerned? We both knew I'd slice off his fucking ear.

This was a hard world. One we'd both grown up in, so we knew how things rolled. Samuel had it pretty easy with me, and he wasn't about to fuck up this job when he was so close to retirement. If he kept his mouth shut, did as I asked, ignored what he may or may not have heard, and drove me wherever the fuck I wanted to go, Sam knew I'd set him and his missus up somewhere nice in Florida. Near the beach, so the moaning old bastard's knees didn't give him too much trouble in his dotage.

See?

I wasn't all bad.

Rapping my fingers against my knee, I studied her, and I made no bones about it.

Her face was tilted down, and it let me see the longest lashes I'd ever come across on a woman. Well, natural ones. Those fucking false ones that fell off on my sheets were just irritating. But as with everything, Aoife was all natural.

So pure.

So fucking perfect.

Jesus, Mary, and Joseph.

She was a benediction come to life.

I wasn't as devout as Aidan Sr. would like me to be, but even I felt uncomfortable thinking such thoughts while sporting a hard-on that made me ache. That made my mental blasphemy even worse.

"Why did you let him touch you? Was it for money?"

I hadn't meant to ask that question.

Really, I hadn't.

It was the last thing I wanted to know, but like poison, it had spewed from my lips.

Who she'd fucked and who she hadn't, was none of my goddamn affair.

This was a business deal. Nothing more, nothing less. She'd fuck me to make sure I kept quiet, and I fucked her so I could revel in the copious curves this woman had to offer.

Simple, no?

She stiffened at the question, and I couldn't blame her. "Do I really have to answer that?"

I could have made her. It was on the tip of my tongue to force her to, but I didn't really want to know even if, somewhere deep down, I did.

"You know why you're here, don't you?" I asked instead of replying.

Her nostrils flared. "To keep silent."

I nodded and almost smiled at her because, internally she was furious, but equally, she was lost. I could sense that like a shark could scent blood in the water. This had thrown her for a loop, and she was in shock, but she was, underneath it all, angry.

Good.

I wanted to fuck her tonight when she was angry.

Spitting flames at me, taking her outrage out on me as she scratched lines of fire down my spine as she screamed her climax. . . .

I almost shuddered at how well I'd painted that mental picture.

"When you're ready, you have my card."

"Ready for what?" she asked, perplexed. Her brow furrowed as she, for the first time since she'd climbed into the car, looked over at me.

"To make another tea room. I've had them move all the stuff into storage."

She licked her lips. "I want to say that's kind of you, but I'm in this predicament because of you."

A corner of my mouth hitched at that. "Honestly, be grateful I was the one who came knocking today. You wouldn't want any of the Five Points' men around that place. Half that china would be on the floor now."

Her shoulders drooped. "I know."

"You do?"

"I pay them protection money," she snapped. "Plus, I grew up around enough Five Pointers to know the score."

That statement targeted my curiosity, hard. "You did, huh? Whereabouts?"

Her mouth pursed. "Nowhere you'd know," she muttered under her breath.

"I doubt it. This is my area, too."

She turned to me, and the tautness around her eyes reminded me of something, but even as it flashed into being, the memory disappeared as I drowned in her emerald green eyes. "Why are you doing this?"

"Why do you think?" I retorted. "You're a beautiful woman—"

"Don't pretend like you couldn't have any woman under you if you asked them."

I wanted to smile, but I didn't because I knew, just as Aidan had pointed out to me earlier that day, that Aoife wasn't exactly what society considered on trend.

She'd have suited the glorious Titian era. She was a Raphaelite, a gorgeous and vivacious Aphrodite.

She wasn't slender. Her butt bounced, and when I fucked her, I'd have some meat to slam into, and her hips would be delicious handholds to grab.

If I smiled, I'd confirm that I was mocking her, and though I was a bastard, and though I was enough of a cunt to blackmail her into this when it hadn't been necessary—after all, before I'd told her who I was, I could have asked her out and done this normally—there was no way I was going to knock this glorious creature's confidence.

"Some men like slim and trim gym bunnies, some men like curves." I shrugged. "That's how it works, isn't it?"

Her eyes flared at that. "But Jenny—"

"Would you prefer she be here with me?" I asked dryly, amused when she flushed.

"Of course not. I wouldn't want her to be in this position."

I laughed. "Nicely phrased."

"What's that supposed to mean?"

Leaning forward, I grabbed her chin and forced her to look at me. "It's supposed to mean that you can fight this all you fucking want, but deep down, you're glad you're here. Your little cunt is probably sopping wet, and it's dying for a taste of my dick. So, simmer down. We're almost at my apartment."

And with that, I dipped my chin, and opening my mouth, raked my teeth down her bottom lip before I bit her. Hard enough to make her moan.

***

Aoife

THE STING of pain should have had me rearing back.

It didn't.

It felt. . . .

I almost shuddered.

Good.

It had felt good.

The way he'd done it. So fucking cocky, so fucking sure of

himself, and who could blame him? He'd taken what he wanted, and I hadn't pulled away because he was right. My pussy *was* wet, and even though this was all kinds of wrong, I did want to feel him there. To have his cock push inside me.

Jesus, this was way too early for Stockholm syndrome, right?

I mean, this was... what was it?

It couldn't be that I was so horny and desperate for male attention that I was willingly allowing this to happen, was it?

Fuck. How pathetic was I if that was true? And yet, I didn't feel desperate for anything other than more of that small taste Finn had given me.

As a little girl, I'd watched Finn. It had been back in the day when his old man had been around and Fiona had lived with her husband and son. He'd beaten her up something rotten. Barely a week went by when Fiona, my mom's friend, didn't appear with some badly made-up bruise on her face.

I was young, only two, but old enough to know something wasn't right. I'd even asked my mom about it, wanting to understand why someone would do that to another person.

I couldn't remember what my mother had said, but I could remember how sad she'd been.

For all his faults, my dipshit stepfather had never beaten her, he'd just taken all her tips for himself and spent every night getting drunk.

Well, Finn's dad had been the same, except where mine passed out on the decrepit La-Z-Boy in front of the TV, Gerry had taken out his drunk out on Fiona.

And eventually, Finn.

Even as a boy, in the photos Fiona kept of him, Finn had been beautiful.

I could see him now, deep in my mind's eye. His hair had been as coal dark then as it was now, and not even a hint of silver or gray marred the noir perfection. His jaw and nose had grown, obviously, but they were just as obstinate as I remembered. Fiona had always said Finn was hardheaded.

When I was little, I hadn't had a crush on him—I'd been a toddler, for God's sake—but I'd been in awe of him. In awe of the big boy who'd been all arms and legs, just waiting for his growth spurt. Sadly, when that had happened, he'd disappeared.

As had his father.

Overnight, Fiona had gone from having a full house to an empty nest, and my mom had comforted her over the loss of her boy.

To my young self, I'd thought he'd died.

Genuinely. The way Fiona had mourned him? It had been as though both men had passed on, except we'd never had to go to church for a service, and there'd been no wake.

As kids do, I'd forgotten him. I'd been two when he'd disappeared, so I only really remembered that Fiona was a mom and that she was grieving.

We'd barely spoken his name because it could set her off into bouts of tears that would have my mom pouring tea down her gullet as they talked through her feelings.

As time passed, those little scenes in our crappy kitchen stopped, yet Fiona hung around our place so much it was like her second home.

One day, my stepfather died in an accident at work. The insurance paid out, Fiona moved in with us, and Mom had started scheming as to how to make her dream of owning a tea room come true. With Fiona living in, I'd heard Finn's name more often, but the notion he was dead still rang true.

Yet, here he was.

Finn wasn't dead.

He was very much alive.

Had Fiona known that?

Had she?

I wasn't sure what I hoped for her.

Was it better to believe your son was dead, or that your son didn't give enough of a fuck about you to contact you for years?

I gnawed on my bottom lip at the thought and accidentally raked over the tissue where Finn had bitten earlier.

"We're almost there," the man himself grated out, and I could sense he was pissed because the phone had buzzed, and whatever he'd been reading had a storm cloud passing behind his eyes.

"O-Okay," I replied, hating the quiver in my voice, but also just hating my situation.

This was. . . .

It was too much.

How was it that I was sitting here?

This morning, I'd owned a tea room. Now, I didn't.

This morning, I'd been exhausted, depressed about my mom, and *feeling* lost.

Now?

I was the *epitome* of lost.

A man was going to use me for sex, for Christ's sake.

But all I could think was: *did I still have my hymen?*

God, would he be angry if he had to push through it?

Should I tell him?

If I did, it would be for my benefit, not his, and why the hell was I thinking like this? I should be trying to convince him that normal people did not work business deals out by bribing someone into bed.

But, deep down, I knew all my scattered thinking was futile.

I wasn't dealing with normal people here.

I was dealing with a Five Pointer.

A high ranking one at that.

It was like dealing with a Martian. To average, everyday folk, a Five Pointer was just outside of their knowledge banks.

Sure, they thought they knew what they were like because

they watched *The Wire* or some other procedural show, but they didn't.

Real-life gangsters?

They were larger than life.

They throbbed with violence, and hell, a part of me knew that Finn was cutting me some slack by asking to sleep with me.

Yeah, as fucked up as that was, it was the truth.

He could have asked for so much more.

He'd have a Senator in his pocket, and to the mob, what else would they ask for if not that?

Yet Finn?

He just wanted to fuck me.

My throat felt tight and itchy from dryness. I wanted some water so badly, but equally, I wasn't sure if it would make me puke.

Not at the thought of sex with this man—a part of me knew I'd enjoy it too much to even be nervous.

No, at what else he could ask of me, that had me fretting.

Was this a one-time deal?

How could I protect my dad from the Five Points when . . .?

I shuddered because there was nothing I could do. There was no way I could even broach any of those questions since I wasn't in charge here.

Finn was.

Finn always would be until he deemed I'd paid my dues. Whether that was tomorrow or two years down the line.

Shit, it might even be forever. If my dad hit the White House, only God knew what kind of leverage Finn could pull if my father tried to carry on covering up my existence. . . .

"We're here."

Something had *definitely* pissed him off.

He'd gone from the cat who'd drank a carton full of cream, to a pissed off tabby scrounging for supper in the trash.

"We're going to go through to the private elevator, and I'm going to head straight down the hall to my living room. You're going to slip into the first door on the right—that's my bedroom."

"O-Okay," I told him, wondering what the hell was going on.

"You're going to stay quiet, and you're going to try to not hear any fucking thing I say, do you hear me?"

"I hear you."

"You'd better," he ground out, his hand tightening around his cellphone. "Coming to Aidan O'Donnelly's attention is the last thing a little mouse like you wants."

A shiver ran through me.

Aidan O'Donnelly was in his apartment?

Fuck, just how high up the ranks was he?

CONTINUE
THE FIVE POINTS' MOB COLLECTION
HERE:
www.books2read.com/FilthySerenaAkeroyd

CONTINUE
A DARK & DIRTY SINNERS' MC SERIES
HERE:
www.books2read.com/CruzSerenaAkeroyd

FREE EBOOK ALERT!!

Don't forget to grab your free e-Book!
Secrets & Lies is now free!

Meg's love life was missing a spark until she discovered her need to be dominated. When her fiancé shared the same kink, she thought all her birthdays had come at once, and then she came to learn their relationship was one big fat lie.

Gabe has loved Meg for years, watching her from afar, and always wishing he'd been the one to date her first and not his brother. When he has the chance to have Meg in his bed—even better, tied to it—it's an opportunity he can't refuse.

With disastrous consequences.

Can Gabe make Meg realize she's the one woman he's always wanted? But once secrets and lies have wormed their way into a relationship, is it impossible to establish the firm base of trust needed between lovers, and more importantly, between sub and Sir…?

This story features orgasm control in a BDSM setting.

Secrets & Lies is now free!

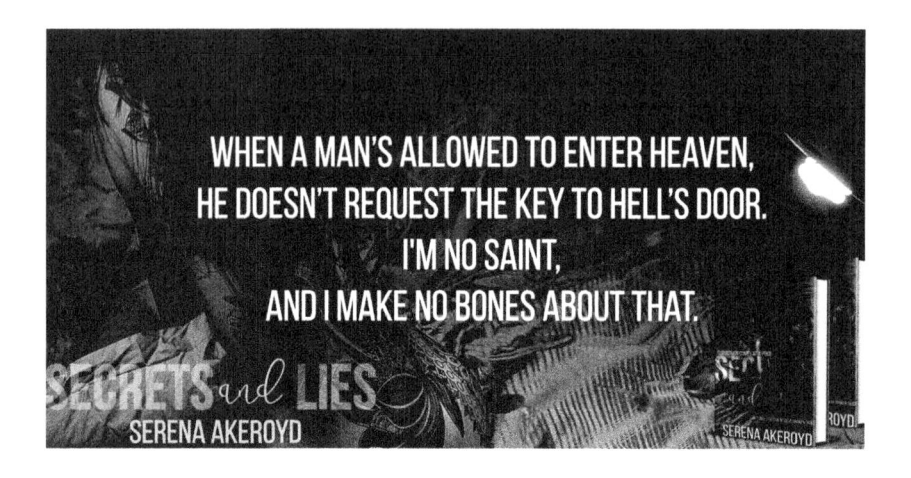

ALSO BY SERENA AKEROYD

For the latest updates, be sure to check out my website!

But, if you'd like to hang out with me and get to know me better, then I'd love to see you in my Diva reader's group where you can find out all the gossip on new releases as and when they happen. You can join here: www.facebook.com/groups/Serena-AkeroydsDivas. Or, you can always PM or email me. I love to hear from you guys: serenaakeroyd@gmail.com.

Until I see you there or you write me an email or PM, here are more of my books for you to read…

The Year of the Wolf
  Wolf Child

The Five Points' Collection
  The Air He Breathes
  Filthy Rich
  Filthy Dark

The Kingdom of Veronia Collection

Theirs

A Dark And Dirty Sinners' MC:
Nyx
Link
Sin
Steel
Cruz

Dragon Bound
Coven
Leman

Eight Wings Academy
The Ascended

HawkRidge High
Dare You To Love Me
Dare You To Keep Me

Hell's Rebels MC
All Sinner No Saint

The Sex Tape **(Co-written with Helen Scott)**

The Professor

The Caelum Academy
Seven Wishes
Eight Souls
Nine Lives

Naughty Nookie
Sinfully Theirs
Sinfully Mastered

The Gods Are Back In Town
Hotter than Hades
The Sun Revolves Around Apollo

FourWinds
Queen of the Vamps

QUINTESSENCE
Hers To Keep
Theirs To Cherish
Hers To Hold

Forever Theirs

Secrets & Lies

The TriAlpha Chronicles
Origin
Trinity
Triskele
Triad
Triumph
Trierna
TriAlpha

Los Lobos
Bound

The Salsang Chronicles (written with Helen Scott)
Stained Egos
Stained Hearts
Stained Minds
Stained Bonds
Stained Souls

ABOUT THE AUTHOR

I'm a romance novelaholic and I won't touch a book unless I know there's a happy ending. This addiction is what made me craft stories that suit my voracious need for raunchy romance. I love twists and unexpected turns, and my novels all contain sexy guys, dark humor, and hot AF love scenes.

I write MF, Menage, and Reverse Harem (also known as Why Choose romance,) in both contemporary and paranormal. Some of my stories are darker than others, but I can promise you one thing, you will always get the happy ending your heart needs!

facebook.com/SerenaAkeroyd
twitter.com/SerenaAkeroyd
instagram.com/Serena_Akeroyd
amazon.com/Serena-Akeroyd/e/B00EC76REA

Printed in Great Britain
by Amazon